BORN TO
DARKNESS

SUZANNE BROCKMANN

BORN TO DARKNESS

BALLANTINE BOOKS

NEW YORK

Copyright © 2012 by Suzanne Brockmann

All rights reserved.

Published in the United States by Ballantine Books, an imprint of The Random House Publishing Group, a division of Random House, Inc., New York.

BALLANTINE and colophon are registered trademarks of Random House, Inc.

ISBN 978-0-345-52127-9
eBook ISBN 978-0-345-52129-3

Printed in the United States of America on acid-free paper

www.ballantinebooks.com

9 8 7 6 5 4 3 2

Book design by Caroline Cunningham

For my readers, who are always willing to boldly go.

Thank you for your trust and your belief that love is a

beautiful gift.

ACKNOWLEDGMENTS

The thank-yous have to start with the real-life U.S. Navy SEALs—the best of the best. Fiction can't touch the reality of who these guys are, and what they do.

I've been writing my sixteen-book Troubleshooters series about Navy SEAL Team Sixteen since 1999, and my eleven-book TDD series about SEAL Team Ten since 1995. That's a lot of Navy SEALs.

So you'd think when I sat down to write an entirely new series—a modern fantasy set several decades into a dark future—I'd have had enough of SEAL heroes.

But I just can't shake my fascination with these tremendously intelligent, powerfully motivated, quietly humble, insanely courageous, and usually seriously funny guys. And thus was created Shane Laughlin, a former lieutenant in the Teams, and the hero of this first book in my new Fighting Destiny series. (Shane's story doesn't end in *Born to Darkness,* either. You'll see plenty more of him in books to come.)

So thank you, real Navy SEALs—and not *just* for providing well over a decade of inspiration.

A big thank-you, too, to the team at Ballantine and Random House including my stellar editor Shauna Summers; my agent, Steve Axelrod; my eternally patient family: Ed, Jason, Melanie,

Aidan, Dexter and Little Joe; and my parents, Fred and Lee Brock-mann.

My first-draft readers should be given medals and a ceremony with a trumpet fanfare, just like at the end of *Star Wars.* Thank you, Deede Bergeron, Patricia McMahon, Lee Brockmann, Ed Gaffney, Deirdre Van Collie, and especially Scott Lutz. (Insert Wookie sound of approval here.)

Thank you to Bill and Jodie Kuhlman for letting me borrow the name "Old Main" for the primary building on the OI campus.

Thanks to the entire cast and crew of *The Perfect Wedding,* the indie feature romantic comedy that I co-wrote, produced, and helped film last summer. Find out more about what I'm doing when I'm not writing novels, at www.ThePerfectWeddingMovie.com.

And as long as you're surfing the Internet, come and see what the main characters in *Born to Darkness* look like inside the murky depths of my head! Meet Shane and Mac and all the others through posts, photos, and video snippets over at my website: www .SuzanneBrockmann.com. Interact with them and with me (and with other readers) on my Facebook page: www.facebook.com/ SuzanneBrockmannBooks.

Huge thanks to Shirin Tinati, photographer extraordinaire, for helping me bring these characters to life; and to my entire gorgeous cast of actors: Aubrey Grant (Shane), Briana Pozner (Mac), Eric Aragon (Bach), Apolonia Davalos (Anna), David Singletary (Diaz), and Jason T. Gaffney (Elliot).

Last but certainly not least, I want to thank *you,* my readers, who trust me enough to follow wherever I will take you, and who continue to give me permission to write the stories of my heart.

As always, any mistakes I've made or liberties I've taken are completely my own.

BORN TO
DARKNESS

ONE

The man had taken his own family hostage.

Mac Mackenzie could feel the fear and hear the joker's wife and three children crying as she quickly scaled the side of the house, all the way up to the roof. Her destination was a small third-floor window, around the back, that was open a crack.

Stephen Diaz's evenly modulated voice came through her radio headset as he and their team leader, Dr. Joseph Bach, waited on the ground below. "Whenever you're ready."

Subtext: *Tick tock, bitch. We're waiting on you. . . .*

Although, okay. The *bitch* was her own embellishment.

In the entire twelve years that Mac had known Diaz, he'd never once addressed her with anything other than respect. Including the night—a *long* time ago—when she'd embarrassed them both by planting herself, naked, in his bed.

Here and now, Mac didn't bother to answer him. She just quickly and soundlessly crossed the rain-slicked roof—which was actually slate.

No doubt about it, someone who spent a truckload of cash on the freaking roof of their house in these trying times had money to burn. And/or money to buy expensive illegal drugs—especially the kind that came with the claim that the user would live forever.

Yeah, that whole *never die, always look twenty* promise that the drug oxyclepta di-estraphen—known by its street name, Destiny—

brought to the table was hard for a lot of people to turn down. Especially those who already had all of the cars and fancy houses and pairs of shoes that their billions of dollars could buy.

Although it wasn't *always* the case that the addicts she and Bach and Diaz helped contain were über-wealthy. Some of them had been using the needle for so long that they'd sold off everything in their lives that had any kind of value. Homes, cars, exotic pets. Yachts, jewelry, designer clothing—none of it worth more than a miniscule fraction of its original price in this craphell economy.

Except for their weapons.

These days, a Smith & Wesson or a SIG Sauer—even in shitty condition—was worth more to most people than a Beemer. Especially considering the skyrocketing price of gas.

But eventually the frequent fliers even sold off their guns and ammo, and the cash went into a vein. But damn, they sure looked good, because Destiny gave them youth and good health, as long as you could ignore the whole violent addiction thing. Although looking hot didn't prevent them from accidentally ODing or worse: hitting the joker-point and going noisily insane.

Some users jokered earlier than others—like their current hostage-taker, who apparently still had enough money to keep the heat on and the lights burning in this three-story mansion here in the richie-richest part of one of Boston's few remaining still-posh 'burbs.

"Okay, I'm finally there," Mac breathed into her lip microphone, knowing that everything she told Diaz would be heard by Dr. Bach, too, even though their leader didn't wear a headset. She dipped her head down over the edge of the roof to get a peek into that partially open window. As they'd suspected, it led into a small bathroom. The shade was up and the light that spilled through came from a fancy fixture out in the third-floor hallway. She reached over and unfastened the screen, pulling it from its frame. "Status?"

"All inhabitants are still on the second floor," Diaz informed her. "In the master bedroom. Dr. Bach thinks our guy's dosing again. What are you picking up? And please don't do it if you can't block the fear."

Fear and confusion from the family was a given. And since, in this case, there were four of them, that fear was a powerful force that left a strangely metallic taste in Mac's mouth when she lowered her mental shields enough to let it in. But three were children, and even though she didn't know for sure, she would bet her life savings on the fact that at least two were under the age of ten. Because, from them, she felt a still-strong blast of hope. *This can't be happening. Daddy loves us—this must be a mistake. . . .*

As for their joker . . .

"I got some serious no-fear from our guy," Mac reported to Diaz. "Just a shitload of rage." She sent the window screen silently flying, like a giant Frisbee, well into the neighbor's yard. "Beneath that? Jealousy, to the point of hatred. He's gone."

"We believe he's double-dosing in an attempt to read his wife's mind," Diaz reported. "Dr. Bach's picking up signs of the vill's increasing telepathic power, but it's bouncing all over the place."

"Maybe he'll do us all a favor and OD," Mac said as she reached down again and pulled up on the bottom half of the double-hung window.

The damn thing jammed.

True, she wasn't in the best position to muscle it up, hanging over the edge of the roof with virtually no leverage.

And even if she got it open all the way, it was still freaking small—just as narrow as they'd all imagined it would be from down on the ground.

And that was why she'd been sent up here instead of Diaz, who was nearly twice her size. Usually, *she* backed up Dr. Bach as he made a first-floor entry, while Diaz climbed the outside walls and gained access through an upper-floor window, easily unlocking and opening it with his mind.

But every other window in this Victorian monster of a house was painted tightly shut. And not even their esteemed leader Dr. Bach had the power to break *that* kind of seal without making a shitload of noise.

Of course, there were times when a shitload of noise came in handy. Sometimes this kind of takedown went more quickly and easily when she and Diaz followed Bach's command to use good old shock and awe. Forget gaining entry by breaking the hundred-and-fifty years of paint that glued the windows shut. Just combine their mental powers to blow all of the glass out of the entire structure while flames erupted from the air-conditioning vents, balls of lightning exploded from every power outlet, and every piece of furniture in the place got up and danced.

Out-freak the frequent flier.

But this time, Bach didn't want to go that way, and Bach knew best.

And that wasn't Mac being snarky, that was Mac being real. Dr. Joseph Bach *did* know best. She wouldn't be a member of his weird little freak-show commando team if she didn't believe that with all of her heart and soul.

She strained to move the window, trying to gain traction on the slippery roof.

"Need help?" Diaz's voice murmured in her ear, just as she finally pushed the window back down and got it realigned.

It went up much easier now.

"Thanks," she said as she rearranged herself, preparing to slip inside.

"That wasn't me," he said.

"I was talking to Dr. Bach," Mac came back. "I'm good to go. Anything else I should know?"

"Joker's name was Nathan Hempford," Diaz replied. "That's all we've got."

And that meant that this particular freak didn't have a file—at least not one that Dr. Bach had been given access to as they'd rushed over here to step in and save the day, after the local Boston SWAT team had already failed to the tune of two body bags.

The villain-formerly-known-as-Nathan was a bullet-bender—they all knew *that* much about him. Thanks to the absurd quantity of Destiny pumping through his veins, he had developed the undeniably impressive mental power to stop a bullet in its path, and return it to the shooter with deadly results.

It was a very rare skill-set. Unfortunately, it wasn't quite so rare among the handful of addicts who'd jokered in the past few months. Must be something in the current local batch of Destiny—something that targeted a particular neural pathway.

And that was unusual. No two individuals had exactly the same powers—even those Greater-Thans like Bach, and Diaz, and Mac herself, who'd all spent countless hours studying and training and practicing, practicing, practicing to control their individual mental talents—talents they'd come by naturally, without sticking a needle in their arms.

Mac's own skills were decidedly different from Stephen Diaz's even though they both had achieved mental integration of a very high and very rare fifty percent. On paper, their skill levels were dead even. But their skills were individual and unique—which was why they shared the job of Dr. Bach's second-in-command. Together, their combined talents made them nearly unstoppable.

And while Mac had talents Diaz couldn't touch, that didn't stop her from being envious of his.

The grass was always greener.

One of Diaz's talents was his ability to maintain telepathic contact with Bach from a relatively longer distance than Mac's erratic two-to-ten-feet, without a SAT signal or a headset. And these days? The SAT towers went down or the signal got jammed more often than not. That was why, also more often than not, Mac was usually the one entering the building alongside Bach, where she was able to communicate silently via hand signals while Diaz did the upper-window shuffle with Bach securely nestled, all snug in his head.

In fact, their current SAT signal now crackled with static as Mac announced, "I'm going in."

Diaz came back, "We'll give you ten. Nine . . ."

It was a tight squeeze through that little window, even for someone as small as she was. Mac went in feet first, which left her feeling vulnerable, particularly when the button at the waist of her cargo pants caught. But she wrestled herself free and in doing so scraped her face on the window's rough bottom edge.

But then she was inside and moving silently toward the hallway, taking a quick scan of the landing and swiftly finding the stairs leading down.

She could hear Nathan, their joker, his voice tight with anger—a common side effect of the drug. "You think I didn't *see* the way you *looked* at him? You think I didn't *notice*? You think I didn't *know*?"

His words were punctuated by what sounded like blows, and what were definitely screams and more crying.

"Don't, Daddy, don't!" one of the younger kids sobbed, as Mac moved faster, as Diaz went straight from *four* to *one*.

"Go. We're go," Diaz told Mac, adding, "Incoming," as Dr. Bach chimed in.

Stop.

He wasn't talking to Mac and his voice wasn't coming through her earpiece. It was inside of her head, and definitely in the joker's head, too. Reverberating, it echoed and permeated, and even though she'd shielded against it, she felt it all the way through her skull and down her spine. It was scary as shit—or it would've been, had she not been on Bach's team.

"I'm gonna fucking *kill* you, you lying *bitch*!" Their joker was back on his feet and threatening his wife sooner than Mac had expected, which was way not good.

STOP.

Bach got louder and stronger, and this time there was no warning from Diaz—only a sharp crackle of static. And Mac thought she was fully prepped and shielded, but she must not have been, because the force of the word hit her, too. It lifted her up off her feet and she hung there for a moment with her brain on fire.

Scrambled and on fire, so that when Bach finally let go, she couldn't snap back quickly enough to keep herself from tumbling down the stairs. She should have tucked and rolled. Instead she flailed her legs like a cartoon character building up speed to run away from an anvil dropping on her head. She felt something in her ankle give as she landed wrong on the edge of one of the stairs.

The pain was hot and fierce and after that first jolt she guarded, so that she wouldn't project it—not just for Diaz's protection, but because it never paid to let a jokering villain know that you had been weakened in any way.

She tumbled and bounced all the way to the bottom, landing with a thud, flat on her back with enough force to knock the air out of her lungs. Still, she managed to keep her guard up and solid.

Never let 'em see you cry. It was her mantra, her mission statement, even back before she'd known she was special.

Besides, this was completely her fault. She should have stayed ready. She should have expected Bach to hit even harder.

On the other hand, the noise she'd made as she'd fallen had drawn tonight's vill away from his defenseless family, and he limped into the hall where he spotted her as she scrambled to her feet.

"*What* did you *do* to me? *Who* the hell are *you*?" he shouted, and even though he was more than ten feet away, it was as if he'd hit her full in the face, with a right hook hard enough to knock her down and make her see stars, and then another and another and another.

And oh, *this* was a new one in the craziest-fucking-shit-she'd-ever-seen category. His words packed a punch—literally.

"*Answer* me!" Boom. He'd made her nose bleed with that one.

But here came Bach and Diaz, thundering up the stairs.

And this time Diaz's voice came through Mac's headset over the static, even as she saw his mouth move. "Again."

She braced for Bach to blast the son of a bitch, to knock him senseless and pin him into place with an *ENOUGH*.

Even with her mental shield firmly in place, Mac knew that her brain was going to sizzle at this proximity, but it did way more than that. It was another full-on deep-fry, and in that fraction of a second before she lost her ability to reason, she realized that their bad guy wasn't just a bullet-bender, he was a *force*-bender. He had the power to reflect the mental attacks that were thrown at him, and to blast whatever he received back at the sender—which resulted in anyone around said sender receiving a double dose of that very same force.

Even Diaz lost his footing at that one. Bach, however, didn't falter.

As Mac's vision returned, she saw him realize that they were going to have to take Nathan down the old-fashioned way. With good old physical might.

Bach threw himself forward into a roundhouse kick that would have knocked out a normal man, but their joker barely even staggered.

It was clear he felt no pain—another common side effect of the drug. But that didn't mean that the man wouldn't eventually shut down and out—if Bach just kept on delivering blow after blow after punishing blow. He would. It was just going to take a while to drop him.

But he started in on his questioning barrage, even as Bach hit him again.

"Get *out* of my *house*! You *think* you can *stop me*?"

With the addict's words directed at Bach, Mac felt only a series of glancing blows. She also felt genuine surprise and even a burst of pain from Bach, which, in turn, surprised the shit out of *her*.

In all of the years she'd known Dr. Joseph Bach—over a dozen of 'em now—Mac had never, *ever* felt him let down his guard. Not like this.

And for the first time in a long time, Mac felt a sliver of fear. The idea that this untrained drug user, this joker, this lowlife unskilled addict, had achieved power that even Bach—a true master and the most powerful Greater-Than in the country—couldn't shield himself against . . . ?

It was pretty damn terrifying.

And even though Diaz didn't have Mac's advanced empathy, she could see that he'd picked up on Bach's surprise, too, because he tried to throw himself on the figurative grenade—springing up and grabbing hold of the bad guy. No doubt he was testing a theory that this type of power-bender might be more vulnerable to something like his own carefully controlled direct-contact electrical shock.

It had taken Mac years to learn to shield herself against this particular power that Diaz brought to the hand-to-hand-combat table. She knew from countless sparring sessions that the greater the amount of body contact and the tighter the bear hug, the higher the voltage of juice Diaz could deliver.

It felt like being tasered.

Here and now, Diaz had scored a direct hit on Nathan and even managed to tackle him to the ground, but his theory was proven dead wrong as he himself jumped and jolted when his own electric current was thrown back at him. To his credit, D hung on, even though the addict was trying to push him away, and even though without that physical contact, the electrical circuit would have been broken.

The bad guy was shouting, too. It was just mindless screaming, but he was making it rhythmic—*"Arhh! Arhh! Arhh . . . !"*—and Mac knew that not only was Diaz taking all that electrical energy, he was also absorbing the joker's vocal punches.

She wanted to help but she didn't know how, until Bach spoke. But her ears were ringing from that latest mental blast. The air around Diaz was crackling, too, and she couldn't make out his words.

So Dr. Bach gained entry into her mind the way he always did, provided he was at a close enough range. He gave a little push asking permission, which Mac granted immediately by lowering her defenses.

And then she felt the warmth and calm that meant Bach was inside of her head. He didn't so much speak as guide her thoughts.

What did you do to me? The addict had asked that when he'd first come out into the hall.

But Mac didn't know what the man had meant—except then,

suddenly, she *did* know. The joker had been favoring the very same foot that she'd injured, the same ankle she'd trashed when she'd fallen down the stairs. He'd been *limping*.

Maybe there were some powers that Nathan couldn't deflect. Maybe . . .

She scrambled to her feet and instead of compartmentalizing and hiding the pain she felt when she put any weight on her left foot, she disintegrated her carefully constructed guard. And she didn't just step onto her injured foot, she jumped onto it. Pain rocketed through her and she heard herself scream.

Nathan screamed, too.

Bingo.

Mac felt Bach pull out of her head, and she knew he must've then paid a visit to Diaz's mind, letting *him* know about the joker's weakness, because Diaz, too, dropped his guard and let out a blast of everything that he was feeling. And to Mac's surprise, that included not just the pain from the mentally looped electrical current, but anger and frustration, and—holy shit—an aircraft-carrier-load of pent-up sexual energy.

Considering he was the Prince of Celibacy, *that* was a stunner.

But that wasn't the biggest shocker of the evening. The fact that Diaz walked around suppressing a forty-thousand-ton urge to screw everyone in sight was nothing compared to the wall of pain that Bach set free.

Unlike Mac's and Diaz's mostly physical suffering, what Bach let loose was a blast of emotional hurt that knocked Mac to her knees.

It was indescribable—the grief, the loss, the regret, the sheer sorrow. . . .

It was too much to bear—not just for Mac, but for Nathan, too.

"He's out, I think that did it, I think he stroked out," she heard Diaz gasp.

Bach agreed with an urgency in his voice that she rarely ever heard. "Nathan's out—and we need the medical team in here, *now*! Let's not lose this one!"

And there was the great irony of what they did. Risk their lives to subdue the joker, but then, when he was subdued? Rush his bad-guy ass to the special hospital unit over at the Obermeyer Institute and work their medical team around the clock to attempt to detox him—to try to keep him from dying.

As the OI med team poured into the house, Mac pulled out of the fetal position she'd curled herself into.

Dr. Bach came over and gave her a hand up. "You should get that ankle checked at the clinic," he told her.

"*I'm* fine," she said, her subtext clear. Yes, she'd been injured, but *he* was the one who needed about a decade of grief counseling. Not that she'd ever dare to say something like that to his face. Still, he was Bach, so he surely knew what she was thinking. "My ankle's not that bad—I can heal it overnight. I'll be back to speed in the morning."

Bach nodded, his brown eyes somber. "Do whatever you have to do. I'll see you back there."

He vanished down the hall, no doubt going to find the former Nathan Hempford's wife and children, to let them know the ordeal was over and that they were safe, to explain what had happened, and what was likely to happen next.

He wouldn't go so far as to tell them that Hempford was guaranteed to die, or that the authorities were already in the process of covering up what had happened here tonight. The official report would no doubt include a home invasion by a fictional meth- or heroin-addled intruder, with the entire family—including Hempford—taken hostage. His obit would read that he'd died trying to save his family from an unidentified man who'd also killed two police officers. And the public would continue to remain blissfully unaware of this new, dangerous drug called Destiny, *and* the existence of Dr. Bach's psychically powerful team from OI.

Not that any of them wanted or needed a ticker-tape parade.

In fact, their very anonymity and lack of recognition helped keep them safe.

But still . . .

Mac blocked her pain and hobbled her way down the stairs

and out of the house, catching up to Diaz out on the driveway, where he'd helped the med team load an unconscious Nathan into the ambulance.

"You okay?" she asked, and Diaz nodded.

"Someone's got a secret," she said, unable to keep her smartass in check, even though he was looking considerably worse for the wear.

She wasn't all that clean and shiny herself—her nose was still bleeding a bit and her lip was definitely split, although it was already starting to heal. Another fifteen minutes, and her face would be as good as new. Her ankle, however, was going to require some significant attention and focus.

Diaz gave her his handkerchief. Who the hell still carried handkerchiefs?

"It's not a secret," he said evenly. "It's just . . . irrelevant." And then he said what he said after every takedown, even though by all rights they should have been rivals, vying to be Bach's official second-in-command. "Good job tonight, Michelle."

So Mac gave him her standard reply. "You, too, D."

"See you back there," he said, and vanished into the night.

TWO

The police station had seen better days. It was grimy and stale-smelling, poorly lit and barely heated, and definitely understaffed.

Anna Taylor had had to wait for two long anxiety-filled hours before the desk sergeant called her number, before she could so much as report the reason why she was there.

"My sister is missing. She didn't come home from school today," she said, working hard to keep her frustration from her voice. This had rapidly turned into a nightmare. But she'd sat, waiting, when what she'd wanted to do was keep searching for Nika, returning to all of her little sister's favorite haunts. Not that there were many of them—they'd only lived in the Boston area for a few months, and were both still feeling their way in terms of making new friends.

Anna hadn't even met their neighbors in their apartment building until this afternoon, when she'd knocked on their doors to see if they'd seen Nika.

No one had.

The heavyset sergeant didn't even look up from his computer. "I can't help you. Until she's been missing for seventy-two hours—"

"Seventy-two?" she repeated, unable to hide her disbelief. "I'm sorry. Maybe I wasn't clear. My sister's a child. She's only thirteen years old."

He looked up at her then, his faded blue eyes vaguely embarrassed, but mostly dull. Time and this job had sucked the life out of him. "Services had to be cut somewhere. Most missing people—including children—turn up on their own within that seventy-two-hour time period. Or they never turn up. Either way, it's a waste of resources."

Anna was staring at him with her mouth open, but she knew it wasn't his fault that cutbacks and layoffs had crippled the entire department. All of Boston's first responders had been decimated. Just last week, while on the bus, she'd seen a building that was on fire. It was just burning unchecked as the tenants of the neighboring triple-decker used garden hoses to keep their own homes from igniting.

Now, she closed her mouth, gathered her frustration-tattered civility, and managed to ask, "So if it's a waste of resources either way, what exactly happens when I come back here in seventy-two hours to report that she's missing?"

He hated his job—that much was clear as he sighed heavily. "Your sister's name gets put on a list. Her photo, description, and last-seen whereabouts go up on the Internet, along with your contact number and the dollar amount of the reward you're willing to pay for her safe return. Citizen detectives take it from there. You'll either get her back or you won't." The sergeant reached beneath the desk for a sheet of paper that he put on the counter and pushed toward her with the tips of his fingers. "Here's the form you'll be asked to fill out, although if you do it online and upload your own photo, the fee's only twenty-five dollars. If we need to rekey your info, it's an extra fifty."

"Fee?" she repeated, stunned by the idea that Nika's life could be in the hands of *citizen detectives*.

"And if you want to skip the waiting period and get her name on the list tonight," the sergeant informed her, "fee for *that's* five hundred dollars. Cash or debit. Five-fifty if you use a credit card."

"What's the fee to actually talk to a detective?" Anna asked, and she was really just being sarcastic. She didn't expect to get an answer. But she did.

"Five thousand'll open a case file," the man said, and her heart sank.

She didn't have anywhere close to that much in cash, and her credit limit had just been lowered again, this time to a meager thousand.

The sergeant shook his head dismissively. "But that only gets you two hours of boots on the ground, which is virtually useless in a situation like this, and there are *no* guarantees." He leaned forward and lowered his voice. "If it was *my* kid, and I had that much money to spend? There are a number of private sector agencies that can help you for a much lower price." He tapped the form. "But I would fill this out, and get her stats on the Net, ASAP. The first three days can be critical, in cases of child abduction."

"And yet there's a seventy-two-hour waiting period . . . ?" This was unreal. "Look, Nika's a really good kid. She's got her own cell phone, I was hoping someone could, I don't know, use some kind of technology to track her . . . ?"

"Again, that's a service you'll spend less on by utilizing a private security firm," she was told.

"Can you recommend—"

He cut her off. "I can't. It's not allowed. And I'm going to have to ask you to step aside—"

"Wait!" This was crazy. "Please. I've heard about these . . . I don't know, kidnapping squads? I thought they were an urban legend, but . . . Nika's a scholarship student at Cambridge Academy. Maybe someone grabbed her, thinking we have money, but . . . I don't even have a full-time job!"

The sergeant sighed. "Best thing to do, miss, is fill out the form and let the citizen detectives—"

"But what if the *citizen detectives* are the people who took her in the first place?"

"If they're one and the same, then it stands to reason that you'll get her back, won't you?"

"Not if I don't have the money to pay," Anna said, as tears of both fear and frustration stung her eyes. "Isn't kidnapping a felony, or has that changed, too? Let me know, because if it's an accepted business practice now, I may have to take it up myself."

He pointed down the hall. "Fee Processing is first door on the right. There are public comm-stations there so you can access the Internet form, save yourself the fifty bucks." He looked down at his computer, tapped a few keys, then raised his voice. "Number 718." He glanced up to find her still there. "Please step to the side, miss."

Anna couldn't let it go. Instead of stepping aside, she leaned forward. "Is this really okay with you?"

"Step to the side, miss." Any glimmer of humanity that she'd seen in his eyes was gone.

Anna moved, telling him, "This *isn't* okay with me." Still, she reached into her backpack for her wallet and the credit card that was already nearly maxed out, and she hurried down the hall.

———

Boston was no different from New York City or Chicago or Dallas or even Phoenix in terms of finding a job.

It didn't matter where Shane Laughlin went—blacklisted was blacklisted was blacklisted, regardless of whether the word was said with a heavy dose of the Bronx or with an accent worthy of a JFK impersonator. And being blacklisted by the corporations that ran the government meant that he wasn't going to get hired. It didn't matter that everyone who still had half of a fortune left after the latest market crash needed personal security to ensure their safety from all of the scary things that went bump in the night.

Shane wasn't wanted.

Not by anybody doing anything legal, that is.

And, here in Boston? Not getting hired due to being blacklisted apparently came with an attached beating.

Three very large men of the no-neck persuasion had followed Shane out of the security firm's personnel office. Two shuffled along behind him on the cracked and pitted sidewalk, and one had hustled across the street—no doubt to cut him off if he tried to run away.

And there, ahead, out of a narrow side street, dimly lit by the flickering streetlamp, came two more bullet-heads—or rather jarheads. Shane would've staked a month of his former pay on a bet that they were, all five of 'em, former Marines.

Of course *that* meant that maybe this beating wasn't related to his being blacklisted, but more about his being a former Navy SEAL. Rivalry between the Navy and the Marines could get pretty intense. Even though, technically, the Marines were related to the Navy. But it had always been very much a dysfunctional stepsibling-type relationship, starting at the very moment some U.S. Navy captain had said, *Hey, I have a good idea. How about we pack the deck of our ships with soldiers who'll storm the beaches to fight the enemy on land, because frankly, these sea battles are getting tedious. And, I know, we'll call 'em Marines and force 'em to get ridiculous haircuts that make their ears look extra stupid— like the handles of a moonshine whiskey jar. And we'll tell our enlisted crew that it's okay to treat 'em like shit. . . .*

The jarheads at twelve o'clock were pretending to window-shop, hands in their pockets, shoulders hunched against the chill of the damp spring wind. Shane might've been fooled into thinking they weren't *really* waiting for him to get close enough to kick his ass, had the window been that of a pawnshop or maybe an old-fashioned video store specializing in porn.

But it was a CoffeeBoy there on the corner—one of the few that had stayed open in this low-rent part of town, probably thanks to its proximity to the private security firm's army of caffeine-ingesting behemoths who regularly dropped by to pick up their weekly paychecks.

Shane picked up his pace, and yeah, when he moved it into a swift jog, the two men behind him followed suit. The two up ahead stopped pretending to be fascinated with the ancient Iced Delight ad that had, no doubt, been put in that window in June, about a decade ago, when CoffeeBoy still featured seasonal variations. These days, the corporate coffee giant was down to caf and decaf.

The two men up ahead turned to face Shane, easy on the balls of their feet, ready to fight.

Although, come on. Five against one wasn't a *fight*. It was a premeditated thrashing.

Instead of feinting right and dashing left around the two men who were blocking his route, Shane just *went* right—and opened the door to the coffee shop and dashed inside, slowing down immediately. Because as long as he was going to get the shit kicked out of him, he might as well be dry and warm when it happened.

"High octane," he told the woman behind the counter, well aware that the four men on his side of the sidewalk had followed him in. Any second now, the gentleman from across the street would be joining them. The bell attached to the door jingled, right on cue—he didn't even have to turn around to look. "Extra large. Black. Please. Ma'am."

He added a hopeful smile, but the woman, close to elderly and clearly exhausted, didn't reach for a paper cup. She barely even moved a muscle in her face as she announced, "We're closed."

"Sign says open twenty-four hours."

"Not today. We're . . . doing inventory."

Shane dropped all pretense. "You're really going to let this happen? It's not going to be pretty and you're going to have to walk past it when you go home."

She was unimpressed. "I'll leave out the back." She looked over his shoulder at the tallest of the men behind him. "Tommy, you take this outside. You know corporate's looking for a reason to shut us down. You bust this place up, it's over. We're gone."

Shane turned around. "Yeah, *Tommy*," he said. "Get down on your knees so you can *properly* suck the dicks of your corporate overlords."

Tommy, completely as expected, lunged at him. No surprises here.

And the blind-rage lunge had always been Shane's favorite form of attack. It was just so defendable, particularly since—even though he was a pretty big guy—he was nimble and fleet of foot.

Shane ducked, dodging Tommy effortlessly. He then tripped the former marine, popped him a sharp chop to the throat that no doubt made him feel like he was going to die, and spun him around. He used the man's own momentum to send him crashing into his buddies, like a giant bowling ball.

As the goon squad cursed and scattered, Shane was already up and over the counter, thanks to the unintentional hot tip from the CoffeeBoy lady about the back entrance.

He was through that rear door, out into the alley, and moving at full speed—which meant he was probably a solid block away before any of the five so much as made it over the counter.

Still, he didn't stop running until a team of police officers in a cruiser eyed him suspiciously. At which point, he slowed to a rather brisk walk, because the last thing he needed was to get picked up by the locals for running-while-unemployed.

It didn't take Shane too much longer to reach the Boston Common—which thankfully was right where the map in his head said it would be. He took the stairs down to an underground station for the T. The first platform he hit was for the Green Line, which seemed like fate, since the Obermeyer Institute was at the end of one of the Green's fingers, out at the end of the D trains, near something called Riverside.

Of course, Shane was assuming that fate applied in times of last-ditch desperation.

And he was assuming, too, that OI's offer wouldn't be reneged when they finally checked their records and realized that he wasn't just a former Navy SEAL, he was a blacklisted former SEAL.

Of course, that was kind of like assuming that buying a lottery ticket meant that he was going to win the billion-dollar jackpot.

The subway turnstile accepted his debit card just as a train stopped at the platform with a squeal of brakes. Shane dashed inside the thing just before the doors closed, but rode it only a few stops to Kenmore Square.

Where there was a public comm-station right on the T platform. He'd used it earlier that evening.

It was open—the place was mostly deserted—so he ran his debit card through the payment slot, keyed in his PIN, and selected the five-minute option. Which would cost him—*shit*—five dollars? He back-keyed and picked three minutes. With only twelve dollars left to his name—nine, now—he'd have to do this fast.

He googled the Obermeyer Institute, cursing himself for spelling it wrong first—he would now forever remember that there were three E's in Obermeyer. When he finally got it right, he followed the website's link to their so-called testing program, clicking on a button that said POTENTIALS.

Which was him. The OI had first contacted him via e-mail, letting him know that he was, apparently, something called "a Potential." Shane had never quite figured out *what* he potentially was. All he knew was that the OI was an R&D facility. And that some of what they researched for future development required human test subjects.

It was all dot-gov approved, which honestly didn't mean that much anymore.

Still, they were willing to pay him, which, in his current situation, was all he really needed to know.

A window opened on the screen, showing a beautiful, bucolic hillside on top of which sat a stately and ornate old brownstone building. *Old Main,* a descriptor beneath proclaimed. It faded neatly into a picture of a more modern building, surrounded by the lushness of flowering bushes in the height of a New England spring. *The Library.* There were people in that photo—of varying ages, but all attractive. They were dressed mostly in street clothes— everything from jeans to business suits, with even a young woman fully clad in BDUs, down to her boots and cover.

Beneath the ongoing slide show—now a bustling scene of some people holding trays, some sitting at long tables in what had to be the nicest, fanciest mess hall Shane had ever seen in his life— a form appeared. It requested his full name, which he typed in: Shane Michael Laughlin. It burped, then requested his NID—his National ID number. He hesitated only briefly. But really, what did he think? Someone was going to steal his identity and empty out his debit account? Buy half a burger with the nine bucks he had left? He typed in the twenty-digit number and hit enter.

And got the icon for *please wait*—the ages-old hourglass of doom.

Shane tapped his fingers as his remaining minutes ticked down, but then a pop-up appeared with the message "Vurp Requested." He clicked "allow," and the computer screen shifted and a man's face appeared. He was in need of a shave, in the time-honored tradition of R&D men-children everywhere, in both the private and public sector. His hair was shaggy and light brown, and kept out of his eyes only by a pair of black-framed glasses. His mouth was wide and friendly, already curling up into a smile. He was wearing a bright blue T-shirt beneath an open lab coat that had the name Dr. E. Zerkowski embroidered over the upper left pocket.

He was sitting in what looked like some kind of computer lab. Shane could see rows of high-tech comm-stations, most of them occupied, in the rather large room behind him.

"Lieutenant Shane Laughlin," the man said, with a genuine smile that touched eyes that were nearly the same color as that shirt. "Former Navy SEAL, twenty-eight years old, in excellent health . . . I was hoping we'd hear from you."

The speaker levels had been turned way down, and with another train pulling up to the platform, Shane searched for the volume control as he said, "Hang on a sec, Doc, I gotta—"

But Zerkowski reached for something on his end and the volume rose as he said, "I'll give you a boost. Some of those older comm-stations need help. I'm Elliot, by the way. I see you're already in Boston—does this mean you're coming in tomorrow?"

"I'm calling to clarify that this isn't a drug-testing program that I'd be entering," Shane said.

"We don't manufacture pharmaceuticals," Zerkowski said. "So, no. But I understand your concern. FYI, you can refuse to participate at any point in the testing process. *And,* to put your mind further at ease, the program you'd be going into involves the study of neural integration, which, in lay terms, deals with the amount—percentage-wise—of your brain that you utilize while doing a variety of tasks—from ditch-digging to complex calculus." He smiled. "And sometimes we'll ask you to combine the two to see what happens when you multitask. Bottom line, Lieutenant, we'll run a lot of tests on you. You might get a little tired of all the medical scans, but we don't use markers—drugs—for any of 'em. In fact, we use no drugs at all in your particular program. It'll be in your release form—our guarantee. And you're free, during the course of your stay with us, to get a scan from an outside medical facility to verify that. We'll cover the cost of one, but after that, you'll have to pay out of pocket."

"Fair enough," Shane said.

"We've got a bed ready for you," Zerkowski told him. "Also FYI, you're exactly what we want in this latest group of test subjects, so please join us. Admission is from oh-six-hundred to noon, with an orientation session at thirteen hundred hours. Right after a delicious lunch. Try to arrive early—housing is assigned on a first come, first served basis, and some of our apartments are . . . pretty lovely."

The slide show was still quietly running in the upper left corner of Shane's monitor, and as if on cue, the picture changed to a view of what was, indeed, a very lovely apartment with a rich-looking leather sofa, upon which a young woman sat beside a little girl—both of them all smiles. *Family housing available,* Shane read.

"Good to know," he told the doctor.

"Although we could probably manage to find room for you tonight, if you need a place to stay . . . ?"

"No," Shane said, "thanks, but . . ."

"Lockdown jitters." Zerkowski smiled. "People hear that word, *lockdown,* and they think draconian conditions, last night of freedom, et cetera, et cetera. I get it. But while we don't allow nonprescription drugs in the compound, we *do* have an on-site lounge that serves alcohol, including some pretty fine wine. You'll get credit for a single drink a day—a half-bottle if wine's your thing. You want more than that, again, you gotta pay for it. And as far as the food goes, it's really quite good. I've been eating here for the past seven years, living here for the past three, and—"

Shane cut him off. "I'm sorry, but my time's running out and I have another question—"

"Oh, no, *I'm* sorry," Zerkowski said, reaching forward again to type something into his computer. "I should have realized. Better?"

The time-clock on the comm-station monitor was now frozen at fifty-eight seconds.

"Thanks," Shane said.

"So how can I help you?" Zerkowski asked, still with that friendly smile on his face.

Shane just said it. Point-blank. "I'm blacklisted." The word still left a bitter taste in his mouth, despite the fact that, if pressed, he'd do the exact same thing all over again. "I was kicked out of the Navy—a dishonorable discharge." No point in saying more than that, in trying to explain what had happened, in attempting to justify what he'd done.

But Zerkowski's expression didn't change. "We're aware of that. We have access to your military records." He shook his head. "We don't believe in blacklisting. A good candidate's a good candidate." He smiled again. "Besides, who are we going to piss off by ignoring the blacklists—that we aren't *already* royally pissing off? You know what I'm saying . . . ? With our pesky scientific facts and all that . . . ?"

Shane couldn't make light of it. "It's a serious deal. My presence could jeopardize your funding—"

"Our funding's secure," Zerkowski said. He smiled again at Shane's obvious disbelief. "Our founder is Dr. Jennifer Obermeyer, the same Dr. Obermeyer who invented the Obermeyer medical scanner—a little piece of technology that's now in every hospital and doctor's office around the globe. Fifteen years ago, she sold her shares in the family corporation, and even if those billions of dollars weren't enough to sustain us indefinitely, she still gets royalties from her patent. So you can trust me when I tell you that our funding is secure."

In the lower right corner of the screen was a photo of Jennifer Obermeyer—a still attractive forty-something blonde with a gleam of intelligence in her blue eyes.

Zerkowski must've made note of Shane's focus because he

laughed. "Don't get any ideas. She's not here all that often. She mostly lets Dr. Bach—Joseph Bach—have full command, but she's also there when we need her. This entire facility is on the former campus of her grandmother's old alma mater. It was an all-women's college that went bankrupt when the so-called Education Opportunities Act first passed. It was boarded up and rat-infested for about five years. But then Dr. O came in and, well, it's this peaceful little secluded bit of rolling hills and brownstone buildings just outside of the city. We're gated and protected. You'll be safe—"

"I'm not worried about that," Shane said.

"Understandably." Zerkowski smiled. "So what else can I tell you? The pay's really just a stipend. Forty bucks a week, but it's nontaxable income, which helps. Of course, we provide room and board—and clothing, if you need it. Most people need it."

Jesus. "That's not employment," Shane pointed out. "That's slavery."

"Hey, as much as we want you, there *are* plenty of applicants for *every* test session, and the cost of feeding and housing them— you—is steep. Plus there's close to a hundred techs, students, and other subjects who live here full time—"

Shane cut him off. "I'll be there."

Zerkowski smiled again. "Excellent. Whoops, gotta go. Busy night. See you in the morning, Lieutenant."

"It's *mister* now," Shane corrected him, but the connection had already been cut.

So okay. He was going to do this. They knew all about him, and still wanted him to attend. Which probably meant that this neural integration testing program was going to involve his doing calculus not only while digging ditches, but also while, oh, say, being waterboarded or otherwise tortured.

But he was going to have a lovely place to sleep and delicious food to eat. And a half-bottle of wine to drink each day.

And, yeah, despite the perks, they were going to lock him up every night. So it was going to be like serving time in a really fancy prison.

With no real freedom.

And quite possibly no access to women. Or at least no ability to be alone with anyone.

The slide show was still going, and it faded up on another large building that was six or seven stories high. *The barracks,* Shane read, which was more like it. Family housing was one thing, but he didn't have a family, so he'd no doubt be given a bunk and a foot-locker in a room with his fellow male test subjects.

Which was fine, but limiting when it came to sex.

And there it was—Shane's agenda for tonight: Get his sorry ass laid. It had been too many months since he'd enjoyed female company.

So far, today, he'd managed to not get beaten within an inch of his life. And he'd finally found employment from an organization that didn't give a shit about the blacklists. Maybe—if the Ober-meyer Institute's work wasn't too reprehensible—he could work his way from test subject to security guard.

A place like that surely needed *some* kind of security.

Maybe—finally—his luck had started to change.

THREE

The Med Center was in turmoil when Joseph Bach returned to the Obermeyer Institute, with the full staff—six doctors and a dozen nurses—all working hard to keep Nathan Hempford alive.

Stephen Diaz was already back in the gated compound, but Michelle Mackenzie was nowhere to be found.

Bach wasn't surprised. He knew from the way she'd looked at him as he'd helped her to her feet, that she'd received a full dose of the anguish he'd fired off at tonight's villain. Stephen, however, hadn't gotten hit by that particular wrecking ball—he didn't have the same empathic skills that Mac did.

But that was to be expected. No two Greater-Thans accessed the exact same neural pathways. And even though Stephen and Mac were both rare Fifties—fifty percent integrated and highly advanced—their mental skill-sets were as varied as their eye color, their skin tone, and even the number of freckles upon their faces.

Annie'd had too many freckles to count, with the main concentration running across her sun-kissed cheeks and nose, beneath her sparkling blue eyes. . . .

Bach had to stop and take a breath, because the magnitude of his loss still made his stomach clench. And while it was true that time healed all wounds, and he'd had plenty of it to work out the guilt and the blame, he hadn't yet mastered the regret or the soul-crushing sorrow. So he'd never progressed beyond more than a thick scab, which he usually easily ignored. Tonight, however, he'd intentionally torn it open.

Someone touched his arm, and Bach spun toward the potential threat, only to find Elliot Zerkowski backing away from him fast, hands raised in alarm.

"Whoa," said the research and support department head. "Whoa, I was just . . ." But then he moved back in, his concern palpable. "You okay there, Maestro? You're looking a little pale. How's your back?"

"My back is fine." Of course, it twinged, just slightly, at that very moment, but that didn't make him a liar. A slight echo of discomfort *was* fine. Bach forced a smile as he waved the other man off. He gave a nod to Haley, one of his top research assistants, who looked as if she were thinking about asking if he needed help. She glanced at Elliot, who nodded a reassurance, so she didn't stop.

"I'm fine," Bach repeated as Elliot turned to look at him. "But it was a difficult night."

"I heard. Let's get you into a room—"

"Not yet," Bach said. "I still need to—"

"Fall on your face in the hallway? I don't *think* so. Kyle," Elliot called to one of the nurses hurrying past them toward the ER, "let the med team know I'm putting Dr. Bach into exam room one. And round up Doctors Diaz and Mackenzie—I want a full on them both tonight." He turned back to Bach. "I was coming to find you anyway. It'll be just as easy for me to ask some debrief follow-ups and to give you a sit-rep while we're checking your vitals."

Bach didn't argue, because he knew it had to be done. He'd already filed a preliminary report on his way back to the Institute, but he'd known there'd be additional questions because he'd been purposely vague.

And *he* had some questions, too. "How's Nathan Hempford?" he asked as he preceded Elliot into room one—just a few convenient steps down the pristine and sterile-looking hall.

"Nuh-uh," Elliot said. "I go first. You know the drill."

Bach did. Still, he had to know. "At least you can tell me about his family. Are *they* okay?"

"They're fine, but you were right about the three-year-old. She has a mild concussion. We're monitoring that." Elliot was also monitoring Bach closely, watching to make sure he didn't do a nosedive as he took off his overcoat and hung it on one of the hooks by the door, kicked off his boots, and stripped down to his T-shirt and shorts—a prerequisite for a full, detailed medical scan.

With Dr. Obermeyer's cutting-edge technology, it was possible to do what many doctors called a shortcut or *jot* scan—with a patient fully clothed and in motion.

But a full, detailed medical scan required complete stillness from the patient, and as few layers of clothing as possible. It took anywhere from one to three minutes, depending on the hardware—which was remarkably quick, considering the information it provided. Blood pressure, heart rate, EKG, full blood work were the basics. It also provided details on any and all illnesses and injuries, including broken bones and soft tissue damage.

Unlike standard hospital med scanners, the equipment at OI had been programmed to include information that most of the medical community still thought was bunk—like the patient's current integration levels.

Not that Bach's levels ever changed.

Still, the medical team here at OI was nothing if not thorough.

"Computer, access EZ," Elliot verbally activated the comm-station as he watched Bach climb onto the hospital bed and lean back. "Prepare full scan of Dr. Joseph Bach."

"Computer, access JB-one," Bach told the computer. "Volume off, please."

There was no need for the computer to go droning on with his scan results.

"Computer, audio notify," Elliot said, overriding Bach's command, "any unusual readings."

"There won't be any," Bach told him.

Elliot gave him a sunny smile. "Getting an official, documented verification of that from your med scan will make me tremendously happy. Now, stay still."

Bach didn't. He sat up. "First, just . . . Tell me if you think Nathan's got a shot."

"He does," Elliot said. "You know that. They all do."

Of course, that was just Elliot being optimistic. They'd yet to save a single jokering addict here at OI. But one of these days, they'd unlock the mysteries of this devastating drug. Bach knew that Elliot was certain of that.

"Brain damage?" he asked.

"Undetermined." Elliot paused. "But likely."

Bach already knew that, too, and he nodded. And then he sat back and held still, and the scanner clicked on.

"Hempford definitely double-dosed," Elliot said, as he checked the test results that were already filling the computer monitor. "And as far as we can tell, the drug was from the same batch we've been seeing over the past few months. That shit is strong, and *shit*'s the scientific term, Doctor. Part of the filler is some kind of electrolyte sports drink and blah blah blah. I've already zapped you a file of my report." He glanced over his shoulder at Bach. "Somehow you always get me talking first. If I didn't know myself better, I'd wonder if you weren't jedi-ing me. *These aren't the droids we're looking for.* My questions for *you*, Obi-Wan, are more along the WTF line. Like, *seriously*? Hempford was immune to *everything* you threw at him, except this mojo you described as a *projected wall of pain*?"

The scanner chimed as it clicked off, and Bach sat back up and shook his head. "He was immune to everything we *tried* throwing at him," he said, reiterating the wording from his own report. "There wasn't a lot of time for experimentation. The reason we knew to try projecting pain was because, early on in the altercation, Mac injured her ankle—pretty badly, I think. You should check, it might even be broken."

"She kinda needs to show up for that, but do go on. She injured her ankle and . . . ?"

"Because Hempford was a force-bender, *Mac* was getting hit by everything I was throwing at *him,* and she couldn't handle that *and* shield her pain. At least not during that initial burst when she was first injured." Bach rotated his own ankle at the memory. It was fine now, but he, too, had gotten a taste of the intense burn. "The joker apparently wasn't able to block her pain *or* bounce it back toward us, so once we figured that out, we blasted him with everything we had."

"Physical pain." Behind his dark-rimmed glasses, Elliot's blue eyes were skeptical. "And that was enough to knock him out?"

"Has Mac submitted her report?"

"Answering a question with a question," Elliot observed, turning to lean against the comm-station, his arms crossed. "Very interesting. No, she has not. And what, pray tell, will I find in Dr. Mackenzie's intentionally brain-numbing dry list of facts when she finally *does* get around to doing her paperwork?"

"It wasn't just physical pain. It was . . ." Bach just said it. "Emotional. Also."

Elliot blinked once, but wisely didn't comment. Instead, he turned back to the computer, checking the final results of Bach's med scan.

"Knowing Mac, she might not mention it," Bach continued. "But I've been thinking about it, and . . . It's important that you know."

"Science over privacy, huh?" Elliot said. "I'm not sure I'd be willing to play *that* game."

"I trust you," Bach told him.

"I'm honored," Elliot said, glancing at him again. "But you know—and you *do* know—that if this turns out to be relevant, it's going to have to go into the official report."

And that was, indeed, the very opposite of private.

"With that said," Elliot continued, "my next question is about the specific nature of—"

"That," Bach interrupted him, "*isn't* important."

"I disagree," Elliot said evenly, as he crossed the room and tossed Bach his pants. "The memories of emotional pain caused by being bullied as a child light up different sections of the brain than, say, memories of pain caused by the death of a parent. And that's different, *too,* than—"

"I lost the only woman I ever loved," Bach said as he slipped on his jeans and fastened them. When he said it aloud, it seemed so simple, but it was, in truth, far more complicated. He stood up and crossed toward his sweater, pulling it over his head before adding, "She died, in part because of me, in part because of circumstances beyond my control. I accept that and forgive myself, but that doesn't make it any easier to live with. And that's . . . all you need to know."

Again, Elliot tried to hide his surprise, but then he just gave up. "I'm so sorry, Joseph," he said. And he was. Bach could feel the sympathy radiating off of the man.

There was envy there, too. For years, Elliot had been in a marriage that he'd thought was rock solid, when in fact his husband, Mark, had cheated on him repeatedly. It had been three years since their divorce, and Bach knew that Elliot was still wounded. He'd come to the conclusion, though, that Mark simply hadn't been able to love Elliot—at least not the way that Elliot had loved Mark. Or so Elliot had told Bach.

"I'm sorry, too," Bach said as jammed his feet back into his boots. "I take it I'm cleared to leave."

"You're showing signs of slight dehydration, and your blood sugar's a little low," Elliot reported. "It's not out of normal range, but I know you better than the computer does. You've also got some blood vessel constriction—again very slight. But it makes me think there's a migraine out there with your name on it, so heads up."

Bach nodded. "I'm already aware of that, and adjusting."

"Your back's fine."

"I know."

"There's bruising on your left cheekbone," Elliot told him, "but it's fading fast. When *was* the last time, I wonder, that you took a hit to the face?"

A good question. "A long time ago."

"I'll bet. Knowing this guy was able to get in a shot like that is alarming," Elliot said. "And speaking of alarming? Here's a fun fact about tonight's joker: He wasn't a frequent flier. Tonight was his very first injection."

Bach looked sharply at the other doctor.

"Yeah," Elliot said, drawing the word out.

"He jokered," Bach needed to clarify. "He went completely insane—on his *first ever* injection of Destiny? You're certain of that."

. "We'll test him again," Elliot said. "But three times so far, the answer's been *yes.*"

"That's . . . not good."

"I hear you," Elliot said with an equal amount of grim. "Oh, and something else came in that you're going to hate. I mean, if you allowed yourself to. You know, hate. And yes, I find myself stalling . . ."

This was going to be bad. Bach made himself breathe. "Just tell me."

"Promise you won't hit me with a wall of pain and fry my brain?"

"Not funny," Bach said.

"Yeah, it kinda was," Elliot pointed out. "The joke being that'd you'd just randomly start unleashing your heretofore unacknowledged inner darkness and—"

"Did I actually *fry* Hempford's brain?" Bach had to ask. "Because Mac got hit by it, too."

"You take things so literally," Elliot said. "And no. The drugs fried his brain. But you definitely added a jalapeño garnish. I doubt, though, that it was something Mac couldn't handle. Although it *would* be nice if she came in so we could check her out."

Bach just waited.

And Elliot finally said, "Nika Taylor, age thirteen. The Twenty who popped to the top of your to-recruit list of Potentials? Her sister *just* filed a missing persons report with the Boston Police.

The girl vanished on her way home from school today." He moved toward the wall station. "If you want I can . . ."

But Bach shook his head. He didn't have to use the computer to access the file. He knew exactly which girl Elliot was talking about. Out of the dozens of recently identified candidates for OI's training program for thirteen-to-fifteen-year-olds, Nika Taylor had an incredible natural talent, and by far the greatest raw potential. She'd appeared on Bach's list a mere hour before the police had called, asking for that assist with Nathan Hempford.

Out of all of the bad news this night had brought, this was the worst.

Nika Taylor's abduction—and it was an abduction, Bach didn't doubt that for a moment—meant that the very bad people who manufactured Destiny, the drug that was illegally distributed and sold to hapless fools like Hempford, had access to the same information that Bach and the Obermeyer Institute did.

Not only that, but they now apparently got that information hours earlier than OI's analysis team.

Bach jammed his arms into his overcoat, because impending migraine be damned—he was going back out into the night. "Send the girl's home address to my car's GPS."

"Already done," Elliot said, raising his voice as Bach went out the door. "Food and drink, Maestro! And do me a pretty and call Mac? She's ducking my calls, but maybe she'll talk to you. I want her butt in here, and I want it now!"

———

"Hey, babe, I'm . . ." *Home,* Mac had been about to say. Except Justin wasn't there. And he wasn't merely out with some friends for the evening. He was gone—and he'd been gone for at least several days. *And* he'd been annoyed with her when he'd left. She could still feel his lingering frustration as she stepped into the apartment—his emotions had been that strong.

She limped farther inside and closed the door by leaning on it. She'd stopped at the drugstore on her way here, and she tossed the bag with her purchases on the sofa, even as she reached for her phone to check her messages.

Bach, Diaz, and Elliot had all called within the past twenty minutes. It was a no-brainer that they were looking for her—they knew she'd been hurt.

Her intention had been to make a quick pit stop here and kill two birds with one stone—get Justin to stop whining by delivering him some immediate gratification, *and* get her ankle healed to a level where she wouldn't be benched for days or even weeks.

She scrolled past Elliot's latest text—*Where ARE you?*—and went back through several days' worth of messages from her OI co-workers to last Wednesday, where there had been three missed calls from Justin, all in a row. She'd made note of it at the time, but had been too busy to listen, let alone call him back. Going backward chronologically, she saw that he'd also called on Tuesday, twice, and once each on Monday, Sunday, Saturday, and last Friday.

Those calls had all slipped past her radar. Damn, she was a shitty girlfriend.

It was possible he'd gotten a job out of town, maybe even gone on tour.

Justin was an actor, and even though he'd been going on auditions steadily since he'd graduated from Emerson College last year, he'd yet to get more than a callback, so she was skeptical. Still, there was a first time for everything.

Fingers crossed, Mac started with his most recent message, highlighting it and putting the phone to her ear to listen.

"It's me." Justin sounded pissed off, which was usually the way his phone messages went. No news there. "I didn't want to do this via voice mail, but since you're not going to call me back or even bother to stop by, I don't have much choice, do I?" He took a deep breath. "Look, I met someone at work—Sandi. I told you about her—she worked the drive-through? At first we were just friends, but then . . . I didn't mean for it to happen, but it did, and . . . God, Mac, you know how much I appreciate all you've done for me. And I can't quite believe I'm doing this, but . . . Sandi's great, and she actually wants more from me than the random booty call, so . . ."

This was entirely Mac's fault. She'd put too much faith in her power to enthrall, combined with Justin's selfishly opportunistic greed, and she'd let too much time lapse between her visits.

"Her dad manages a Big Box, back in Ohio, outside of Columbus, and he can get me a job," Justin's voice mail went on. "I suck at being an actor, and I suck even more at being a fry-cook, so . . . I'm going to Ohio with Sandi, and . . . I'm sorry, Mac. I really am. I didn't want to tell you like this. I hope . . . Well, I hope, someday, that you find what you're looking for."

And with that, he ended the message.

Truth was, he *wouldn't* have told her any other way than over the phone. If she'd called him back and he'd asked her to come see him . . . ?

All she would have had to do was step through the door, and he'd instantly be dazzled, all of his childish petulance gone. He'd be like, *Sandi who?* In fact, last time Mac had been here he'd brought the other girl up in conversation. But then he'd looked a little puzzled, as if he'd forgotten what he was going to say about her.

Mac hadn't thought twice about it. It was all just part of what they did whenever she showed up. Justin told her what he'd been doing since they'd last connected—usually not a lot—and she . . . Well, she gave him a list of excuses—all true—for why she hadn't called, why it had been so long since her last visit. Work was crazy, she'd had to travel, and this time she'd even lost her phone. And even though he never really understood, he forgave her.

Always.

And then the talking part of their visit was over and he would drill her. There wasn't much that Justin was good at, but when it came to sex, he was a natural.

The last time, it had happened right on the kitchen table. He'd swept the clutter off onto the floor, as she'd laughed and kissed him back and sent him into orbit, too.

The table was clear again now—the entire place was tidy, the garbage was out, there were no perishables rotting in the fridge. He'd cleaned up before leaving, which was so not a typical Justin thing to do that Mac was pretty certain this Sandi girl had been involved.

Part of her still couldn't believe that he'd actually left. He'd *left*. But his clothes were gone from the closet, and he'd taken the quilt off the bed—the one that his grandmother had made. He'd left his cell phone behind on the bedside table—no doubt because Mac had bought it for him.

He'd also left her last month's electric bill—another expense she'd always picked up, along with the rent.

She stashed both items in the pockets of her cargo pants as she stared at the bed, wondering if he and Sandi had . . .

Okay, don't go there. She could feel the girl's presence in the apartment. She could practically taste the bitch's happiness, but it was more about going home. Or maybe not. *She was finally going home, and Daddy would love Justin, but not half as much as the way* she *loved Justin when he—*

Yeah, he'd had sex with Sandi-with-an-i in that bed. More than once. Nice.

It made her think about Tim, and she hated thinking about Tim—or her father, or her father's third wife and Tim's mother, Janice. None of whom Mac had seen or even e-mailed in over a dozen years.

Mac limped back into the living room, well aware that she'd thought about Tim every time she'd visited Justin. It had been impossible not to. It sucked, and she would have stayed away, if she didn't need to use the sex to help her heal. Yeah, *that* was why she'd come here as often as she had.

It certainly hadn't had anything to do with real emotion—with anything as laughable as love.

She knew that Justin didn't love her. He'd never loved her. Instead, she'd inadvertently used her crazy-ass Greater-Than mental powers to make him *think* that he did, to make him want her, to desire her. She'd charmed him, dazzled him, entranced him. And then she'd given in to temptation, hating herself for her weakness, and kept him like a self-walking, self-feeding puppy in this apartment that she'd paid for, telling herself that he was using her as much as she was using him.

And every now and then she'd dropped by to get shagged and adored by the kind of guy who would never have adored her, let alone been faithful, had she not been a Greater-Than.

There'd been a time, before Mac had learned to use and control her talents, when out of sight very literally meant out of mind. She'd discovered at an early age that when she was with a man— any man—she had the power to make him want her, ardently. But as soon as she walked away, those feelings vanished—instantly forgotten. Over the years, that had changed. She'd not only learned how to control her powers, which, most of the time, kept total strangers from following her down the street, tongues hanging out. But she'd also developed her skills to the point where a lover could well remain charmed and faithful for weeks.

Justin had pursued her—relentlessly—when she'd first met him. She'd tried to shut him down, but he hadn't let up. And she was probably going to go to hell—if it existed—for not being strong enough to walk away. Although she *did* pay for her sins by letting him live here for free.

But now he was gone.

Mac left the apartment, locking the door behind her, and as she went down the stairs that led out to the street, she jarred her ankle hard enough to bring tears to her eyes, despite her ability to block physical pain.

Yeah, *that's* why she was crying. Her fucking foot hurt. God, she was a pathetic idiot, weeping over some stupid man.

Justin hadn't really meant all that much to her, either. If he truly had? *She* would've left *him*—a long time ago.

Mac went down to the sidewalk, jamming her hands into her gloves and then her pockets, because even though it was spring, the night wind was cold. Hunching her shoulders, she limped toward Kenmore Square, unsure of her long-term plans—what to do with the apartment now that Justin was history, how to deal with her injured ankle—but dead solid when it came to the next twenty minutes of her life.

She was heading to the nearest bar on Beacon Street—a dive called Father's that had been there forever.

It had been one total hellfest of a night, and she needed a drink.

—————

Shane was winning when she walked in.

His plan was a simple one: spend a few hours here in this low-life bar and win enough money playing pool to take the T down to Copley Square, where there was a cluster of expensive hotels. Hit one of the hotel bars, where the women not only had all of their teeth, but they also had corporate expense accounts and key cards to the comfortable rooms upstairs.

But drinks there were pricey. Shane had spent his remaining fifty-eight seconds at the Kenmore comm-station checking menus, and he knew he'd need at least twenty dollars just to sit at the bar and nurse a beer. Fifty to buy a lady a drink. And expense account or not, you had to be ready to start the game by buying the lady a drink.

But then *she* walked in—or rather limped in. She was smaller than the average woman, and slight of build. She'd also injured her foot, probably her ankle, but other than that, she carried herself like an operator. She'd certainly scanned the room like one as she'd come in.

Which was when Shane had gotten a hit from her eyes. They were pale and he couldn't tell from this distance whether they were blue or green or even a light shade of brown. But the color didn't matter, it was the glimpse he got of the woman within that had made him snap to attention—internally, that is.

She looked right at him, gave him some direct eye contact, then assessed him. She took a very brief second to appreciate his handsome face and trim form, catalogued him, and finally dismissed him.

Of course, he *was* playing the role of the hick just off the turnip truck—he would have dismissed himself, too, had he just walked in.

Shane watched from the corner of his eye as she sat at the bar, shrugged out of her jacket to reveal a black tank top, then pulled off her hat and scarf. She was completely tattoo-free—at least in all of the traditional places that he could currently see.

Her light-colored hair was cut short and was charmingly messed. But it was the back of her neck that killed him. Long and slender and pale, it was so utterly feminine—almost in proud defiance of her masculine clothing choices, her nicely toned shoulders and arms, and her complete and total lack of makeup.

And Shane was instantly intrigued. He found himself restrategizing and forming a solid Plan B almost before he was aware he was doing it.

Plan A had him missing the next shot—the seven in the side pocket and the four in the corner—which would lead to his opponent, a likable enough local man named Pete, winning the game. After which Shane would proclaim it was Pete's lucky night, and challenge the man to a rematch, double or nothing, all the while seeming to get more and more loaded.

Because Pete was a far better player than he was pretending to be. Pete was hustling *him,* and all of the regulars in this bar knew it, and at that point the bets would start to fly. Shane would drunkenly cover them all, but then would play the next game in earnest, identifying himself as a hustler in kind as he kicked Pete's decent but amateurish ass. He'd then take his fairly won earnings and boogie out of Dodge.

Because if there was one thing Shane had learned from the best pool player in his SEAL team—an E-6 named Magic Kozinski—it was that you didn't hustle a game and stick around for a victory beer. That could be hazardous to one's health. Resentment would grow. And resentment plus alcohol was never a good mix.

Plan B, however, allowed Shane to stick around. It gave him options.

So he called and then sank both the seven and the four, then called and missed the two, which put the balls on the table into a not-impossible but definitely tricky setup. Which Pete intentionally missed, because making the shot would've ID'd him as the hustler that *he* was.

They finished the game that way—with Pete setting up a bunch of nice, easy shots, and letting Shane win. Which put five dollars into Shane's nearly empty pocket.

Which was enough to buy a lady a drink in a shithole like this.

"You're on fire tonight," Pete said, when Shane didn't do an appropriate asshole-ish victory dance. "How 'bout a rematch, bro?"

And Shane wanted to sit Pete down and give him a crash course in hustling, because this was a beginner's mistake. You never, *ever* suggested the rematch yourself, not if you'd just intentionally lost the game. The mark had to do it, otherwise the hustle was too much of a con. The mark had to think he was going to screw *you* out of your hard-earned pay.

Pete's suggestion made him significantly less likable and more of the kind of sleazebag who deserved his ass handed to him on a platter.

"I don't know, man," Shane said, massaging the muscles at the base of his skull as if he'd had a hard day at the construction site. "You're pretty good. Let me think about it . . . ?"

Pete thankfully didn't push. "I'll be here all night. But, hey, lemme buy you another beer. On account of your winning and all."

Better and better. As long as Pete didn't follow him over to the bar. "Thanks," Shane said. "I'm going to, um, hit the men's and . . ."

But instead of going into the bathroom in the back, he went to the bar and slid up onto one of the stools next to the woman with the pretty eyes. She was drinking whiskey, straight up, and she'd already ordered and paid for her next two glasses—they were lined up in front of her in a very clear message that said, *No, butthead, you may not buy me a drink.* She'd also purposely left an empty-stool buffer between herself and the other patrons. And the glance she gave Shane as he sat let him know that she would have pre-ferred keeping her personal DMZ intact.

Her eyes were light brown, but she'd flattened them into a very frosty *don't fuck with me,* dead-woman-walking glare. It was a hell of a talent. The first chief Shane had ever worked with in the SEAL teams—Andy Markos, rest his soul—could deliver the same soulless affect. It was scary as shit to be hit with that look. Even to those who knew him well and outranked him.

But here and now, Shane let this woman know that he *wasn't* scared and *didn't* give a shit that she didn't want him sitting there, by giving her an answering smile; letting his eyes twinkle a little, as if they were sharing a private joke.

She broke the eye contact as she shook her head, muttering something that sounded like, "Why do I do this to myself?"

Any conversational opener was a win, so Shane took it for the invitation that it wasn't. "Do what to yourself?"

Another head shake, this one with an eye roll. "Look, I'm not interested."

"Actually, I came over because I saw that you were limping," Shane lied. "You know, when you came in? I trashed my ankle about a year ago. They giving you steroids for the swelling?"

"Really," she said. "You're wasting your time."

She wasn't as pretty as he'd thought she was, from a distance. But she wasn't exactly not-pretty either. Still, her face was a little too square, her nose a little too small and round, her lips a little too narrow. Her short hair wasn't blond as he'd first thought, but rather a bland shade of uninspiring light brown. She was also ath-letic to the point of near breastlessness. The thug he'd tangled with earlier that evening had had bigger pecs than this woman did be-neath her tank top.

But those eyes . . .

They weren't just brown, they were golden brown, with bits of hazel and specks of green and darker brown thrown in for good measure.

They were incredible.

"Be careful if they do," Shane told her. "You know, give you steroids. I had a series of shots that made me feel great. They really helped, but ten months after the last injection, I was still testing positive for performance-enhancing drugs. Which was problematic when I tried to earn some easy money cage fighting."

She turned to look at him. "Is that it? You done with your public service announcement?"

He smiled back at her. "Not quite. I did a little research online and found out that that particular drug can stay in your system for as long as eighteen months. I've still got six months to kill."

"Before you can become a cage fighter," she said, with plenty of *yeah right* scorn in her voice. "Does that usually impress the girls?"

"I've actually never told anyone before," Shane admitted. "You know, that I stooped that low? But it *is* amazing what you'll do when you're broke, isn't it?" He finished his beer and held the empty up toward the bartender, asking for another. "Pete's paying," he told the man, then turned back to the woman, who'd gone back to staring at her whiskey. "I'm Shane Laughlin. From San Diego."

She sighed and finished her drink, pushing the empty glass toward the far edge of the bar and pulling her second closer to her and taking a sip.

"So what are you doing in Boston, Shane?" he asked for her, as if she actually cared. "Wow, that's a good question. I'm former Navy. I haven't been out all that long, and I've been having some trouble finding a job. I got a lead on something short term—here in Boston. I actually start tomorrow. How about you? Are you local?"

When she turned and looked at him, her eyes were finally filled with life. It was a life that leaned a little heavy on the anger and disgust, but that was better than the flat nothing she'd given him earlier. "You seriously think I don't know that you're slumming?"

Shane laughed his surprise. "What?"

"You heard what I said and you know what I meant."

"Wow. If anyone's slumming here . . . Did you miss the part of the conversation where I admitted to being the loser who can't find a job?"

"You and how many millions of Americans?" she asked. "Except it's a shocker for you, isn't it, Navy? You've never *not* been in demand—you probably went into the military right out of high school and . . . Plus, you were an officer, right? I can smell it on you." She narrowed her eyes as if his being an officer was a terrible thing.

"Yeah, I was officer." He dropped his biggest bomb. "In the SEAL teams."

She looked him dead in the eye as it bounced. "Big fucking deal, Dixie-Cup. You're out now. Welcome to the real world, where things don't always go your way."

He laughed—because what she'd just said *was* pretty funny. "You obviously have no idea what a SEAL does."

"I don't," she admitted. "No one does. Not since the military entered the government's cone of silence."

"I specialized in things not going my way," Shane told her.

"So why'd you leave, then?" she asked, and when he didn't answer right away, she toasted him with her drink and drained it. "Yeah, that's what I thought."

"I'm proud of what I did—what I was," he said quietly. "Even now. *Especially* now. But you're right—partly right. About the shock. I had no idea how bad *bad* could be, before I was . . . kicked out and blacklisted." Her head came up at that. "So, see, *you're* the one who's slumming. You could get into trouble just for talking to me."

She was looking at him now—really looking. "What exactly did you do?"

Shane looked back at her, directly into those eyes as he thought about his team, about Rick and Owen, about Slinger and Johnny, and yes, Magic, too. . . . "I disobeyed a direct order—which is something I did all the time out in the world, as a SEAL team CO. But this time? It was apparently unforgivable. And that, combined with my need to speak truth, even to power, and my inability to grovel and appropriately kiss ass . . . It got ugly. In the end, someone had to go, so . . ." He shrugged, still convinced after all these hard months that he'd done the right thing. "I was stripped of my rank and command—and dishonorably discharged."

She sat there, gazing at him. His answer had been rather vague and even cryptic, but it was still more than he'd told anyone since it had happened. So he just waited, looking back at her, until she finally asked, "So what do you want from *me*?"

There were so many possible answers to that question, but Shane went with honesty. "I saw you come in and I thought . . . Maybe you're looking for the same thing I am. And since I find you unbelievably attractive . . ."

She smiled at that, and even though it was a rueful smile, it transformed her. "Yeah, actually, you don't. I mean, you think you find me . . . But . . ." She shook her head.

Shane leaned forward. "I'm pretty sure you don't know what I'm thinking." He tried to let her see it in his eyes, though—the fact that he was thinking about how it would feel for both of them with his tongue in her mouth, with her hands in his hair, her legs locked around him as he pushed himself home.

He reached out to touch her—nothing too aggressive or invasive—just the back of one finger against the narrow graceful-ness of her wrist.

But just like that, the vaguely fuzzy picture in his head slammed into sharp focus, and she was moving against him, naked in his arms, and, Christ, he was seconds from release as he gazed into her incredible eyes. . . .

Shane sat back so fast that he knocked over his bottle of beer. He fumbled after it, grabbing it and, because it had been nearly full, the foam volcanoed out of the top. He covered it with his mouth, taking a long swig, grateful for the cold liquid, aware as hell that he'd gone from semi-aroused to fully locked and loaded, in the beat of a heart.

What the hell?

Yeah, it had been a long time since he'd gotten some, but *damn*.

His nameless new friend had pushed her stool slightly back from the bar—away from him—and she was now frowning down at her injured foot, rotating her ankle. She then looked up at him, and the world seemed to tilt. Because there was heat in her eyes, too. Heat and surprise and speculation and . . .

Absolute possibility.

"I'm Mac," she told him as she tossed back the remains of her final drink. "And I don't usually do this, but . . . I've got a place, just around the corner."

She was already pulling on her jacket, putting on her scarf and hat.

As if his going with her was a given. As if there were no way in hell that he'd turn her down.

Shane was already off the stool and grabbing his own jacket, as she—Mac—went out the door. Her limp was less pronounced—apparently the whiskey had done her some good. In fact, she was moving pretty quickly. He had to hustle to keep up.

"Hey," he said, as they hit the street, and the bar door closed behind him. "Um, Mac? Maybe we should find, you know, a dealer? I'm not carrying any um . . . So unless you have, you know . . ." He cleared his throat.

She stopped walking and looked up at him. Standing there on the sidewalk, he was aware of how much bigger and taller he was. She was tiny—and significantly younger than he'd thought. More like twenty-two, instead of pushing thirty, the way he'd figured her to be, back in the bar.

Or maybe it was just the glow from the dim streetlight, making her look like youthful beauty and desire personified.

"Why do men have a problem saying *the pill*?" she asked.

Shane laughed. "It's not the words," he told her. "It's the concept. See, what if I'd misunderstood and—"

"You didn't. And FYI, this is Massachusetts. It's still legal here. No need to back-alley it."

"Well, good. But . . . we still need . . . some."

She smiled, and Jesus, she was beautiful. "Don't worry, I got it handled." Her gaze became a once-over that was nearly palpable, lingering for a moment on the unmistakable bulge beneath the button-fly of his jeans. She looked back into his eyes. "Or I will, soon enough."

No doubt about it, his luck had changed.

"Please promise that you're not luring me back to your apartment with the intention of locking me in chains and keeping me as your love slave," he said. "Or—wait. Maybe what I really want is for you to promise that you *are*."

She laughed at that. "You're not my type for long-term imprisonment," she told him. But then she stood on her toes, tugging at the front of his jacket so that he leaned down. She was going to kiss him and they both knew it, but she took her time and he let her, just waiting as she looked into his eyes, as she brought her mouth up and softly brushed her lips against his.

Shane closed his eyes—God, it was sweet—as he let himself be kissed again, and then again. And this time, she tasted him, her tongue against his lips. He opened his mouth, and then, Christ, it wasn't sweet, it was pure hunger, white-hot and overwhelming, and he pulled her hard into his arms, even as she clung to him, trying to get even closer.

The world could've exploded around him and he wouldn't have cared. He wouldn't have looked up—wouldn't have stopped kissing her.

And through all the layers of clothing, their jackets, their pants, his shorts, and whatever she had on beneath her cargo BDUs— God, he couldn't wait to find out what she wore for underwear— Shane felt her stomach, warm and taut against his erection, and just that distant contact was enough to bring him teetering dangerously close to the edge.

And by the time he made sense of that information and formed a vaguely coherent thought—holy shit, just kissing this woman was enough to make him crazy—it was almost too late.

Almost. But only because she pulled away from him. She was laughing, her incredible eyes dancing as she looked up at him. As if she knew exactly what he was feeling.

She held out her gloved hand for him, so he took it, and then— bad ankle be damned—she pulled him forward.

And together, they started to run.

FOUR

Anna's cell phone rang at a little before midnight, and she dug through her backpack for it, even though it wasn't Nika's ring.

The word *private* appeared on the phone's tiny screen instead of a typical ten-digit number, and she took a deep breath before answering, half-dreading and half-hoping that Nika's abductors were on the other end with their ransom demands.

"This is Anna Taylor," she said, hoping she sounded less exhausted and more in control than she was currently feeling, having repeatedly and fruitlessly walked the route from Cambridge Academy to the tiny studio apartment that she and Nika shared.

Her breath hung in the cold night air as she closed her eyes, waiting, hoping . . .

"Miss Taylor, this is Dr. Joseph Bach from the Obermeyer Institute. One of my colleagues informed me that you've filed a missing persons report for your sister, Nika?"

Whoever he was, his voice was pleasant. It was evenly modulated, and it hinted at formal training—his elocution was quite good. *Moses supposes his toeses are roses. Singin' in the Rain,* that old movie about old movies, was one of Nika's favorites.

Maybe Dr. Bach was an elderly man in good health, with still-excellent breath-control.

But he'd asked her a question.

"Yes, I did," Anna answered quickly after that long and probably strange pause. "My sister didn't come home from school this afternoon. And yes, I know she hasn't been missing for that long, and that she's thirteen and capable of breaking rules, but she's not . . ." *Normal,* she'd been about to say. But that made Nika seem like a freak, and she wasn't. "Prone to going off the radar like this," she said instead. "Not ever. She's a good kid, and she knows I've made a lot of sacrifices for her to go to Cambridge Academy. She's a scholarship student there. We're not wealthy."

She emphasized that last bit, just in case he was one of those *citizen detectives*—the kind who'd snatched Nika up in the first place.

"I'm aware of that," he said. "I'm outside of your apartment, and I know you're not here, that you're probably still searching for your sister, but it's important that you spare a moment to talk with me. If you tell me where you are I'll—"

"Do you know where Nika is?" Anna was just around the corner from her building, and she began walking again, picking up her pace.

He hesitated. Just a little. "Not exactly."

"What does *that* mean?"

Another pause. "It means I have an idea as to who took her—and why she was taken. But I don't know precisely where she's being held. Not yet. Miss Taylor, it's urgent that—"

"Who took her?" Anna demanded as she crossed the street. Her building was in sight, and she could now see a tall, slender man in a long, dark overcoat, with his phone to his ear, standing on the sidewalk out in front. She slowed her pace. He was unaccompanied—or at least he appeared to be. Still . . .

She was suddenly very aware that she was alone on a dark, deserted street. And that at least one of the neighbors she'd met in her apartment building this evening had been some kind of drug addict. Meth, probably. The woman's teeth had been terrible.

"It's . . . complicated," Dr. Bach told her, turning to look directly at her, even though she was moving quietly and he couldn't possibly have heard her approach.

"I'm pretty smart," she said, closing her phone as she stopped a safe-feeling ten yards from him. If she had to, she could run, and she was fast. "Why don't you try me?"

He wasn't elderly. Not even close. His shoulder-length hair was dark and his eyes were brown, and the phrase *black Irish* came to mind, although, really, that meant his eyes should have been blue. Despite the brown eyes, his complexion was properly United-Kingdom-pale, his face lean, his features strong yet aristocratically perfect.

Cruel lips.

Anna had read that description once, in a romance novel. The hero had had *elegantly cruel lips.* She'd always thought that was a load of hyperbolic bull. Or at least she had before tonight.

Nika would've thought that Dr. Joseph Bach, with his elegantly cruel lips and pale complexion, looked like a vampire. The hot kind, with a soul—like Angel or Spike from *Buffy.*

And had Anna been just a few years younger, and had her fear and worry for her little sister not been consuming her, she might've agreed. This man *was* unnaturally handsome. But since there were no such things as vampires, either with or without souls, and since she was solidly grounded here in this current dreadful-enough-without-demons-and-monsters reality, he looked like *exactly* what he was—a slightly tired, very good-looking young man who no doubt knew all about the incredible stress that came with a missing child, and who purposely spoke and dressed the part of the gallant prince in a fairy tale, come to the rescue.

A gallant prince who spent a lot of time indoors, and didn't even remotely share her own racially-mixed, melting-pot heritage—which was all part of being a prince. The whole purebred-to-the-point-of-inbred thing came with the territory.

He was looking her over as carefully as she was inspecting him, and she knew that she didn't look like most people's idea of a Cinderella princess, with her wild mass of dark curls, her coffee-colored skin, and her hint-of-Mayan-ancestor's nose.

Of course, he wasn't much of a real prince himself if he made his living kidnapping girls and "finding" them for their distraught families.

He still hadn't tried to explain his *it's complicated,* so she asked him point-blank, "How much?"

"I'm sorry?"

"How much is it going to cost me to get Nika back?"

He didn't answer her. Instead, he said, "Let's go someplace a little warmer—and safer—to talk."

Anna laughed and crossed her arms. "Yeah, sorry, *Dr.* Bach, I'm not inviting you inside."

"I'm not asking that," he countered. "In fact, that's the last thing I want. I have no doubt that your apartment's been bugged."

"If the kidnappers bugged our apartment, then they know I have no money to pay any kind of ransom." And they also knew that, at twenty-five years old, she slept in the bottom rack of a bunk bed in a tiny room that she shared with her thirteen-year-old sister. If they'd been inside the place, they'd probably also guessed that she and Nika felt profoundly lucky to have their own kitchen and bathroom, rather than having to share with a bunch of strangers.

Although, if Anna didn't get a real job soon, they'd have to move into that kind of a rented-room arrangement. Assuming, that is, she was going to get Nika back. Her throat tightened.

"They're not looking for ransom," Bach told her somberly, in his Golden-Hollywood-era voice. "If I'm right about who they are, sometime in the next few hours—if they haven't done it already—they're going to decide that they want to keep Nika. Badly. At which point, they're also going to realize that they'll have to get rid of you."

What? "Get *rid* of . . . ?"

"Kill," he said, nodding. "You. Although first they might try taking you, too. If Nika's as talented as I think she is."

"Talented . . . ?" Now he was really freaking her out. "This doesn't make sense. Why would they want to kill me and keep her?" Anna asked. "If the whole point of kidnapping is to make money from ransom? And don't say *it's complicated.*"

He smiled rather ruefully as he took a set of keys from his pocket. "But I'm afraid it is." He pushed a button and a little car

that was parked right there at the curb flashed and the doors unlocked with a click. "Why don't you come with me to the Obermeyer Institute, and I'll do my best to explain."

Anna took a solid step back. "Why don't you just *do your best
to explain* right here and now?"

He sighed. Almost imperceptibly. "I know that the idea that
you're in danger isn't easy to process, and that you have no real
reason to trust me."

"Why *should* I trust you? Why should I believe *anything* you
tell me?"

This time he didn't hesitate. "Because I can get Nika back—
I *will* get her back. I'm one of the good guys, Miss Taylor."

And time seemed to hang as she gazed into Dr. Joseph Bach's
dark brown eyes. He exuded such absolute confidence, and she
found herself wanting to believe him. It would be so easy, in fact,
to believe him—to just throw herself into his extremely attractive
arms and beg him to rescue both her and her sister, to let him take
care of them, forever.

Instead, Anna took another step back, away from him, and
drew in a deep breath. Exhaled hard. And asked, "What kind of
doctor are you, exactly . . . ?"

He took his time answering. "I'm a surgeon," he finally said.

She laughed her disbelief. "I'm sorry, but it's just . . . *Before* you
lie? You really need to do your research. My mother was a doctor
and . . . Seriously? You're just too young. Next time try *intern.
Intern over at Mass General* might work a little better for you."

He smiled. "I'm not as young as I look. And I usually *do* hide
what I do, but . . . I didn't want to lie to you. I'm actually a *brain*
surgeon, Miss Taylor, although that's even harder for some people
to swallow. I have a variety of other degrees, too. Internal medi-
cine. Psychiatry."

"What, no rocket science?"

His smile broadened, revealing charming creases—too elegant
to be called dimples—along the sides of his mouth. "Actually, yes.
But I tend to leave that off the list. It makes people take me less
seriously."

"As opposed to that degree you got from clown college . . . ?"

He laughed. "I haven't done *that* yet," he admitted. "But I wrote the book—the Western one, anyway—on neural integration."

This was a little crazy, because part of her actually *wanted* to believe him, particularly when he let his amusement shine in his eyes.

"And that brings us back to your sister," he said, sobering and instantly serious again. "Did you know that she's twenty percent integrated? Has she had any outside training or . . ." He trailed off, no doubt because he could tell just from looking that he'd completely lost her.

Twenty percent *what*? "What does this have to do with finding Nika?" she asked him.

"Everything," he told her. "It's the reason she was taken. She's special and . . ." He frowned slightly and took his phone out of his pocket. He must've gotten a text because as he looked at the screen, his frown deepened. "I'm sorry, but we really do have to get out of here. Immediately." He opened the passenger-side door to his car.

"Mmm," Anna said. "Still not keen on getting into a car with someone I've just met."

"I can understand that." He gazed at her for a moment, and then sighed. Just a little bit. "I can help you . . . to trust me."

"By . . . How? Showing me your *citizen detective* ID card?" she asked. "Or a note from your mother saying, *Trust my son*?"

"My mother's dead," he told her.

She winced. "Sorry," she said. "I'm *so* sorry. That was . . . I didn't mean to . . ." She was unable to stop the sudden rush of tears to her eyes. "Mine is, too, and, God, what I wouldn't give for her to be here right now."

He looked at her and other than the sympathy and empathy that she could see in his eyes, he didn't move. He just stood there and did nothing, and nothing happened, except . . .

Anna was suddenly flooded with warmth, with peace, with a sense of calm certainty.

Joe Bach is going to find Nika.

Joe Bach is going to bring her home.
Joe Bach can be trusted.
She and Nika, both, will be completely safe with him. Always.
Mommy would've loved him. . . .

"We have equipment at the Institute," he said quietly, "that can track Nika's cell phone. I know that's something that you want to do as soon as possible. Although I have to be honest, Anna. Whoever took her isn't an amateur. They ditched or destroyed her phone right after they grabbed her. We're not going to find her that way."

Anna nodded. "I want to do it, though. Is it very expensive?"

"No," he said and he stepped out into the street, crossing around to the driver's-side door and opening it. "Come on."

It's time to go.
Joe Bach is a friend.
Anna nodded again and got into his car.

———

Mac fumbled as she unlocked the apartment door, wishing—not for the first time—that she shared Bach's and Diaz's telekinetic skills. While she had the ability to move large objects—cars, buses, the occasional jet plane—she'd yet to develop the small motor skills needed to finesse the inner workings of a lock. Of course, compared to Bach and D, she was still a relative newbie at this.

"Want me to . . . ?" Shane asked her, but she shook her head, pulling off her leather gloves so that she could use her fingers to get the key where it needed to go.

"I got it." The door finally opened, and as she led the former sailor inside, she realized that, if she'd been thinking clearly, she could've taken control of the thermostat back when they'd still been in the bar, so that heat would have begun ticking its way through the ancient radiators. Instead, the place was cold.

But she hadn't been thinking clearly. At least not about any of the Susie Homemaker shit that made an apartment feel all welcome and warm.

She'd never done more than furnish her various living spaces with the basics. She didn't hang pictures or curtains, didn't collect knickknacks or doodads or even old-fashioned DVDs or hard-copy books, the way some people did.

Stephen Diaz's quarters at OI had shelves on almost every available wall space. He had throw pillows, and expensive cookware, and art.

But Mac traveled light and saved nothing.

And an apartment like this one, in a crappy part of town, was just a place to crash.

Or keep some guy that she occasionally liked to screw.

She pulled off her hat and scarf, but kept her jacket on as she made her way to the thermostat over by the kitchen door, and pushed the arrow up to a walk-around-naked seventy-five degrees. It would take awhile to get there, though. Until then, they'd have to create their own heat.

Yeah.

She shrugged off her jacket, and turned to find the sailor still standing by the door, watching her.

Damn, he was attractive—tall and lean, with broad shoulders, narrow hips, and long legs. He was almost impossibly handsome, too, with that head of thick, reddish blond hair, a straight nose, a strong chin, and an almost elegant, gracefully shaped mouth that was quick to quirk up into a smile.

Kind of the way it was doing right now.

He was well-educated, and well-mannered, and his intelligence gleamed in his perfect-cloudless-sky-blue eyes.

And as scornful as she'd pretended to be about the whole officer-and-a-gentleman thing, it was a total turn-on.

He was the anti-Justin—a full-grown man to Justin's often-petulant boy.

His smile broadened at her perusal, and she didn't doubt for a second that a man this handsome knew exactly how good-looking he was. She would've bet her entire month's pay that he knew just how to make his eyes sparkle like that, in order to make a woman's heart beat a little harder.

It was working.

But she, too, had her own tricks in the charm department, so she couldn't blame him or cry foul.

He let a little heat into his eyes as he continued to just stand there, and her mouth actually went dry.

"You got another name," he whispered. Even his voice was sexy. A rich, accentless baritone with just a hint of smoke to give it a unique texture. "Besides just *Mac*?"

"I do," she said.

He waited, but when it was clear that she had no intention of telling him what it was, he laughed a little. His laughter was almost musical. "Okay," he said.

"Is it?" she asked.

"It has to be, doesn't it?" He took off his jacket then, and tossed it onto the sofa, but still didn't come any closer.

"You could leave in a huff," she pointed out.

He laughed even more at that, genuinely amused. "I suppose, in some alternate universe, I could, in fact, leave in a huff. But that's not going to happen here." He looked around then, at the small, austerely furnished living room, the attached dining area, the pass-through to the tiny kitchen, the hallway that led—just a few steps—to the bedroom. And then he looked back at her, clearly waiting for a cue.

So Mac gave him one. "I'd offer you a beer, or something to eat," she said, as she went down that little hall, "but I haven't been here in a while, and I'm pretty sure the cupboard's bare."

"I'm good. But . . . can I ask you something?" he asked as he followed her into the bedroom, where she turned on the bedside table lamp. He didn't wait for her to respond. "Am I here because—or in spite—of being blacklisted?"

"Neither," Mac said. "You're here because you were honest." She looked at him over her shoulder as she sat on the side of the bed that was farthest from the door. There was real irony in her words, because no way in hell was she going to be honest enough with *him* to say, *You're also here because just touching you put my self-healing mental powers into overdrive. I can't wait to see what happens to my ankle when we actually have sex.* "I happen to really like honesty."

"Note to self: Be more honest." He'd stopped in the doorway again, just leaning against the jamb as he watched her unfasten the laces of her boots.

"Don't forget the smiley face emoticon," she said. Her right boot came off easily and hit the floor with a thump. The left was going to be more of a challenge and she hesitated.

He laughed. "I don't think I've ever included a smiley face in a note."

"No?" she asked.

"Nope." He let the P pop.

"I didn't really think so," Mac said. It was probably better if she just kept her left boot on for now. Although *that* could be awkward when it came time to get out of her pants—which was going to happen soon. She hoped. "I was kidding. You're just such a . . . Boy Scout."

"Hardly." He laughed again at that as he broke eye contact to look around the room and take it all in: Cheap platform bed, secondhand dresser, mirror, closet door. Mac knew from the change in his body language that she'd inadvertently hit a nerve.

"That's not a bad thing," she hurried to tell him. "In *this* world? It's not. I didn't mean it to be. Bad."

"Still not leaving in a huff," he pointed out as he met her eyes again.

"But this time you thought about it," she countered.

Shane laughed. "No, ma'am, I most certainly did not."

"Okay, I'm sorry, but you just, like, proved that you're a Boy Scout. Who says *ma'am*?"

"I'm not a boy," he said.

"Believe me, I'm highly aware of that."

And in that moment, with that much heat in his eyes, she was sure he was going to move—pull off his T-shirt, join her on the bed, and kiss the shit out of her, the way he'd done out on the street. But he didn't. He just kept standing there, looking at her, smiling a little bit—which really worked with the full-on smolder from his pretty eyes.

"So what does that make you?" he finally asked, folding his arms across his chest in a way that made his biceps look huge. Also not by accident. Nor was it a fluke that his T-shirt was deliciously snug. "If I'm a Boy Scout. You're . . . the girl with the dragon tattoo?"

She answered his question in part by pulling her tank top up and over her head. "No tattoos," she said. "Of dragons or anything else. But feel free to check more thoroughly."

Heat flared again in his eyes, but he was observant and he'd clearly noticed that she hadn't yet taken off her left boot. And he finally moved closer, coming around to her side of the bed. "You need some help with that?"

"I'm a little afraid to take it off," she admitted.

He stopped. And it was clear he was going to ask a question, like, *When, exactly, did you hurt yourself?*

She didn't want to lie to him, certainly not by more than omission—not after he'd been so honest with her. So she said, and it wasn't a lie, "It's been feeling much better, but I think that's partly because the boot provides support. I've just mostly left it on. Since the injury." She left out the part where it had felt startlingly better after he'd touched her in the bar. And after that kiss, as well . . .

"That's one way to go," he said. "What did the doctor say?"

"Well . . ." Mac made a face.

Shane laughed, and his smile was like a sunrise and God, wasn't *that* some of the corniest shit that had ever sashayed through her brain. What she *should* be thinking, right about now, was *Justin who?* No need for any rainbows after a storm on a tropical island, or the perfect silence of an early morning snowfall, or a glorious sunrise or sunset or moonlight or spring flowers or puppies or fluffy newborn bunnies. And yet . . .

He'd crouched next to her still-booted foot and looked up with a neon-blue flash of eyes to say, "You *do* know that there're a lot of little bones in your feet and ankles, right? You might have a stress fracture, and not even know it. You really should get it scanned. If you want, I'll go with you, to the hospital."

He was just so beautiful and sincere in his kindness—and okay, yeah, he totally wanted to fuck her. That was really why he was here. But he was sincere in his desire, too. There was no ugliness involved—at least not that she could feel from him. He didn't have any issues at all with sex. He liked having it, and he was okay with himself for liking it.

And he absolutely wanted her to peel off her sports bra—she knew *that* because he kept looking at it, like he was trying to figure out where the clasp was so he could get it off of her.

"No clasp," she told him, as he knelt there before her, like some kind of knight in shining armor come to rescue her. "It pulls off, over my head. And going to the hospital isn't a good idea."

He instantly took her words the wrong way. "Of course. I understand. I wasn't thinking—"

"Not because you're blacklisted, Navy. I don't give a shit about that," she told him. "But medical records aren't private anymore—something you should be aware of, as you adjust to life in the real world. There's actually a Med Center where I work, where I can see a doctor and it *can* be kept confidential."

He nodded, looking up at her with those eyes, that face. "If you want, I can help you get over there."

Mac had to clear her throat. "I think it's okay," she said. "My foot. I think I just . . . Could use some help. Getting my boot, and these pants. Off. Kinda right now?"

"But if you're in pain—"

"I am," she agreed. "In pain. But it has nothing to do with my foot."

"That's not good," he murmured, so she pulled off her bra, and okay, sue her, but she adjusted as it went up over her head. She'd never be buxom, but there wasn't a woman alive who didn't have at least a *little* bit of extra body fat. Unlike most women, Mac had skills that allowed her to move it around and make it work for her, when she wanted.

And with this man looking at her like that, she wanted.

And he liked what he saw when her bra came off—that was clear. He was also surprised, although he tried not to show it. But he couldn't help himself from glancing at the bra that she tossed onto the bed and saying, "Wow, those things really . . ."

"Squash you flat," she finished for him. Also not a lie. Not completely.

And Mac knew he wanted to take his time and look at her, but he also wanted what *she* wanted, and that wasn't going to happen until she got her pants off, so he focused on the task at hand.

"How about I anchor your boot in place, and let you . . ." He did just that, bracing the bottom of her foot against his thigh, like the sexiest shoe salesman alive, while he held both sides of her boot in his big hands, careful not to twist her ankle. "That way you can do it as quickly or slowly as you like."

Mac was breathing hard. And not just because this was going to hurt, but because she could feel him, even through the thickness of her boot. His leg. His hands. What the hell kind of power did he have, that just by touching her, her own power was exponentially greater than?

Like, one plus one equals four hundred and eighty-five.

Like, if he touched her again, skin against skin, she was going to go up in flames. And since she didn't want to jump this man with one boot on and her pants flapping around her leg . . .

"Band-Aid pull," she told him. "Hard and fast. Hold on tight, okay?"

"You got it."

"For the record? Hard and fast works in other departments, too."

"Duly noted." He met her eyes. "I find myself inspired enough to start using smiley face emoticons, so . . ." He gave her a big, happy, toothy smile.

She was laughing as she yanked her foot free. "Oh, shit! *Shit!*" Tears rushed to her eyes, and she knew she'd really fucked up her ankle on those stairs, if it still hurt this badly despite her ability to block her pain. Of course the fact that she'd been walking around on it probably hadn't helped.

Shane was hovering now, afraid to touch her as he said, "Hey, hey, you okay? Let me see. May I see it?"

Mac shook her head swift and hard, no. She didn't want to take off her sock, because if just *thinking* about having sex with this man had made her injury heal to the point where she could run . . . And yeah, sure, her boot had been on, giving her the support she'd needed, but *still* . . .

Imagine what was going to happen when he pushed his way inside of her. Dear God . . . She unfastened her pants and shoved them down her thighs. "Help me."

"Mac, come on, I don't want to hurt you—"

"I'm fine. Just grab the legs of my pants, Laughlin, and pull!"

He certainly was a good little soldier, because he followed her command, which left her flat on her back on her bed, wearing only her panties and that single sock. Shane, however, was still completely dressed.

But not for long. He dropped her pants, then quickly adiosed his T-shirt, tossing it, too, onto the floor and revealing an upper body that was worthy of the cover of the priciest men's fitness e-zine. Shoulders, arms, abs—he was sculpted like an athlete. But those muscles weren't for show. They were fully functional.

And unlike Mac, he *did* have tattoos—a collection of art that you'd expect from a boy who'd been idealistic enough to join the Navy. The barbed wire that encircled his bicep, the requisite anchor on his forearm, a cartoon frog in dive gear grinning from his shoulder. But there were unexpected words and symbols, too. A line from that old John Lennon song, *Imagine all the people living for today,* a single rose, a peace sign, and the Chinese characters for truth and honor positioned gracefully over his heart.

While she was looking, reading, admiring, he was kicking off his own boots and taking off his pants. He pushed down his shorts—tightie whities, no big surprise there—along with his jeans. He got his socks off, too, which left him even more naked than she was, speaking of big surprises.

Which, again, was no real surprise, considering his height and weight—and quiet confidence. He was the whole package, all that and more, and he knew it.

He was also that rare creature—a fair-haired man who actually tanned—and he'd obviously recently been somewhere warmer and sunnier than spring-means-it's-thirty-seven-and-raining Boston. And yeah, that's what she was admiring—his tan and the sun-bleached hair on his muscular arms and legs.

She pushed down her panties, cautious of her injured foot, aware as hell that he was watching her, too, taking care to give her the space she needed, even as he lowered himself next to her on the bed.

He was still all about her injured foot, but as he said, "I really think you should let me see—" she reached for him, and she was right.

The skin-on-skin contact was unreal—blistering-hot and blinding—and she heard herself laughing as she kissed him, as he damn near devoured her in kind.

"What the hell . . . ?" she heard him breathe, between kisses, but even with his disbelief, he was laughing, too. And when they both tried to get even closer—Mac by rolling him on top of her, between her open legs, and Shane by trying to pull her up to straddle him—she had to resist him only slightly. He instantly surrendered, as if he trusted her to know what would hurt her and what wouldn't.

He trusted her, too, to know how much of his weight she could take, and when she pulled him even closer, he didn't hold back. He just kept on kissing her, with the solidness of his chest against her breasts, his powerful legs intertwined with hers, and his erection . . . It wasn't until she reached for him, to wrap her fingers around the hard length of him, to move him into position, that she bumped into his exploring hand. And she realized he was doing the equivalent of one-armed push-ups as he stopped kissing her for just long enough to pull back and look into her eyes.

He looked a little stunned, and she must've looked equally shell-shocked as he pushed his fingers inside of her, just a little at first, but then deeper, touching her, stroking, even as she took hold of him and did the same. And then his expression wasn't surprise, it was pure, found-heaven ecstasy.

And he breathed, "Holy shit," and she felt him start to come, so she lifted her hips, and he got his hand out of the way to let her push him hard and deep inside of her.

And it didn't feel as good as she'd imagined—it felt better—as he took control. He'd taken her *hard and fast* comment to heart, and, again, trusted that she wouldn't let him hurt her, trusted that she wasn't some delicate and fragile flower that he might crush or break.

Mac could feel the pleasure—overwhelmingly absolute—crashing through him, and if she hadn't already started to come herself, it would've pushed her over the edge. As it was, her own orgasm blasted through her, and she closed her eyes because that same white-hot, blinding light was back, like they were making some kind of return entry from outer space, burning up through the atmosphere. And she clung to him, her body straining to meet his, to receive him, as the heat, the rush, the thrill kept surging, rocketing, spinning . . .

This shit was fully out of control, and she was, too, and she knew it—and she loved every freaking second of it.

God, when was the last time she'd felt like this?

Never.

She'd never felt anything even remotely this crazy. But like all good things, it came to an end. And there they were, out of breath and gasping for air, atop the blankets and sheets on the bed that she'd bought all those months ago, where Justin had screwed his new girlfriend before leaving town for good, thus putting into place the chain of events that had put Mac into Father's bar at the same time as this Boy Scout who'd just sent her to heaven.

She could hear him panting, catching his breath, and feel the pounding of his heart—he was still pressed that close.

"Holy fuck," Shane gasped, and she laughed because, really, that said it all, didn't it?

He laughed, too—a warm rumble that she felt more than heard.

It was then that he kissed her, his lips so soft against hers. It was such a contrast to the hard-core sex they'd just shared. It was sweet. Tender. The kiss of a lover, not that of a hookup she'd met mere minutes ago in a bar.

But then he laughed again, and said, "Did we do that?"

And Mac realized then that her eyes were open, but the room—the entire apartment—was dark. All of the lights had gone out.

"Just kidding," he said, as he kissed her again—a shadow back-lit by the dim light from the streetlamp on the corner, filtered in through the cheap window shades she'd bought and installed when she'd realized the ancient mini-blinds were transparent. "Must've been a power surge. Where's the circuit box?"

"In the kitchen," she managed to say, even as his question echoed. *Did we do that?*

Before she knew it, he'd pulled away from her and out of her—all that heat and full body contact just suddenly gone. And she must've made some kind of sound of distress, because he was in-stantly back, kissing her again—his mouth possessive but no less sweet.

"Don't go anywhere, baby," he breathed. "I'll be right back. I promise."

And Mac couldn't stop herself from grabbing his arm. She couldn't keep herself from asking, "Who *are* you?"

Shane laughed again—more heat in the darkness, his breath warm against her cheek. "Funny, I was going to ask *you* that. Right after I asked the more important question: Can we do that again?"

"I'm ready whenever you are," she managed.

He leaned in to kiss her, longer this time, slower, and she felt herself melting against him. "Hmm," he said. And then he got off the bed, but not to vanish into the kitchen. Instead he went to the window and pulled up the shade, just a little. Just enough to let some silvery light shine into the room so that Mac could see him. So that he could see her.

"That's better," he said, as he rejoined her on the bed, smiling into her eyes. He then proceeded to look her over very thoroughly.

Mac laughed as he turned her over slightly, then lifted first one of her arms and then the other. "What are you—"

"So far no tattoos," he confirmed. "Although maybe under that sock . . ."

Her ankle barely hurt at all anymore, and she reached down and pulled off her sock. She wiggled her toes, rotated her foot to the left and then to the right. She'd always healed faster when she had sex, but she'd been right. Because this time? It had been off-the-charts.

"Wow, it really doesn't look that bad," Shane said.

"It cramps sometimes," she said—again not a lie, but not exactly the truth. "But see? No tattoos."

"Hmm," he said. "One more place to check . . ." He gently but very firmly pushed open her legs as she laughed again. "Definitely no tattoos. Although maybe I should look more closely . . ."

Smiling, she pushed herself up onto her elbows to watch him as he kissed the inside of her thigh.

Shane looked up into her eyes, smiling back at her. "For the record," he said. "If you want more? I'm *always* ready. And if I'm not? I'll improvise." He looked back down at her, then met her eyes one more time before leaning in to kiss her again. And again. And . . .

Mac heard herself moan.

And this time?

She came in slow motion, with her fingers laced through Shane Laughlin's beautiful hair.

FIVE

The line between being a man and a god was a thin one that was far too easy for a Greater-Than to cross.

Bach couldn't help but think about that as he drove Anna Taylor to the Obermeyer Institute.

She hadn't given him her consent.

Of course, once they arrived at the Institute, and she saw the guard at the gate and the sign-in procedure, she'd feel more at ease. And then she'd see the bustle of activity, even this late at night. And *then* she'd meet Elliot and talk to him, and all of her remaining doubts would vanish. Elliot had that effect on people.

Elliot would also help Bach explain who had taken Nika and why.

Until then, Bach had to keep up the constant reassurances so that Anna wouldn't panic—which meant that he was going to spend the next twenty minutes inside of her.

And okay, *that* came out wrong. Even as just a fleeting thought, shared with absolutely no one, it was inappropriate.

He was going to spend the next twenty minutes *inside of her head*.

Which was probably a thousand times more intimate than any sexual act could ever be.

Bach carefully double-shielded his own thoughts, because letting slip the fact that he was thinking, even peripherally, about sex right now, while he *was* inside of Anna's head . . . That wouldn't be good.

He focused on the positive. He *was* going to find Nika.

Still, he could feel Anna's discomfort rising as he signaled for the entrance ramp onto the Mass Pike. He glanced over to find her watching him, her dark brown eyes wide, and her pretty face illuminated by the light from the dash.

"We're going to find your sister," he said, echoing the very words he was planting in her mind, along with *Joe Bach can be trusted, you're safe with him, everything will be explained at the Obermeyer Institute.* "But it'll help me to know the details of her abduction—who was the last person who saw her and when. Do you know if she made it to school today, or was she grabbed before she got there?"

Anna nodded. Bach knew she believed that the sooner they found her sister, the better—although she had no *real* idea of the danger that Nika was in, that she herself was in, too. She was also a firm believer in action, and she hated the fact that—for at least the next twenty minutes—she was being forced to sit still.

And even though Bach was inside of her head, there was a difference between providing calming assurances—and tromping around, uninvited, while helping himself to her memories and thoughts. He also knew that talking about this would make her feel—at least a little bit—as if she were doing *something* to help get her sister back.

"The last person to see Nika," Anna told him, "that I know of, so far, is her English Lit teacher, Erika Hodgeman. I spoke to her on the phone. Nika was in her final class of the day. Nothing seemed unusual, she wasn't upset, she'd handed her homework assignment in, aced a pop quiz. I asked Ms. Hodgeman if she knew whether Nika had made any new friends recently, and . . ." Anna shook her head. "She said she didn't really know, but that Nika came into class alone, and left alone. Same way she always did."

"So she left school," Bach said through Anna's burst of sadness that her little sister was still struggling to fit in, "at *what* time?"

"At 2:27," she told him, and then smiled wanly at his questioning glance. "She texted me then. See, I'm usually there to meet her—I make a point to walk her home after school—we meet at the corner. But I got a call that morning, for a job interview. So I texted Nika, telling her where I'd be. She texted me back after classes were over, at 2:27, with a *good luck.*"

"Where was the interview?" Bach asked.

"Downtown," Anna said, frowning slightly. There was something bothering her about it—the interview.

So he pushed. "What was it for?"

"Does that matter?" she asked.

"It might."

She sighed, then said, "It was for a secretarial position at Montgomery and Lowden, a law firm specializing in bankruptcies. It's down near Government Center. I knew when I walked in that it was a waste of time. They were looking for someone older. There was confusion, too, about my appointment. I wasn't on the list and they didn't even have my résumé on file. So that was . . . awkward."

"And yet someone called you to go in," he pointed out.

She looked at him again, and he could both see and feel her realization. And as she suddenly turned and opened her daypack, he knew she was looking for her cell phone.

He watched her, one eye on the road, as she searched.

She was lovely, with a riot of dark curls cascading down her back, and dark brown eyes that would've revealed everything she was feeling, even if he hadn't set up camp in her mind. Her face was pretty enough, with gorgeous mocha-colored skin and a smooth complexion, but it wouldn't launch one ship, let alone a thousand—until she smiled.

When she'd smiled . . .

He tried to dissect what he'd seen, so that it would make sense, but it didn't and he couldn't. Her mouth was a mouth, perhaps slightly more generous than most, with lips that made him think a little too much about the simple pleasure of a kiss, so much so that he had to stop watching her and focus on the road.

It was strange, what he was feeling. Strange—and unwelcome.

Bach had always felt that he was lucky. He appreciated beautiful women. He enjoyed their company, their conversation, their companionship. But he'd never let himself get sidetracked or distracted by sexual attraction. He'd succeeded in shutting down that part of himself.

And if he ever did feel a glimmer of desire's deep pull, it was never something that he couldn't immediately control.

It made his life significantly less complicated.

Back in the monastery, there had been quite a few Greater-Thans who'd had trouble with the idea of celibacy. And, as Bach had found out tonight, Stephen Diaz apparently still struggled with their monk-like lifestyle.

But Bach never had.

His theory was that he'd succeeded, at an early age, in completely and irrevocably linking sexual attraction to the idea of romantic love. He hadn't done it on purpose—it had just happened that way, for him. And if the war hadn't interrupted, he and sweet Annie Ryan would've been one of those couples who'd married after high school and lived out their lives in deep contentment and harmony.

But the war *had* interrupted. The war—and a whole lot more.

And now Annie was gone, and Bach was alone. And since love at first sight was a ridiculous concept—one *couldn't* love someone they didn't know, the idea was absurd—he'd traveled through most of his life certain in his knowledge that, because he didn't love? He didn't desire.

Enter Anna Taylor. Whose richly complex mind Bach had entered with barely any hesitation.

Whom he certainly now knew a whole lot better than he had ten minutes ago.

She'd found her phone, and scrolled her way back to the call she'd received earlier that day. "It's a 781 area code," she told him triumphantly. "They called me to come in for the job interview just before noon."

"Don't use your phone to call them back," he said, handing her his own phone. "Use mine. And after you input the number, shut your own phone off."

He felt her doubt surge. Who was he, what was she doing in his car, and why should she trust him?

Joe Bach will find Nika.

Joe Bach will never hurt you.

All of your questions will be answered. . . .

He felt her surrender again, and she did as he'd instructed, key-ing the number into his phone, and then putting it to her ear so she could listen, her arms crossed, her face intense, her eyes slightly unfocused.

"It's ringing," she murmured, glancing at him.

Bach nodded, and activated the backup phone that was here in the car, pushing the buttons on the steering wheel that would con-nect him with OI. "If it goes to voice mail, don't leave a message," he advised her, and she nodded.

And then he could feel her disappointment as she cut the con-nection. "It just stopped ringing," she reported, "and then there was a beep."

Over at OI, Elliot picked up. "I see from your GPS that you're on your way back in."

"I am," Bach said. "With Anna Taylor. You're on speaker. We have a phone number that we want looked up. You want to con-nect me to—"

"Hell no, Maestro. I can do it," Elliot said. "Piece of cake. Hello, Anna, sister of Nika Taylor. What's the number?"

Bach glanced at Anna, who read the digits off his phone.

"I'm Elliot, by the way. I'll meet you when you get here and . . . Huh. According to our computer, that number belongs to an as-of-yet unactivated disposable cell phone."

"That doesn't make sense," Anna said.

"It actually does," Bach told her. "If a hacker had access to the number—"

"Hang on *just* a sec," Elliot interrupted. "I'm getting a little more info. . . . It's part of the Blacklight communication network, and they sell both their hardware and airware at . . ." He sighed dramatically. "Just about every mega-store in America. Sorry. That doesn't help you very much at all, does it? Did you get a ransom call from that number?"

"No," Bach answered him. "But someone used it to call Anna— Miss Taylor—to make sure she was tied up at the time she usually walks Nika home from school—which was when we believe the girl was kidnapped."

Anna was pissed. And upset with herself. "I should've called the firm to verify."

"Why would you?" Bach asked her. "It was a job interview. Whoever did this knew you were looking for work. And that's probably not all they know about you. I think we can be thankful they didn't use a more permanent approach to get you out of the picture, right from the start."

The next girl's family was probably not going to be that lucky.

From over at OI, Elliot said, "I got your ETA at about ten minutes. We'll be ready for you."

"Thanks," Bach said. "Hempford's status?" He asked, even though he knew the answer. It was kind of obvious, since Elliot was not only out by the computers, but he'd taken the time to track down the cell phone info, instead of handing it off to a subordinate.

"I'm sorry, Joseph. He didn't make it," Elliot told him.

Shit. "I want to know what this man had in common with every other addict who jokered at first use," Bach said. "I want details. Nothing should be considered insignificant or irrelevant."

"I'm already on it," Elliot said. "His bathroom was blue. His car was a BMW. He wore silk boxers. He was married to his third wife, who was thirty-one years younger. He drank boutique merlot, shipped from Sonoma, California. He graduated from Boston College in 1985 . . ."

"Over and out," Bach said, and cut the connection.

"Jokered," Anna Taylor said as she gazed at him. She repeated his words. *"Every other addict who jokered . . . ?"*

Bach nodded. Maybe this was a good place to start the explanations. "You ever watch *Batman*?"

"The old movie. With . . . was it George Clooney?"

"Clooney played Batman, too. But I'm thinking of the one with Christian Bale. There's this character, a super-villain, who calls himself the Joker. He's particularly frightening because he's completely insane."

Anna was watching him, listening carefully. "And addicts who *joker* . . ."

"Are drug users who lose their minds," he told her. "There's something in this particular drug that makes a significant portion of the population go insane."

"Crystal meth?" she asked anxiously. "Because I think one of my neighbors is a meth user."

"Not meth." Bach shook his head. "This is where," he told her as he took the exit for Route 30, "it gets a little strange."

———

Shane woke up to find himself alone in the bed, still in the dark.

Or near dark.

A little bit of light was still streaming in through that crack he'd made between the bottom of the shade and the window frame. And then he realized that there was a glow coming from the main part of the apartment, too.

From here, it looked like candlelight.

He pulled off the blanket someone—Mac—had put over him, and found his jeans where he'd dropped them. He stepped into them and was still fastening the buttons as he went into the kitchen.

Where Mac had, indeed, lit a candle.

She was wearing his T-shirt. And even though he would've liked to believe that she was wearing it because it belonged to him, it was probably just the first thing she'd grabbed off the floor as she'd gotten out of bed.

Still, it looked great on her. It hit mid-thigh—she was that short—and he liked the idea that she was wearing it with nothing else beneath.

Holy shit, he was hot for her. Again. Already.

Although, if they were keeping score? She'd had three orgasms to his two. Which kind of meant he was winning, didn't it?

"Hey," she greeted him in that husky voice that belonged to a much bigger woman. "It was getting cold, so I, um, came out here to . . ."

She'd gotten the heat working again. Shane reached out toward the ancient radiator, which was definitely living up to its name.

"There must've been some kind of power surge," she continued. "All of the circuits in the box were thrown."

She had the built-in microwave running, but the light was off inside of the thing, so it was just whirring as the LEDs counted down from forty-seven. Forty-six, forty-five . . .

"I got the thermostat and the appliances back on line," she reported, "but the lights . . ." She shook her head.

"Bulbs might've burned out. Power surges can do that," he said, as part of him stood off to the side and gave himself a skull-duster at the inanity of their conversation. Why wasn't he falling to his knees before her, and pledging his unending devotion and adoration?

Why wasn't he over there next to her, kissing the hell out of her, and lifting her up onto the counter, which was the perfect height for him to push his way inside of her again?

She wanted him to do it. He could see it in the way she was standing, breathing, looking back at him—her nipples already tightly peaked beneath his T-shirt.

But the microwave dinged, and she turned away and reached up to open the door, which made his shirt ride up and . . .

Yeah, she was not wearing anything under there.

As she set her mug of tea on the counter, she glanced at him and he could see his reflection along with a whole lot of heat in her eyes. But then she sighed and said, "I have to go. There's a situation at . . . Work."

Her hesitation before saying that—*work*—made *him* hesitate. Was he reading this—and her—wrong? Was it really trepidation in her eyes that he was incorrectly interpreting as heat? Was she look-ing for an easy excuse to get him to leave?

He kept his voice level, easygoing. "Okay. I'll walk you over there."

But she was already shaking her head.

"I'll walk you to the T?" he tried, hoping that she'd say, *I won't be that long. It's kind of obvious that you woke up with a hard-on, and since I know just what to do with it, why don't you wait right here until I get back?*

But a woman who didn't want to give him her full name wasn't going to be comfortable with him hanging here, alone, at her apartment—assuming it was her apartment, as temporary and im-personal as this place appeared to be.

Instead she said, "I've got a bike," which could have meant Trek, but probably meant Harley, as she brushed past him with both that candle and her mug, down the hall and into the bedroom.

The fact that she hadn't offered him some tea of his own was another hot clue that she didn't see him as anything more than a trick—a one-night hook-up. A quick shag and then *Have a nice life.*

But Shane had learned that if you didn't ask the question, the answer you got was an automatic *no.* So as he followed her, he said, "I'd love to see you again."

She didn't respond right away, and he stopped in the doorway to the bedroom, watching her as she put both the candles and the mug down on the bedside table, and then pulled his shirt up over her head.

Mac.

Naked and candlelit.

Holy shit.

He was struck, again, by the fact that her breasts were fuller than he'd thought back in the bar. And he knew from experience that her skin was smooth and soft. All over. And—as she'd pointed out—completely unmarked. Which was unusual for a woman her age.

And for some reason, even though he loved seeing art on women, Mac's lack of a single tattoo was a turn-on. Maybe because it was part of her mystery. Why *wouldn't* she get one? When he'd asked her about it, she'd shrugged it off. But, she must have had a reason, and he was intrigued.

And how old *was* she, really? Her body screamed early twenties, but her attitude was older. And that attitude was another pretty hefty turn-on.

Along with her size. Which was weird. Shane had always been drawn to tall, slender, willowy women, while Mac was petite and compact. But even as small as she was, she was strong. Her shapely arms and legs were muscular—her thighs a little too big because of that. Too big, that is, according to the dictates of today's screwed-up, looking-for-perfection world, where beautiful women regularly went under the knife.

Her hair was too short—also according to the world's current interpretation of beauty—and her face . . . In certain light, she was breathtaking and almost angelic. In other light, she was what some would call quirky-looking, but others would use words that were far less kind.

Still, it would be hard for anyone to claim that there wasn't something unique and compelling about her. Something that Shane found utterly appealing.

She glanced at him as she reached down to get her panties from where she'd tossed them onto the floor. As she met his gaze, it was all he could do not to crawl across the bed toward her, pleading for her not to leave.

She smiled then, a touch ruefully, as if she knew exactly what he was thinking, as she pulled her panties on. And then she reached for something that was on the bedside table, and said the words that made his heart leap. Truly. The damn thing did a full workout in his chest. "You got a cell?"

She wanted his number. She was standing there, holding her phone in her hands, ready to input his info into her address book.

Fuck.

"I don't," he had to admit. Jesus, he was a loser. But she said she liked honesty, so . . . "It was too expensive, so I, um . . ." He cleared his throat, in part because she was giving him her full attention, which was pretty darn distracting since she was still bare-breasted. "But I've got a freemail account. You can always reach me that way. I mean, yeah, there's lag-time, because sometimes it's not easy for me to get online. Except I'm betting I'll have access to the Internet at this new place, where I'm . . . sort of working . . ."

"So . . . you gonna give it to me?" she asked.

And Shane met her eyes and smiled, because even though he knew she didn't mean it *that* way, he couldn't not smile at the images her words conjured up.

Mac realized, too, what she'd said and how it had sounded, and she laughed. "I meant your e-mail address, Navy. But believe me, if I had the power to stop time, we'd be back in that bed, and you'd be rocking my world again."

Thank you, Mighty Creator. He'd rocked her world. He'd suspected as much, but it was fan-fucking-tastic to know for sure.

"Doberman7580 at gmail dot com," he told her.

She spelled doberman, glancing up questioningly as she keyed in the address.

"Like the dog," Shane said, shrugging. He had nothing to hide. Not from her. "It's a random word and number. I had to change my address because the men in my old team were trying to contact me, and that wasn't healthy for them."

Mac nodded as she stepped into her pants, and stashed her phone in one of her many pockets. "I thought it might be some cute nickname leftover from . . . What's that training called . . . ?"

"BUD/S," he told her. "Basic Underwater Demolition slash SEAL training." There was nothing about the SEAL teams or their insanely competitive training that was even remotely cute, but Shane let it slide as he tossed her her sports bra. It had ended up on the floor on his side of the bed.

She pulled the bra over her head, then put on her tank, but then she said, "Shit, I almost forgot."

She hurried around the bed and past him, back into the living room, and at first Shane thought she was . . . going for his jacket?

But she moved it aside and he saw her pick up a plastic Pharma-City bag, which she opened and . . .

She had a fresh box of the drug that had been nicknamed *the pill*. It worked as an STD annihilator, and the women's version doubled as a powerful contraceptive. It didn't matter when you took it—before, during, or after sex. It was good for a solid twenty-four hours in either direction. She cracked the box and tossed him one of the little baby-blue foil packets.

"Thanks." And, huh, he just now realized that the entire box she was holding was blue—which was code for male only. The women's pill was color-coded pink. They usually were marketed and packaged in combo packs—a pink with a blue. Of course there were blue/blue and pink/pink packs available, just as there were pinks without contraceptive, and blues that contained some bonus Viagra. He'd never paid much attention to them, other than to make sure he didn't grab them by mistake when he was in the store.

The pills containing contraceptives had been outlawed in forty-eight states, with a forty-ninth coming fast, but the black market demand for them was still booming.

Mac took the blue box and the entire drugstore bag back into the bedroom with her as Shane opened the packet and swallowed the pill. She'd obviously already taken one, and okay, as he followed her, he didn't want to think too much about that because the questions generated weren't helpful. When had she taken hers? Recently, after getting out of bed? Or up to twenty-four hours ago, when she was with someone else?

Yes, ladies and gentlemen, that *was* jealousy he was feeling, and he tamped it back down. He didn't even know this woman's real name, so it was unlikely she'd be okay with him expressing his desire to own her.

So Shane kept his mouth shut and just breathed and watched while she stuffed the box and the bag into the drawer of her little bedside table. And when she bent down to pick up first one and then the other of her socks, he realized that she'd been walking around barefoot, and she hadn't been limping.

At all.

"Your ankle seems much better," he said as she sat on the bed.

"Yeah," she said. "It is." She rubbed her foot, then rotated it, and even seemed kind of surprised herself at how little it was bothering her. She looked over at him. "Thanks."

"Hmm," he said. "I'd like to think I'm responsible for, I don't know, maybe . . . Relaxing you? So in that spirit, you're very welcome."

She didn't laugh. She just sat there looking at him, almost as if she were trying to get inside of his head and read his mind.

Shane let her look, trying to emote a calm lack of desperation. Come on, Mac. Ask him to stay . . .

But then she said, "Shit," almost under her breath. And she picked up his T-shirt off the bed and tossed it to him, before returning her focus to putting on her boots.

So much for his hopes of hanging here until she came back from work. But despite that ominous-sounding *shit,* the battle had not been lost. In fact, it had barely begun. He just had to be cool. After all, he knew where she lived, knew the bar where she hung out.

Shane breathed in deeply as he pulled his shirt over his head. God, she smelled impossibly good. He sat on the other side of the bed to put on his own socks and boots. "Can I ask you what you do?" he asked.

"You can ask," she replied, "but I can't answer."

Can't was better than *won't.* "So . . . CSO?" He was teasing, but he felt her stiffen, so he added, "It's a lifelong fantasy. Gorgeous Covert Security Org operative takes me home, lets me rock her world . . ."

She did laugh then. "Yeah, sorry to disappoint but I'm seriously not CSO."

"Which is what you'd say if you *were.*"

"For all I know," she countered, "*you're* CSO."

"Yeah, well," Shane said, "the CSO *is* where former SEALs tend to go, but that door kinda slams shut with the whole black-listed thing."

"That still seems surreal to me," Mac told him. "You're so . . ." She searched for the right word.

"Don't say cute," he requested. "Or anything with the word *boy* in it."

She laughed and crawled across the bed toward him. He turned to meet her. To kiss her back. And Jesus, just kissing her was better than most of the full-on sex he'd had in his entire fairly long life.

But then she pulled back, and he realized she was straddling him as he lay on his back on her bed looking up at her, out of breath, as he dry-humped her. Nice.

"You're a straight-arrow," she said even as she, too, struggled to catch her breath. "In a good way. You're gleaming and . . . true."

She meant it. He could see her respect for him in her eyes. Respect and admiration.

And he wanted . . . Damn, it scared him—what he wanted. So he defined it in terms of sex.

"Sixty seconds," he whispered. "Come on, honey, just give me sixty more seconds . . ."

Mac laughed down at him. "A true romantic, huh?"

If she wanted romance . . . "Meet me back here tomorrow night," he said, "and I'll cook you dinner and give you the massage of your life." And yes, he could see that the idea appealed to her. "But right now? I want only sixty seconds of your time. Because I know I can make you come as soon as I'm inside of you." He pushed himself up, against her.

And God, she was going to do it.

Shane could see it there, in her eyes—the fact that she wanted to. And sure enough, she kicked off one boot and pulled one leg free from her pants, even as he quickly unfastened his jeans and pushed them down off of his hips, as she threw her bare leg back across him, as she came down hard, and he thrust up . . .

"*Yes!*" Jesus, this was unbelievable—how good it felt.

"Oh, God," she gasped as she pushed him deeper, as he, too, helped. "Oh, God!"

She was laughing, and he was, too—it was that fricking great as she moved on top of him, as he pushed himself up to meet her, as he gazed into her eyes.

He'd already learned what she liked and where to touch her, but he'd been dead right, and it didn't take anything more than his being inside of her to make her unravel, and he, too, let himself fall right over the edge into his own powerful release, surging inside of her again and again and again.

The intensity nearly made his eyes roll back in his head, and he struggled to stay present in the aftermath, even as his heart continued to race, and his breathing was ragged, and his brain wanted to disconnect so he could float in this happy moment.

He'd expected her to make an immediate dismount—she was, after all, in a hurry, but she didn't move from where she'd collapsed on top of him, her face pressed against his chest, her head tucked beneath his chin.

He gave her an additional sixty seconds, and when she still didn't do more than breathe, he spoke. "So. Tonight?"

Mac sighed. "I'm not sure I'll be able to get away." She lifted her head then to look at him. "My work is . . . Important. I've learned not to make promises."

"So don't promise," Shane said. "Just try. Give me your cell. I'll call *you*. Around six. See where you're at."

He could see the great big no in her eyes. But instead of shaking her head, she said, "How about—tentatively—a week from tonight? That'll give you a chance to find out your schedule. If you're starting a new job, you might want to go into it being flexible."

"Yeah," he said, "I don't think that's going to be a problem. This job isn't . . . It's basically some kind of medical testing. You know, *Hi, my name's Shane, and I'll be your guinea pig today?*"

Mac sat up. "That's dangerous shit. There are drugs out there that'll screw you up, big-time." She shook her head and her vehemence was fierce.

"Whoa," he said. "No, it's not drug-testing. I wouldn't do that—"

"But they tell you it's not, and then you get inside and you sign the release and . . ." She exhaled hard. "Most of those programs are lockdown. You go in, you're in."

"There's no lockdown in the world that I can't get out of," he assured her.

She wasn't convinced. "In some of the programs, you're strapped to the bed. And unless you're Houdini—"

Okay, so *that* was an unpleasant thought. "I'm not going to participate if they're going to do that."

"You really think they'll tell you in advance?" she asked, then exhaled her exasperation. "Which lab hired you?"

"It's not a lab," Shane told her. "It's an R and D facility. Something called the Obermeyer Institute . . . ?"

She froze. She was sitting there with her body still locked together with his, but she'd suddenly gone completely, totally blank.

He said, "They were very clear when they recruited me that there wouldn't be drugs involved." She still didn't move, so he tried to explain, "They study something called neural integration. It's—"

"I gotta go," she said, and just like that she was off of him. She grabbed the candlestick and took it with her. And when she left the bedroom and went into the bathroom and closed the door, Shane was plunged into total and absolute darkness.

What the hell . . . ?

He waited a few seconds for his eyes to adjust to the dim light coming in through the window—except that light wasn't there anymore. He fastened his pants by touch, then went to the shade and lifted it and . . .

The streetlight right outside the window had gone out.

But that wasn't the only light that had vanished.

He heard the toilet flush, and the bathroom door opened, and the pulse and sway of the candlelight was back.

Mac, however, had already left the building. So to speak.

"Let's go." She'd turned back into the cold stranger he'd first approached in the bar. She put on her scarf and hat and jacket, then tossed him his. She picked up the candle and unlatched the door to the apartment's landing. She propped it open with her foot, her impatience barely concealed as she waited for him to get out.

It didn't make any sense. "What just happened here?" Shane asked as he went past her.

She didn't meet his eyes. She put her key into the deadbolt, and then blew out the candle and tossed it back inside. The power outage had clearly affected the common areas of the building, too. It was dark as hell in there.

He could hear Mac, though, latching the bolt and then swiftly going down the stairs to the door that led to the street.

He followed her outside, feeling his way. "Mac."

She didn't stop. So he chased. Not far—her bike was right there. And it *was* a Harley. She set to work unlocking it. In this neighborhood, she'd needed a variety of methods to keep it safe.

"What the hell did I say?" he said, and she still didn't turn around.

But she did speak. "This was a mistake."

"The Obermeyer Institute," he said. "It was when I said—"

"What do you know about neural integration?" she asked, finally turning to face him, a heavy chain in her hands.

"Not much," Shane admitted. "I mean, it's common knowledge that the average person only uses ten percent of his or her brain—"

"That's a myth," she dismissed it.

"Then I guess I don't know very much," he said, searching her face, her eyes, for some kind of clue—and getting nothing but massive regret. "Is it the science?" he asked, reaching for her, touching her shoulders—only to have her almost violently shrug him off. And turn away to stow that chain and mount her bike.

"Are you . . . really religious?" he asked. It was hard to believe, but . . . "Is that why no tattoos or—"

She started the Harley with a roar.

"Because I don't have to do it," Shane shouted to be heard over the engine. "I'll find another job."

But Mac shook her head. "No," she said. "You have to go. It's important that you go. You're a Potential, right?"

"Yeah," he said, "but I don't even know what that means."

"It means," she told him, over the noise of her Harley, "that I can't see you again. I'm sorry."

She adjusted the throttle, and the bike leapt away with a roar, leaving him standing there, still freaking clueless, watching her taillight vanish in the darkness of the night.

SIX

Anna sat at the conference room table inside the gated former college campus that was now the Obermeyer Institute, clutching a mug of coffee that the friendly doctor, whose name was Elliot Zerkowski, had given her. They were waiting for the results of the GPS search for Nika's phone.

OI had a variety of different departments, including one called "Analysis." The many busy and bustling staff members who made up Analysis's night shift were also searching satellite images, trying to see if they could find pictures of Nika's abduction—and ID her abductor as well as the car or van into which she'd no doubt been tossed.

This is where, the dark and mysterious Dr. Bach had told her, back in his car, as they drove over here, *it gets a little strange.*

You think?

Apparently, there was a dangerous new drug out there called oxyclepta di-estraphen, street name Destiny, that users injected into their veins.

It was illegal, but sparingly available in virtually every major city around the world—provided you made the right connections and could pay the exorbitant price.

The drug allowed its user to access the otherwise underused parts of his or her brain that controlled regenerative cell growth.

In plain English, that meant that, with this drug, theoretically at least, a seventy-five-year-old cancer patient would not only be able to cure his own illness, but could use the power of his own brain to create the hormones and enzymes necessary to naturally transform his entire body into that of a strapping, healthy twenty-year-old, with decades of life ahead of him.

With this drug? A human being could conceivably live forever.

The catch, besides the high price tag, was the fact that the drug was immediately addictive. One injection, and boom. The user was instantly hooked. And detoxing was not a possibility. Addicts needed to continue taking the drug, or they would, without exception, die.

The whole live-forever thing was undeniably a major enticement in spite of the drawbacks—particularly for those who were facing terminal illnesses and certain death. Provided the user had truckloads of money to continue buying the drug, forever and ever, Amen . . .

Although, along with the instant addiction came delusions of grandeur. Since most Destiny users were rich, it was possible that their feelings of superiority and belief that they were above the law were there from the start. But the drug appeared to break down the users' morals even more, further corrupting their sense of right and wrong.

But the *biggest* problem with Destiny was that only a very small percentage of the population was able to absorb the drug without eventually suffering the very serious side effect of violent insanity, also known as *jokering*.

Joseph Bach and his team of scientists had recently been called in by the Boston police to contain an addict who'd jokered after only one injection of Destiny.

"Why did they ask *you* to apprehend this man?" Anna asked Bach now.

He took a sip from his own mug—he drank herbal tea instead of coffee—before replying. Dr. Zerkowski, who'd instructed her to call him Elliot, was also watching Bach, as if he, too, were curious as to how the dark-haired man would answer.

"Because the police often find themselves outmatched. You see, people who are addicted to Destiny have access to a wide variety of neural pathways," Bach said, then broke it down even further for her. "The drug allows addicts to cure their diseases and to re-build strong, healthy bodies, it's true, but it also allows them to develop other mental powers. They might have, say, telekinetic or telepathic abilities."

"Be able to move things with their minds, or read others' thoughts," Elliot interpreted.

"Or they might be able to manipulate electricity—"

"Shoot lightning bolts from their derrières."

Bach looked at Elliot, one eyebrow slightly raised.

"What?" Elliot said. "We had one of those last month." He turned to Anna. "Talk about bad surprises. Last night's joker was less amusing. He was able to stop a bullet with his mind, turn it around, and send it rocketing back to kill the SWAT team sniper who'd tried to take him down."

"Dear God," she breathed.

"He could also use vocalizations—words—to punch people," Elliot said. "I know that sounds crazy, but while he was talking, if he emphasized a word, you'd feel it like a punch in the face. Total comic-book super-villain stuff. That's where the verb *to joker* came from."

"Batman," Anna said. "I got that, yes."

"The bottom line," Bach interjected, "is that when someone makes the choice to try Destiny, they—and we—have no idea which neural pathways they'll be able to integrate."

"That means we don't know if they'll only have the ability to play the piano and sight-read music at a professional level, or maybe the power to melt all the wood-glue in the furniture to make your desk fall apart," Elliot again explained. "*Or* if they'll be more dangerous, like that bullet-bender. We also can't know how long they've got before they joker and become a danger to themselves and everyone around them."

Anna looked over to find Bach watching her. "And you," she

said. "You have similar powers even though you haven't taken this drug?"

"It's absolutely possible—for those of us with potential—to achieve a more fully integrated neural net, drug free," he told her, "with training and many years of hard work and discipline."

This was crazy. "And you don't risk those same side effects?" Anna asked. "Jokering, or . . . ?"

"There've been no documented cases of that."

"How many of you are out there?" she asked. "Potentials—or whatever you call yourselves?"

"Potentials are the people we believe to be more inclined to develop powers after participating in our training programs," Elliot answered for Bach. "The people who learn to more fully integrate, to use their brains more completely, like Dr. Bach . . . We call them Greater-Thans."

"There are currently just over eight hundred known Greater-Thans living here in the U.S.," Bach told Anna. "Most are integrated at thirty percent. About a hundred are Forties, a few dozen have reached fifty, and only a handful have gone beyond that. At least that we know of."

"The average person," Elliot chimed in, no doubt because he could see that Anna didn't quite understand, "like you or me— we're called *Less-Thans* or *fractions*. We spend our lives at about ten percent integration, give or take a few in either direction. There's a myth that says we only use ten percent of our brains, but that's not true. That's not what that ten percent means. You and me . . . ? We *do* use all of our brains. But we tend not to use more than about ten percent at any given time. But it's not just about being able—or unable—to use more of the different areas in our brains *simultaneously*. It's about having the potential to learn to use those relatively underutilized and definitely unexercised parts more *completely*."

Anna nodded. She was following now—at least she thought she was.

But Elliot sat forward. "Let me give you an example that'll make it easier for you to understand," he continued. "Part of our brain regulates the way our blood is pumped by our heart through our body. That's a fact. You and I are doing that, while we're sitting here. But it's not conscious—thank God, right? But Dr. Bach over here, he's a Greater-Than. He's seventy-two percent integrated."

Seventy-*two*? Anna turned to look at Bach as Elliot went on. The dark-haired man was sitting there, legs crossed, as he sipped tea from a mug that bore a picture of Godzilla engaged in battle with a giant moth. Even holding that mug, even without his royal-looking overcoat, even dressed down the way he was in a cable knit sweater that was a muted shade of blue and a pair of jeans that stacked above his clunky boots, he *still* looked like a fairy-tale prince.

But then again, he would probably still look like a fairy-tale prince if he were naked and in chains.

"Like all Greater-Thans, Dr. Bach has studied and trained for years, and he's identified which of his neural pathways lead to the areas of his brain that regulate blood flow," Elliot said. "Now you wouldn't know this to look at him, but tonight's joker landed a very solid blow to the good doctor's face. Ow, right? Well, someone like me or you—a ten-percenter—we would have one heck of a black eye after that. But the maestro here took that hit, and about a half a second later he started the healing process. He not only had his brain instruct his body to repair the broken blood vessels that would've created a very colorful bruise, but he also manipulated the circulation in his face. He got the blood flowing through the injured area and . . . look at him. No injury to speak of. And that's just one of many seemingly superhuman things that he's learned to do."

Anna glanced over at Bach again, and this time, he was looking rather pointedly into his tea.

Oh, God.

"Can you read my mind?" she asked him.

He looked up at her and took his time to answer. "Yes. But not without your permission."

"How does *that* work?" she asked.

"I shield myself," he said, "from everyone's thoughts. If I didn't, it could get overwhelming. If I want to . . . share thoughts with someone, I . . . approach. And I ask permission to, um, enter their mind."

"So it's not a *can't* thing," Anna clarified. "Like, you *can't* read our minds without asking permission. It's a *won't*. You *say* that you won't."

"I won't," he agreed, with a flicker of something that she couldn't read in his eyes.

"But how do we know that you're not just saying that, just so that it doesn't get awkward?" Anna argued. "I mean, if we had to sit here, *knowing* that you're tapping into every thought . . ."

"I don't do that," Bach said.

"Well, just in case you're lying," she said. "Sorry." She turned to Elliot. "I made the mistake of thinking about him naked, before I knew he could read my mind."

Elliot had been following their exchange with a half-smile, but now he laughed aloud.

"It wasn't sexual," she told him—Bach, too. Again, just in case. "It was more of an art-appreciation thing. Although, I have to admit that once you know someone can read your mind, it's really hard *not* to think about them naked."

Joseph Bach was actually blushing as Elliot continued to laugh.

"What else can you do?" Anna asked Bach directly. "Can you stop a bullet with your mind?"

"Yes," he said. "And create an energy shield to protect myself from just about anything that gets thrown my way. But that's a pretty basic skill."

"Can you . . ." She started over. "Have you made yourself look significantly younger than you actually are?"

"Yes. But it's not just about *looking* young. I control my body and generate new cell growth and I actually *have* the health of a twenty-five-year-old."

The concept took her breath away. It was one thing to hear about it in theory, but another entirely to see the results of that kind of mental power. "How old are you, really?" Anna asked.

Bach shook his head. "I don't want to freak you out."

Anna looked at him pointedly. "Too late."

He smiled at that. "I *am* sorry about that."

"So . . . can you rearrange the furniture in this room without getting out of your chair?" she asked, looking around the conference room at the heavy bookshelves and wooden sideboard, the enormous table . . .

He didn't blink. "Yes."

"Knock down a building?"

"Or rebuild one," he countered pointedly, taking another sip of his tea.

"Can you . . . unlock locked doors?"

"Yes."

"Can you make people get into your car with you, even though they really don't want to?"

He didn't answer that one right away. But he finally sighed and said it. "Yes."

This time, he didn't look away first. This time, she did. She finished her now-cool coffee, and set the mug on the table.

"So there are eight *hundred* people out there, like you, with superhero powers," Anna said, and it still seemed surreal to her.

"Only a handful can do all that Dr. Bach can do," Elliot reminded her. "Most have limited talents and abilities."

"Still," she said. "Why haven't I heard anything about this?"

Bach and Elliot exchanged a glance.

"Is it a secret?" Anna asked.

"Not by choice," Bach said. "We regularly publish papers on neural integration, but . . ."

"The corporate-controlled media has mocked our research— and that of all the other research facilities in the country," Elliot said. "There are four other labs similar to OI, but we're the only one that's privately funded, so the others are always in danger of being closed. Particularly when the media insists that neural integration researchers are little more than a fringe group spouting crazy theories—while wearing tinfoil hats."

"The entire Destiny problem has also been swept under the

rug," Bach told Anna, "allegedly to keep the public from panicking, but in fact to suppress the truth about the drug's dangers as the pharmaceutical companies lobby to get FDA approval."

"But if people are jokering as violently as you described," Anna started.

"The cost of a single syringe of Destiny is around five thousand dollars," Elliot said and she gasped, because even though he'd already told her it was expensive, she'd never imagined it cost *that* much. "Yeah. And until the expense of production is streamlined and the price drops—which it will—the number of users, and jokers, will remain relatively low. Relatively. We get a call from the police around once a month to assist with a jokering addict."

"The families of the jokers also work to cover-up the incident," Bach added. "The stories that do break are quickly tagged as urban legends."

Anna looked from Bach to Elliot and back. "So . . . How do I know you're the good guys?" she asked. "If you can do the very same things that these jokers can do?"

"The jokers are the symptom, not the problem," Bach told her. "The problem starts with the Organization—the unscrupulous people who manufacture and distribute Destiny."

Elliot chimed in. "They're the ones who took Nika."

"And this . . . Organization took her because they think she's . . . a Potential?" Anna still struggled to understand this part of it. Apparently her little sister was, without any training, already twenty percent integrated. But what would the people who made Destiny want with her?

"They don't just think Nika's a Potential," Bach told Anna grimly. "By now, they know it."

———

Nika screamed.

And screamed.

But the grotesque man with the surgical knife kept coming toward her.

His face was badly scarred—as if he'd survived a fire. One of his ears and most of his nose was completely gone and the scar tissue twisted one side of his mouth up into a relentless grimace.

There was nothing she could do—the restraints were unbreakable.

She'd woken up with no idea how she'd gotten here, into this darkened room. She was locked in place, on her back, unable to move.

But then, moments after she'd woken up, the light had come on, glaring and bright, and Nika had seen that she was in a hospital bed, wearing a hospital gown, in a room filled with other girls who were also restrained on hospital beds.

There were about two dozen of them in there, some much younger, but none too much older than Nika. Some of them had started to scream, and then they were all screaming—Nika, too—as she turned and saw the man who'd come in through the door, carrying that glittering knife. He was looking at Nika and pointing to her as he advanced, closer and closer.

He was so close now that she could smell his breath—rancid and foul. "This won't hurt," he told her as he brought the blade of the knife to the inside of her left arm.

But it *did* hurt and Nika screamed as he cut her, as her blood sprayed and splattered, bright red against the white of the bedsheets, the walls, the floor, the man's white coat. And the screams of the girls around her grew more frantic, more terrified at the sight.

"What do you think?" the man asked though his misshapen mouth. "Should I just let you bleed? Should I allow you to die?"

Nika shook her head frantically. "No, please, no!"

And he laughed—at least she thought it was laughter, that sound he was making—and he took something from the pocket of his no-longer-white lab coat and pressed it into the open wound in her arm.

The pain nearly made her black out, and she screamed and sobbed, with a chorus of screams echoing her, as whatever he'd put into her arm pinched and burned and stung, and she realized he was stitching her up, sticking and pulling a needle through her skin, with whatever he'd put there still inside her arm, poking out.

It was blue and it had a little transparent tube attached. It was some kind of medical shunt or port—her mother had had something vaguely similar inserted beneath her skin when she'd started her chemotherapy.

The man finished the stitches and cut the thread, and God, it still hurt, but at least she wasn't dead, and she lay there, trapped and crying—unable to wipe the tears and snot from her face as, around her, the other girls continued to scream.

But Nika caught her breath, watching as the man took his knife and his needle and his thread, and limped back to the door, opened it, and left the room.

Her arm was still bleeding, blood oozing out from those Frankenstein-worthy stitches, and the man had done nothing at all to clean up the rest of the mess he'd made.

Some of the girls just kept screaming because of it. All that blood . . . It had soaked through her sheet and she could feel it wet and cold now against her stomach.

"It's all right," Nika said, as the slow closing door finally latched behind the man. "I'm all right. I'm okay."

Some of the girls were still crying—some noisily, some more softly.

One of them—a girl about her own age, who was strapped into a bed almost directly across from Nika—said, "Last week, he killed Leesa. He just slit her throat and let her bleed." The girl started to cry again in earnest. "Right in that same bed you're in."

Nika had been working hard to keep herself from panicking, but with that dreadful news, her heart again began to pound. But she took a deep breath and then another and another. And when she could speak again without crying, she asked, "Where *are* we?"

But no one knew. Not one of the girls had the slightest clue.

———

Elliot was playing part-chaperone, part-interpreter for Joseph Bach and the incredibly lovely and charming Anna Taylor—who'd actually told the maestro to his face that she'd pictured him naked, oh snap!—when he got a text message from Mac.

ETA: now.

Bach was deeply into his explanation of why Anna's sister Nika had been taken. The bottom line was that because the girl was a rare raw Twenty, she was going to be strapped to a hospital bed and kept in a state of near terror to keep her adrenal system active, so that her captors could, essentially, milk her of a hormonal complex found in its highest concentrations in preadolescent girls. Those hormones would then be used to manufacture Destiny.

Bach was being much more tactful and far less alarmist as he explained the science to Anna. Eventually, however, he'd have to get to the horror of it all, because the truth was the truth. Nika had been kidnapped by some real asshole-bastards who belonged to a group called the Organization, who were going to terrorize her and possibly beat or even rape her to keep her in a constant state of fear that would allow them to increase production of a drug that killed nearly everyone who used it.

A drug that made its manufacturers and dealers insanely rich . . .

Elliot pushed himself to his feet, and Bach trailed off mid-sentence to look up at him questioningly. There were shades of *don't leave me here alone with her* in his eyes—which, okay, could really just be a figment of Elliot's creative imagination. Joseph Bach was, after all, afraid of nothing.

He was especially unafraid of attractive young women who pictured him naked.

"I gotta . . ." Elliot pointed to the door. "Mackenzie surfaced."

Bach looked across the conference table at Anna, then back at Elliot as he took a deep breath and managed a curt nod. And wasn't *that* interesting? Maybe Elliot *wasn't* imagining Bach's trepidation at being alone with the woman.

"Good," Bach said. "Tell her I want to see her before she vanishes again."

"I will." Elliot looked from Bach to Anna. "Did anyone show you to your quarters yet?"

She blinked up at him, then looked to Bach for confirmation. "Quarters?"

"We're going to want you to stay here," Bach told her. "At least until we find Nika."

He hadn't gotten even close to what they all hoped would come *after* they rescued Nika from the nightmare in which she was trapped. They hoped that Nika would sign on for training here at OI—which would mean that she and her older sister would become full-time residents.

Here and now, however, Anna was nodding. "And if I don't want to stay here, you'll . . . use your powers to muck around inside my head and make me *think* that I do."

*Awk*ward.

Apparently Anna wasn't just going to forget about that little unauthorized personal B&E that Bach had performed on her, in order to get her here safely.

Elliot took that as his cue to exit stage right, and he slipped out the door. He loved Joseph Bach like a brother, but the man was on his own for this one. As he hit the corridor, he set his phone on its intercom feature and buzzed the nurses' desk. "Kyle, send Dr. Mackenzie into exam room one when she arrives."

"Yes, sir."

"Oh, and she injured her ankle while she was out there tonight, so be aggressive in checking to make sure she doesn't need assistance."

"I'm on it, Doctor," Kyle's voice came back.

This had been one long, awful, total bitch of a night, and it wasn't over yet. And after Elliot gave in to the fatigue and collapsed in his bed, he knew he was going to stare at the ceiling, unable to sleep because he was going to be thinking about Nika. The kid's night wasn't anywhere close to over, and daybreak wouldn't save her. She was going to have to endure whatever nightmares were being thrown at her until they could pinpoint her location and kick down the doors and get her the hell out of there.

It was at times like these that Elliot wished he were on Bach's door-kicking-down team, instead of merely being in charge of research and support. And as long as he was wishing for things that would never happen, he also wished he could learn how to become more fully integrated.

But he couldn't. He was—without a doubt—a mere fraction. Early on in his career, he'd thought he might be one of the gifted ones, since he tested, at times, at a higher-than-average fifteen percent. But try as he might, he was unable to move beyond that.

Eventually he'd come to accept that there was no chance of his ever learning how to fart lightning bolts. Fate had sidelined him, and the best he could do was provide assistance and support to the Greater-Thans like Bach and Mac. And Diaz.

Elliot sighed as he opened the door to exam room one. It was dark inside and the automatic sensors didn't make the room light up, which was odd. So he slapped the wall switch, and the fluorescents sparked to life.

And illuminated Stephen Diaz, who was sitting on the floor in the corner with his knees drawn up to his broad chest, his head in his hands.

"Oh, sorry," Elliot said. "I'm *so* sorry—I didn't know you were in here."

Diaz was up and on his feet so quickly, in one smooth motion, that Elliot almost doubted what he'd just seen. Almost. But he closed the door and stepped directly in front of it, blocking the exit, as he asked Diaz, "Are you okay?"

The other man couldn't—or wouldn't—meet Elliot's eyes as he shook his head no, even as he ran his hands down his face and said, "Yeah, I'm just . . . I needed a minute. It was a really rough night and . . ." He made a sound that was vaguely laughter-like as he shook his head again.

"Yes, it was a rough night," Elliot agreed. "Come on. Quick med scan. Off with your clothes and up on the table. Computer, access EZ. Prep full scan of Dr. Stephen Diaz. I know you did this when you first came in, but . . . It'll take us two minutes, tops."

Diaz looked as if he were going to give birth to a water buffalo, right there on the exam room floor. "Oh," he said. "No. No, I just . . . I really need to be alone right now. I need to *not,* um . . ."

Elliot made a face. "Stephen. I gotta scan you, man. You know the rules. We can't play games with your health and well-being. If you're having a problem—"

"I'm *fine,*" Diaz insisted. "It's just overwhelm. Please, Dr. Z, I need you to give me a break." He closed his eyes. *"Please."*

If he'd wanted to, Diaz could've gone right through Elliot. Not only was he bigger and stronger, but at fifty percent integrated, he could've picked up Elliot without laying hands on him, floated him through the air, and moved him away from the door.

But a significant part of the training program here at OI focused on choosing when and where to unleash one's powers. And in dealing, respectfully, with all of the many fractions who inhabited the world. Between Diaz and Mackenzie, Mac was the one who had trouble in that department.

Diaz, however, completely embraced the zen-related philosophy and monk-like lifestyle that was supposed to allow him to train more easily as he strove to be even more highly integrated.

A man of few words, he usually moved quietly through the halls at OI, doing his work and keeping to himself—which couldn't have been all that easy for him, considering the amount of attention he generated just by looking the way he did.

The Greater-Than was jacked. He was also about three inches taller than Elliot, and Elliot had passed the six feet mark back before he'd turned fifteen. Diaz walked around on legs that were like tree trunks, and had those arms and shoulders that . . . Yes. The man was in excellent physical shape. And with his dark hair worn short, those stormy-ocean green eyes, perfect nose, and chiseled features . . .

Needless to say, Diaz's visits to the OI gym had become something of a spectator sport for the female R&D staff.

Even though—at least as far as Elliot knew—Diaz took his training vows and accompanying celibacy very seriously.

But the truth was that Elliot *didn't* know. He and Diaz weren't friends. They were co-workers. Acquaintances who shared a mutual respect for one another. They knew each other well enough to not be thrown if they were matched during the holiday season as each other's Secret Santas. But while Elliot regularly hung out with Mac and occasionally shot the shit with Bach, he'd never sat and chilled with Diaz.

Not once.

But that wasn't because Elliot hadn't tried. For the seven years he'd worked here—including the past three that he'd lived on campus—he'd kept the friend card at the top of his deck whenever he'd dealt with Diaz.

It was Diaz who'd carefully kept his distance.

For a while, Elliot had thought that it might have been a gay thing—that Diaz was uncomfortable with Elliot's sexual orientation. But as time went on, he'd realized that Diaz kept his distance from everyone.

"Okay. You can go," Elliot said, but he didn't move away from the door as Diaz opened his eyes to look at him. Eye contact. Finally. His pupils weren't dilated and his eyes weren't glazed. That was good. "But if I don't see a report that you've been scanned again, sometime within the next thirty minutes? Don't make me come and find you. Because I will. And *that's* a promise."

Diaz clenched his teeth, the muscles jumping in his jaw as he just stood there, staring back at him.

"You understand?" Elliot pushed.

Diaz closed his eyes and nodded. He even laughed a little as he whispered, "I understand," as if something Elliot had said was funny.

"Good." Elliot didn't get the joke, but he stepped to the side.

Diaz moved swiftly toward the door and threw it open. . . .

And collided with Michelle Mackenzie who was on the other side, about to come in.

Diaz was moving so fast that he couldn't stop himself even though he tried, and she was almost literally half his size, so they both went down, hard, onto the hallway's tile floor.

"Holy shit!" Mac said, then, "Sorry! *Sorry!*" as Elliot scrambled after them, intending to help.

But Mac was already back on her feet, so he turned to Diaz, who was still on the floor.

"You all right?" he asked them both.

"I'm good," Mac said, "but I kinda gave D a pretty enthusiastic knee to the junk. Auto-pilot kicked in and . . . Sorry, about that."

Elliot knew from the endless testing and reports, that that kind of pain was difficult to block. It was one thing for a Greater-Than like Diaz or Bach—or even one of the trainees like Charlie or Brian—to go into an altercation with their ability to block pain already in place. In those cases, they could conceivably endure a full-on electrical current to the gonads without blinking. But the male anatomy was such that, if they *weren't* blocking pain, and they accidentally got whacked, masking that pain was like stopping a stone that had been thrown into water. You might be able to freeze the stone in place, but you couldn't still the ripples that its impact had created.

"I'm okay," Diaz said, although he sounded anything but. "It was more the surprise than the hit."

Elliot extended his hand to help him up, but Diaz looked at it and shook his head. He reached to help Diaz anyway, taking hold of the bigger man's arm and—

Holy crap!

He got slammed by a wave of heat and power that came with an image that was bright and full-color: *Diaz, in a room that Elliot had seen before—but where?—half-sitting, half-lying back, exactly as he was there on the floor, except he was on a bed and he was naked. And instead of reaching to help him up, Elliot was joining him, reaching for Diaz in a different way entirely as they both smiled . . .*

The image shifted suddenly, almost before Elliot had even processed it, turning into a rapid-fire sequence of pictures that flashed through his brain with an accompanying soundtrack of something that might've been a thunderclap with each new burst.

That contact, with Elliot's hand wrapped around Diaz.

Diaz's gasp of pleasure . . .

The intensity of a kiss, deep, long, hot . . .

Sex—Elliot on top, their bodies straining . . .

It happened so fast and filled Elliot's mind so completely, there was no room for other thoughts. In fact, he could barely remember how to breathe.

The images might've continued, but the sheer force of it all knocked him back onto the floor, on his ass. And when he let go of Diaz, it stopped—both the images and that incredible heat.

"Hey," Mac was saying, as she swiftly moved to help him. "El, you okay?"

Elliot couldn't do much more than stare at Diaz, who was pushing himself to his feet.

"Did he shock you?" Mac asked. "D, you need to be careful. I had this weird power surge tonight. I don't know if it had to do with the joker we contained, or maybe it was having Bach's skills slapped back at us, but . . . I've had some strange shit happen tonight, myself."

"Yeah, maybe that's it," Diaz murmured, but he didn't meet Elliot's eyes as Elliot managed to grind out, "I don't think *that* was an electric shock."

"I'm gonna . . ." Diaz pointed down the hall. "Go."

"Now I *really* want that full med scan done in the next thirty minutes," Elliot said, as Mac helped him to his feet.

"Or you'll come and find me," Diaz repeated his earlier words. "I got it." And then he did meet Elliot's eyes—for a mere fraction of a second—before he jammed his hands in his pockets and hurried away.

Elliot stood there, dumbstruck, watching him leave. Holy crap. That definitely hadn't been an electric shock—it had been a *projection.* Elliot had experienced the phenomenon before while doing tests with Joseph Bach, who, at appropriately close-range, could project his thoughts quite easily into another person's head—even someone as less-than as Elliot.

Bach often used the method to communicate with his team while they were apprehending a joker.

Diaz's projection had been similar in some ways to Bach's—the unfamiliar warmth and the sensation of having one's mind filled, completely, with another's thoughts.

But in other ways? It had been *extremely* different. Elliot hadn't received structured thoughts and clear messages from Diaz, but rather something more jumbled and chaotic.

In fact, it was entirely possible that Diaz was completely unaware of all that he'd just shared.

"What just happened here?" Mac asked, as Elliot exhaled what probably sounded to her like a laugh.

He glanced over to find her watching him, so he shook his head. "Nothing," he said, as he motioned for her to go into exam room one. "I definitely have a boatload of questions for you about this power surge you experienced, but first I need to give you a scan."

He looked back, one last time, in the direction that Diaz had gone, but the man had finally turned the corner, way down at the end of the hall.

Holy, *holy* crap.

Whatever that was that Elliot had just experienced, one thing was crystal clear.

Stephen Diaz was gay.

SEVEN

"And if I don't want to stay here," Anna Taylor was saying, "you'll . . . use your powers to muck around inside my head and make me *think* that I do."

Bach agreed completely with Elliot, who'd left the room very quietly, with the faintest click from the door closing behind him.

This *was* awkward.

And although there were a number of ways he could've responded to what Anna had just said, he went with the truth.

"In order to control your thoughts," he told her, "to that degree, I'd have to take up permanent residence inside of you. Your head."

She was silent, just gazing at him, so he cleared his throat and continued.

"I do the best I can," he said quietly. "That's all I can ever hope to do. And I did what I did tonight because it was imperative that you leave the area immediately. The police were on their way to your apartment with a warrant for your arrest in connection to Nika's disappearance."

She reacted to that, leaning forward in her chair, her brown eyes blazing. "But that's absurd! I'm the one who filed the missing persons report. Even if they had reason to believe I'd harm Nika—which they don't!—do they honestly think I'd cover my tracks by spending five hundred dollars that I don't even *have*?"

"It doesn't matter what they think," Bach told her evenly. "What matters is that they would have taken you into custody. And once you were in the system? The people who took Nika would have had access to you, but I would not have. I couldn't let that happen." He sat forward, too. "I know you don't want to hear this, but if you leave here, you *will* be picked up by the police. It doesn't matter why, it doesn't matter if you can answer all of their questions and even provide a legitimate alibi. I'm sure that you can. But as they're checking that alibi, you'll be put in a holding cell with people who have already been given the order to kill you. You need to believe me, Anna, when I tell you that the people who run the Organization have a *very* long reach."

He was scaring her. But he knew that she still didn't believe him. Not completely. "I thought the police were understaffed. Why would they spend any time at all on this one missing little girl?"

"Because they've also been given an order," Bach told Anna. "The Organization has connections everywhere."

"Even here?" she asked. "At the Obermeyer Institute?"

"No," Bach said. "Not here. Everyone who enters the compound gets screened."

"Screened," she repeated. "By you and the other Seventy-twos?"

"There are no other Seventy-twos at OI," he told her. "We've got two Fifties. A fair number of Forties. Forty is considered very high. But even the Fifties can't screen to the level that I can."

"So you *are* like the prince," she said. "Or maybe I should say *king*. King of the Thought Police. Nika must be very important to the Institute, to get you involved. Can I assume that I've been cleared? Since I've already been *screened*?"

"Yes," he said.

"That makes it sound so much better than calling it, say, mental invasion or privacy annihilation."

"Most people who come here, do so willingly," he said a tad more sharply than he would have liked. "They welcome the protection."

And there they sat, staring at each other across the conference table.

"I'm not any kind of king," Bach added. "I'm far from perfect. But like I said, I do my best." He stood up. "Why don't I show you to your quarters? The facilities here are very comfortable. Maybe seeing your apartment will help you decide to stay."

"I've decided," she said, looking up at him. "To stay."

The rush of relief made it hard to speak, so Bach nodded. And finally managed a "Good."

"Since I don't care *where* I stay," Anna told him as she, too, got to her feet, "and I *do* care about finding my sister, maybe you could show me the part of the compound where your analysts are tracking Nika's cell phone GPS and searching through those satellite images of her route home from school."

Bach nodded again. That he could do.

————

Elliot was still flustered and freaked out. And aroused.

Mac could feel it—it was still radiating off of him in waves as they headed for the OI lounge, leaving the more sterile-feeling Med Center's wing and going into the far more lavish and old-fashioned part of the brownstone building known as Old Main.

The doctor had absolutely no ability to block his emotions. And, as an occasional fifteen-percenter or maybe just as a highly intelligent gay man, he also had a naturally heightened empathy. And yes, okay, Mac was guilty of stereotypical thinking, but in Elliot's case, it was true. He *was* more empathic than most people, *and* he was indisputably, openly gay—which was one of the main reasons he and Mac had become such close friends. As a gay man, he was unaffected by her ability to cast a sexual spell. Because of that, Mac knew his friendship with her was real.

She also loved Elliot because the man was incapable of bullshit. What made it even better was that he had no clue that he was so transparent to most of the Greater-Thans—which made his obvious choice to never even *try* to sling any BS doubly refreshing.

And that also made the *nothing* he'd said to her outside the exam room extra odd.

What was he hiding?

If it had been anyone besides Diaz in the hallway with them, Mac would've guessed that El had recovered sufficiently from his damaged-by-an-asshole broken heart to finally engage in a little unauthorized something-something—and more power to him.

But it *was* Diaz, which meant there was absolutely nothing going on. At least on Diaz's end. He was totally blocked when it came to his sexuality.

Elliot opened the lounge door and held it for Mac to go in first.

The dark-paneled room had been a gentlemen's club in the building's precollege days. At this time of night, it was deserted. Most of the staff were asleep, and the Potentials were still in lockdown. But the lounge remained open. Always. The private bar at OI was on Vegas-time, open 24/7. There was never a last call.

Mac slid into her favorite booth, way in the corner, and Elliot sat across from her. "So when did *you* start crushing on D?" she asked her friend.

Elliot rolled his eyes, but he didn't deny it. "Is there anyone at OI who *doesn't* have a crush on Stephen Diaz?"

"You mean, besides me?" she asked, and he gave her a very pointedly raised eyebrow. "Hey. I got over my thing for him years ago."

"I have the occasional—okay, more like frequent—hot dream," Elliot told her with his trademark honesty. "It's triggered, apparently, by walking past him in the hallway. And if you repeat that to anyone, I'll deny it. The last thing I want to do is make him uncomfortable."

He shut up fast as the nightshift bartender and cook—a tall, flaxen-haired woman named Louise—brought them their usual. She didn't even bother to take their order, she just delivered a glass of wine for Mac—she never drank anything harder than that while in the compound—and a coffee for Elliot.

"Thanks," Mac said and Elliot nodded, too, watching Louise meander back to the bar, obviously waiting until she was well out of earshot.

And here it came.

"Okay, we're here," he said. "In the lounge. Spill, Mackenzie. What the hell's going on?"

Back in the med-wing, Elliot had scanned her, giving her a longer-than-normal full, and while she was up on the table in her underwear, he'd started frowning at the test results. Apparently her integration was up a little—she was at fifty-two, instead of her usual forty-nine-point-five.

"*Which* ankle did you injure . . . ?" he'd asked.

"The left," Mac had told him. "But I don't think I hurt it that badly. It healed pretty quickly."

"Yeah, I don't think so," Elliot had said and brought over a handheld wand called a DEET that he waved across the foot in question, looking for a more detailed analysis.

"I'm fine now," she'd insisted as he again frowned at the computer screen. "I'm walking on it. No pain."

And that was when he'd dropped the bomb. "It's registering as a fully healed break," he told her. "You broke it. In more than one place. And there was damage to ligaments, too, plus a slight tear in your plantar fascia . . . All healed with readings of scar tissue that I'd expect to see from an injury that's at least a year old. At *least*."

Mac had stared at him. "Seriously?"

"Yup," he'd said. "And FYI, if you'd come in with this severe a break, I would have scheduled you for surgery. How the *hell* did you do this?"

"I was coming down a flight of stairs," she'd told him, "and I fell—"

"No," Elliot had said. "Hello. I know how you *did* it. It was one of the few things you actually included in your report, but we'll get into everything you left out later. What I want to know now is how you *healed* it. Talk about *quickly* . . . What I'm seeing is . . ." He was as serious as she'd ever seen him as he looked up from the computer. "It's impossible."

"Apparently not," Mac had said. And then she'd told him that she had a theory, but that she wanted to go to the lounge to talk about it.

To her surprise, he'd actually agreed—which probably had more to do with whatever had happened out in the hall with Diaz than any desire to appease Mac.

Still, she was glad, because this wasn't a conversation that she wanted to have sitting in her underpants on a table, with him in the role of her primary care physician. This was a conversation that she wanted to have with her friend, El.

But now here they were, and Elliot was giving her his full attention, waiting for her theory as to how and why she could heal a seriously broken ankle in a matter of hours.

Mac took a fortifying sip of wine. And then she just said it. "I've found that I heal significantly faster when I have sex."

Elliot laughed. Just a little. Then he leaned forward slightly and asked, "Really?"

Mac nodded.

He took a deep breath and exhaled hard, and then admitted, "I have so many questions and comments running through my head right now, I'm not sure where to start." He rubbed his chin as he stared first into his coffee, and then at the table, and then at the wall before looking back at her. "Okay, I give up. I'm not going to try to organize. This is just going to be random reaction. Nothing I say is in order of importance, so I'm just going to start with *How long have you known about this?* Followed by, *I thought we were friends. How could you not tell me?* Followed by, *So who, exactly, are you sleeping with?* And please don't say *random strangers.*"

"I've known for years, and I should have told you a long time ago," she admitted. "I'm sorry about that. But it was hard to separate the friend from the researcher, and I didn't want a report drawn up on the subject."

"Well," he said, sitting back in his seat. "Thanks *so* much for your faith in me."

"I *do* have faith in you," she said. "This job is your entire life, El."

"And isn't that the pot calling the kettle black!"

"You know damn well that you're going to have to write up a

report," she shot back. "What happened with my ankle is . . . It's too big. You're honestly going to withhold *that* from Bach?"

"*You've* been withholding it from Bach," he countered.

"Actually, I haven't," Mac said, "because, before tonight, the boost I've gotten in self-healing hasn't been all that drastic—which is where we get into the answer to your last question. Who am I sleeping with." She took another sip of wine. "Up until tonight, I've had, well, a boyfriend. Justin. You don't know him. We had an apartment in the Back Bay. We were together for . . . a couple of years."

"Years?" Elliot repeated with heavy disbelief.

"Look, I'm sorry," she said again. "It was easier if you didn't know. I didn't want you to have to lie to Bach." As if he actually could've . . .

He knew what she was thinking. "You suck. You were with this Justin guy for all that time . . ." But then he realized that they were talking about Justin in the past tense. "Up until tonight, you said. What happened tonight?"

"He dumped me," Mac admitted. "He just moved out. I got there and he was gone. It was kind of a shock, if you want to know the truth."

Elliot exhaled hard and reached across the table to take her hand. "I'm so sorry," he said. "You still suck, but . . . I *am* sorry."

"It's really not as bad as it sounds," she said. "Or . . . maybe it's worse, because I . . . I didn't really love him, El. At least not enough. I'm sure, on some level, he knew that, and . . ."

"Still, to do it that way?" Elliot said. "With no warning? That's pretty shitty." He sighed. "I just wish you'd told me. I mean, here you had this whole secret life outside of OI, and . . . I honestly had no clue."

"No one knew," Mac said. "Well, except for Diaz. I'm pretty sure he suspected."

Back when she'd first arrived at the Institute, when she was still a Potential, she'd tried to seduce first Joseph Bach and then Stephen Diaz. Tried and failed. And Diaz had not only turned her down, but he'd also stopped her when she'd later gone shopping for a lover among the other trainees and recruits. He'd told her, in no uncertain terms, that if she were going to ignore the strong suggestion that she remain celibate, she should get her groove on well off-campus.

She looked at Elliot now. "Did you seriously think, all this time, that I've actually been celibate? *Me?*"

He blinked. "I guess . . . I didn't think about it. I mean, in retrospect, it's kind of ridiculous. Although . . . You've been busy, and busy people don't always . . . I mean, I haven't. Had sex. For three years now." He frowned. "Whoa, that's a long time, isn't it?"

Mac nodded. "And there's a difference between not having sex and being celibate in the way that the trainees are encouraged to be celibate. Come on, seriously? Does anyone *really* believe that we gain anything from redirecting our sexual energy? Obviously, I don't, because I haven't been redirecting. But Diaz? He's definitely been following the program. Except we both hit fifty-percent integration at the same time, and I did it without torturing myself. I didn't put this in my report tonight—you know, the one on the Hempford takedown . . . ? But I wanted you to know, in case it had something to do with Diaz electrocuting you in the hall—"

"He didn't electrocute me," Elliot said.

"Whatever. But that wall of pain that we used to hammer the joker?" Mac said, "Diaz's contribution was to open up a giant can of sexual-frustration whup-ass. He not only hasn't had sex in years, but he hasn't allowed himself *any* kind of sexual release, so . . ."

Elliot laughed his disbelief. "You can't possibly know *that.*"

"Yes," Mac said, nodding emphatically. "I can. The guy doesn't even masturbate. When he opened *that* up, and aired it out, it was kind of like getting hit with a wrecking ball. Or, more accurately, a pair of wrecking blue balls."

"Holy crap." The joke was lost on Elliot, who was back to staring into his coffee, his eyes slightly out of focus.

"You know, if you'd asked," she told her friend, "I would have told you. About Justin. But you never asked."

He looked up at her, and it was clear he accepted that. "Okay. But there's more to this story, am I right? What happened tonight? You get home—"

"It's not home," she interrupted. "It's just some shitty apartment."

"The point is," he said, "that you get there, the boy-toy's gone and . . . what?"

"I went to a bar," Mac told him. "And I must've been sending out a signal. You know, the whole enhanced-charisma thing I do, to make guys think I'm really hot . . . ? I must've been adjusting and sending out pheromones—my powers just kind of on autopilot—probably because I was bummed about Justin. At least that's what I thought at first. But then . . . It's entirely possible that the guy I picked up was doing some adjusting of his own."

"Oh, no." Elliot focused on the wrong part of what she'd told him. "The guy you picked up?" he repeated with dismay.

"Listen to what I'm telling you," Mac said, leaning across the table. "This guy that I met in that bar . . . ? I don't think I've *ever* met anyone as attractive. Not ever. There *had* to be powers— charismatic powers—involved."

As Mac watched, Elliot took a moment to do the math, but he finally realized what she'd just told him. "You hooked up tonight with another Greater-Than?"

"I think so," she said. "I mean, he's not yet. A Greater-Than. He's had no training, but . . . I swear I didn't find out until *after,* that . . . Well, he told me that he's a Potential. He enters the program tomorrow."

Elliot's mouth dropped open. "Here at OI?"

"Yep."

"Oh, shit," he said.

Mac nodded, and to her horror, her eyes actually filled with tears—which was stupid. Her eyes had been bone dry when she'd told Elliot about Justin. She quickly forced the excess moisture away before Elliot could see. "When I found out, I told him I couldn't see him again."

"Who is he? Did you get his name?" Elliot asked.

Mac just looked at him, letting her disgust show on her face.

"Well, it sounded to me like it was rebound sex, and I don't know how you do these things," he said. "I mean, if you were sending out your super-hot vibe, and he was, too . . . That could've gotten pretty intense, pretty quickly. For all I know, your foot got healed in the men's room of the bar."

"Wow, thanks," she said.

"Look me in the eye, and tell me you've *never* had sex in the men's room in a bar," Elliot countered.

"I haven't," she said.

"Okay then, ladies' room," he said. "Or unisex bathroom—you *know* what I mean. Hello. I was young and foolish once, too."

"Said the ancient man—who's what, two years older than me?—who hasn't gotten laid in three years."

"Touché."

"For the record," Mac said, "the accelerated healing of my foot started while we were sitting at the bar. He touched me and . . . It was crazy, El. And I thought, okay, Justin's gone, so why not experiment? But then when we were outside, I kissed him, and after that? I could run."

"Are you kidding?" Elliot said. "With *that* injury . . . ?"

"When we actually had sex," she reported, "there was some kind of electrical power surge—I think he must've done that, too. You know, unconsciously. But after, all the circuit breakers needed to be reset. Plus I'm pretty sure every lightbulb in the apartment building was blown. Later, I lit a candle and . . . At first I thought it was just a shitty candle, but I've been thinking about it, and I'm pretty sure he did that, too—you know, caused the wax to burn extra fast."

"So you think *he* somehow healed your foot. This mysterious Potential that you've yet to name."

Mac laughed her despair as she nodded. "I know that I have to tell you who he is," she said. "He's a former Navy SEAL. He's really suited to the program—except for the celibacy bullshit. We'll get some serious resistance there."

Elliot laughed at that. "But, staying on topic—healing *other* people is something we've never seen before," he reminded her. "I'm still not convinced that that wasn't all you. You *did* start this by saying that even before tonight you'd made note of a correlation between sex and healing." He took a sip of his coffee. "You ever try, um." He cleared his throat. "Healing yourself?"

Mac sighed. "Yes," she said. "And no, it doesn't work when I'm alone. God, the tests you're going to run to prove this theory are going to be *really* awkward, aren't they?"

"What if all these years," Elliot asked, "Bach's been wrong? What if sex enhances one's ability to integrate, instead of hampering it? That's something he's going to want to know."

Mac wasn't entirely sure about that. She finished the rest of her wine in one large swallow. "His name's Shane Laughlin."

Elliot nodded. "I know. I had him at *Navy SEAL*. FYI, on paper, he's nothing all that special. A Seventeen. So okay, he's maybe a *little* bit special, but still. He's nearly thirty years old. It's not like he's thirteen and his powers are still developing. And it's also not like he's coming in at thirty-percent integrated, the way you did."

"Test him," Mac told her friend. "Pull him out of the group and put him through the paces."

"I will," Elliot said. "And you can help."

"No." She stood up. "I'm going to take a few days off." She didn't want to see this guy in the hallway, or even in the lab. Although, if Shane was as powerful as she thought, he was going to be there when she got back. God, that was going to suck.

But Elliot was shaking his head. "Crap, you don't know, do you? You didn't hear, of course you didn't, you weren't back until . . ."

"Hear what?" Mac asked.

"Nika Taylor got grabbed."

"The thirteen-year-old?" Mac said. About two minutes before she got the call to help out with jokering Nathan Hempford, she'd gotten an e-mail from Bach about the girl. He wanted Mac with him when he went out to recruit her.

Elliot nodded.

"What the hell was Bach waiting for?" Mac exploded. "God, *some*one's got to protect these girls!"

"Hey, turns out she was taken before we even knew about her," Elliot said. "The abduction happened this afternoon, but we didn't know she existed until this evening. We can only do what we can do."

"Well, whatever we're doing," Mac said, heading for the door, "we need to start doing it freaking better!" She spun back to tell Elliot, "You know what those assholes are doing to this girl? *Right now?*"

"I do know," he said quietly. "Mac, I'm sorry, I didn't mean to—"

"Where's Bach?" she asked.

"He's with Nika's older sister," Elliot said. "Trying to get her acclimated."

"Tell him I'm going out," Mac said. "I'm going to troll for dealers. I'll find someone who's seen this girl—someone who knows where she's being held. And then I'm going to go in, and I'm going to bring her home."

Because if this job was going to rule her life the way that it did, to the point of her having to discard promising new lovers in the street? She was going to make it goddamn worth it.

"Mac, wait!" Elliot hurried after her, but she didn't slow her pace until he said, "I just got a text message from Analysis. They found what they're pretty sure are the satellite images of Nika's abduction. You're gonna want to see that before you go anywhere."

EIGHT

"These images may be disturbing," Bach told Anna as they took the elevator up to the floor of Old Main that was devoted to OI's Analysis department. "There's no need for you to see them."

"Yes, there is," she said. "What if you're wrong about this Organization? What if whoever took Nika is someone I recognize? And even if it's not, I want to know exactly what happened to her, so I can help her deal with it after we get her back."

Unlike Joseph Bach, she wouldn't be able to read Nika's mind.

"Fair enough," he said evenly. "But if it's too much for you—"

"I'm pretty sure that I'm going to have nightmares," Anna told him, as the elevator dinged, and the doors opened, "regardless of what I see."

He led the way out and Anna found herself in an ornate, old-fashioned elevator lobby area with a corridor at one end. This part of the beautiful old building had clearly been restored to its original splendor, with gleaming wood paneling that was rich and dark, and shining marble floors.

The elevator doors were brass, and the second one opened with another mellifluous ding as Anna followed Bach past it.

"Hey." Elliot emerged, and he was with a diminutive woman dressed in olive drab cargo pants, clunky boots, and a black leather jacket. Her dirty-blond hair was cut extremely short and her face was a little too cute to be called beautiful. Yet there was something oddly, strikingly compelling about her, and had Anna been pressed to deliver a one-word description of the woman, that word would have been *gorgeous*. "We got the message about the SAT images. Have you seen them?"

"No," Bach said, "we just got the call, too." He looked at the petite woman. "You okay?"

"I'm great, Maestro," she said. "You?"

"I've had better nights," Bach told her, and for an instant, she seemed to be genuinely surprised at his candor. She covered it quickly, though, as Bach gestured to Anna. "This is Nika's sister. Anna Taylor, Dr. Michelle Mackenzie. Mac's one of my Fifties."

Dr. Mackenzie held out her hand, and Anna shook it—the Fifty may have been small, but her grip was strong.

"We're going to find your sister," Mac promised, and Anna turned to find Bach watching as the elevator dinged again.

"Hopefully the satellite images will give us some help," he said as the first elevator door opened again, and a ridiculously good-looking man stepped out.

The man stopped short when he saw them standing there, but then he took a deep breath and forced a smile as he came toward them. "I guess we all got the same message," he said in a rich baritone voice that was as beautiful as he was.

He was as large as Mac was petite. He was taller than Elliot even, and he towered over Dr. Bach—who managed to look no less royal and still completely in charge. Probably in part because the double-XL greeted Bach with a nod and a very respectful, "Sir." He then turned to Anna. "Ms. Taylor."

"This is Dr. Stephen Diaz," Bach told Anna. "My other Fifty."

Anna reached out her hand to greet him, when Elliot suddenly stepped forward. *"Be careful—"* the doctor said, but then cut himself off as she clasped Diaz's hand.

"I'm sure there'll be something in the images that'll point us toward Nika's abductors," Diaz said, exuding rock-solid confidence as he gazed down at Anna. His eyes were a beautiful shade of green that seemed even lighter in contrast to his dark complexion.

"I hope so," she answered him, glancing over at Elliot

questioningly—be careful of what?—but the fair-haired doctor just forced a smile and shook his head.

"Let's do this," Mac said.

"You ready?" Bach asked Anna, who nodded. "We've got a room set up to view the images. We're in study three," he told his teammates as he led the way.

"I haven't read the reports yet," Mac said to Bach. "What time, exactly, did the girl go missing?"

As Bach filled her in on the details of Nika's disappearance, Elliot spoke quietly to Diaz. "I saw your med scan," he said. "Thanks for making sure that I was cc'd on that."

"Oh," Diaz said. "Yeah. No problem, Doctor."

"You seem . . . Fine."

"Yeah," Diaz said again. He cleared his throat. "It was a rough night though."

"One that's not over yet," Elliot pointed out. "It's barely three A.M.—or should I say oh-three-hundred."

Diaz laughed a little. "Three A.M. is fine, and . . . Believe me, I'm well aware that we've still got hours to go before dawn. Excuse me, Dr. Z. I want to, um, make sure we have enough chairs in the room." He picked up his pace, pulling ahead of them all.

Elliot sighed almost inaudibly, but then smiled when Anna glanced at him. "Kinda hard not to picture *him* naked, too, huh?" he said to her, out of the corner of his mouth.

She laughed, but doing so somehow triggered a rush of tears to her eyes, and she inhaled, hard, so that her laughter didn't turn into an audible sob.

But Bach glanced sharply back at her, as if he'd heard her anyway. Or maybe he'd just felt a disturbance in the Force—this was *so* weird.

Elliot slipped his arm around her and gave her a squeeze. "Hey," he said, warm and solid against her. "With these three on your side, there's no way we're not getting Nika back. You gotta have faith."

"It's just all so strange," Anna admitted. She forced a smile as she looked up at him. "Particularly since the best-case scenario puts me in a world where my little sister is going to learn to read my mind."

Elliot laughed. "I know, scary, huh?" he said as he led her into a small room with a flatscreen that almost took up an entire wall. There were plenty of chairs. And as Elliot pulled her by the hand to the row of seats, she couldn't help but notice that tall, dark, and handsome Dr. Diaz stayed standing, off to the side, over by the door.

Bach took some kind of remote control device from its port on the wall, and sat, leaving an empty seat between himself and Anna. "Let's just get this over with," he said. "Computer, access JB-one. Dim lights. Picture on."

The lights in the room dimmed as a picture appeared on the flatscreen. It was an aerial map of the part of Boston where Cambridge Academy was located. Nika's route from school to their apartment was marked with a bright blue line.

Anna forced herself to keep breathing as the Bach commanded, "Computer, zoom in."

The image on the screen wasn't a dead-on aerial. The satellite must've been positioned to the south, because although it gave them a view from above, it was angled enough for them to see that yes, that was Nika, walking home from school, her backpack slung over one shoulder, her jacket unzipped.

Her head was down, though, as she looked at her phone, no doubt sending that text message to Anna.

Sure enough, the time clock running down the seconds up in the right-hand corner of the video read 14:26:43. As it clicked over to 14:27, Nika must've pushed send, because she finally looked up from her phone.

"God, is she your sister, or what?" Mac said.

"She does look a lot like you, doesn't she?" Elliot said.

Anna nodded, her heart in her throat, as a car—a black sedan with tinted windows—pulled up alongside her sister, keeping pace with the girl.

Nika didn't notice it at first, but then she did, looking at it

Born to darkness 119

askance, over her shoulder. She shifted her bag, increased her speed, and raised the phone she was still holding up to her ear.

"Smart girl," Mac said. "Calling someone—or at least pretending to."

"Pretending," Bach confirmed. "Her phone records don't show any calls out after that last text."

"Why doesn't she run?" Anna breathed.

But then Nika *did* run—and she proved herself to be a *very* smart girl, because she ran back the way she'd come, toward the school.

The street was heavily trafficked enough to make it impossible for the car to follow her by backing up. Instead, a large man jumped out of the passenger side and chased after Nika.

Bach used the remote to adjust the view.

And it looked—for a moment—as if Nika was going to do it, as if she were going to get away. She flung her backpack at the man who was following her, and it slowed him as he tripped and nearly went down.

But then there was a break in traffic, and the black car went surging in reverse, all the way back to the corner, where it jerked to a stop. And the driver got out and Nika was trapped between the two men.

"Shit," Mac said. "With his hood up, I can't see his face. Can you—"

"Let's just watch it through once," Bach murmured.

There was nowhere for Nika to go on the otherwise empty sidewalk—the building on her side of the street was boarded up and surrounded by a dilapidated chain-link fence.

So she stopped and focused on her phone, and Anna knew that she was trying to call for help, trying to dial 9-1-1.

But the hooded man from the car slapped her phone out of her hand, then slapped her in the face, and Anna gasped as the force of the blow sent her little sister reeling back, right into that fence.

And still, Nika tried to run, but the man with the hood blocked her and hit her again. And again. And again.

This time the flurry of blows sent her to the ground, and Anna was unable to keep silent. "Oh, *God . . .*"

But the fight hadn't been beaten out of her sister yet, and even though Nika could barely push herself up off the broken and pitted concrete, she again reached for her phone.

But the bigger man who'd been chasing her down the sidewalk finally caught up to them. He saw what she was doing, and he stomped on her phone with one of his big, clunky boots, then kicked the pieces into the street before turning to kick Nika in the stomach. God, Anna was going to be sick. She couldn't help herself—she started to cry.

And still Nika tried to crawl away.

The two men then exchanged what looked to be angry words. The driver jogged back to the car as the bigger man dropped the pack, and dug into his pocket for something.

He turned and reached for Nika, pulling up the girl's jacket and shirt.

"What is he doing?" Anna couldn't keep her horror from her voice.

"Giving her an injection." Bach's voice was tight, too.

"Probably something to knock her out," Elliot murmured as he reached over and took Anna's hand.

And sure enough, Nika finally slumped, unconscious.

The big man scooped up Nika's pack and then picked the girl up almost as easily, carrying her to the car. He tossed her inside, then climbed in himself, and the car pulled away from the curb.

Throughout the video, Bach had been pushing buttons on the remote, and a series of small pictures now lined the margins of the screen—including some still shots of the two abductors. "Computer, pause video," he said now, as he used the remote to highlight the stills, going through them one at a time.

The first was of the car, and he zoomed in to reveal the plate number. That was good, wasn't it? Anna pulled free from Elliot's hand to use her sleeve to wipe her eyes. Crying wasn't going to help get Nika back.

Diaz spoke up from the back. "Analysis already ID'd the car as a government vehicle reported as stolen—which explains, at least in part, why no one stopped to help."

"I would have stopped," Mac said grimly.

"For all they knew it was official business," Diaz said.

"Two men? Beating a child . . . ?"

"It doesn't matter. People don't want to know," Diaz pointed out.

Bach had already clicked to the next photo—of the larger man getting out of the car—but it was blurred so he kept going. "Let's just get through this as quickly as possible," he said, again, stopping on a much clearer shot.

The man was heavyset, with a wide, fleshy face, and light-colored eyes that broadcast anger and what looked to Anna like more than a touch of crazy. His hair was dark and thinning, and he had a bald spot in the back.

She felt Bach glance at her, and she shook her head as she gazed up at the man. "I'm sorry, I don't know him," she said, fighting another rush of tears.

"We didn't expect you to," he said quietly. "Anyone else?"

"No, sir," Diaz murmured, as Mac said, "Nope."

"Computer, analysis," Bach commanded and a window with information popped up onto the screen. Apparently, whoever this man was, he was six feet tall, and weighed 270 pounds. His approximate age was thirty-four. Face recognition software was flashing an icon as it searched its archives, but it came up with a very disappointing *Unknown*.

"He's either not in the system, or he's using some kind of shielding device," Elliot leaned in to tell her. "There's a new product on the black market—a cell phone app—that creates interference with digital imaging technology. It's illegal and it's expensive—which tells us something right there. If thugs like this have that technology? We can be pretty certain they're connected to people with money, i.e., the Organization."

"We can still use these images to try to make a visual match," Mac pointed out.

"Analysis is already on that," Diaz said. "But that takes time."

Bach was already flipping through the stills of the man wearing the hood, and going back to the only one that showed his face.

His features were contorted, his mouth an ugly gash, and Anna had to look at it through her eyelashes. The picture was from right after he'd hit Nika, and the girl was in mid-air, having not yet landed on the sidewalk. Anna couldn't speak. She just shook her head no, even as Mac spoke up.

"I know this one," she said. "His name is Rickie Littleton. He's a low-level dealer, lives in Southie, but peddles his shit at Copley Square and the Chestnut Hill Mall. He's something of a hard-on—" She glanced at Anna as his stats appeared on the screen. He was significantly smaller than his compatriot—not a whole lot taller than Anna herself. But again, the face recognition program came up blank. "Look, I'm not going to lie. He has a rep for being brutal, but he's not real bright, either, so . . ." She exhaled hard. "It really could be a lot worse."

"Looks like he's gone into acquisition," Elliot said. "Maybe trying to move up the Organization's food chain?"

"Yeah, I can't see that actually happening," Mac scoffed. "We've been tracking him for a few years now. We haven't taken him out because he's so transparent that it's better for us to keep him in the game. We get more information from watching him work."

"The real question is," Bach said, "does he know what he's got?" He made an adjustment with the remote, and the screen went back to the paused video of the stolen car leaving the abduction scene. "Computer, highlight the car," he ordered, and the vehicle glowed bright yellow. "Let's see where they take her. Computer, fast-forward."

The image not only fast-forwarded, but it zoomed out to a map of the area, so that the movement wasn't too dizzying. Anna could easily follow the yellow dot. "But how will we know they didn't stop and remove Nika from the car?" she asked.

"The software'll bring us in closer if the car so much as slows," Bach said, as the image on the screen did just that. The car pulled up to a red light and idled. No one got in or out. "But someone in Analysis will watch the footage in real-time, just to be sure."

The yellow dot was moving again, faster now. And it didn't slow until it pulled up to what looked like a mechanic's garage that was, indeed, in South Boston.

The bay doors opened and the car pulled inside, and the doors shut tightly behind it.

Mac stood up. "Let's go kick his ass."

"The girl may not be there anymore," Bach warned, although he got to his feet, too.

"On the other hand, Rickie really might *not* know how important Nika is," Mac repeated Bach's words. "Seriously, sir. There's no way the Organization would've farmed this job out to him. This was entrepreneurial initiative. Had to be. Rickie somehow got hold of the acquisition list and went after the name at the top. How much you want to bet we find a stolen shipment of Blacklight disposable cell phones somewhere in that garage?" She turned to look back at Diaz. "Who wants to come find out?"

Bach looked toward the back of the room, too, as Diaz said, "I'm good to go."

"Let's do it," Bach decided. "Go ahead and start surveillance. I'll be right behind you."

The two Fifties left the room as Anna and Elliot, too, stood up.

"Mac's right," Bach told Anna as if he could sense her anxiety—which he no doubt could. "They aren't as smart as they think they are. It was amateur hour—as soon as they broke Nika's cell phone, we were well on our way to finding them."

Anna didn't understand. "But breaking the phone meant we couldn't track them by its GPS."

"Except they broke the phone," Bach said, "at the precise location where they abducted Nika, which was the equivalent of sending us a message saying *start searching here.* And we *did* start our search of the SAT images at the longitude and latitude where we lost Nika's signal. Without that critical information, our analysts would still be sifting through footage. Do you remember how I had you turn off your cell phone while we were on the Mass Pike?"

Anna nodded.

"*That's* the way to do it, if you don't want to be tracked. There was a lot of traffic at the time—you could have been in any one of those cars. Or maybe you weren't there at all, but you'd put your phone in someone's vehicle and . . . Because you turned off your cell phone at that moment, the police now have no idea where you are."

"Unless they find me from SAT images." Anna gestured toward the screen. "When they search the footage taken outside of my apartment, they'll see me getting into your car."

"No, they won't," Bach said, as he put the remote control back on the wall. "Before I arrived, I, uh, made a few adjustments in the satellite positioning. There are no pictures. At all. Any security cameras in the area experienced a blackout during that time. You're completely safe here, Anna. And even if they produce a warrant, we have the means to hide you."

Dear God. Anna searched his eyes, looking for what, she wasn't sure. "I really hope you *are* one of the good guys," she said.

"He is," Elliot assured her.

"Yeah, well, you work for him," Anna said. "You kind of have to say that."

Bach smiled as he exchanged a glance with Elliot. "Everyone here works *with* me, not *for* me." He turned to leave, but Anna stopped him with a hand on his arm.

"What can I do?" she asked him. "Please, I want to help."

He covered her hand with his, and Anna felt shades of that same incredible warmth she'd experienced in his car. Although, this time there was an undercurrent of . . .

Turmoil. Intensity. Ferocity.

Heat.

"You *can* help," Bach told her. "I made arrangements for your things to be packed up and moved here, into the OI compound."

"What?" She pulled free from him.

"Why don't you use this time to unpack?" he continued. "That way, if we do find Nika, we'll be bringing her back to a place that feels at least a little bit like home. That'll help her more than you can know."

He was out the door before Anna recovered from her surprise, before she could find her voice. Still, she ran to follow, calling after him, "When I said I'd stay, I didn't mean *forever.*"

But Bach was already gone, almost as if he'd vanished into thin air.

"I hate when he does that," Elliot said. "Come on, I'll show you to your rooms."

––––––––

Shane figured it out.

Important.

Mac had used the word twice—once to refer to her job, and then again when talking about his position as a Potential at Obermeyer Institute. *My work is important,* and then, *It's important that you go.*

It was that, plus the nagging question: how many people out there even knew the word *Potential?* It led him to the somewhat shaky conclusion that the woman he'd had sex with, multiple times last night, *worked* at OI.

Possibly in the very same security department that he'd fantasized would hire him after his time as an R&D test subject came to an end.

What he couldn't figure out was why her working there made her so skittish and absolute in not wanting to see him ever again.

Until after he was buzzed in to the place.

He'd gotten his seabag from the rental locker where he'd stashed it, and then, because the T had stopped running for the night, he'd hitched and humped his way on foot to the compound.

It looked, absolutely, like the former college campus that it was. Beautiful brownstone buildings on a grassy hillside, with gardens and shade trees—surrounded by an electrical fence, with both a kick-ass high-tech security system *and* manned guard towers in intervals around the perimeter.

Shane was kept waiting outside of the gatehouse even after the guards took his name, searched his bag, walked him through a metal detector, and then gave him a pat down—and no doubt a probe while they were at it. Medical scan technology was improving in leaps and bounds, and a jot scan, also known as a partial scan, could be done without a subject's knowledge or permission, since your clothes stayed on and you didn't have to stay still. It was illegal in public places, hence the nickname "probe." It violated personal privacy laws, up the yin-yang. There was currently a battle going on in Congress, where lobbyists were attempting to redefine all places of employment as "private." But the truth was that jobs were so scarce, that even if the bill *didn't* pass, no one in their right mind was going to raise a stink if their employer probed them, even on a daily basis.

Still, it was disturbing.

But most people believed that freedom and privacy was for shit if they couldn't feed their children.

After about twenty minutes, the gate finally opened, and Shane was ushered into a security vehicle and driven up the hill by an uncommunicative guard to a resplendent old building with arched windows and doors. The place had to date from the turn of the nineteenth century. It was the building called "Old Main" from the OI website slide show.

It was pretty damn impressive.

There was a small area off to the side where a variety of vehicles were parked—including a pair of motorcycles. Shane couldn't tell from the distance, in the dim streetlight, if either of them were Harleys, let alone if one was Mac's.

Still, it was enough to make him hope as the guard left his cart out by the curb and walked Shane inside.

There was a manned desk right at the entrance, with another metal detector—which impressed the hell out of Shane. Most organizations relied solely on their perimeter security, which meant that once an intruder was inside, he had free rein. But not so, here.

Apparently, the Obermeyer Institute was run by someone with brains.

It was then, as Shane was spread-eagled to allow for an even more detailed pat down from the guard, that Mac appeared, heading for the doors.

His heart leaped—it actually did gymnastics—when he saw her.

Except she was walking with a man whose picture could have appeared in the dictionary next to *tall, dark, and handsome.* He moved the way she did—whoever he was, he was a warrior, too. And wherever they were going, there was real purpose to it. The dark-haired man said something to her and she laughed, and the look they exchanged . . .

It said it all.

That look was filled with intimacy and trust. Whoever this man was, he was Mac's teammate—probably in every sense of the word.

And it was then that Mac saw Shane. She did an almost imperceptible double take, and her eyes widened only slightly before she turned her face into an expressionless mask.

She didn't look up at her giant friend, and she didn't look over at Shane again—she just walked out of the building with the man by her side.

A blast of cold air from the open door hit Shane as the guard searching him gave a nod. He could put his shoes and jacket back on. There was a bench where he could sit, so Shane sat where he could look out of the windows in the big doors, and sure enough. He heard it before he saw it—the sound of not one but two motorcycle engines being started. They pulled out of the lot, and he could see their twin taillights—red and bright in the pre-dawn darkness—disappearing down the hill.

Mac and her boyfriend had his and her bikes—wasn't that sweet?

Shane carefully kept his voice even as he asked the guard who'd walked him in, "Who was that who just left?"

"Sorry, sir," he said. "I'm not at liberty to say."

Of course he wasn't.

"If you'll follow me to processing . . ." The guard gestured down the hall, in the opposite direction from where Mac had appeared.

Shane grabbed his bag, which had been thoroughly searched a second time, and followed him, a little queasy and a whole lot disappointed—and far more jealous than he knew he had a right to be.

And it was only because jobs were so scarce that he didn't just turn and walk out the door.

Besides, Mac had said it was important that he show up.

Although it was kind of clear that she hadn't expected him *quite* so soon.

NINE

The mechanic's garage in South Boston was deserted by the time they arrived. The place was a total ghost town—Rickie Littleton had clearly known that someone would be coming after him.

Mac stood in the middle of the vacant center bay and lowered her mental shields, closing her eyes to get a better sense of . . .

The slap of fear she could feel was strong, but it wasn't sharp, and she knew it was a residual from the past. Still, it was enough to make her gasp and quickly reshield—someone had been killed here. Raped, and then killed.

God.

But not recently—which meant it hadn't been Nika.

Mac felt nothing from the girl, which was either good or bad, depending on how you looked at it. It was good in that while Nika was here, she hadn't awakened to find herself at the mercy of two very nasty-ass men. It was bad in that it suggested Nika hadn't been here long enough to wake up from whatever sedative she'd been given during her abduction.

And that meant that their trail was cold and getting colder with every passing minute.

Diaz was already on the phone to OI, reporting what they'd found and requesting SAT images of the garage for the entire afternoon and evening. Analysis needed to track every car and truck that had left this place—although there was room in here for at least twenty vehicles. More, if they'd been parked tightly. It was going to take time to track them all to their destinations, and even then, it didn't mean that Nika hadn't since been moved again. And again.

Mac took a deep breath, and bracing herself for the awfulness of that rape, she lowered her mental shields again. She had to ignore the now-dead girl's fear and pain, and focus on the other emotions in the room, hoping for a clue that would lead them to Rickie and his cohort.

But the rapist had bitten his victim over and over again as he'd slammed his body into hers, and—God, the murdered girl had been only a child, sobbing and pleading for him to stop. Her voice echoed with fragments of memories that Mac had long-buried: *Don't, Daddy, please don't . . .*

The force of the horror and pain pushed Mac down onto the cold concrete on her hands and knees, as she fought to stomp back her own ugly memories and to feel beyond it, to get to the emotions of the people who'd been here today.

And there it all was—there had been a lot of people in this garage, not too long ago. Dozens, if not more. Again, not a good sign—they were probably the drivers, hired to move cars out of the place—to make it impossible to track the one carrying Nika.

Mac searched among them for the strongest emotions and found a sense of triumph and glee. His ship had come in, he was going to be rich . . .

And then, from someone else . . . An intense sense of need. Someone was jonesing—not just for drugs, but for . . .

The girl. He knew he couldn't do it, but he wanted to bite Nika like he'd bitten the other one and—

Jesus.

Mac threw up, right there on the concrete. But then Diaz was there—not just picking her up and wrapping his arms around her, but he was also inside of her head, helping her get her defenses back into place, helping her breathe, helping her stop shaking.

"Maybe you shouldn't do this anymore," Diaz said.

"Maybe you should suck my dick," Mac countered before she threw up again.

She tried to push him away, because he couldn't do anything to calm her stomach—it needed to be emptied, and there was really only one way for that to happen. Plus, Diaz didn't have very much control when he walked around inside a fellow Greater-Than's head—not the way Bach did. Bach could stay away from private thoughts if he wanted to. And right now, Mac knew she was an open book when it came to her sordid past. From childhood to adolescence to last night's hookup with Shane . . .

She found that she was clinging to those memories of the former SEAL, focusing on the way he'd smiled into her eyes before he'd kissed her and . . .

God.

She felt Diaz turn away from her too-graphic memories, kind of the way someone polite might do if they stumbled upon you taking a dump with the bathroom door wide open. But he didn't let go of her. He didn't stop trying to absorb at least some of her nausea.

And finally her stomach was empty and it was over. She'd thrown up the crackers and tea, the whiskey and the wine, and whatever else was still in her system after a long day and night with too little food.

And then she and Diaz just sat there. She'd knew he'd gotten a glimpse of everything she'd felt from this hellhole of a garage, so there was no point in discussing it in detail.

One of Nika's kidnappers was a serial child rapist and murderer. As if the threat from the Organization weren't bad enough.

But Diaz felt compelled to say, "They grabbed her for the money. There's no way the greedy one is going to let the other kill her."

"But he might let him . . ." Mac couldn't say it.

Steady. She felt Diaz beside her, and she let him breathe for her for a moment.

"I know this is hard for you," he said quietly.

"Yep," she said. "And I couldn't tell which one was which. So when I find 'em? Littleton and his partner? I'm going to kill 'em both." After she squeezed every little last bit of information out of them.

Even though Diaz was no longer inside of her head, he knew what she was thinking, and he nodded. "Sounds like a plan."

She glanced at him. "Sorry about . . ." She didn't need to be specific. Again, he knew precisely to what she was referring.

And he shrugged. "Yeah, well, I have some pretty fierce fantasies, too."

So okay. He either honestly thought those pictures in her head of her and Shane had been make-believe instead of memories, or he was pretending that was the case, in order to make her feel less embarrassed.

But then he surprised her by saying, "He was really hot—that man we saw in the lobby at OI, but I've discovered that I'm kind of a one-man man, even when it comes to daydreams."

The look she gave him must've been an odd one, because he added, "What? You know my secret." And as realization no doubt dawned in her eyes, he *then* added, "Except, okay, you didn't *really* know." But then he backpedaled. "Not that I was intentionally keeping anything a secret. It just wasn't . . ."

"Relevant?" Mac finished for him and he nodded. "What I knew is that it's hard for you. The celibacy thing. No pun intended. And, for the record, you know as well as I do that the no-sex rule *is* bullshit."

"No, I don't know that," he said on a heavy exhale. *This* part of the conversation they'd had plenty of times before.

"It's not even a real rule. It's just a suggestion. I've had boyfriends—the kind that I get intimate with—for years," Mac confessed. "And here I am—as much of a Fifty as you are."

"Maybe you'd be a Seventy if you'd abstained."

"I doubt it, but for the sake of argument, let's say you're right. Maybe I'd be a Seventy, but I'd also be a completely bitchy Seventy," she told him.

"Hard to imagine you bitchier than you already are," he murmured, and she actually laughed.

And that was when the most personal conversation they'd ever had ended, because Bach arrived.

"Don't unshield completely," Mac warned the maestro as he swept in and did a slow spin, looking around. He made note of everything—of her puke on the floor in the center of the room, of the way she and Diaz were sitting off to the side on the cold concrete with their backs against the brick wall. He closed his eyes briefly as she told him everything that she and Diaz had discovered here.

Well, not quite everything . . . She left out the personal 4-1-1 about Diaz being gay and her desire to keep on shagging one of their new Potentials.

"Analysis just called," Bach informed them. "Littleton and his friend were ready for us to track them. The SAT images show twenty-three different vehicles leaving this facility after Nika and her abductors arrived. We're in the process of tracking them all, but . . ." He shook his head.

There was no way of knowing for sure which car or truck Nika had been in when she was moved from this place.

Diaz stood up, and turned to help pull Mac to her feet. Because, like Mac, he knew what was coming.

"Let's find them—Littleton and his cohort," Bach told them. "Split up, but keep in touch. Mac, head over to the abduction point, see if you can't get a traceable read on Nika's emotional grid."

"Yes, sir."

That, along with the rapist's grid—which Mac would now recognize instantly, and be able to pick out of a crowd at a close enough range—would help them find the girl. Of course, Rickie would be even easier to trace, because the Analysis team at OI knew most of his hangouts and haunts. Assuming, that is, that he hadn't already left the city.

"Remember, please," Bach added, "we need them both alive."

Mac nodded, and as Bach swept back out the door, before she followed him, she turned to Diaz and said, "FYI, nothing's changed."

She didn't wait for him to nod, but she could feel his relief—and a very genuine affection that almost made her pause—as she turned and walked away.

———————

Dr. Zerkowski had been right. The living quarters at OI were fricking great.

Shane had expected a barracks-quality living situation for the unmarried test subjects, or maybe—because the place so closely resembled an ivy-league college campus—something more like a dorm. A lack of privacy. Shared bedrooms, bathrooms, and common areas. Narrow cots with cheap mattresses that were designed for eighteen-year-old co-eds.

Instead, he'd been given a suite of rooms, right out of those pictures on the OI website, one of which contained a luxurious king-sized bed.

The place had hardwood floors that gleamed—tile in the kitchen and bathroom—and furniture that was both pleasing to the eye and comfortable. Both the sofa and the easy chair in the living room were covered with rich leather, and the rest of the furniture was solid wood.

The kitchen had old-style granite, gleaming wood cabinets, and top-of-the-line appliances. Plus—hot damn!—the cabinets and fridge were stocked with all kinds of food, and a bowl of fresh fruit stood out on the counter.

The towels were plush, the sheets were soft, the blankets were fleece, the bathroom floor was *heated*.

One entire wall of the living room was windows—a slider opened onto a balcony, which overlooked a garden that hid what appeared to be a parking lot behind it. Or at least it would overlook that garden in the daylight—which was coming soon. Dawn already lit the sky to the east.

The view, like the entire lush accommodations, was lovely.

And Shane would've traded it in a heartbeat to be back at that dumpy little apartment near Kenmore Square, where Mac had told him he'd rocked her world.

And it wasn't just about sex.

He liked her.

A lot.

Shane stood at the window, eating a banana that had somehow achieved the perfect state of ripeness, thinking about all the material he'd just read about neural integration. He'd been given an e-reader by a terse, gray-haired woman named Clara, down in Processing, who—like all the other OI staff he'd encountered, hadn't so much as blinked at the fact that he'd arrived in the middle of the night.

Sleep be damned—he'd already plowed his way through most of the files Clara had given him.

And he still didn't quite know what to make of any of it.

Apparently, according to the "scientists" here at the Obermeyer Institute, some people were born with the ability to integrate significantly more of their neural net, aka their brain. Doing so allowed them to develop some serious superpowers. But control of those powers required some equally serious training—a concept Shane well understood as a former SEAL.

But still . . .

It was off-the-scale in terms of the whoo-whoo factor. Probably because, also as a former SEAL, he well understood physical limitations. A body could only do what a body could do. It was as simple as that.

But according to the good folks at OI, a body could do almost anything that an integrated brain told it to do.

And apparently? Those same folks believed that Shane was a good potential candidate—aka a Potential—for their training program.

They were going to be disappointed, because their entire line of research was a total pile of bullshit. They were wasting their time, whether they spent two minutes or two months trying to get him to move a pencil with his mind.

Time he'd far rather waste in other ways.

Which brought him back to Mac.

He'd been playing and replaying all that he'd seen in the main OI lobby, and he'd come to the conclusion that he really *couldn't* make any realistic conclusions about any of it.

Mac had been walking next to a man who'd said something that had made her laugh. Big fucking deal. Shane had spent time with plenty of women that he'd never so much as touched.

They both had motorcycles—Mac and her giant friend. So what? The Harley was a vehicle of choice for security specialists all around the globe.

When Shane pulled back his heavy shroud of jealousy and looked objectively at what he'd seen, he saw two people—one of whom he'd recently slept with—heading off purposefully on some kind of mission.

And yet he couldn't help but hear an echo of Mac's voice, right before she left him standing alone in the street, outside of her apartment. *It means I can't see you again.*

There were quite a few reasons why she might've said that—only one being because she was already in a relationship with someone she worked with.

Shane threw away his banana peel, and picked up the phone that was out on the counter and punched zero.

It rang only once before it was picked up. "Lieutenant Laughlin," a cheerful voice greeted him. "This is Robert in Hospitality. What can I get for you, sir?"

"Yes, hi," Shane said, "I'd like to leave a message for Mac. I saw her leaving, so I know she's not here at the Institute right now and, um, I'm wondering the best way to do that since I don't have her phone number."

There was a somewhat longish silence before Robert cleared his throat and said a whole lot less cheerfully, "Your request is . . . most unusual, sir. I'm not sure how to . . . Well, I *do* know that I can't give out anyone's private number. I'm sorry, but—"

"Nuh, nuh, no, I'm not asking you for that," Shane said, even though he hadn't exactly *not* asked for it. This was a fishing expedition. He didn't even know if Mac really did work here, and he still didn't because Robert hadn't given him much to go on. Although maybe he had. When Shane had asked for Mac, he hadn't said, *Who?* Still, Shane wanted more. He made his voice match Robert's initial joviality as he laughed. "If you *did* do that, I'd have to call Security to kick them in the ass, right? I just thought maybe you could, I don't know—connect me to her voice mail?"

Another long pause. Come on, Robert. At least drop him a clue. Did Mac even have voice mail here?

The throat was cleared again, then, "I'm sorry, sir—"

"How about *you* leave her the message?" Shane tried. "Ask Mac to call me, okay? Whenever she gets in. It's kind of urgent."

"If it's urgent, sir," Robert said, "I can connect you to one of the other staff members."

Hah. He was right. Mac was staff.

"Or," Robert continued, "I can send someone up to escort you over to the health center . . . ?"

Staff at OI's health center . . . ? Was Mac a doctor or maybe some kind of paramedic?

"Oh, nah, that's okay," Shane said. "I'm sure I can find my way over there, if I need anything."

"Well, no, sir, I'm sorry, but you can't," Robert told him. "You haven't been cleared for movement throughout the facility. Besides, all of the Potentials go into lockdown from midnight to oh-seven-hundred."

Shane went over and tried to open first the slider to the balcony and then the door to the hallway. Sure enough, he was locked in. Sort of. The slider could be taken off its tracks and the main door's hinges were on the inside, all of which made the lockdown mostly symbolic—at least to anyone who absolutely needed to get out. Although there were probably security cameras outside of the building and in the halls . . .

"I'm putting in a request for someone to come to your room," Robert decided, and as Shane started to speak, he added, "*And* I'll leave your message for Dr. Mackenzie, although I have no idea when she'll be back."

Dr. Mackenzie. Holy shit. Mac *was* a doctor. "Thanks," Shane managed. "But—"

"Someone will be with you immediately," Robert said.

"That's really not necessary," Shane said as the bell on his door buzzed. "Wow, that was fast."

"Have a pleasant morning, sir," Robert said, and cut the connection.

Shane hung up the phone and went back to the door—which he still couldn't open. But there was some kind of intercom system right near a standard peephole, so he leaned on the button. "I'm kind of locked in."

The peephole revealed a tall man wearing a lab coat and . . . Yeah, it was Dr. Zerkowski. He was just as rumpled, but a lot more tired than he'd looked all those hours ago, when they'd spoken via Vurp. "I have a master key," the doctor said now. "May I come in?"

"Knock yourself out," Shane said, and the door opened. "I'm sorry you were bothered, Doc. I really don't need anything—"

"Yeah, I know," the doctor told him. "I scanned the transcript of your phone call—the beginning of it, at least. Did you get the information you wanted?"

Shane laughed his surprise, which kind of killed his ability to play dumb. He tried anyway. "I'm sorry . . . ?"

"Not entirely, huh?" Zerkowski said. "Thanks, I *will* come inside for a minute. And it's Elliot. Please." He stepped forward, a move that forced Shane to shift back, and the door closed behind him. "Actually, I was in the building when I heard that you'd arrived. Since you're obviously still awake, I thought I'd drop by." He smiled at Shane. "And keep you from giving another entry-level worker the third degree about Mac, who happens to be a friend of mine. Didn't it occur to you that it might be problematic for a Potential to be asking a lot of questions about her, leaving her messages . . . ?" He answered his own question as he went into the living room. "Probably not. Same way it probably didn't occur to her that you'd put two and two together and show up here with a lot of questions needing answers."

"I just want to talk to her," Shane said.

Elliot gave him a pointedly *oh really?* look as he sat on the sofa. But he changed the topic. "You have any questions about the program?" He gestured toward the e-reader. "I see you've been given an overview."

"Yeah, I guess my biggest question," Shane said as he stayed standing, leaning against the wall that separated the main room from the bedroom, "is about how to handle the anticipation. I mean, I'm not sure I can wait to find out whether my big superpower is going to be flying or invisibility."

The doctor laughed. "A nonbeliever. Better and better. For the record, Mac thinks you could be very special."

Shane had to work it, overtime, to keep himself from reacting, and this time he was pretty sure he'd pulled it off.

"And excuse me for the incredulous staring," Elliot continued, "because you're even more . . . *military* in real life than you are over Vurp, and you come across as pretty intensely military, even over the Internet. I think I'm also having a bit of a disconnect because you're not at all what I'd imagined as Mac's type for a bar hookup."

As accurate as his being a bar hookup was, it was entirely possible that Elliot was on as much of a fishing expedition as Shane had been on earlier. So Shane kept his face blank and his mouth tightly shut.

After a good thirty seconds of sitting there in silence, Elliot nodded and stood up. "Good, then. I like you. A fast learner. You'll do." He headed for the door, but then turned back. "Have you ever broken a bone?"

It was an odd question, coming out of left field like that. But Shane nodded. "Yeah. My collarbone. I was fifteen, playing baseball . . ."

"Okay," Zerkowski said. "So much for *that* theory."

"What theory?"

"My theory that your *big superpower* is an ability to instanta-neously heal yourself—and anyone else that you come into, um, intimate contact with. And as far as big goes, that would be *really* big, in the superpower world that we've documented here at OI. We haven't seen anything like that before. I mean, aside from some vaguely mythical superhero-type, who allegedly lived over two thousand years ago."

"Why would you think that I could . . . ?" Shane shook his head.

"I should probably let Mac tell you," Zerkowski said. "But on the other hand, she's probably gonna go into serious avoidance mode, and you might not see her for a while, so . . . I'll just say it. Mac broke her ankle tonight. Badly. And something happened be-tween the time that she broke it and the time she showed up back here, with the injury completely healed. And I'm pretty sure that the something that happened was *you*."

Shane was now guilty, himself, of some incredulous staring. "I don't believe that," he said. "There's no way her ankle was bro-ken." He'd seen her running on it, but he stopped himself from saying that—he'd already given away too much.

"I can show you the results from her med scans," the doctor said. "Yesterday's, without any indication of a break, and then today's, with the break fully healed. But it's unethical for me to do that without her permission. So we'll have to wait for her to return before we can completely blow your mind." He clapped his hands together. "In the meantime, what do you say we get started on some of those tests that were outlined in your overview material? Since it appears that neither one of us is very good at sleeping . . . ?"

Shane shrugged. "I'm up for anything. But I've got to warn you, you're going to be disappointed. You might be better served recalibrating your medical scanner."

"I've done that," Elliot told him. "Twice."

"Maybe you should let me lay my special Jesus-hands on it," Shane said.

Elliot laughed as he unlocked the door and held it open, gesturing for Shane to exit first. "Sarcastic mockery of my life's work—that *never* gets old."

"Just tell me this," Shane said as they headed down the hall, toward the elevators. "In all your years of research, have you ever found anyone who can actually *do* the things described in those reports?"

Elliot smiled. "There are dozens, currently right here, training at OI. Of course, most of them don't make it beyond more than thirty-percent integrated, so they have beginner-level skills, at best. The training is intense, and progress is slow, so attrition tends to be high. About ninety-five percent of each class drops out—that should sound familiar to you."

Shane nodded. SEAL BUD/S training also had a notoriously high candidate dropout rate. "But if five percent stay in the program," he pointed out, "that means you've got people walking around, right here at the Institute, with scientifically proven telepathic and telekinetic powers."

"That's right," Elliot said as he pushed the down button for the elevator.

"Okay, then. I want to meet someone," Shane said, "who can do a whole lot more than guess what I had for breakfast or push a pencil across a table without the use of hands—or gravity."

Elliot smiled as the elevator door opened, and he gestured for Shane to get in. "You've already met someone," he said, "who can pick you up and throw you, while standing twenty feet away."

Shane knew what he was implying, and he couldn't help but laugh. "Mac?"

The doctor nodded serenely. "Mac Mackenzie can kick your ass—without her foot getting anywhere near your posterior."

"Yeah," Shane said. "Sorry, but I'm going to have to see that to believe it."

"That can be arranged."

Shane nodded. "I can't wait."

But what he really couldn't wait for was a chance to see Mac again.

And even though Elliot didn't say as much, Shane was well aware that the doctor knew that, too.

———

Anna didn't think that she'd be able to sleep.

But the word came back—pretty quickly—that the mechanic's garage in South Boston was deserted. Sometime during the past afternoon or evening, Nika had been moved to a different, as-yet-undetermined location.

Joseph Bach had called Anna himself to deliver the bad news. "We'll find her," he said, but at this point, his words sounded a bit hollow.

"I don't know how," she admitted quietly.

"Have faith," he said and ended the call.

The fatigue that replaced her spark of hope was overwhelming, and Anna curled up on the sofa in the OI apartment's spacious living room, and closed her eyes. It seemed impossible that she would actually fall asleep, but she must've done so, close to immediately. Because it wasn't long before she began to dream.

Nika was back in the hospital, getting an outpatient medical scan for the chronic sinus infections that had been troubling her for nearly two years. Her new scholarship to Cambridge Academy had included health care, so for a hundred dollar co-pay, they were finally able to buy her the tests needed to make sure the situation wasn't something more serious.

It wasn't. The doctor had called Nika's sinuses a *swamp* and had prescribed a heavy-duty, long-term dose of antibiotics, which had finally begun working to clear up the recurring infections.

It was obvious, upon waking, why Anna had dreamed about that somewhat mundane and insignificant hospital visit.

Because Elliot Zerkowski had told her it was those very hospital records that both the Obermeyer Institute and the underworld Organization had hacked that identified Nika as a Potential. It was through that medical scan that both groups had realized that the girl was already a Twenty, which was very rare.

Apparently, even though a standard med scan wasn't calibrated to report integration levels, it *did* provide information on brain activity. And certain activity combined with various hormone and enzyme levels was found, more often than not, to occur in Potentials.

If Anna hadn't been sick and tired of Nika's constant coughs and sore throats, if she hadn't pushed Nika finally to go to the doctor's . . .

In her dream, Nika had looked balefully up at her from the table where the doctor—tall and dark-haired and oddly familiar—had scanned her, as if to say that this was all Anna's fault.

But then the dream shifted, and suddenly *she* was Nika, and the table where she was lying became a hospital bed with restraints that bound her arms and legs. The white cover that had been pulled over her was stained with a horrible spray of blood, the sight of which still made her terribly, breathlessly afraid. Her left arm burned and throbbed with pain, and she realized that some sort of medical port had been inserted, giving access to her vein. A tube was connected to the port, leading down to a bag that was slowly filling with her blood, as her heart continued to pound.

Around her, other girls, most much younger, were screaming and weeping. They were all trapped in beds like hers, and there were about twenty of them in the room.

A badly scarred man was making his way around the room, attaching tubes to the ports in the remaining girls' arms. He was wearing a bloodstained white lab coat and carrying a surgical knife. He used it not merely to frighten or threaten. Occasionally he would strike and slice, and blood would flow, which made his threats to the other girls that much more potent.

Not all the girls were screaming, though. One girl, her name was Zooey, several beds down, just watched silently, expressionlessly, with dull eyes. The man stopped and looked at her, and the girls around her screamed as if to try to rouse her, but she didn't move, didn't speak, didn't look up from some invisible point on the far wall. And finally the man moved on.

He traveled the room twice—once to attach the empty bags, and then again when they were filled with blood, to collect them, detach the tubes, and reinsert the plugs in their ports.

But for Zooey, he didn't remove the tube or reinsert the plug. He just left it open and flowing, and her blood soon soaked the sheet that covered her legs.

Nika expected him to return to the little girl, especially when she seemed to awaken and started to cry and moan, but he didn't. He left the room without looking back, closing the door behind him with a solid-sounding *thunk*.

"Help me, please help me," Zooey sobbed, but the man was gone.

All of the girls were crying then, and Nika shouted above them, "Pinch the tube! You can reach it with that same hand. Just grab it and bend it and the blood flow will stop! Come on, Zooey, *do* it!"

And Zooey finally heard her, but like Nika, she was dizzy from lack of sleep, from the constant interruptions and visits from the awful scarred man. She had to be dizzy, too, from giving so much blood without any solid food.

It was awful to lie there, trapped and helpless, as the little girl's strength ebbed, as she finally fell asleep, exhausted. Nika tried to wake her by shouting and screaming, but by then Zooey was unconscious and there was no way to save her, nothing to do but watch that blood dripping, dripping, dripping onto the floor as the girls around her wept.

Nika must've dozed off, because she jerked awake to the screams of the other girls, and she saw that the man with the scarred face had finally come back into the room.

Hope bloomed as he went to Zooey's bed, but he didn't remove her tube and plug her port. Instead, he unfastened her restraints and as he picked her up, her head lolled back. And Nika got a nightmarish glimpse of the girl's small, pale face, with her eyes wide open and staring at nothing, before the man threw her lifeless body into a garbage bin.

And he took out his knife and asked, "Anyone else want to go out with the trash?" as he slowly spun to look at each one of them.

He pointed at Nika, maybe because she didn't scream, maybe because she looked at him with all of her hatred for him burning in her eyes. But he said, "You. You are a fountain. Devon Caine will be rewarded for bringing you to us. I'll let you choose one of your new friends. She'll be given to him as a gift."

"Fuck you," Nika said, even as her heart again began to pound. Devon was the name of one of the men who'd kidnapped her—the bigger man. The man who bit her on the shoulder, the man she'd been terrified was going to do awful things to her, before the other, smaller man yelled at him and made him back down.

The man with the scar smiled—or at least she thought that his grimace was a smile. It contorted his face and made him look even more frightening, and the girls around her screamed and screamed and *screamed* . . .

TEN

Bach awoke with a gasp.

He'd stopped for a quick combat nap in the Star Market parking lot in Newton. But now, awakening from that mind-blowing nightmare about Nika and the scar-faced man—if that was indeed what it was—he put his car back into gear. He quickly pulled out of the lot, hurrying back toward OI, taking the Pike west, with the dawn lighting the sky behind him.

He turned off the heat in the car and opened his window several bracing inches as he drove. He let the early morning air slap his face as he made a quick call to Analysis, asking them to pull whatever files they could find on a Devon Caine.

Finding Rickie Littleton and his unidentified cohort had been Bach's highest priority, past tense. Tracking them down was, of course, still way up there on his to-do list. Except now his newest high priority was to check in with Anna Taylor.

And run some more detailed tests on the woman, because, what if . . . ?

Bach still couldn't quite wrap his brain around what had just happened while he was asleep, but he'd lived long enough to know that just because he hadn't imagined something was feasible didn't mean that it wasn't.

A joker delivering punches with the sound of his voice was tonight's Exhibit A.

And yes, it *was* possible that Bach had simply had a nightmare about Anna's little sister, and that his mind had conjured up that name—Devon Caine—from a memory of something he'd read or heard or perhaps a photograph he'd seen in the past.

But there were other possibilities, too.

One was that Anna—whose head he'd spent some significant time inside of tonight—was, like her little sister, in possession of significant power that hadn't shown up on the med scan she'd received upon arrival at OI. And that Anna's power, plus Nika's, plus *Bach's* had combined to . . .

What? Create a telepathic ability to project thoughts over distances that heretofore had been unheard of?

Again, in Bach's world, *unheard of* wasn't really all that big of a shocker.

Another possibility was that Bach had suddenly spiked—gone from seventy-two to seventy-three. Increases of power rose tremendously as integration levels got bigger, so that while the difference between a Ten and a Twelve wasn't that significant, the difference between a Seventy-Two and a Seventy-Three was vast.

Bach had been training and working for years now without the slightest increase in his integration. It was time for a bump upward. And maybe the ability to receive some type of thought projection from Nika was one of his newest skills.

Of course, there *was* the possibility he'd received that thought projection from the girl because she was somewhere in the close vicinity of that supermarket parking lot—a fact that would also be very good to know.

Bach waited as patiently as he could for his car to be searched at the entrance to OI, and when the gate finally opened for him he went significantly above the campus speed limit as he buzzed up the hill and then over to the main housing building.

Anna Taylor had been given apartment 605. High floor. Great view. It was a three-bedroom—one room for her, one for her little sister, and one to emphasize the perks that would come when she gave Nika permission to enroll in the training program here.

When, not *if*.

There was no way Anna could afford a three-bedroom apartment out in the real world. No way at all.

Bach parked and beeped his car locked as he ran toward the more modern architecture of the building that had been lovingly dubbed the "barracks." The nickname had been given by someone who obviously had never in his or her life lived in military housing. Still, it had stuck.

The guard at the door ran her security wand over Bach—the security team had long since learned that waving him through was a surefire way to get canned.

She did a thorough job, and even though he used the time both to stretch out his back and exchange some quick texts with Analysis—they'd found info on a Devon Caine and were attempting to locate a current picture—he was tapping his toe by the time it was over. When she told him he could go in, he thanked her for her thoroughness, but then headed for the elevators at a run.

One opened right away, and he pushed the button for the sixth floor. It took too long to get there, so when the doors finally opened again, he dashed down the hall.

Apartment 605 was an end unit—he knew it well since he lived directly above it, on the top floor. He could feel Anna's presence—she was awake—so he leaned on the buzzer.

The intercom clicked on almost immediately.

"Did you find Nika?" Anna asked, no doubt having ID'd him through the peephole, then added, "I can't open the door. I think I'm locked in."

She was. But Bach used his mind to click the lock open and there she stood, hair slightly rumpled, looking at him with such hope in her eyes and on her pretty face.

"We haven't found her yet," he said, "but we've got a possible new lead. May I come in?"

"Of course." She stepped back and as he went inside, he saw that she'd done as he'd instructed and unpacked. She'd flattened the empty boxes that had held her few belongings, and they leaned in a neat stack against the island counter that separated the big kitchen from the rest of the main living area. "What kind of lead? Do you know where they took her?"

"Actually, this is going to sound a little crazy," Bach realized as he took off his coat and put it over the back of one of the counter's stools, "but I just had an unusually vivid . . . dream."

"A dream?" she repeated, frowning slightly.

"Yes, I know, maybe not just a *little* crazy, am I right? At least not in the world you're used to." A framed photograph was on the coffee table in front of the sofa and he picked it up after he sat down.

In the picture, Nika was a toddler, which meant that Anna had been close to Nika's current age when it was taken. A woman who had to be their mother, with slightly darker skin but the same wide smile, held the younger girl on her lap as Anna hugged them both.

It was true that the two sisters looked very much alike, but there was a somberness, a seriousness in Anna's brown eyes that had been absent in the SAT images Bach had seen of Nika.

He looked up from the photo at the real Anna, who now had her arms tightly folded across her chest as she stood there, gazing at him with unconcealed dismay.

"I'm sorry," she said, "but are you honestly telling me that your *lead* is from a *dream* that you had . . . ?"

"Telepathic powers include something called *thought projection*," Bach explained. "It's a highly advanced skill, and we've only documented cases sent and received at close proximity— where the sender and receiver were mere yards from each other. The visual images sent can be remarkably realistic. And detailed. And yes, I do believe the projection I received, just a short time ago, was from Nika."

He could see, just from the expression on Anna's face, that she was unwilling or unable to understand.

So he quietly told her about the nightmare he'd had in the supermarket parking lot—about the scar-faced man and the room filled with screaming little girls.

Anna slowly sank down in the leather chair opposite the sofa as he described the badly stitched port in Nika's arm.

When he ended with the scar-faced man's casual disposal of Zooey's body and his words to Nika about a man named Devon Caine, Anna silently spoke the name along with him.

He sat forward at that. "Did *you* receive the projection, too?" he asked, intrigued.

She nodded. "I thought it was a nightmare."

"It's possible Nika was somehow subconsciously projecting to you, and you then projected to me—" Bach cut himself off. Even though the idea that a thirteen-year-old girl had the power to project to not just one person but two, across great distances, was fascinating, *how* it happened was a mystery they'd focus on later. Right now . . . "May I?" he asked as he reached out to Anna with his mind. His silent request was more specific. *May I check to make sure there were no other details in this projection that we both might have missed or overlooked . . . ? It would help if I could combine our two memories.*

She nodded, her eyes wide as she gazed back at him.

It was unnerving and oddly intimate to be looking directly into the eyes of a person whose head he was entering. He usually turned slightly away, or even closed his own eyes to avoid the forced intimacy.

But this time he didn't. Turning away felt too much like he was abandoning her, and he wouldn't do that. He couldn't.

And as Bach moved into Anna's mind, he felt all of her trepidation, her confusion, her disbelief, her attraction. Yes, she was definitely attracted. She was also afraid of him still—afraid to trust him, to believe him. And yet she was willing and even eager to let him in—if it was going to help them find her sister.

He moved into her memory centers, and there was that name again—Devon Caine—and a glimpse of the brightly lit hallway on the other side of the door outside the room where Nika was being held. He saw numbers on the side of the trash container that the scar-faced man had wheeled into the room—a two and a one, but the rest were obscured. He saw an image of that same man's deformed face that was so clear he could have drawn it. And he *would* draw it, with Elliot's help. The doctor possessed a natural artistic ability that Bach didn't share, despite countless years spent trying to hone those skills. Music had always been more Bach's thing, but it was far less practical given his line of work. He just couldn't imagine that the day would ever come when he'd play *Rhapsody in Blue* or a Mozart piano concerto to woo some joker down from some mental ledge.

But maybe this man with the scar isn't real. That was Anna, interjecting and pulling him back on track as she followed his thoughts. He was far more tired than he'd believed, and it was a good thing he hadn't wandered into thoughts of—

He cut himself off abruptly, but Anna was focused and didn't notice. *Maybe he's just a symbol of the danger that she's in,* she continued. *If Nika's projections are subconscious—and it's hard to believe that she knows how to do this—isn't it possible that this is, I don't know, just a nightmare that Nika had? Couldn't it all just be fantasy?*

"I don't think it's a dream." Bach answered her by speaking aloud, even as he gently pulled out of her. She gasped, just a little, at his sudden departure, and he added, "I'm sorry, I should've warned you that I was going to—"

"No," she said quickly, "it's just odd. It's going to take some getting used to."

"It's really not something I'll be doing all that often," he tried to reassure her. "And . . . you can see that—now that you know what it feels like—it's not going to happen without your knowledge. Again," he added somewhat lamely, since he *had* not only invaded her mind but had also put his own thoughts in it, completely without her knowledge, simply to get her into his car. He quickly pushed on, bringing them back to the vision they'd shared. "I don't think Nika was dreaming. It was too linear, Anna. Too real. Too organized—dreams tend to jump and shift." He put it as clearly as he could. "I believe that Nika was projecting what she was actually experiencing and seeing."

"So that name—Devon Caine . . . ?" Hope was back in her eyes.

"I've already sent a request to Analysis," Bach told her. "We're working to track him down. We'll bring him in and find out what he knows." He didn't tell her that he believed Devon Caine was also the man responsible for raping and murdering a girl at the mechanic's garage in South Boston. That headline could wait until they had the man safely in their possession.

"He called Nika a fountain," Anna remembered from the vision. "The man with the scar. What did he mean by that?"

"They took your sister's blood," Bach explained, "and they no doubt tested it and discovered that she's an abundant source of the crucial ingredient needed to make oxyclepta di-estraphen. The good news is that they'll keep her alive. The bad news is that they're going to try to keep her in a near-constant state of terror, which is *really* bad news for the girls in the room with her."

"Oh, God," Anna breathed. But she took a breath and sat up a little straighter. "So . . . What now?"

"We run some tests," Bach told her. "I want to see if you've got any powers that we might have missed, since it's highly unusual for a non-Greater-Than to receive a projection of any kind. At the same time, I'll see if maybe I'm the one whose integration is spiking, or . . . Maybe it's all Nika. We're going to gather as many facts as we can. I know it's early and you haven't had much sleep, but if you're willing, we could go into the lab and—"

Anna stood up. "I'm willing. Just let me get my sneakers."

––––––

Rickie Littleton was in the Oasis Restaurant on Route 9, up by the Chestnut Hill Mall. He was eating their $14.99 Recession Special breakfast, the way he always did when he was flush.

He didn't recognize Mac when she walked in—but then again, he wouldn't. Through the years, she'd worked hard to make sure that he never saw her. Up until now, it had served OI to use Littleton as an informant of sorts, following him and gathering information when needed.

Up until now.

She could've kept her distance, let him finish his breakfast, and then trailed him around the city for a few days to see where he went and who he talked to. But a few days would seem like an eternity to their missing little girl, and picking Littleton up and bringing him in meant that they'd know everything that he knew in a matter of minutes. That's how long it would take for Bach to stroll through the drug dealer's mind.

So Mac sat down at the counter next to him, her charm set on stun.

Still, he didn't even look up from his plate until she said, "Don't you hate it when they undercook the bacon?"

He looked a little surprised then, because, really, what woman in her right mind would initiate a conversation with someone who looked and smelled the way he did? But then she gave him a flash of the Rolex and gold-and-diamond bracelet that she'd borrowed from OI's local bank box, specifically for this purpose. As she pulled the sleeve of her jacket back down, Littleton's second glance at her was filled with understanding. She was here to score some Destiny.

"I've had both items appraised and I'm fifty dollars short," she told him, catching her lower lip between her teeth in a move that she knew he'd find hypnotizing. She didn't have to work to sound desperate—she just had to think about the child who'd died at the garage that this man owned. Either Littleton was a murderer and rapist, or he'd let his murdering rapist friend use his place for his evil deeds. "I was hoping we could . . ." She lowered her voice even more. "Trade?"

His *yes* was in his eyes, even as he returned some of his attention to shoveling his home fries into his mouth. "I'll be done here in five."

"My car's out in the lot," she told him as she slid off the stool and headed out the back door.

There was no way he wasn't going to follow her. But just to be safe, as she left the establishment she nodded at Diaz, who was lurking near the Dumpster. And when he nodded back, she knew he'd used his power to jam shut the restaurant's front door, so that no one could enter or leave any way but through the back.

Mac climbed into the driver's seat of the car that Diaz had

traded for his bike when she'd called him after guessing—correctly—that Littleton had taken at least part of his payment for Nika's capture in product.

When she'd hit Chestnut Hill, she'd picked up on his emotional grid almost immediately.

She was glad to be right, because she hadn't picked up an empathic reading on Nika at the abduction site—the stretch of sidewalk where the little girl had been grabbed.

Sometimes, after trauma, the remnants of a person's emotional grid were so loud that Mac could search for that person and pick them out of a proverbial crowd, even though she'd never laid eyes on them before.

But it was hard to do that if the event had occurred outside versus indoors, and as she'd stood on the spot where Nika had been attacked, she'd felt almost nothing. A mere glimmer of fear.

She'd found Nika's phone, broken, in the street, but that hadn't told them anything they didn't already know, and she'd picked up nothing from touching the plastic.

Mac now rolled down the heavily tinted window and pulled the car up so that she was idling near the restaurant's back door.

And here came Rickie Littleton, his hood up and his hands in his pockets. He spotted Mac right away and she smiled at the dirt-wipe and he didn't look away.

Because he didn't look away, he didn't see Diaz coming up behind him.

One hand on Littleton's shoulder was all it took for Diaz to zap the dealer into full submission.

Mac was already out of the car. She opened the back door and helped catch the unconscious scumbag and throw him neatly into the backseat. Part of her was pissed off that, despite all of her various skills and tricks and talents, it was the simple fact that she had a vagina that had most expedited Littleton's capture.

It bothered her that she still struggled to control her powerful telekinetic skills, even after years of training. While Bach and Diaz could use their minds to pop open a window or door lock, she was limited to larger, less precise movements. She could blow a hole in a building just by thinking about it, sure. She could toss an adversary across a city street. She could turn up a thermostat so that the heat would kick on in a room.

But she couldn't set the thing precisely at seventy-two degrees, the way Bach or Diaz could. She'd invariably turn it up as high as it could go, and then have to make the adjustment in person, by hand.

And if she tried to hold a man's arms behind his back, creating a force-field version of handcuffs in order to subdue him? More than likely, she would dislocate both of his shoulders in the process.

Her telekinetic fine motor skills were for shit. She still spent hours working on her control. Her current project was a thousand-piece jigsaw puzzle, done entirely by moving the tiny pieces with her mind. She'd been working on it for three weeks now, and had accidentally sent the damn thing flying around the room— destroying the part that she'd already pieced together—five separate times. What a pain in her ass.

Bach had commented that this was also an exercise that provided a workout for her patience.

No shit, Sherlock.

Here and now, Mac had already used one of the plastic restraints she always carried to cuff Littleton's hands behind his back. She stepped away after closing the door behind the scumbag and said, "See you back there."

Diaz nodded as he climbed behind the wheel. He was already out of the parking lot as Mac took one last look around, checking to make sure no one had witnessed their little kidnapping.

There were people coming into and out of the drugstore next door, and others pulling into the parking lot, but no one was anxious or upset—at least not about anything having to do with Rickie Littleton.

There *was* a woman who was frantic about her four-year-old's devastating illness, and a despondent elderly man with terrible arthritis whose wife had died last month, and who was now unable to get his run-down car to start. Neither of them had eaten in several days. Their problems were so much more severe than Mac's, and she kept her emotional shields down longer than she usually would have, just to remind herself of that.

The fact that she'd met some random guy with a nice smile, a guy she had to stop sleeping with because they were both going to work in a place that not only frowned on fraternizing, but encouraged across-the-board sexual abstinence . . . ? And yeah, okay, that was just a handy excuse for Mac not seeing Shane again. In truth it was more complicated—more about her not wanting to use him like he was just another toy for her amusement.

But whatever the reason was, the bottom line was that she and Shane were history.

And boo-freaking-hoo. She was going to have to sacrifice a little immediate gratification and a whole lot of hot sex.

And *that* was a great big nothing on a cosmic scale that included starvation, pain, dead spouses, and dying children.

Life would go on.

She'd deal.

She always did.

Besides, even if she'd gone ahead and met Shane next week for dinner and a massage—and more of that awesome sex, let's be honest—it wouldn't have been long before the guilt kicked in, bigtime. Shane Laughlin was no Justin. And even if she could have pretended, since the man was blacklisted and couldn't find a job, that letting him live in her apartment was an act of generosity and kindness on her part, she would have eventually done the right thing and let him go.

This was just the accelerated version of that very same path.

So Mac took a deep breath and grew her hair long and lush, and made her lips pouty and full. She gave herself boobs that would've made Shane weep with joy. And that really was enough to disguise her. A woman's body was still too often the only thing most people bothered to notice.

Mac took her boobs and went inside the drugstore, to the ATM, but the damn thing had a limit to how much she could withdraw from her account in the course of a single day. Even though she'd never done anything like it before, she managed to short the fucker out so that it burped wads of cash at her—close to sixteen thousand in the new five-hundred-dollar bills—nearly her entire savings. She left the store with it, dividing it into two piles—one of which she handed to the distraught mother, walking away without a single word.

It took her a bit longer to find the old man and once she did, she had to tap on the window of his car to get him to roll down the glass. He was crying, and the wave of loss and pain that hit her was so much like the emotion she'd felt last night from Bach, that she just stood there staring at him like an idiot.

Was it possible that the seemingly unmovable Joseph Bach had lost someone that he'd loved as much as this man had loved his deceased wife . . . ?

And the real irony—the real stop-her-in-her-tracks, slap-in-the-face truth about *that* was that she was freaking jealous of them both. She wanted what they'd both once had. Yes, they'd lost it, but you can't lose something that you've never experienced. And Mac thought of Shane, and of what he'd never mean to her—of what he could never have meant to her, even if she said to hell with her conscience and spent the next two years with him in her bed, every night.

The old man wiped his face as he peered up at her with watery blue eyes that were magnified by his old-style glasses. He spoke in a quavering voice, "May I help you, dear?"

He wanted to help her—this man who had less than nothing.

He lived in his car. Mac could see that the backseat was packed with his belongings—including a teapot with roses painted on the side, and a pink cardigan that was probably new back in the 1980s—and she realized that even if she gave him *twenty* thousand dollars it wouldn't be enough to truly help him.

Still, she held the money out for him. "Get your car fixed."

His eyes widened as he looked at it, but then he looked up at her again, and shook his head. "I can't take that," he told her. "You'll make better use of it than I will. I've already called . . . some friends. They'll be here to pick me up in about an hour."

But Mac could see the brochure for Johnston, Lively, and Grace Drug Testing Labs on the passenger seat next to him, and she knew he was lying. He had no real friends—at least not at JLG.

"You don't have to do that," she said. "Go to JLG? They'll treat you like a lab rat. When they say *lockdown* they mean it." She tossed the money across him, onto the seat beside him, atop that brochure. "This way, you still have some options."

It was then, as she was turning to walk away, that he said, "It doesn't matter anymore. Not for me. But *you* still have time to make the right choice."

Mac turned back to look at him, and he was holding out her money.

"Love," he said, as if he were answering a question that she'd asked him. "The only real right choice is *love*. It's worth any risk. And it's well worth the pain. I had her for sixty-three years. Over twenty-three thousand days. Can you even imagine . . . ?"

She looked into the old man's eyes and shook her head, thinking about the single night she'd spent with Shane—a night that, by comparison, didn't even count, because love wasn't involved.

And she found herself thinking, then, about her father, about her little brother Billy, about Tim . . .

"I'm sorry for your loss," Mac said, and turned and walked, and then ran to her bike, and got the hell out of there.

———

Elliot was still in the examination room finishing up a set of prelim-tests on Shane Laughlin when he got the message that Mac and Diaz were on their way back in, and that Diaz had Rickie Littleton in his possession.

Bach also sent a quick text: "Already here, escorting Ms. Taylor back to her room, on my way," which was good since Elliot needed a visual aid. All of the former SEAL lieutenant's test results were coming out remarkably unremarkable, and Elliot was pretty certain that the man had erected a very large block of disbelief that was inhibiting or counteracting any natural talent that he may have had.

The brain worked in mysterious ways.

So Elliot popped out into the hall, hoping to catch Joseph Bach before the pair of Fifties arrived and they all vanished behind a locked door with their suspect.

He just needed the maestro for a brief show-and-tell—maybe pick Shane up and move him over to the other side of the little room, along with a quick demonstration of what Elliot, who'd clearly spent too many hours watching his father's DVDs of *Star Trek,* still thought of as a *mind meld.* It *was* mind-blowing—extremely fantastic and a little scary—to experience the sensation of Bach tiptoeing through one's head. It wouldn't take more than a few seconds of that to take Shane's nonbeliever status and give it a quick one-eighty.

Thinking about that kind of mental power brought Elliot back to the wall of images he'd experienced a few hours earlier, when he'd tried to help Stephen Diaz up from the floor. He was still fairly positive that Diaz had had no idea he was broadcasting those thoughts. Although, to be honest, it was hard for Elliot to believe that Diaz was *having* those thoughts in the first place. And it wasn't the fact that he was gay that was so hard to swallow. Neither was the idea that he was attracted to Elliot a problem. Okay, maybe that *was* a little mind-bending—a little *holy crap.* Okay, it was a truckload of *holy crap.*

But still, really, it was the idea that Diaz might be thinking about something other than a serene rose petal suspended mid-air, or the powerful ripple caused by a single raindrop moving across the Atlantic Ocean that was shocking.

As Elliot opened the door and stepped out into the hall, Stephen Diaz was right there, mid-stride, outside the exam room. And even though Elliot had tested himself again and again and again, and was completely convinced of his status as a lowly fraction, it was almost as if he had conjured Diaz up, just by thinking of him.

"Oh, hey," Elliot greeted him. "I thought you were only just on your way back in." He checked his phone for the status of the message Diaz had sent and . . . "Oops, there's that dang time delay again. It took . . . twenty minutes this time, for your message to come in. You nearly beat it back here."

Diaz had stopped walking, although he glanced almost longingly down the hall in the direction he'd been going. "Infrastructure decay," he said, shaking his head in disgust. "It's getting worse. I've noticed it, too." He cleared his throat. "We're going to have to work on getting ourselves a dedicated satellite." He couldn't quite hold Elliot's gaze and he looked down the hall again and even pointed a little. "Long night. I was getting . . . something . . . to eat?"

"And . . . we don't have people who'll do that for you?" Elliot asked.

Diaz smiled briefly, ruefully, and Elliot's heart actually sped up. "Busted," he admitted. "The guy I brought in . . . I didn't want to have to help move him from the car to the holding cell. The temptation to snap his neck was a little too strong. I was really just giving myself a time-out."

Now Elliot couldn't help but think about the way he'd found Diaz, sitting on the floor in the corner of that darkened exam room. Had that been a *time-out,* too?

Across the hall, Diaz's body language got even tighter. He was perceptive enough to know just where Elliot's thoughts had gone, even without telepathic assistance.

And Elliot didn't have to be a Greater-Than to know that if he mentioned that earlier incident at all, Diaz would run away. So instead he said, "I'm doing some preliminaries on a promising new Potential, but I'm thinking he might be experiencing a significant block, due to massive disbelief. I was hoping to grab Dr. Bach to do a little demo, but as long as you're here and looking for a distraction . . . ?" He gestured toward the exam room door.

"Oh," Diaz said, looking again down the hall, as if wishing he had the power to be rude and just walk away. "Yeah. Sure."

"It'll only take two minutes," Elliot reassured him, leading the way back into the room where Shane Laughlin was pretending that he hadn't been messing with the comm-station on the wall.

"Oh, it's you," Diaz said as he shook Shane's hand, and Elliot introduced the two men.

Elliot was watching closely, and Shane *wasn't* flung against the far wall the way Elliot had been earlier when he'd touched the Fifty.

So . . . maybe that power had been Elliot's. And wasn't *that* a ridiculous theory, since he was as un-special as they came.

"I, um, saw Lieutenant Laughlin come in," Diaz told Elliot, a tad self-consciously.

And yes, it made sense that Diaz would have noticed Shane Laughlin. Kind of hard not to. Elliot thought of himself as a fairly good-looking man, but standing beside both Diaz and Shane, he felt both dweebish and nearly invisible. *And* simultaneously flabby and skinny—which came with the knowledge that it was both time to hit the gym *and* time to accept the fact that he should never bother going to the gym again, because why make the effort?

Shane nodded coolly as he greeted Diaz. "You were going someplace in a hurry. With your . . . friend."

"Shane's former military and still a little suspicious of us," Elliot told Diaz, leaving Mac out of it, since Shane had done the same. Although that use of the word *friend* was certainly interesting.

He hit the button that turned the med scanners on, using the keyboard to call up Diaz's profile, too—no point in announcing it, though. While it wasn't standard to scan Greater-Thans who were participating in an experiment, Diaz was still looking tired and as if he were under some kind of physical strain. *Long night* was an understatement.

And even though both men were in motion and fully clothed, Elliot could still program the computer to make a partial or jot scan—which, here at OI, included a readout of their neural integration levels.

Diaz was smiling at Shane. "You ready for a demonstration?" he asked.

"What the fuck . . . ?" the Potential said. He took a step forward, but then jerked to a stop. "What is this?" He then said something more, but his words were muffled and indiscernible, as if he were trying to talk with his lips tightly shut.

"First I bound your arms," Diaz told him evenly, "then your legs, then I gave you a mental gag. I'm going to release you now. You need to relax, stop fighting me and regain your balance, or you'll fall over. Ready?"

Shane nodded, his eyes almost wild with a mix of disbelief, frustration, and what on another man might have been fear. And maybe it *was* fear. Elliot had been used as a training dummy a time or two hundred. Being bound and gagged by telekinetic power was not for the claustrophobic or faint of heart.

"On one," Diaz said. "Three . . . two . . . one."

"Holy shit!" Shane fell forward and would have landed hard on his knees if Diaz hadn't caught him. He turned to Elliot. "How the fuck did you do that?"

"Typical," Elliot said to Diaz with mock disappointment. "Blame the guy who runs the fancy equipment." He held out both of his hands as he turned to Shane. "I'm not doing anything. Didn't touch the comm-station. Didn't give the computer a vocal command. It's all him." He gestured toward Diaz with his head.

Now, with Elliot's empty hands still held out in full view, Diaz used his power to pick up Shane, and deposit him over on the other side of the small room. Not as impressive as moving him across one of the main meeting rooms, but still astonishing to the former SEAL.

"I bound you before I picked you up," Diaz told the Potential, "because the initial reaction to being moved like that is to flail, and I didn't want to dump you on your butt. Be ready to really relax this time, because I'm going to release you on three . . . two . . . one."

This time Shane only wobbled slightly. He'd caught on fast, but he still wasn't completely convinced. He opened the exam room door. "I want to see you do that again, out in the hall," he challenged Diaz, who followed him out and did just that as Elliot reviewed the information on the computer from both men's jot scans and . . .

Okay, *that* was weird. Shane hadn't budged from seventeen percent integrated, which was exactly where he'd started. His reading hadn't changed at all, out to three decimal points.

Instead *Diaz* was the one who'd popped. He usually scanned at anywhere from forty-eight to fifty percent. His scan from earlier tonight had had him at a higher than usual fifty-point-nine-two-five. But right now? He was showing an *amazing* fifty-eight. Fifty-eight-point-four-three-nine, to be painstakingly precise.

Elliot was just about to call Diaz back into the room—he'd re-calibrated the equipment and was going to give the Greater-Than another scan—a full this time—when the overhead speakers began to trumpet an alarm.

They ran drills every month, so he easily identified the three-blast pattern. His "What the heck . . . ?" was meant as more of a rhetorical question.

But Diaz answered as if he were serious—or maybe he was re-sponding to Shane's questioning look. "Intruder alert. Compound's going into lockdown." He came over to Elliot's computer and all but hipchecked him aside, working the controls himself, overrid-ing the medical file with one from security.

"The prisoner we just brought in," Diaz announced as he scrolled through the reports on the computer screen. "He jokered. He's going one-on-one with Mac, downstairs. She needs help."

Most newcomers wouldn't have understood half of what he'd said, but Shane, despite his Alice-in-Wonderland status, followed completely. He got all Alpha male and naval officer and said, "Where is she?" and "I'm going, too."

"No, you're not," Diaz said, tossing Elliot a "Keep him here," as he headed for the door.

But Elliot reached to stop Diaz with a hand on the bigger man's arm—and the world went weird. He was suddenly bathed in warmth, and his vision seemed sharper. Colors were brighter, but they had a slightly yellow hue, as if he were wearing those tinted glasses that fighter pilots sometimes wore.

Diaz froze. Elliot did, too—which was stupid. He'd stopped the Fifty because he had to warn him. Diaz needed to be told that he was suddenly integrated at nearly sixty percent, that his powers were enormously enhanced. He had to be made aware of this. If he used his ability to manipulate electricity to control the joker, he could well kill the man with his augmented talents.

Seriously? I'm at sixty percent?

Holy crap, was that . . . ?

Yeah, and I'm reading your thoughts, too. Very clearly. Holy crap, indeed. That was definitely Diaz, deep inside of Elliot's mind. *I'm not sixty, I'm fifty-eight-point-four-three-nine.*

Close enough.

No, it's not. Two percentage points is . . . All right, I'm not gonna . . . You really think it's . . . Shane *who's doing this to me?*

Elliot did. His theory was that Shane had the power to somehow enhance or augment the Greater-Thans—the way he'd done with Mac, to help her heal herself and . . .

Mac really had sex with him? Okay, I don't want to know that. Shit, he's heading for the elevators.

Diaz pulled his arm away, and without the contact, it was all gone—the warmth, the tint, and Diaz's powerful presence inside of Elliot's head. The shock of the sudden withdrawal made Elliot grab for the comm-station's keyboard to hold himself upright. He clung to it as Diaz used his power to bring Shane all the way back into the room, to place him on the examination table, and to lock the physical restraints firmly around the former SEAL's arms and legs.

"Don't you goddamn do this!" Shane was saying. "I can help! For Christ's sake, let me *help!*"

Diaz looked back at Elliot as he went out the door. "Lock this behind me," he said, and then he was gone.

"God *damn* it!" Shane was practically foaming at the mouth and as Elliot turned to look at him, he could see the man visibly working to calm himself down. "Okay. Okay. Dr. Zerkowski. Elliot. Let's be reasonable. I *can* help. Whatever's going on, I can be an asset, with my training. So, look, we can make a deal. Unlock me and let me go down there, and I'll do whatever tests you want me to do and . . ."

He kept talking, but Elliot had already turned back to the comm-station, because the thought suddenly occurred to him that Shane's *presence* might be necessary for him to enhance both of the Fifties' power.

Elliot quickly keyed in the command for the computer to find Diaz and to jot scan him from a distance. The results would be less than accurate, but it would be better than guessing and . . .

Crap, according to the computer, Diaz's integration level was already down to fifty-three and continuing to drop.

If Elliot's theory was right, Shane's presence downstairs in security would not only boost Diaz's power, but Mac's and Bach's, too.

And since this was a brand-new scenario—they'd never had to deal with a jokering addict here at OI before—Elliot wanted to give Diaz more than a mere home court advantage. And Mac and Bach, too, of course. He turned to the table and unlocked Shane's restraints. "Come on," he told the former SEAL. "Let's do this."

And they both headed for the elevators at a run.

ELEVEN

"This facility is in lockdown!" one of a crowd of ten guards shouted as Shane rounded the corner, with Elliot on his heels. The security team was positioned in front of what looked like a heavy steel door. "Containment shields are in place!"

According to Elliot, who'd gasped out the information as they ran through the brightly lit tunnels that connected the buildings in the compound, the Obermeyer Institute had never had an incident like this before. All of the jokering addicts they'd dealt with had already been in medical distress before arriving at the facility's med-wing.

And while OI had holding cells in a designated brig, in a building close to but separate from Old Main, they'd rarely used it.

OI was, first and foremost, a research and training center.

Which meant that even if their security detail was carefully trained, they were inexperienced.

The intruder they were facing, however, was deadly.

He'd broken free from the brig area of the main security building, and had been trapped up on a higher floor.

That building, Elliot had informed Shane, was an older structure that also housed OI's theater, and a ballroom-sized function room that was being set up to hold today's meet-and-greet luncheon for the newly arriving Potentials.

"Sirs!" another guard started yelling, too, as neither man

slowed down. Her stress was evident in her strained voice. "This is not a drill! Turn around immediately! Seek shelter—"

"Research override," Elliot bellowed over her. "Computer, access EZ! Jot scan and identify! Vocal verify!"

The computer's voice—male and bland—clicked on through the overhead speakers as Shane and Elliot skidded to a stop. "Dr. Elliot Zerkowski and newly processed Potential Shane Laughlin," the computer reported. "Warning—"

"Warnings received and understood," Elliot said, then looked at Shane and nodded.

"Warnings received and understood," Shane repeated, adding, "Open the fucking door. *Now*."

"Do it," Elliot ordered the stressed young woman who was obviously the detail's CO. She obeyed, but didn't look happy. "Computer, continuous jot scan of myself, Laughlin, Joseph Bach, Stephen Diaz, Michelle Mackenzie, and any other Greater-Than in the immediate vicinity of the altercation with the intruder."

"*Michelle* Mackenzie?" Shane repeated as they went through the door. Doing so put them in a small, airlock-like holding area that had another heavy steel door on the other end.

"You didn't know that?" Elliot asked, glancing at him as they waited impatiently for the first door to lock and the second door to open.

"Nope," Shane said, heavy on the P. "Mac. She only volunteered *Mac*. How do we get the computer to give us a sit-rep— situation report?"

"I know what a sit-rep is," Elliot said as he moved toward the comm-station on the wall. "Our system's not designed for that kind of information." He raised his voice. "Computer, visual of Mackenzie. For what it's worth, I think Stephen Diaz might be the only one who calls her Michelle."

And that made sense, going with Shane's earlier hypothesis. Although if Mac had a boyfriend or—shit—a husband who was fricking Captain America, why the hell was she stepping out on the man? But there would be plenty of time to think about that later. Hopefully he could ask her that question to her face.

On the computer screen, Shane could see a grainy picture, no doubt from that ballroom where . . . "What the *fuck* was that?"

"Crap, this joker's a flier," Elliot said. "And—shit!—it looks like he's already taken Mac down."

"What?"

Before Shane could see what Elliot meant by *down,* the doctor had commandeered the comm-station keyboard, his fingers flying as the screen flipped quickly through what looked like a series of medical reports.

"Define *down,*" Shane demanded, past his heart in his throat.

But before Elliot could answer, the door finally opened, and Shane bolted toward it.

"She's alive," Elliot reported, following him, "but unconscious from a blow to the head."

"Fuck!" The door had opened into another corridor—an empty one that stretched in two different directions. Like many of the other ornate hallways at OI, there were comm-stations spaced out about every twenty-five meters along the walls, as if ready for the research scientists to use, should they have a brilliant idea on their way to dinner. "Which way?"

"This way," Elliot said, going left, "to the main function room."

Shane raced down the hall and then around a corner—and there was another team of security guards hunkered down far back from a partly open door. Whatever was inside of that room was making a hell of a lot of noise. It was as if a lot of furniture was being thrown against the wall and broken. There was an odd roaring, too, and an even stranger crackling sound.

None of it slowed Shane. Mac was in there—unconscious and vulnerable.

Another man—dark hair, grim face, slighter of build and lighter complexioned than Stephen Diaz—was running toward them from the opposite direction.

Elliot knew him. "Mac's down, Dr. Bach," he called.

"I know," Bach called back. "Diaz needs help getting her out. A team of Thirties and Forties are on their way, but I've ordered them to stay back. Laughlin, you *cannot* go in there."

Somehow this guy knew his name. "Like hell I can't," Shane said, but before he could pull the door open farther and do just that, he was put in one of those fucking mental body-locks. "God damn it—" he started, but then he was gagged, too.

"If you go in there," Bach told him as he continued to approach, "you'll be just another casualty that we'll have to deal with before we can help Mac."

And okay, that was probably the only thing anyone could've said to keep Shane from going through that door. Assuming Shane could move. But then, he could—he'd been released—as if Bach knew precisely what he was thinking. And maybe the man did know. He was clearly one of those freaky Greater-Thans.

But then Elliot spoke up, from over at yet another commstation. "I'm jot scanning you, sir," he reported, and there was urgency in his voice, as if the information he was providing was vital, instead of the non sequitur that it seemed to be. "And you're . . . still only a Seventy-two—which blows up my theory. Unless . . ." He turned to look at Bach, who was reaching for the door. "Wait. Before you go in, shake hands."

Bach was as perplexed as Shane was. "This isn't the time for—"

"Just *do* it," Elliot insisted. "Even though Shane's registering as only a seventeen, he has the power to . . . I don't know exactly what it is that he does yet, but he can somehow enhance both Mac's and Diaz's integration levels. Diaz was up to fifty-eight, just from shaking hands with the guy, and I'm pretty sure Mac was up even higher from, well . . ." He looked at Shane. "Sorry to have to tattle, but this could be vital information." Back to Bach. "Apparently, Mac had sex with him last night."

Bach blinked—just once. And he and Shane spoke simultaneously. "And you think that *elevated* her neural integration?" Bach asked as Shane said, "You *seriously* believe that *I* was the one who—"

"I do," Elliot told Bach, who immediately reached out to shake Shane's hand. "They connected, physically, and her self-healing ability went through the roof and crap, sir, your levels are unchanged. So much for the theory that Shane enhances all Greater-

Thans." The doctor turned to Shane. "Still . . . What did you do to Diaz, that—"

"I don't know." Enough with the science experiments. "But if I *did* give Diaz a boost, then I'm going in, so I can do it again," Shane announced and he did just that. Bach didn't try to stop him—in fact, he was right on his heels.

But after Shane went through that door and cleared the entrance, he stopped short. He wouldn't have believed what was happening in there if he wasn't seeing it with his own two eyes. And he *still* couldn't fully accept the craziness.

The former prisoner—short and slight and wearing a hooded sweatshirt that looked as if it had been dragged through the city streets after a rain—was freaking *flying* back and forth up near the high ceiling in the rear of what was a still-formal old-time ballroom, his sweatshirt flapping as he dipped and bobbed like some kind of remote-controlled toy dragon. The effect was emphasized by his apparently newly developed ability to breathe flames.

All of the tables and chairs that had no doubt been evenly spaced throughout were being flung continuously back and forth, in a wide swath of destruction, from one side of the expansive room to the other. It created a dangerous barrier of sharply broken legs and huge slabs of wood between the joker and the entrance to the room that was virtually impossible to cross.

Diaz stood several meters back from the moving shards of furniture, clearly in constant battle with the joker, working his mental mojo, no doubt trying to get the man into one of his body-locks. It made the joker's movement even more erratic. Diaz would get a grip on the bad guy, who would start to plunge to the floor on the other side of that wall of moving furniture pieces, before he broke free and flew back up to the ceiling.

It was mind-blowing to realize just how powerful the joker must've been, if he was able to get away from Diaz.

"His power seems to be growing," Diaz shouted as Bach moved to stand beside him. "I'm working to contain the furniture, too. I've tried to crush it into sawdust—eliminate the threat—but he's stopping me!"

Every now and then, a piece of broken wood was haphazardly flung in Diaz's direction, and he had to duck or deflect it.

Four people—clearly kitchen and wait staff—were huddled against the wall, almost directly beneath the joker, uncertain of which way to run.

And—shit!—there was Mac, on the floor near the curtain of crashing furniture, where she'd been thrown against the wall and knocked unconscious. Lying there, perfectly still like that, she looked small and almost fragile. Shane's heart went into his throat. Please, God, don't let her die. . . .

"Why don't we just shoot this fucker and end this—get Mac the hell out?" Shane shouted, moving closer to get a better look at that marauding furniture as Elliot accessed the comm-station inside the room, over near the door. With a closer look, there seemed to be a small space, maybe six inches, at the bottom of the parading crushed wood, that Shane might be able to slip beneath, to get to Mac. He was willing to try, anyway.

"Security already hit him about a dozen times, with trank," Diaz reported. "He's hyper-resistant." He did a double-take. "What are *you* doing here?" He caught sight of Elliot, too, and his eyes widened even more. "You shouldn't be in here!"

"I can't break his lock on the furniture, either," Bach shouted. "Let's focus on bringing him down together—try to weaken him that way!"

Diaz was obviously distracted by Shane and Elliot's presence, but he joined the other Greater-Than in their struggle against the joker. For a moment, Shane thought they had him, because the man went down, hard and fast, hitting the shining hardwood floor with enough force to break a normal human's bones or at least to knock him unconscious.

But he still writhed and kicked and screamed, which made fire shoot in flames about a yard long from his mouth. And even though Diaz and Bach were just standing there, they were both clearly working, the physical strain showing on their faces and in the tightness of their bodies.

The broken furniture, meanwhile, went even more crazy—

starting to spin in a series of miniature tornados that left behind deep grooves in the floor.

So much for his six inches of clearance. Shane wasn't getting to Mac that way. "Let's take him out with a real weapon," he said again, directing his words at Elliot this time, because he didn't want to distract the two Greater-Thans. "You *do* have weapons here?"

"Actually," Elliot said, his intense focus on the computer, "we don't."

That was a jaw-dropper. "You're telling me that your security team," Shane persisted, "has nothing but *tranquilizer guns?*"

"That is correct."

A tabletop came flying at them, and Shane leaped forward to push Elliot out of its way. But another was right behind it, and shit, this one was going to hit them.

But suddenly Diaz was there, moving at a speed that Shane couldn't quite believe, tackling them to the ground. "I said get *out* of here!" he roared, as they all went down in a tumble of arms and legs.

Shane quickly scrambled free, because their need for rescue had pulled Diaz away from his mission. Not only had the joker escaped, but he'd also hurled an enormous ball of fire in their direction. Now there really *was* nowhere to go and Shane tried to shield Diaz and Elliot from its impact, hoping the flames would quickly disperse when it hit his back. God help him if the joker could somehow manufacture a substance like napalm.

But it never hit because Bach, bless him, intercepted it and flung it back toward the joker, who had resumed his crazy floating around near the ceiling. It hit the bad guy squarely—good aim— and he screamed as his clothes caught on fire. He dipped and flailed as he tried to use his hands to beat out the flames.

Bach was no doubt continuing to fling all kinds of crazy shit at him as Diaz looked at Shane and put him into a mental body-lock. "I want you *outside. Now!*" He used more traditional physical might to muscle Elliot up and onto his feet. "You, too! *Out* of here!"

But something on the comm-station's monitor caught Elliot's eye, and he pulled away from Diaz to say, "Okay, *now* you're spiking again. Sweet Jesus, you're up to sixty this time!"

But Diaz wasn't having it and he grabbed Elliot from behind, as if to manhandle him out into the hallway as Elliot said, "It's Shane—he's giving you that boost and holy crap, it's—" He broke off suddenly, and Diaz let go of him, fast, almost as if he'd been burned.

"*Use* it," Elliot urged, his eyes blazing as he turned to look at Diaz. "For God's sake, man, don't fight it, *use* it!"

The joker managed to fling another fireball at them, but Diaz turned toward it with a roar and the damn thing disappeared. It just vanished in a spray of sparks.

"Mac's vitals are dropping," Elliot reported, back at the computer as Shane, too, was released from Diaz's hold. "We need to wake her up—right now!"

Bach and Diaz must've been having some kind of silent communication, because they turned in unison, and the joker went down again in a nosedive to the floor. He was still thrashing, though—probably because the two Greater-Thans used a portion of their combined power to push that wall of furniture back, like opening a curtain, to the side of the room away from Mac.

Shane wasn't sure what had happened, what had changed— where Bach and Diaz had gotten the extra power to gain the upper hand—but there'd be plenty of time later for his *What the hell?* Right now he used the opportunity they'd given him, and with Elliot right behind him, he rushed to Mac's aid.

"Go! Now!" Shane shouted at the kitchen staff, and the four civilians scrambled past both the joker and the still-heaving furniture, and out the door.

And there was Mac.

Shane hesitated, afraid to just scoop her into his arms, thinking that if she'd injured her back or neck, he might do more damage.

But Elliot seemed unconcerned about that. The doctor grabbed Mac's upper body, so Shane took her legs, and together they carried her back to the comm-station by the door. Shane wanted to take her all the way out into the more protected hallway, but Elliot had already started putting her down. Jesus, with her eyes closed and her head lolling back, she looked lifeless—vulnerable and broken—like a doll that had been cast aside and forgotten.

"We need to get her to the medical center!" Shane was as close to frantic as he'd ever been in his life. He was ready to pick her up again, but the other man stopped him.

"There's no time." Elliot ran a portable medical wand across her. "She's bleeding internally, plus there's a head injury."

What, was he going to do field surgery, right there on the floor? "We should at least bring her into the hall!"

"I need to be in here." Elliot opened the med kit he'd been carrying in the pocket of his cargo pants and pulled out a syringe. "It's nothing she can't fix herself, but she's got to be conscious to do it. Just relax."

"Relax?" Was he kidding?

But Elliot was intent upon selecting the correct dose. "Remember her ankle?" he said as he gave her the injection. "This is easier. This one she could probably even do without your help."

Shane understood the concept—that Mac could allegedly heal her injuries herself, right here and right now. Allegedly.

He looked back at the furniture that was heaving and pulsing and pushing at Diaz and Bach's mental restraint. The joker was doing the same on the floor—occasionally sending badly formed fireballs up toward the ceiling as the two Greater-Thans strained to keep him in place. It was only a matter of time before he broke free again. When they'd first come in, Diaz had said that the man's power was growing.

"We should get Mac and Elliot out of here," Shane said, raising his voice loudly enough for both Diaz and Bach to hear him, "then get me some kind of real weapon—an M-16 or, shit, a grenade launcher—so I can blow this motherfucker to hell while we still have the chance!"

Bach spoke, his voice tight. "We want him alive."

"We *need* him alive."

Holy shit, that was Mac. Shane turned back to see Elliot helping her sit up. Whatever was in that injection had brought her around.

"What is *he* doing in here?" she asked, and she was talking about him. Her face was pale and drawn with pain, but her eyes were sharp and alert—and as beautiful as he'd remembered them to be. Except she was the icy-cold stranger who'd left him alone on the street, not the laughing, passionate woman he'd made love to in the warmth of her bed. "Get him out of here, Elliot. *Now.*"

"Use him," Elliot told her, his voice low, "to heal even faster. You were right, Mac, he's special. Just by being here, he's enhancing your power." He looked at Shane. "Touch her."

"What?" Shane wasn't sure what the doctor meant, and that combined with the chill in Mac's eyes made him hesitate. Her body language screamed *stay back*.

"Look, I'm not asking you to have sex right here on the floor," Elliot said. "Just touch her. For God's sake, are you an idiot? She needs your help. Take. Her hand!"

It was Mac who reached out first, real turmoil in her eyes. Shane met her halfway and they intertwined their fingers. And it was just like back in the bar, when he'd touched her wrist. Except this time the images that flooded his mind were memories. *Mac, kissing him, devouring him, as he pushed himself deeply inside of her . . .*

And this time, instead of pulling away, she clasped his hand even more tightly. And Shane realized that she was in tremendous pain. Whatever they were doing here, it was hurting her—more, even, than she was already hurting—and he tried to pull free, but she wouldn't let go. In fact, she gasped, "More," and God, talk about stepping through the looking glass. But here he was, and this freaky world was apparently where this incredible woman lived. And the hard truth was that if she was here, he wanted to be, too. And if she really believed that he could help her, simply with body contact . . . ?

Hands still clasped, Shane pulled her up into his arms so that he was cradling her against his chest, so that she was in his lap.

Her ass pressed against his raging hard-on—way to be a sick, twisted bastard. She was badly injured and in some crazy amount of pain while just a few yards away her boyfriend or husband or whoever-the-hell-he-was-to-her was battling some insane super-villain, while Shane . . . ? He wanted to shag her.

Nice.

Across the room, the joker had started to scream, as if he were being tortured. It was blood-curdling and hair-raising, and just as abruptly as it started, it stopped.

And with that, the joker stopped fighting. He collapsed on the floor in a very small, unthreatening, slightly smoking heap, while the furniture vanished—instantly pulverized into huge sprays of sawdust.

Mac clung to Shane for only a fraction of second longer, too, before pulling free from his arms and scrambling up to her feet to meet Bach, who was already heading toward her.

Diaz, however went toward the joker, announcing, "He's out! Medical team, we need you in here, *now*!"

"Are you all right?" Bach asked Mac.

She glanced back at Shane, her expression unreadable, before she nodded. "I am now. What the hell happened? Littleton wasn't using when we picked him up. If he was, I would have known it."

"Belay that, med team." Diaz called. He was down on one knee, beside the joker. "He's not just out, he's flat-lined."

"*What?*" Mac went toward the fallen man, obviously horrified.

"Flat-lined?" Shane repeated as Elliot, too, went over to the joker, his medical wand in hand. "As in . . . ?"

"His neck's broken," Elliot reported as Diaz stood up and backed off. "But if *that* hadn't killed him, the massive brain hem-orrhaging would have. Whoa, his brain practically imploded."

"Aw, shit," Mac said. "*Shit.*"

Bach looked at her. "What did you do to him?"

She was instantly defensive, chin high. "It wasn't intentional."

"I know that," he said evenly. "I'm merely gathering informa-tion."

She didn't look convinced. "It hurt," she told him. "The heal-ing process." She glanced at Shane again. "Accelerated, it was more painful and . . . So I didn't block it, I flung it at him, the way we did with that other joker, last night. I thought maybe . . ." She shook her head, clearly pissed. *"Shit."*

Bach nodded. "Whatever you did worked."

"Yeah, but I double-whammied him," Mac said. "The drug made him paranoid and I found his fears and I took them and somehow . . . amplified them back at him. That, combined with the pain I was throwing . . ." She shook her head again. "I don't really know how I did it, sir. I've never been able to do anything like that before—definitely not to that degree."

"You're integrated nearly ten percent higher than normal," Elliot told her.

Mac again turned to look first at him, then at Shane, with an expression of complete surprise that she tried to hide. She was clearly exhausted, though, and she covered it with her anger and frustration over killing the joker.

"You're up to fifty-nine," Elliot continued, as he moved back to the comm-station. "Diaz is . . ." He cleared his throat. "Still at sixty."

"D is enhanced, too?" Mac looked over at Diaz then, and Shane realized that, even with all of the near-death drama, this was the first time he'd seen either of them exchange so much as eye contact.

And whatever he'd seen—or imagined he'd seen in the lobby when he'd first come in . . . There was nothing there now. Friend-ship, sure. They knew each other well. They were teammates—he'd recognize that bond anywhere, having lived it with his SEAL team for years. Why he hadn't seen it that way earlier was . . .

Probably because jealousy, which he was prone to experienc-ing, made him not just crazy but stupid, too.

"You believe *Shane's* responsible for this boost in their power?" Bach was asking the doctor.

Elliot hedged. "Partly. I have a new theory that needs a little modification and . . . a bit more research. Let's all take a break, and meet in Dr. Bach's office at . . . fourteen hundred hours should do it."

"I may not be back by then," Mac said flatly, arms folded across her chest. "With Littleton dead, we need to find—"

"Yeah, actually you *will* be back," Elliot cut her off as he turned toward her. "Because you're not going anywhere. Until you can control your enhanced power . . . ?" He shook his head. "You're not leaving the facility."

She started to argue, but he cut her off.

"Not going to happen. Besides, according to your most recent scan, you haven't slept in nearly sixty hours." Elliot looked at Diaz. "You could use some downtime, too."

But Mac was not one to go silently into the night. Or morning as it now was. "We've got a missing girl," she informed them, her self-disgust heavy in her tone, "and I've just killed one of two men who can tell us where she is. And—oh yeah—we have no idea who or where the other man is."

"We've got a name for our second man," Bach told her, told all of them, even though Shane wasn't in the loop. Missing girl? What missing girl? "Devon Caine. Analysis is already working to find him."

"Still," Mac insisted. "I should be out there, on the street. And obviously, the enhancement only works when I make contact with Laughlin. My integration levels were only slightly elevated when I was med scanned earlier, which means—also obviously—that enhancement drops rapidly without that contact. If I go out, without him—"

"That's not an *obviously*," Elliot countered. "Not to me, anyway. Plus, it doesn't take into consideration the fact that the human body needs to rest. That goes for all of you."

"Fourteen hundred in my office," Bach decided. "Fully rested."

For a moment, Mac looked as if she was going to argue, but she wisely zipped it, even though she grimly shook her head in obvious disgust.

"We'll want you at the meeting, too," Bach said, and Shane realized that the man was talking to him. "But until then, we can't have you wandering the compound. Mac will see you to your quarters."

"Sir," she started, this time ready to get into it.

But Bach cut her off. "Apparently, you and Lieutenant Laughlin have a few things to discuss."

"No, sir, we don't," she said.

Shane spoke, quietly but absolutely. "Yes, we do."

Mac looked at him. And nodded. "Fine. Let's do this, then. Right now. Let's go." She turned and headed briskly toward the door. Shane hurried to keep up as she raised her voice so that the others could hear her. "I want a report on what the hell happened— how Littleton went from dumbass dealer to Puff the Magic Dragon. I want to know who fucked up by not taking his product away from him when he was admitted into our holding cell. And I want that info sent to me, ASAP."

She didn't wait for an answer. She just slapped the door open and led Shane into the hallway, past the security guards, and all the way back toward a bank of elevators.

It wasn't until she pushed the button that she turned to look at him. "So," she said, obviously through gritted teeth. "Dorothy. Welcome to fucking Oz."

TWELVE

This was going to suck.

Shane was standing there, just looking at her, as the elevator doors opened with a *ding*.

In the hours since she'd left him in the street outside of her apartment, Mac had nearly managed to convince herself that he couldn't possibly be as fabulous as she'd remembered. His eyes really weren't that blue nor was his smile that sweet—except they were and it was.

Even after being as frazzled as she knew he had to be from witnessing Rickie Littleton joker so horrifically, Shane still managed to exude a cool calm.

Mac also knew that he was still worried about her, no doubt a result of having found her knocked stupid by the fire-breathing freak.

"Are you sure we shouldn't hit the Med Center and get you checked out?" Shane asked in his black-velvet voice as he followed her into the elevator. "Dr. Zerkowski said you were bleeding internally. And a head injury isn't anything to sneeze at."

"I'm fine now." She pushed the button for the lower level, intending to escort him back to the barracks, as ordered, through the tunnels that connected all of the buildings on the Institute campus. That would get them there the quickest. "Do you really think he would've let me walk away from him if I weren't? And he really *does* prefer being called Elliot."

Shane was frowning slightly as he looked at her. "You just look a little . . ."

Mac caught a glimpse of herself in the mirror on the elevator's back wall and . . . Great. They were going to start with *this*. Fabulous.

"Shitty?" she finished his sentence for him. She'd stopped at the CoffeeBoy on Route 9 and used the pair of plastic scissors she always carried with her to quickly cut her hair short again. The job she'd done had been lacking in both skill and finesse. But it wasn't her hair that he was looking at. "That's not because I was hurt. That's because, in reality, I usually look, well, kinda shitty. That's just . . . my face. This is what I actually look like when I'm not trying to get laid."

"Pale, was what I was going to say," he told her. "And tired. You don't look—"

"Yeah, well, tired's a given," she spoke over him, because really, what was he going to say in response to her *shitty*, no matter how accurate a descriptor it was. "I still haven't learned to control my sleep cycles. Bach can get by on maybe six hours, once a week. I'm not even close to doing that. But that's not why I look . . . the way I look. Today."

The elevator opened into the sub-basement and she led the way out into the main lobby for the tunnels. It was, thankfully, empty.

"The tunnels are color-coded," she interrupted her true-confession session—thank God—to give him the standard tour-guide spiel, but he stopped her.

"I got it," he said. "Dr. Zer . . . *Elliot* gave me all the info last night. The blue path'll take me back to the apartments. Yellow goes to the Potential training classrooms. Red's medical." He laughed a little, which made charming crinkles appear around his eyes. "In case I forget how to read the signs."

"Not everyone who comes here *can* read," Mac told him a tad sanctimoniously as they started down the brightly lit path with the blue line of tiles on the wall, because staying on that inane topic was better than telling him the truth. If she kept talking long enough, she could time it so that she didn't have to tell him before they reached his apartment. At which point, she could drop her bomb and exit. Fast. "Some are very young children. And some of our Potentials can't read English. Not many, but some are recruited from other countries."

Shane took her conversational ball and ran with it as their footsteps were muffled by the tunnel's skid-proof floor. "I'm still not exactly sure how I got onto OI's recruitment list. I got an e-mail—out of the blue—inviting me to enter the program, but . . ."

Mac glanced at him again—to find him looking kind of sideways at her. No doubt he still couldn't quite figure out what was different about her. He probably just thought it was morning-after reality, rearing its ugly head. So to speak. Except she wasn't picking up any revulsion from him—just confusion. Along with—damn—a genuine chime of desire, and—shit—a whiff of affection. Perfect.

Clearly the sex they'd shared had been good enough for him to want a replay—regardless of what she now looked like.

But of course it was possible—highly likely in fact—that whatever she'd done to him with her charismatic power hadn't yet worn off.

"How long have you been out?" she asked him, forcing herself to focus on his question about his own recruitment—how OI had found him. "Of the military?"

"Not quite a year," he told her.

"Well, that's not it, then," Mac said. "I was thinking maybe you just left, and your medical records only recently went public and . . . You visit a hospital any time in the past few months?"

"No," Shane said. "But I did get a full medical scan about two months ago. Drug testing for, you know. That cage-fighting thing."

Mac looked at him, a bit sharply.

"What?" he said, picking it up, still watching her. "You thought I was BSing you about that? I'm really blacklisted, too, *Michelle*. I'm not the one with all the secrets—including the fact that you had a broken ankle while we were getting it on. Jesus. Did *that* hurt like hell when it was healing, too?"

"No," she told him, surprised and rattled by his point-blank approach. This was where they were both awkwardly supposed to pretend last night had never happened, not bring it up or discuss any aspect of it. And still he watched her, as if he couldn't believe his good luck at finding her again. She, however, was having a moment of serious surrealness. Last night, while she was letting him rock her world, she'd never, in a million years, imagined that she'd ever be walking with him, like this, through OI's tunnels. "It's, um . . . Well, I'm not really sure what happens, but having sex is, um . . ." She cleared her throat. "For me, it accelerates the healing process and . . . It . . . *doesn't* hurt—really doesn't—when I'm . . . Not when, um . . . I think the pleasure drowns out any pain, so . . . no." He didn't say anything so she kept going. "Plus, you need to understand that—this morning—I was *leaning* on the pain, so I could project it and . . . I was trying, actively, to use it to take down Rickie Littleton—the joker."

And take down Littleton she'd done—to the tune of killing him and bringing them back to less than square one, in terms of finding Nika Taylor.

God damn it.

"Ah," Shane said. "So . . . It's not *me*, necessarily. It's *sex* that allows you to heal faster . . . ?"

"It's sex," she agreed, but then admitted, "And you." She cleared her throat again and changed the subject. "It *was*—probably—the med scan. That you had for the cage-fighting thing. I bet that's how we found you. Those records go into the international medical database and . . . We hack 'em, pretty regularly. Your integration level is seventeen, which is significantly higher than the average fraction's ten percent, which is why that e-mail went out to you. That plus your military training . . . You're disciplined. You're, like, the perfect Potential. You know, aside from being male and . . . Too old."

He looked at her, but didn't comment.

So she continued. "Our usual recruits are girls. Estrogen naturally boosts integration levels and . . . But the best age for us to acquire a Potential is around ten or eleven. Pre-puberty. Of course, it's the hormones that create the spike in most girls' levels, so we often don't identify them as Potentials until it's already too late. And I mean it's too late only because most girls who are recruited when they're older don't stay with the program—I don't know if it's a fear of being different or . . . Ironically, it's the rare boys who usually excel, regardless of when they join. That's why we still look to recruit men your age as Potentials."

His brow was furrowed as he attempted to interpret her babbling. "So . . . the Obermeyer Institute hacks into the medical records of people—mostly children, and among those children, mostly girls—from all over the world?" he asked.

"There are still some countries whose med records aren't online," Mac said. "We've gotten some of our best Potentials from them. But it's unconventional—the way we find out about them. We keep a constant watch for reports of disturbances—so-called poltergeist activity or accusations of witchcraft, or even stigmata or other unexplained physical mutilations or illnesses that can be a part of a belief-induced fervor. Really, they're looking for anything unexplained that might be traced to an untrained, out-of-control Greater-Than. With the poltergeist thing being the most common."

"Poltergeist," Shane repeated. "I'm not sure I'm following. Are you saying that poltergeists—like that old horror movie—are . . . real?"

"Yes, but, no." Mac shook her head. "Not like the movie, or . . . Not like your old dead creepy Uncle Moe who was also a serial killer and is now terrorizing the new owners of the house where he sliced and diced his victims . . . No spirit-world shit. I'm talking about unexplained events—doors opening and closing, furniture moving, dancing teacups without a Disney animator in sight. Even, yeah, statues crying tears of blood—all of which can be the result of a living person—usually a teenage girl—who has uncontrolled telekinetic powers. Most poltergeist disturbances take place in a home that includes a female child between the ages of eight and sixteen. Sometimes it's a boy, but that's, well, it's really rare. Anyway, in a majority of the cases, the telekinetic activity takes place unconsciously, usually because the child is under some kind of duress. Sexual abuse being a biggie."

"Jesus," Shane said. They'd reached the end of the tunnel, where there was a bank of elevators to take them up into the barracks.

"Yeah," Mac agreed, pushing the button. They were almost there. God help her. "A few years ago, we pulled a girl out of Iraq after she'd essentially burned her village to the ground. She was thirteen years old at the time. She'd lived most of her life in London, but she was illegal and hadn't been to see a doctor. So no med scans and no records, right? When she was identified as a noncitizen and sent back to her grandfather—her parents had died—she was immediately given away in marriage. Her husband-to-be was Kurdish and about a million years old, and he insisted that she get circumcised—here in the West, we call that FGM. Female genital mutilation. The scar tissue that's created acts as a chastity belt—that's if the girls who are cut actually survive the procedure."

"I know what FGM is," Shane said quietly.

"They dress up the maiming with a fancy ceremony," Mac told him. "But this girl? She wasn't having it. She tapped into some pretty crazy powers when the village elder first began cutting her. We're still not sure if she actually started the fire spontaneously, or just used standard telekinesis to knock some stuff into an open flame. Either way, the blaze spread really quickly, and the old man she was supposed to marry was killed. She escaped, and was being hunted when our research team heard the stories about the *devil bride*. Our rescue squad went in, and we found her first. She's pretty powerful, but she's also still pretty messed up."

"I can imagine," he murmured. The elevator opened and they got in. Shane was silent as he pushed the button for his floor, so Mac kept going.

"We've got a three-person research team down in Analysis dedicated to searching for that type of story," she told him. "In chatrooms, on YouTube, on all the Internet blogs. Of course, we look for the extra-freaky here in America, too, since so many people can't afford health care. Did you know there are over thirty million children in this country who've never seen a doctor—who've never received a medical scan?"

"I didn't know the number was that high," he said.

"It is," she said, "and it's growing."

"So this girl you mentioned, the one who's missing . . ."

"Her name's Nika Taylor. She was on our list of Potentials—and there should be another category for girls like her, and like the girl who torched her village. We should call them Definites. Anyway, Nika was kidnapped by the scumbags who make Destiny—the drug that made Littleton joker. They do what we do—search for girls who are Potentials. Only they don't train them. They use them. They literally bleed them for the hormones that make the drug."

"Jesus."

"Yeah."

They rode the rest of the way in silence, and it wasn't until the doors opened on the third floor that Mac cleared her throat again. "So, which suite is yours?"

"Three-fourteen," he told her, leading the way down the hall.

She could feel his surprise as she took out her master key.

"I would've thought you wouldn't need that," he said. "I read—in the material I was given—that opening locked doors was a pretty basic skill—"

"Telekinesis isn't one of my strengths," Mac admitted. She glanced over and found that he was watching her again. She held open the door and gestured for him to go in first. "What did . . ." She started over, sounding as lame as she felt. "Didn't Elliot tell you anything . . . about me?"

Shane shrugged as he looked back at where she was still standing in the open doorway. "Not much," he said. "He said that you're one of these Greater-Thans, and . . . Frankly, I didn't really believe any of it until . . . Well."

He scratched his head, bringing his hand down to rub the back of his neck, and it was hard not to think about the way he'd tried to entice her to see him again, with his offer of dinner and a massage. Mac knew how good his hands would feel on her shoulders, her neck, her back . . .

She sighed, because that part of their relationship was over. It had to be. It *would* be after she told him the truth. It was one thing to use her create-an-instant-boyfriend abilities on a stranger, another entirely to seduce a co-worker. "Yeah, some people really have to see it to believe it. And some don't accept it even then. There's this crazy group of Fundamentalists, a fringe group of about twenty Bible-thumpers from freaking Kansas, who *do* believe we're real—and that we're evil. Satan's foot soldiers, they call us. They picket out front every few months or so. But most people don't know we're here."

"I sure as hell didn't," Shane told her.

"So Elliot didn't tell you anything about my particular skill-set?" Mac asked.

"Aside from the accelerated-healing thing," he said, "no. Your friend Diaz, he, um, managed to put me into some kind of wrestling hold from across the room. I was totally immobilized. Bach did it to me, too. I guess I was assuming that you could do the same . . . ?"

"Yeah," she said, shaking her head. "No, I can't do that. As far as telekinesis goes, I'm only good for the big things. I can knock down a wall or tear off a roof. I *could* throw you across the room, sure, probably farther than Diaz could dream of doing, but . . . Your landing would be a little messy and you'd probably be killed, so it's really not a good idea to try it unless we're in a padded testing lab. You know, one of the basic skills that most Greater-Thans master is an ability to shield—to protect ourselves from violence—to make ourselves bulletproof. But that's a form of telekinesis, too—it's related. And I'm about a second-grade level when it comes to that. I can shield, but only if I focus completely on it—to the point that I'm virtually useless when it comes to utilizing any of my other powers."

She kept going. "I also suck at telepathy. Dr. Bach can read your mind, but not me. I don't know what you're thinking—but I *do* know what you're feeling. My specialty is empathy. I can read emotions. Pretty clearly. I can even pick up on emotional events from the past—just by being in the place where they went down."

He was silent, just standing there in the entryway of his recently assigned apartment, listening, so she kept going.

"I'm also highly skilled at self-healing, which you already know," she told him. "And, connected to that—it's a similar neural pathway—I can change my physical appearance at will. To a degree, of course. I mean, I can't turn myself into a bat, or a panther, or even a man, although that would be useful if I could. I'm stuck with the basics of what I've got."

Mac paused then, because this was where it was going to get difficult, and she found herself searching for the right words.

But Shane took her silence as a signal that she was finished, and he asked, "Aren't you coming in?"

Before she could answer, he added, "Or are these apartments monitored the way that all of the corridors and elevators and tunnels are?"

"No," she told him. "There are no cameras in the private residences. So feel free to jerk off in the shower." Okay, that was stupid—to bring up sex in any way, shape, or form.

Shane smiled, still just briefly. "I was asking because I was assuming you'd want privacy before I said . . . some of the things I was waiting to say to you."

They wouldn't have that privacy with the door wide open.

Mac stepped into the apartment, letting the door close behind her with a *clunk*.

For some reason, her coming inside made him happy. Happier, anyway. "Can I get you something?" he asked as he went into the kitchen, like she was actually there on a social call. "Coffee, or—"

"No," she said, purposely leaving off the *thank you*. "And I'm not coming in. Not any farther than this. But you're right, privacy is better for what *I* still have to say to *you*, too, so—"

"I understand why you couldn't tell me where you worked." Shane came back out of the kitchen to say. "I get it. And I also get why you thought you needed to break it off. You're one of these super powerful Greater-Thans, and I'm . . . Not. I understand the hazards of fraternization within an organization, I really do. But all that has to mean is that we keep it on the down-low. You've got that apartment in Kenmore Square. I say we meet there—"

Damn, she must've still—somehow—been doing it. Charming him. She didn't think she was, and yet . . . She'd learned to control her abilities, post Tim, thank God, yet it was possible that her attraction to Shane made it kick on, without her awareness, and despite her attempts to stifle it.

"You don't know what you're saying," she said.

He laughed. "Like hell I don't." His smile faded. "Look, there's something between us that I want to pursue—and it's more than just sex."

"No, it's not."

"Yeah, it is. I've never been so certain of anything as I am about the fact that we . . . We just *fit*. Mac, I know you felt it, too." He came toward her, his intention to pull her into his arms and kiss her written all over his face.

Mac backed up, hands up, and smacked her head on the door. "Shit! Stop!"

He stopped his advance, but only physically. "We can make this work," he insisted. "You and me, Mac—it was magic. You can't deny that."

"No," she agreed. "I can't. Although, I'm more inclined to use a slightly more scientific word for what happened last night. It was biology and psychology—but mostly biology." She forced herself to look him in the eyes as she just said it. "One of my biggest skills is my biological ability to attract men." She corrected herself. "Others. It works with gay and bi women, too."

It was obvious that Shane didn't truly understand what she meant—he didn't understand why he should care. Because his response was to shake his head and shrug as he exhaled a laugh. "You say that like it's some kind of unique talent. I'm pretty sure this won't be a newsflash, but last night, I was looking for some action. It's not like I was bound for the seminary and you waylaid me en route. Pun intended."

She didn't laugh. But that didn't stop him.

"I think I'd have a better time believing you," he continued, "if that was the case."

"You went into *Father's* to get laid?" Mac asked skeptically. "That place is a dive."

"I went in to hustle a few games of pool," Shane told her honestly. "I needed some cash so I could hit one of the nicer hotel bars, downtown. But then, you walked in."

"And it was *lust* at first sight." She leaned on the word, hoping that he wouldn't embarrass them both by using the other L-word. "That's exactly my point. That's what I do. In this case, unintentionally, but still."

Shane was clearly unconvinced. "I wasn't the only man in there who noticed you."

"And again, you prove my point."

"Have you ever been in a bar—anywhere—where the men *don't* look up when a woman—any woman—walks in?" Shane laughed. "I hate to burst your bubble, but the biological ability to attract applies to all women, everywhere. All you have to be is female for at least *some* men to say *I'd tap that.* It's a given. It's kind of like my saying that I have a special talent when it comes to eating dinner. My body's really skilled at turning food into energy. And yeah, metabolism's involved. Mine's better than most. Same way you turn more heads when you walk into a bar."

"This is more than that," Mac told him. "Do you know how I caught Littleton this morning, before he jokered? I found him at the counter in a greasy spoon, and all I had to do was sit down next to him. I offered to trade him sex for drugs and—"

"Jesus," he breathed. "You really are out there on the front lines, aren't you?"

"He would have followed me anywhere," Mac said.

Shane laughed again, but it was obviously an expression of his disgust. "You say that like it's some kind of miracle. Do you ever even *look* into a mirror, Michelle? Do you *really* not have a clue—"

"Oh, please," she scoffed. "And I am *not* being coy or cute or trying to—"

"Beauty is more than supermodel-perfect features," he countered. "Which, by the way, any fool with money can buy from any doctor with a surgical knife, along with perfect tits and ass."

"And what *I'm* saying," she shot back, "is that beauty isn't, ultimately, what attracts. Although it helps—I'm helped by being able to alter my appearance, which is what I did last night, FYI, before taking off my bra? That wasn't me—that was me, *adjusted*—for your enjoyment."

Shane still didn't understand. She could pick up his bewilderment, along with his amusement. "Am I supposed to apologize because I thought you were hot?" he asked. "When you did something I had no idea you were doing . . . ?"

And okay, when he put it like that, she definitely sounded crazy. "Of course not," she said. "But you're not letting me explain."

"Please," he said. "Do."

"It's not only the adjustments to my physical appearance that make me attractive," Mac told him. "I also release pheromones and my pupils dilate and . . . I tune into individual body chemistry—when you sat down next to me, I was able to make myself smell really good, specifically *for you*. I can read body language—subtle things that you might not even be aware of, and send back messages that inform your subconscious that we'd be—yes—a perfect fit. I can do this instantly and, apparently, subconsciously. The bottom line is that I can dial up the charisma factor—that's the best way to explain it—whenever I want to. And that makes me irresistible to men. Most men. I must've done it without thinking when I went into the bar last night. Otherwise you never would have approached me."

Shane waited several beats, no doubt to make sure that this time she truly was finished. But then he said, "You can't know what I would or wouldn't have done."

"On the contrary," Mac said. "I can. You say you went in there to get laid? Well, I did, too. At the time, I wasn't really thinking that clearly, but in hindsight? Why else would I have gone there? I walked in, and when I saw you—"

"You dismissed me," he countered.

"As any kind of a threat," she shot back. "But as a fuck-buddy? Apparently, I locked in on your potential right away. Sometimes eye contact is all it takes."

Shane laughed again. "So because you *looked* at me, that was it? My free will was gone? I *had* to go over and sit next to you— I had absolutely no choice . . . ?"

"You used the word *magic* before," she admitted. "In a way, you were exactly right, since I cast a spell on you."

He was shaking his head. "I don't believe that."

"And you also probably didn't believe that Diaz could pick you up and move you across a room," she pointed out.

And there it was—she finally felt it. Doubt had put a chink in his certainty, which wavered as he gazed back at her.

"It probably hasn't fully worn off yet," she told him quietly. "Whatever it was that I did to you. But it will. It always does. And then you'll believe me, too."

She'd managed to silence him. She turned toward the door, aware that there was only one more thing that she had to say. She forced herself to turn back and meet his still-steady gaze. "I *am* sorry—"

He cut her off. "I'm not," he said. "Whatever that was that happened between us? And it sure as hell felt like free will, but even if it wasn't? I'm not *sorry*. It was fucking great, Michelle."

Oh, God. "Please don't call me that."

"It was fucking great," he repeated. "Mac."

She'd expected his anger or indignation. She didn't quite know what to say, particularly since she now felt the sudden pressure of tears. Dear God, don't let her cry. "Somehow I doubt you'll still feel that way tomorrow."

"And if I do?"

"You won't." She had to get out of here. She opened the door.

Shane didn't stop her, other than to say, "Elliot thinks I helped fix your ankle—that I helped you heal today, too. How does that crazy shite fit in?"

"I don't know," Mac admitted, glancing back at him over her shoulder. She didn't know how the fact that just touching this man brought her up to nearly sixty percent integrated fit in with any of this, either. But she *did* know that she was unwilling to keep on deceiving him. "But thank you for . . . that."

He was still watching her, and despite his still-new doubt, she felt it again—that distinct chime of his desire. Despite everything she'd told him, he wanted her to stay.

And God, wouldn't that be nice—to be able to use sex to release some of her anger and grief at killing Rickie Littleton, at failing to find Nika Taylor, at her own blind and dumb luck for crashing into this incredible man in the first place?

And then, after, she might even be able to fall asleep without assistance, next to his solidness and warmth . . .

"I'm so sorry," Mac told him again as she closed the door gently behind her, and the latch caught, locking him in, because Bach didn't want him wandering the compound while all of his babysitters had been ordered to rest.

He didn't complain about the lockdown. But he found the intercom. The speaker clicked on, and his voice followed her as she walked away.

"I'm not," he said again. "Sorry. I'm not . . ."

"Give it time," Mac said, even though he probably couldn't hear her. "And you will be."

THIRTEEN

Stephen Diaz lived on the very same floor as Elliot, in the OI building known as the barracks.

Elliot stood outside of the Greater-Than's apartment, afraid to ring the bell and wake him up, but knowing that he had to do it. He had to talk to Diaz *before* the meeting in Bach's office. And that meant that this conversation had to happen now.

Regardless of how tired he was.

Regardless of the fact that Diaz might be asleep.

So he raised his hand to ring the bell—and the door opened before his finger hit the button.

Diaz wasn't sleeping. In fact, it was kind of obvious that he'd recently showered. His chiseled face was freshly shaven, his short, dark hair was artfully arranged. He was dressed for company in a really nice, soft-looking shirt that was a vibrant shade of blue—with its sleeves rolled up to his elbows and the collar comfortably open.

Or maybe this was just the way he spent his alone-time at home. In faded jeans that he *had* to know made him look like a million bucks, and brown leather sandals that exposed his perfect toes . . .

In contrast, Elliot felt rumpled and messy. Although, even when he tried to dress up, he still managed to look disheveled, so it shouldn't have bothered him.

But it did.

"Hey," Elliot said, because one of them had to say something, instead of just standing there, staring in silence. "Um, sorry. About the late hour. I mean, it's morning, sure, but . . . I know you were up all night, because I was, too, although, now that I think of it, it's probably not your night to sleep, although Dr. Bach *did* give the order to rest, and it really felt—to me—like you needed at least a nap, so . . ."

Okay.

He sounded like a moron, but close proximity to Diaz usually made him yammer as if his IQ had suddenly dropped. Recent events had made that phenomenon worsen.

The man was clearly embarrassed by Elliot's somewhat obvious mission—he was hardly able to meet Elliot's gaze. But he did open the door wider and even stepped back to let the doctor come inside. "I was pretty sure you'd be, um, coming by," Diaz murmured. "So . . ."

So, indeed.

It was difficult not to think about what had happened, down in the main function room after Rickie Littleton had jokered—when Diaz had tried to push Elliot out into the hallway. With his telekinetic powers occupied by locking Shane Laughlin into place, Diaz had had to use physical force. He'd grabbed Elliot from behind, wrapping his arms around him and pulling him back against his chest.

And just as it had happened down in the exam room, Diaz had suddenly and instantly been deep inside of Elliot's head.

The Greater-Than's thoughts had been a rapid-fire jumble of words and images.

Elliot was in danger simply by being there. Shane, too, but Elliot . . .

Elliot caught a flash of himself—a memory from months ago—as he laughed at some test of one of the trainee's powers that had gone ridiculously wrong.

But then Diaz had realized that Elliot could hear his thoughts, and he'd addressed him directly. His vehemence was strong. *You should have kept Shane in the exam room, where it was safe!*

But it was because they were here that Diaz was up to sixty percent, Elliot tried to tell the Greater-Than.

How can I concentrate on rescuing Mac? God damn it, I want you safe! I want . . .

"It's Shane!" Elliot had said, speaking over Diaz's thoughts, saying the words aloud. "He's giving you that boost and holy crap, it's—"

You. God, I want you.

And the flood of erotic images was back, and it was all so vivid and overpowering that, for a heartbeat, Elliot wasn't sure where he was. It was only because Diaz was holding him that he didn't fall over. And it was, finally, *that* that grounded him and brought him back—the fact that he was pressed so tightly against Diaz that the other man's very physical attraction was both unavoidable and unmistakable.

Diaz obviously couldn't and didn't fail to notice it either, and he let go of Elliot—fast—breaking the intimacy of their mental connection.

And just as quickly as Elliot's theory about Shane fell apart, a new theory blossomed. What if *he* were responsible for Diaz's boost in power? Not because he was special, but because of Diaz's attraction?

What if Mac was right, and sex didn't hinder a Greater-Than's progress, but instead *helped*?

"*Use* it," Elliot had urged Diaz. "For God's sake, man, don't fight it, *use* it!"

He had no clue what Diaz was feeling or thinking—because their connection was no longer active. But he *did* know that Diaz combined his ramped-up power with Bach's, and together they were suddenly able to contain both the joker and the rampaging furniture so that Elliot and Shane could reach Mac.

After the battle had ended, there'd been no chance for Elliot to talk privately to Diaz.

Until now.

So Elliot walked through the door, hyper-aware both of the bigger man's presence and the fact that he'd never been inside of

Diaz's apartment before. The Greater-Than had obviously brought in his own eclectic furnishings—including bookshelves aplenty—and he'd adorned the walls with boldly colorful artwork that had a distinctly Mexican flavor. He'd renovated, too—opening the place up so that instead of having two separate bedrooms, he had one single, much-larger main room, with his bed tucked away in an alcove and . . .

Okay, *that* was the exact same bed Elliot had envisioned earlier, both when he'd tried to help Diaz up off the floor in the hall, when those shockingly intimate images had first flashed through his mind, and again, down in the function room, just a few hours ago. It had looked familiar to him, he realized now with a jolt, because he'd seen it before, in his dreams.

He'd been here before, in this apartment—*in his dreams.*

Holy crap.

"Can I get you some coffee?" Diaz's voice came from right behind him, and Elliot quickly turned.

"Yeah," he said. "Thanks. Wait. You don't drink coffee."

Yet he could smell it brewing—rich and fragrant. And sure enough, there was a fresh pot in a small coffeemaker that was out on the kitchen counter, hissing and spitting its last.

Diaz slipped into the kitchen area, behind a breakfast counter that separated it from the otherwise open room. There were two brightly colored mugs already out and waiting. One was filled with hot water that steamed as a tea bag brewed.

As Elliot watched, Diaz pulled the pot from the hot plate and poured the coffee into the blue mug, filling it close to the brim. He pushed the mug forward, handle out, clearly aware that Elliot drank his coffee black.

Maybe kinda the way Elliot knew that Diaz was a fan of vanilla chai, with milk and just a touch of sugar . . . ?

Holy crap. All these years they'd worked together—how could Elliot not have known that Diaz . . . ?

As Elliot took the mug, Diaz glanced up at him, his eyes somber. And this time, Elliot was the one who quickly looked away, uncertain as to how to start the conversation. *So. Despite insisting you remain celibate, you apparently and somewhat desperately seem to want to have sex with me . . . And oh yeah, we should probably also discuss the fact that I am now probably the only person at OI who knows that you're gay—and we're about to go into a meeting where it's extremely likely that I'm going to out you. And as long as we're discussing WTF topics, do you have any idea why I've had extremely vivid dreams set in your apartment, even though I've never stepped through your doorway before today?*

He took a sip of his coffee, and—"God, that's good. You make a mean pot of coffee for a tea-drinker."

Diaz stirred his tea, his spoon clinking softly against his mug as he leaned back against the counter, his long legs casually crossed at the ankle. "I used to be a coffee addict myself."

"There are worse addictions," Elliot said, and okay. Were they really going to make mundane chit-chat like this? Any second now, they were going to talk about the weather. *Nice day. It's finally starting to warm up out there. . . .*

Except, suddenly all he could think about was the vehement certainty with which Mac had informed him that Diaz didn't so much as masturbate, and oh, sweet Jesus, this man could conceivably read his mind—especially if Elliot were right, and his own mere presence created a boost in Diaz's integration levels, and great, now he was *mentally* yammering. Don't think about sex, don't think about sex, don't think about sex. . . .

Except, particularly after the past day's surprises, it was impossible to look at Diaz and *not* think about sex, or the fact that it had been three long years since Elliot had gotten any.

Although, forget *him.* Three years was a heartbeat, compared to how long it had probably been for Diaz, who was standing there with his ridiculously broad shoulders and those gorgeous eyes, quietly sipping his tea as he watched Elliot.

Elliot abruptly turned toward the window, where a sofa and various other comfortable-looking chairs were positioned. He gestured toward them with his mug. "May we sit? I think we should, you know, probably sit. I've done a bit more research on the fluctuations in your integration levels and, um, thought you'd want to know what I've found."

"Absolutely." Diaz nodded and pushed himself up out of his lean, but Elliot didn't wait for him to lead the way.

"First, I reviewed all of the various jot scans from . . . before. You integrated at a high of sixty-point-seven percent down in the function room," he said as he went over to the sofa—a buttery-soft light-brown leather—and sat before he realized that there was no flatscreen TV on the any of the walls. Of course not. It was clear from those crowded bookshelves that Diaz was a reader. An old-fashioned-real-book lover. He most likely spent his rare free evenings quietly lost in a book instead of, like Elliot, glued to the thirty-somethingth season of *So You Think You Can Dance.*

"I looked at those scans, too," Diaz was saying as he moved toward the chair. "Trying to make sense of it and—"

"I'm sorry," Elliot interrupted him. "I didn't bring my computer, and I didn't think that you might not have a TV to hook into the OI mainframe. Do you, um . . . ."

"Oh," Diaz said. "Sure. I've got a laptop. Of course. I'll just . . . Get it." He set his mug down on a coaster on the coffee table and crossed over toward the part of the room that held his neatly made bed.

He moved gracefully, with a smooth efficiency that didn't read as hurried.

During all the years Elliot had worked here, he'd always really enjoyed watching this man walk—which sounded pathetic or maybe even a touch creepy, but really wasn't. What was it that Anna Taylor had said earlier? It was definitely an *art-appreciation thing.*

But there was art, and there was *art,* and he had to look away as Diaz put one knee up on his bed, leaning over to reach his computer from where it had been stored on a shelf that was inset into the wall, above the curve of the bed's sleigh-styled wooden headboard.

Exactly where Elliot knew it would be—which kind of blew his mind.

"Maybe we should go over to my office to do this," he blurted.

Diaz had already brought his laptop all the way back to the sofa, but now he hesitated, holding on to it instead of setting it down on the coffee table in front of Elliot. "If that would make you more comfortable—" he started.

Elliot cut him off. "*I'm* fine. Okay, that's a lie. I'm completely freaked out. But I'm not going to be any more or less freaked out here or in my office or on the fucking moon. I just . . . Stephen, I'm trying to make *you* more comfortable."

"Comfortable?" Diaz laughed at that as he put his laptop down, his amusement briefly touching his eyes. But only briefly. It was replaced far too quickly by something that seemed shockingly like self-contempt or even disgust. "I'm a Fifty, Doctor. I'm not supposed to be *comfortable*. I'm supposed to train," he continued. "I'm supposed to focus all of my energy and effort into becoming a Sixty, and then, maybe even—someday—a Seventy or higher. My comfort doesn't play into that. It never has. But it's not fair for *you* to have to—"

"I'm fine," Elliot repeated. "I just didn't want—"

"You just said you're freaked out." Diaz actually started to pace, his movement sharp and tight. "That I freaked you out."

"—*you* to feel uncomfortable," Elliot continued over him, "because we're alone here in your apartment"—he tried to make things lighter—"where we've apparently both set quite a few of our fantasies—"

Diaz turned to face him and he definitely wasn't amused. "Those were *my* fantasies. I saw your memories of them while I was inside your head the second time—in the function room. They were mine, and I forced them on you. And you know it."

Elliot had to laugh. Forced? "Do you seriously think I haven't had plenty of nearly identical fantasies of my own? You know, I've got this one dream—it's recurring. And I'm talking about like clockwork, sometimes twice a week. We're in this beautiful house in, I don't know where—maybe Italy? We're in the middle of a vineyard and . . . What?"

Diaz had actually turned pale and now he slowly sank down into the chair across from Elliot. "Wednesdays and Sundays," he whispered.

Elliot shook his head. "I'm sorry, I'm not following."

"Is that when you dream it?" Diaz asked. "Because Wednesdays and Sundays are when I sleep. I'm down to only two nights a week."

"Wait a minute—what?" Holy crap. Was it actually possible . . . ? "But, no, you're not," Elliot said, pulling the computer closer so he could access its keyboard. "You're still on a three-night-a-week schedule." He called up Diaz's file. "It's Wednesday, Friday, Sunday." He looked up, suddenly uncertain. "Isn't it?"

"Fridays I'm down to a combat nap," Diaz told him. "Well, it's longer than that. About an hour and a half. Usually sometime in the early afternoon, when . . . you're probably awake."

And there it was—the change in Diaz's sleep schedule notated in the margin of his file. That meant, indeed, he was now on a Wednesday/Sunday cycle. Elliot tried to remember exactly when he had those dreams, but came up cold.

"I can start sleeping during the day," Diaz said. He was really upset. "God, I'm so sorry—"

Elliot shook his head. "Are you saying . . . ?" He looked over at that bed that he'd dreamed about so many times and started over. "I'm sorry, what are you saying?"

"I'm saying that . . ." Diaz forced himself—miserably—to hold Elliot's gaze, as he exhaled hard. "Those dreams you've been having? They're mine, too."

Elliot leaned forward. He hadn't actually believed . . . He'd really thought he must've seen a picture of Diaz's apartment, maybe from Mac or . . . "Can you actually *do* that? Broadcast your dreams? From an unconscious state?"

"I don't know," Diaz said. "I didn't know I was doing it, but—"

"Maybe I'm just dreaming about you on my own initiative," Elliot suggested. "I really don't know how often or which nights—"

"So you think it's a coincidence?" Diaz asked, his skepticism heavy in his voice. "Okay. Last dream—do you remember the last dream? It was . . ." He nodded. "Where you said. At the vineyard."

Elliot did remember. He'd woken up with his heart pounding and a hard-on of epic proportions. He'd realized some time ago that whenever he had a sex dream about Stephen Diaz, he always— *always*—awoke before either of them climaxed. And he always regretted waking. This time, he'd lain there in his bed, cursing and replaying the dream in as much detail as he could recall. So, yes, he remembered.

"We're in a beautiful house, on a hillside covered in rows of vines." Diaz exhaled hard. "It's not Italy, it's California. We're at my grandmother's house, near Sonoma. Do you remember the photograph that hung over the bed? Last time I had the dream, I came in to the room, and you were looking at it."

"Holy crap," Elliot breathed. He did remember that. "It was an old snapshot of the house, from the . . . 1920s?" He'd been looking at it quite closely—at the collection of people posing out near the front porch, when Diaz had come into the room, just out of the shower. At which point Elliot's attention had shifted. Dramatically.

"It was from 1914," Diaz corrected him now, his voice tight. "My grandmother loved that photo—her brother was in it, he died in the war, and after *she* died my father gave it to a local museum." He reached for the computer, pulling it in front of him, and quickly hopped over to the Internet, where he typed in a URL and clicked through a few links and . . .

"Holy *crap*," Elliot said again, as Diaz pushed the computer back toward him. On the screen was the photo that he had, absolutely, seen in that dream.

He also remembered—even more clearly—the way Diaz had smiled into his eyes before kissing him and then pushing him down onto that big bed.

"You were wearing a blue T-shirt and jeans," Diaz said, his voice low. "I had . . . only a towel around my waist."

A towel that hadn't stayed on for long. Elliot remembered that, too.

"*Holy* crap," Elliot whispered. It was clearly becoming his refrain. "Okay, so we definitely had the same dream. You honestly have no idea how you did it? How you broadcast it to me?"

Diaz had closed his eyes. He shook his head, and it was clear that he was mortified.

"Or maybe *broadcast* isn't the right word," Elliot said. "Thought projection isn't *that* unusual. Bach can do it. Although I'm not sure he can do it through several walls, down a hall—while in his sleep. This is an impressive new skill."

"Oh, yeah," Diaz said, laughing his disbelief and disgust. "This is great. I'm thrilled." He rubbed his forehead as if he had a terrible headache.

"Although I'm definitely making some assumptions, here," Elliot corrected himself. "When you were inside my head earlier today, it seemed as if we were having a kind of a conversation. A give-and-take. It's completely possible that the dream wasn't entirely yours. I mean, maybe your id picked the locale, and mine, you know, chose the activity."

"No." Diaz turned to look at him. "That was *my* dream."

"You can't know that absolutely," Elliot argued. "We're in uncharted territory."

"Yes," Diaz said. "I can. The sex was . . . *My* fantasy. I've been capable of something I call controlled dreaming for a while now. It's an augmented form of wake-initiated lucid dreaming, and I started doing it to let my subconscious work on certain problems and . . . I discovered there was a . . . recreational appeal. I haven't made the research team aware of it for obvious reasons." And now the look on his face was both apologetic and embarrassed, and for a half a second he looked as if he were about to cry. But then he was up and on his feet and pacing again, running his hands down his face. "God, I'm sorry, Dr. Z. This is so inappropriate."

"You really have to start calling me Elliot. I'm pretty sure we're on a first-name basis by now, at least in your dreams. And okay, being a smartass obviously isn't helping. Why don't you slow down and just breathe." Elliot stood up, too. "Come on, Stephen—I'm not offended. I'm flattered. I'm more than flattered. I'm—"

"Freaked out," Diaz finished for him.

"Yeah," Elliot said, "but—for the record—I'm not freaked out because you apparently want to do me, every chance you get. As far as *that* goes, I'm mentally running laps around the room and giving myself high fives and fist bumps. When I said I was freaked out it was because I know how seriously you take your training, and I respect both you and that, even though I haven't found even the slightest hint of scientific evidence backing your belief about your celibacy's impact on your mental skills." Diaz started to speak—no doubt to disagree—but Elliot held up his hand and stopped him. "And please, I don't want to argue about that right now. Can we focus on your elevated integration levels? Let's start with the scientific facts—with what we already know, what we can prove."

Diaz didn't say anything, didn't move, but he seemed to be breathing again, so Elliot sat back down in front of the computer, calling up the research he'd done over the past few hours. He focused on keeping breathing, too. There'd be plenty of time, later, for him to hyperventilate over the fact that Stephen Diaz *chose* to dream about having sex with him. With *him*. Holy crap.

"I've gone back and looked closely at the history of fluctuation in your integration levels," Elliot said, somehow managing to sound calm and in control. "And there's definitely a correlation between a slight rise in those levels and my presence in the room. I appear to give you a mental hard-on." He looked up at Diaz, who'd closed his eyes again. "Okay, not funny. But remember that. *You're* not the inappropriate one. *I* am, got it? But back to the facts—we're talking about the relatively insignificant difference between your being a Forty-Eight when I'm *not* in the room, or a Forty-Nine or true Fifty when I am. But then suddenly, today, you soar up to fifty-eight and then sixty. Both of those numbers were after . . ." He cleared his throat. "There was physical contact. Between us." He resisted the instinct to clear his throat again. "That's easy enough to test, to see if it happens again. Although, I don't think I remember ever coming into contact with you. Before this. Even casually, like . . . shaking hands when we first met."

Diaz nodded. "That was intentional. When you first came to work at OI, I was early in the process of controlling my ability to deliver an electrical current. The *no touching* was for your protection."

"Ah," Elliot said. "Of course."

"You thought I had a problem with your being gay."

"I did think that," Elliot admitted.

"I didn't."

Elliot looked up from the computer at that, and chose his next words carefully. "Do you have a problem with *your* being gay?"

Diaz shook his head. "No."

"I mean, I know I just said I didn't want to get into a conversation about the factual value of your celibacy, but . . . Is it possible that you've embraced abstinence so *fiercely* because of—"

"No."

"So it doesn't bother you—the idea of going into that meeting with Dr. Bach in a few hours, and being outed—"

Maybe Diaz hadn't really been breathing that well after all, because he exhaled a large burst of air. It was almost a laugh. Almost. He started pacing again. "You seriously think I care about *that?*"

"Don't you?" Elliot asked.

"I've known that I was gay since I was *five*, okay?" Diaz turned and told him. "I've always been gay. I don't have a problem with being gay. What I have a problem with is putting *you* in this incredibly awkward position. And that was *before* I even knew I was *invading* your dreams with my broadcasts or thought projections or whatever the *fuck* it is that I'm doing to you when I *sleep!*"

"Whoa," Elliot said. "All right, okay. Let's talk about this dream-invasion thing, or so you call it. I'll go first and say that since those dreams are the highlight of my sex life—and I'm talking past, present, *and* future—you need to be aware that I do *not* object to them, whatsoever. As a matter of fact, as long as we're discussing it, I'd like to put in a request that next time? Since you get to control what happens, can you at least let *me* get off? I mean, it's kind of clear that you've been consciously stopping the dreams before—"

"Don't," Diaz said, his voice low. "Don't mock me."

"What?" Elliot said. "Wait, no, I'm not—"

"I get that it's just not that big of a deal for you," Diaz said roughly. "But it's *huge* for me."

"I'm sorry," Elliot apologized. "I didn't mean to be disrespectful."

"You *honestly* don't think that my celibacy has anything to do with my integration levels?" Diaz forced himself to sit down in the chair, but he was on the very edge of his seat as he looked at Elliot with the same intensity. "You think I should just say to hell with it?"

"Okay, *now* I think we're moving into radically inappropriate territory," Elliot said. "How am I supposed to answer that question?"

"Honestly."

"As a scientist," Elliot asked him, "or as a man who is dying to stage a reenactment of that dream from your grandmother's house?"

Diaz was silent, the muscle jumping in the side of his jaw.

"It's hard for me to separate the two," Elliot continued. "Sure, the scientist seems pretty adamant that your sudden surprise sixty wasn't *merely* the result of your putting your arms around me this morning, but that it came from . . . more *intimate* contact—and I know *you* know exactly what I'm referring to. But I'm human, Stephen—which means I'm biased. Are there ways to fight that bias? Of course. But do I really want to fight it? Good question."

Diaz still didn't say a word, but he was clearly listening, so Elliot kept going.

"Completely aside from *that,* here's the thing about testing whether celibacy increases your integration levels. We can't really test the impact of your doing nothing—although you've been doing that nothing for . . . how long now?"

Diaz exhaled again—just a little puff of air this time. "Fifteen fucking years."

Jesus, really? Elliot's years of being a researcher allowed him to hide his surprise, but he turned his attention to the computer, because he couldn't look at the other man. Especially since he had the urge to correct him and say that those had been, more accurately, fifteen *non*-fucking years. Instead, he clicked his way into and then through Diaz's file. And he found out . . . "That's exactly how long you've been here, at OI."

"That's correct."

From out of the corner of his eye, Elliot saw Diaz reach for his tea mug and take a fortifying sip.

"You came in as a Thirty," Elliot saw as he reviewed the file. A few quick clicks and the computer organized the data into a simple graph, showing Diaz's obvious and swift improvement in the first year he'd spent at OI. Within days of arrival, he was up to thirty-five; after eight months he was a Forty-two. After that, his increase in neural integration was slow and steady, leading to his current near-fifty.

Those facts made today's bump to sixty a major event.

"I was training out in California," Diaz volunteered, "and not getting anywhere. I came to OI for a workshop with Dr. Bach. A cleanse. I had a breakthrough, so . . . I stayed."

"I can see that." Elliot turned the computer so that Diaz could see the graph, too. "You know, as a researcher, I would look at this and be unable to come to any absolute conclusions about the cause of your abrupt improvement at that time. Yes, I can assume that as part of Dr. Bach's workshop, you embraced his no-sex suggestion. So *that* was probably different for you. But your diet—while you were here? That was different, too."

"No, it really wasn't," Diaz said.

"We buy locally grown fruits and vegetables," Elliot corrected him gently. "Your diet *was* different—assuming your training center in California didn't ship their produce in from Massachusetts, and I think we *can* assume that. It's certainly easy enough to check.

Other potential reasons: Our tap water is different. Even if you drink bottled water, you're still showering and brushing your teeth with the stuff that comes out of our reservoirs. You were at a different longitude and latitude—the sun hit your body at a slightly different angle. Sunrise and sunset were at different times of the day versus what you were used to in California. You probably experienced some form of jet lag upon arrival—that might have kick-started something. Oh yeah, and you were working with a new teacher—that's the Occam's Razor reason for your sudden improvement—you know, the best explanation for an event is usually the simplest? Did refraining from sex help you in your work with your new teacher? Yes, probably at first, it may absolutely have helped you to focus and make those initial great strides, but . . . For most of this time period, Stephen, your gains have been unremarkable. Until now."

Elliot pulled the computer back toward himself. "If it's okay with you, I'm going to request a jot scan from the OI mainframe," he continued. "Check your integration level. See where you are right this moment."

Diaz nodded, exhaling hard again as he set his mug back on the coaster.

"Here," Elliot told him. "Come over here. Because we're in your apartment, and you've got privacy shields in place . . ." Not everyone at OI opted for that feature. Elliot knew for a fact that Mac didn't give a crap, and actually preferred having standard med scans performed on her while she slept. But Stephen Diaz had had privacy shields installed. "You'll need to be closer to the computer, and I need access to the keyboard and monitor in order to . . ." With Diaz next to him, if he moved the computer slightly, the laptop's sensor could scan Diaz even as Elliot controlled the keyboard.

Of course, it also meant that Diaz needed to sit beside him on the couch.

Diaz slowly did just that as Elliot told him nothing he didn't already know. "Of course, with this kind of scan, done via your laptop, we're not able to be all that accurate. We'll have to go into the lab for precise to-the-decimal-point integration levels, but this will give us a rough sense of where you are, and what happens when we, um, change things up a bit."

"Change things up?" Diaz repeated as the jot scan was completed, and Elliot squinted at the screen.

"Whoa, okay, you're already up to fifty-five," Elliot reported. "Again, roughly. But that's still a marked increase in your normal . . ." He turned to look at Diaz. "How are you feeling? Any new abilities—can you belch fire or reanimate your dust bunnies—strike that, you have no dust bunnies." This was, quite possibly, the cleanest apartment he'd ever been in, in his life.

Diaz managed to laugh—just a little bit—as he shook his head. "Nothing I've identified. I mean, the world seems to be a little more in focus—colors are brighter, sounds are sharper."

"An increase in visual and aural acuity, okay. That's interesting." Elliot reset the computer to jot scan Diaz continuously. "How about telepathic abilities? Where are you with those?"

"I don't know."

"Why don't you try to read my mind?"

Diaz nodded, took a deep breath, and closed his eyes.

And Elliot felt the Greater-Than at the edge of his consciousness—felt a slight bump that quickly faded. Another, but it, too, was rapidly gone. On the monitor, Diaz's integration level dropped like a stone to fifty-four. *That* was interesting. Perhaps a reaction to failure . . . ?

"No," Diaz said, frowning as he shook his head. "Sorry. I'm not able to . . ."

"No worries," Elliot said. "Keep breathing. You're doing great. And okay, so now is when we're going to, you know, change things up. Because before, your telepathy with me was dependent on contact. And that wasn't the first time I made note of that. Remember what happened in the hall? After Mac plowed into you? I, um, kind of got a brainful when I tried to help you up."

Diaz closed his eyes again. "You must think that all I do is walk around thinking about . . ."

Elliot kept his eyes on the screen, watching as Diaz's integration level rose again to fifty-five. Wasn't *that* interesting? But it wasn't just the scientist in him who wanted to push Diaz outside of his comfort zone. It was the man who filled in Diaz's unfinished sentence with the words he'd said earlier, half in jest. "Doing me?"

It was that same guy who turned and looked directly at Stephen, with enough heat simmering in his eyes to let him know that such a possibility was more than okay with him.

Because it sure as hell would be.

And sure enough, when Elliot glanced back at the computer, Diaz was up to fifty-six this time. Fascinating. And they hadn't even touched.

But Diaz didn't look happy. In fact, he looked extremely grim.

"That *is* what you think, isn't it?" he said quietly. "That it's all about the sex, but . . . it's not. I've been in love with you, Elliot, for the past seven years."

FOURTEEN

Mac nose-dived back to fifty pretty freaking fast after leaving Shane in his third-floor suite in the barracks.

She went into her own apartment, just a floor above his, but on the other side of the building, showered, lay down, and with the help of some heavy-duty self-hypnosis, she slipped into body-healing REM sleep.

Elliot had been right about *that*, anyway—she'd needed it.

But forty minutes was plenty for emergency conditions and she woke up easily, without needing to set an alarm. The computer in her quarters was permanently set on voice recognition—she hated to type whether with her fingers or thumbs, she never invited anyone over, and she'd programmed the thing to recognize her ringtone so that it knew when she was on the phone. Except for those rare phone calls, anything she said while at home was directed to the computer. So even before she got out of bed, before she opened her eyes, she issued the order, "Activate full medical scan. CC the report to Elliot Zerkowski. Vocal confirmation when scan is complete, announce anything outside of personal normal with the exception of integration level. Give me that, regardless."

She waited, holding still, until the computer responded with, "Scan complete," and then she got out of bed and rummaged through her underwear drawer, looking for . . . Damn, all she had left were the wedgie-makers. Served her right for her failure to do her laundry.

She slipped them on along with a sports bra, and found—of course—no clean cargo pants in her closet. That left her with the choice of wearing motorcycle leathers or fishing through the dirty laundry for a pair of BDUs that weren't too gross. And since the leathers wouldn't do for what she had in mind . . .

"Current integration level fifty-point-two-four percent," the computer informed her.

"Hah!" she said. "See?"

"Command unclear," the computer chastised her mildly. "Please repeat."

"CC that report to Dr. Joseph Bach as well," Mac ordered as she found a pair of olive drabs that managed to not smell, at the bottom of the laundry pile. She pulled them on. "With an e-mail cover to him only, in a small font, reading, quote, *Unless otherwise directed will see you at fourteen hundred.*"

She put sneakers, instead of boots, on her feet.

Her usual black tank would work just fine—although, she was going to need some kind of sweater or . . .

She took a clingy red blouse—lightweight, made of a nearly filmy, gossamer fabric that she would never willingly be caught dead wearing—from the back of the closet. She'd bought it for a situation just like this one, and it would, absolutely, do the trick. She tossed it on the back of the kitchen stool where she'd draped her jacket earlier.

"Any response from either Zerkowski or Bach?" she asked her computer as she went into the bathroom.

"Negative," the computer told her.

Good. Even though it had only been a few minutes since the e-mail about her scan had been sent, it was likely that if either Bach or Elliot was awake, alert, and/or near his phone or computer, Mac would have been zapped an immediate WTF response.

Mac looked at herself in the mirror as she splashed water on her face and brushed her teeth, and as she did so, she adjusted, making her breasts even smaller than they normally were. She couldn't make them completely disappear, but she could certainly look more like a pubescent thirteen-year-old.

She put most of her excess body fat into her arms and shoulders, taking away their definition.

She changed her face, making it rounder, smoother, putting just enough baby fat back into her cheeks, around her eyes, and beneath her chin. She changed her underarms, too—smoothing and tightening her skin—because that was one of the telltale giveaway places where most women failed, when trying to hide their true age. Unless, of course, they had a skilled plastic surgeon—or Mac's particular talents.

Or unless they were a Destiny addict.

As she put her toothbrush back into the mug that she kept on the sink counter, she adjusted again. Back to her regular body shape and features. It was easy to do so without thinking—it was her own personal reset or default. But then she turned her back on the mirror and adjusted again, this time without looking—just by memory.

And when she turned and faced the mirror, that petulant tweenager gazed back at her again.

And for a half a second, it was weird. It was like she'd somehow traveled back in time to when she was fourteen and her brother Billy and her mom had died, and she'd moved into the shitty apartment that Janice and her son, Tim, shared with Mac's father. From the get-go, Janice had hated Mac, who'd never quite understood why.

But as Mac now stared into the surly uncommunicativeness of her adolescent eyes, she felt—for the first time—a twinge of sympathy for her father's third wife, who'd been dealing with financial stresses for years, and whose own son, Tim, was no huge prize. Janice's relationship with William Mackenzie was going south, too, and then Mac showed up, with a barge-load of attitude.

That had to have sucked.

Mac now adjusted back to herself, then sprayed a little detangler into her hair to lose the dried-while-she-was-napping look, going instead for simply messy.

She transferred her plastic scissors and wrist restraints into one of her pants pockets along with her lock pick and her keys, loosely folded the red blouse and stashed it in the flat pocket on her lower right leg, and she was good to go.

Mac grabbed her jacket and went out the door, not looking back.

———

Bach got off the elevator on the sixth floor.

He could sense that Anna was sleeping even as he approached the locked door to her apartment.

He felt her total exhaustion beneath an anxiety that was so solid and deep he didn't need Mac's empathic skills to feel it.

So he didn't ring the bell to wake her. He just stood there a moment, undecided—until he recalled just how eager Anna was to help find Nika, in any way possible.

So he clicked open the lock and let himself in. Anna had pulled the living room curtains, and they blocked all but a narrow ribbon of light, leaving the room dim.

Bach stood for a moment, aware that Anna had left her bedroom door open. He could hear the steady, quiet sound of her breathing.

There was paper over at the comm-station, in the printer. And he powered the thing up because his handwriting was lacking. But he changed his mind and instead of typing the note—which might have awakened her—he took a piece of paper from the tray, and used a pen from the desk drawer.

Anna, he wrote, working carefully to print the letters legibly. *I'm in the living room. I didn't want to wake you. Even though I still don't know how Nika managed to project those visual images you and I shared, I thought it would be a good idea to re-create some of the conditions—and perhaps make it easier for her to contact us again. I thought if I took a nap, this time in closer proximity to you, while you sleep, too . . .*

Well, I'm not sure what I think, other than that we're in un-charted territory, and anything's worth a try.

Wake me if you rise before me. If there's time, we'll return to the lab for additional tests. I have a meeting at 1400 (2 p.m.) with Elliot and my Fifties. If you like, you can be present for the end of that, when we're discussing the next step in our search for Nika.

They'd be talking about the girl only *after* they'd discussed the fact that Mac's integration level was up to sixty after having been intimate with one of their new Potentials.

And wasn't *that* going to be fun?

He signed the note, *Joseph,* but then added *Bach,* which looked stupid. How many Josephs did Anna know here at OI, anyway? Although he really couldn't remember the last time he'd signed a note Joseph or Joe instead of just Bach. Of course, he also couldn't remember the last time he'd handwritten a note instead of simply sending a text.

Dearest Annie,

I couldn't bear to wake you, but I had to get back home before my father discovers I'm gone . . .

Yeah. It had been a good long while.

When he stood up his back twinged—a reminder that it had been awhile since he'd last stretched—but he pushed away the vague residuals of discomfort as he carried the note toward Anna's open bedroom door.

It was darker in there, and he stopped for a second to adjust his eyes.

And there she was, her black curls spread out across the pillow, her eyes closed, and her lashes long and dark against her cheeks.

Something stirred inside of him and he tamped it gently back down because that was what he always did. Effortlessly. Uncon-sciously. Except this time he was aware of what he was doing. And a part of him watched, wondering what would happen if he ever let himself truly feel that desire.

This woman was attracted to him, too. Bach would have known that even if he hadn't spent time kicking around inside of her head. And after they found Nika, she was going to be living here at OI.

For years, probably, as Nika trained. They'd find Anna a job, if she wanted one—and Bach was willing to bet that she'd want one.

She was beautiful and smart and funny.

And she wasn't Annie, despite their similar names.

She was sleeping, curled up, on top of the spread, as if she'd only intended to lie down for a few minutes.

Bach knew that there was a throw on the back of the sofa in the living room, and he raised his hand to catch it effortlessly as he moved it toward him with his powers. He carried it into the bedroom with him, and he set the note on the bedside table where she'd see it right away when she awoke. He used his telekinesis to open the blanket and float it gently down to cover her without waking her.

He then went back into the living room and stretched for just a moment before he sat on the sofa and closed his eyes.

And he opened his mind to any and all possibilities—at least in terms of receiving contact from Nika.

It wasn't long before he, too, slept.

———

Shane dozed in the sunshine, on the lounge chair out on his previously inaccessible balcony.

He'd gotten the locked sliding door open within minutes of Michelle Mackenzie's leaving him in his cushy but freedom-restricting temporary quarters. His inner asshole needed to flip the bird to the people here at OI who wanted to keep him contained.

Or maybe he'd thought Mac would come running back when the alarms went off. But nothing happened. No bells, no buzzers. No flashing red lights, either—at least not that he could see—as he stepped out into the spring morning.

And that was fine. Because he wasn't going anywhere.

He just wanted to make it clear that if they really wanted to contain him, they'd have to chain him, literally, to the wall in some cell in their brig.

He assumed they had real cells in their brig, over in the security building. But then again, he would've assumed their security team had real weapons besides tranquilizer guns, so maybe they didn't.

Shane ate a bowl of cereal and had another of those perfect bananas as he sat and thought about everything that Mac had told him—that she'd used her superpowers to make him lust after her and that he wouldn't have looked twice at her if she hadn't engaged her voodoo. He supposed it *was* possible—in this new world he was in where drug addicts could fly and professional types with doctorate degrees could completely restrain a Navy SEAL with a simple thought.

But he didn't quite believe it.

And then he stopped thinking about it—but didn't stop thinking about Mac. She was a far more pleasant subject for his musings than his worries about Johnny and Owen and all of the other good men who'd served under his command in SEAL Team Thirteen.

Lucky Thirteen . . .

Shane let himself focus, instead, on his memories of last night as he put his head back and his feet up and closed his eyes.

His exhaustion levels were high, and he fell immediately into a deep sleep, convinced that someone—hopefully Mac herself—would come to get him in a few hours, for that mysterious meeting in Bach's office, wherever that was.

He hadn't been asleep for all that long when he woke up suddenly. He was instantly alert, which wasn't a big surprise. He'd trained extensively, as a SEAL, to have all synapses firing before he opened his eyes. And this time, when he opened his eyes, he found he was already on his feet.

He knew exactly where he was, and why he'd woken up. Mac was in his apartment. He could practically feel her. He turned toward the sliding screen door that separated him from the living room, expecting to see her standing there, glowering at him. But his apartment was empty.

It was then that he heard the sound of footsteps on the pathway that led through the garden to the parking lot.

And there she was, three stories below him.

And again, at just the sight of her, Shane's heart did another gymnastics routine. And he found himself smiling.

"Hey!" he called, his voice rusty from sleep. He cleared his throat. "Mackenzie!"

Her shoulders tightened and she spun back toward the building, looking first toward the door she'd just exited. But it didn't take her long to find him, her gaze jerking up to his balcony.

"Where are you going, Michelle?" he asked, leaning his elbows on the railing.

"What are you doing out there?" she countered.

"Just getting some air. I thought Elliot grounded you."

"My integration levels are back down," Mac told him. "I've been cleared to leave. I'll be back in time for the meeting. Get your ass back inside."

"Yeah, I don't think so," Shane said, swinging his legs over so that he was outside of the railing. It was a piece of cake to climb down from this balcony to the one below, and then to dangle and drop to the ground. He landed lightly on his feet as he smiled at her. "I'd rather go with you."

She made a sound of disgusted outrage, then said, "Like hell." But since she didn't reach for her phone to call either security or her buddy Elliot, Shane knew she'd been stretching the truth with that *cleared to leave* crap.

"Where are you going?" he asked again. "I know this has something to do with finding that girl. Nika Taylor. Maybe I can help."

"Look," she said. "Navy. I get that you're a rule-breaker. You're a badass, blacklisted, cage-fighting rebel. Point made. But you can't help—"

"Come on, we do this right, no one will know I was gone," Shane persisted. He knew her words were designed to piss him off—calling him a *badass rebel* when he knew she thought of him as a Boy Scout—so he ignored them. "I looked at the security at the front gate. You're checked going in, not out. We'll just breeze past the guard—"

Mac shook her head, absolute. "No. Nuh-uh."

"Of course, your alternative is to leave me behind," he pointed out. "Possibly get stopped—wow, that would suck—before you even reach the gate."

"Possibly," she repeated, looking hard at him with those crazy-beautiful eyes.

Shane nodded, turning away to squint out at the budding trees in the garden. It *was* a lovely day. "I'd say there's a pretty high probability."

"You're going to call security on me," Mac said, and it was clear she didn't believe he'd do it. In fact, she dug into her pants pocket and took out her phone. Held it out to him. "Okay. Go on. Tell on me. Tattle. Turn me in."

And just like he'd called her bluff, she'd called his.

"I'm not going to do that," he admitted.

She put her phone back and turned to leave. "Get back up-stairs."

"But I *am* going with you," Shane said. "You can keep me out of your car, but that's okay. I can ride on the top. Although *that* might raise some eyebrows as we approach the gate."

Mac turned to look back at him, and he could see that she knew he was serious. *This* he'd do. Absolutely.

"I know you're taking a car instead of your bike—otherwise you'd be wearing boots," he told her, pointing to her sneakers.

Her gaze never left his face. "So this is blackmail," she said. "You're blackmailing me. I take you with me, or I'm busted. That's pretty low, Laughlin."

He laughed. "I'm sorry, but aren't you the woman who recently confessed to tricking me into having sex with her?"

That hurt her. Shane didn't have any special talents when it came to empathy, but even *he* could tell that one had hit below the belt. So he quickly apologized, "Wow, that was harsh. I'm sorry. I think it was supposed to be funny or clever or—"

"I don't need any help," Mac told him flatly, "with what I'm doing. I'm going to the hospital ER, all right? The same one that

Nika Taylor went to. When I get there, I'll go in as a child. I'll pay in cash, they'll med scan me, and I'll get on the Organization's radar."

"You're setting yourself up as bait to be kidnapped the way Nika was," Shane realized. "But, honey, I'm sorry, no one on this planet is going to mistake you even for a sixteen-year-old. It's just not going to happen."

Except, Jesus, she changed herself into a kid—right there, while she was looking at him. Her chest flattened and her face became that of a girl, not a woman.

Shane took a step back, involuntarily, and she laughed—and turned back into herself.

"Okay, so I'm wrong about that," he said quickly. "But . . . They're really just going to let you walk in there, to the ER, without an adult? Aren't there rules—"

"I'm going to be my own mother," she said. "I have another shirt to put on. I've done it before—people are too busy to pay attention. Mom's parking the car, or she's in the bathroom, or taking a phone call . . ."

"But won't it be easier," Shane asked, "if you're there with your, I don't know, your mother's boyfriend, or your Uncle Shane?"

"What's the deal?" Mac asked him abruptly. "You're tired— I can tell you're still tired. Why is it so important that you come with?"

"Because I know I can help. Because I *want* to help."

She laughed, but Shane knew that it wasn't because she found any of this funny. "You want to come," she told him, "only because whatever I did to you still hasn't worn off."

Shane laughed, too, genuinely amused. "Yeah, I don't think so. I mean, even if it hadn't, that you-being-suddenly-thirteen thing would've done the trick."

"No, it wouldn't. You'd still want me. You'd just hate yourself for it." Mac's mouth tightened. "How about we both just climb back up into your apartment? I'll give you what you want, and then you'll let me leave."

"Hmm," he said, and for the first time he could actually feel it—the whatever it was that she did to make herself more attractive. It was crazy. He could feel himself responding—shifting a little closer, his pulse quickening, his body actually stirring from the increased blood flow. He forced himself to take another step back, away from her. "Tempting, but, no. I'd much rather take the field trip. Besides, if I touch you, your what-cha-ma-call-it, your integration level goes through the roof—I'm pretty sure that's a given. You'll have to wait for it to drop back down."

He could see from her face that he was right about that.

"This way, as long as we don't touch," Shane continued, "you can pretend you don't realize that just *standing* next to me elevates you, right? *And* I'd also like to point out that hospitals have security cameras and metal detectors at the door. If someone gets suspicious, they'll definitely realize there's only one of you, which could come back and bite you on the ass. So let's just do this the easy way. I'll walk in with you, we'll get this done, and then walk back out."

Mac turned abruptly, heading for the parking lot. "Slow me down, and I'll leave you behind."

"I wouldn't dream of it," Shane said, keeping his smile inward as he jogged to catch up.

———

Stephen Diaz closed his eyes.

He'd just taken the biggest leap of faith ever in his life and told the man that he adored that he did, in fact, adore him. *That is what you think, isn't it. That it's all about the sex, but . . . it's not. I've been in love with you, Elliot, for the past seven years.*

But now Elliot was uncharacteristically silent. He was no doubt remembering the nonstop action that Stephen had broadcast into his dreams, which surely made it seem as if, despite what Stephen had just said, it *was* all about sex.

Elliot finally spoke. "You ever going to look at me again?"

So Stephen opened his eyes.

Elliot was sitting there, beside him on the sofa, and behind his glasses, his blue eyes were soft. "That's better," he said quietly.

The heat that had been in his eyes just a few moments ago was gone. It had been replaced by . . . kindness?

Oh, God, Elliot was going to tell Stephen that his confession was flattering but entirely crazy, and that there was no room in his life for insanity, only he was going to do it gently, kindly, patiently and with humor—the way he always did everything, and—

"I'm not sure what to say," Elliot admitted. "I mean, you're this . . . paragon. Everyone's just automatically in love with you. Including me—but it's never been a real possibility, connecting with you that way, because of who you are. Never. I *never* thought . . . I never even *hoped* . . . I'm not even sure I really know you, Stephen—the real you. I didn't even know you were gay."

Here it came. The *I think we should just be friends* speech. Stephen's heart had leapt at that *including me*—but that absolute-sounding *never* had put him back on guard. He braced himself for the disappointment. Forcing himself to keep his eyes open, he nevertheless couldn't hold Elliot's gaze for a second longer. He had to look down at the floor.

"But I'd very much like to get to know you," Elliot said quietly. "And then, we can . . . I don't know. See where it goes?"

Stephen looked up at him, his surprise no doubt apparent on his face, because Elliot laughed and added, "Seriously, you thought I might, what? Shut you down cold? You *do* know who you are, don't you? This higher-integration thing hasn't created some kind of weird amnesia, has it? You want to take a minute and go look in the bathroom mirror?"

Stephen laughed, too, as he let himself gaze into Elliot's eyes. "The way you were leading up to it, I was expecting—dreading—that you were going to *friend* me." His heart was actually pounding, and he wondered, inanely, if Elliot could tell that from his ongoing jot scan. Of course, he could. Except the researcher hadn't looked at the computer's monitor once since Stephen had dropped his L-bomb.

Elliot's gaze dropped to Stephen's mouth—just for a brief moment. Just long enough for Stephen to know that Elliot was thinking about kissing him—which no doubt sent his pulse rate soaring even higher.

"But I do want us to be friends," Elliot told him, back to being serious again. "I'd like for us to be friends. It's really up to you, though, with your whole celibacy-as-part-of-your-training deal, whether or not we move beyond that friendship. I have to confess that I'm just not enough of a romantic to be *more* than friends with someone I can't be intimate with."

"I would never ask you to do that," Stephen said.

"Says the man who's apparently loved me for years without getting any," Elliot pointed out. "At least not that I remember."

"You were married."

"Only at first."

Stephen was, indeed, aware that Elliot's divorce had gone through three long years ago. He shook his head. "I know. I just thought that . . ."

As he trailed off, Elliot lifted one eloquent eyebrow, waiting for him to continue. And as Stephen looked into his eyes, he knew that—with this man—the truth was always the way to go.

So instead of making it be about Elliot's need for a little time and space after his heartbreak—which *was* true, but only to a point—Stephen admitted, "I thought I couldn't allow myself to have a relationship like the one I wanted to have with you. I thought I had to deprive myself—to abstain from that part of life—to become more fully integrated. And yes, I *was* willing to make that sacrifice."

"But now . . . ?"

Stephen held Elliot's gaze. He didn't waver. "Just sitting next to you, I'm at fifty-six. It seems that I was wrong, and that getting closer to you will actually *help* me more fully integrate." He swiftly added, "And when I say that, I don't mean to sound as if I'm discounting how important the idea of having this relationship is to me, on every other level. Because it is. It's massively important. Nearly as important as my training—and I know you understand what that means to me. You live and breathe this job, too."

"I do understand," Elliot said quietly.

"I view this as potentially the biggest win/win of my life," Stephen told him, then added another truth. "The celibacy thing was wearing me out—which is . . . not very romantic, I know. But it's true."

Elliot smiled at that. "I appreciate your honesty. About all of this. More than you could possibly know."

"I *could* know," Stephen told him and held out his hand in a silent invitation.

Elliot looked down at it, and then up into Stephen's eyes, his expression unreadable. "Point of no return. You know what happens when you touch me." He made the sound of an explosion.

Stephen didn't take back his hand. "Point of no return," he agreed, past his heart, which was securely lodged in his throat.

Elliot smiled again—hot and fierce. And that heat was back in his eyes as, no longer hesitant, he took what Stephen offered, clasping their hands, intertwining their fingers.

The connection was immediate—and intense. Stephen was deep inside of Elliot's incredibly complex mind, which was disorienting and dizzying, but somehow already familiar and wonderful— a rapid-fire barrage of both conscious and half-formed thoughts, of emotions and reactions and instincts and beautiful reason.

Sex was in there.

Elliot was thinking about it—Stephen knew it would have been kind of hard not to, considering. There were shreds of memories of his fantastic dream from Grandma's house flying around, along with plenty of other images—and not all had come from Stephen's dreams, which was both comforting and terrifying.

But mostly Elliot's thoughts were bouncing from that first time they'd met—he remembered it clearly, and no doubt about it, their attraction had been immediate and mutual—to the way he'd stumbled upon Stephen in the exam room last night. *Don't make me come and find you . . .* Stephen could see that Elliot understood, now, why Stephen had laughed the way he had. But back then? He'd honestly had no clue.

Elliot smiled, now, into Stephen's eyes. *So, here you are. Hello. That was easy enough this time.*

I guess there has to be contact for the telepathy to work, Stephen hypothesized. *What's my integration level?*

Elliot turned to look at the computer. *Sixty. Damn, Skippy. That was fast.*

Stephen moved his leg, just a little, so his thigh was pressed against Elliot's. "You want to see what happens when I kiss you?"

His intention was to release Elliot's hand so he could take off the man's glasses, but Elliot beat him to it, setting them on the table as he turned to smile at Stephen.

"I very much do," he murmured, his gaze dropping to Stephen's mouth. But when Stephen leaned in, he backed off. *Please just . . . Reassure me that this is more than an experiment for you. I mean, I get that it's an experiment. And in the name of science, I support that, you know I do. I just need you to know that, for me, it's a hell of a lot more, too. I know I joke, and I pretend, but . . . I wouldn't do this with just anyone.*

You can't read it? Stephen asked in response, his heart back in his throat. *What I'm feeling?* God, he was feeling so much of it, too. Elation. Euphoria. Terror—in a good way. Heat.

But Elliot shook his head. *I can sense you in my mind, which is very nice, and I can read the thoughts and images that you put there, but . . . It's not like it was downstairs—when you seemed to be unconsciously projecting. This feels more organized and controlled. As if you're . . . Are you guarding?*

"Not intentionally," Stephen spoke aloud as he closed his eyes and focused on finding and unclenching his mental shields. There was no longer a reason to hide himself, to hide anything that he was feeling—not from Elliot. And slowly, rustily, he felt himself start to unravel and then, in a rush, like dominoes in a row, his guard came undone.

"Holy crap!" Elliot's grip tightened on his hand, and Stephen opened his eyes to find the other man laughing. *Yeah, this is more*

*like it. Yeah, this is . . . This works. This is . . . You . . . You're . . .
Whoa. You were serious . . .*

Stephen didn't try to organize any of what he was thinking and feeling—he just let it blast free, and he could tell that Elliot was doing the same.

Elliot's joy was nearly tangible, and he was trying to figure out what should happen next—should he go ahead and kiss Stephen and follow wherever that led, or should he back away and give them both some time to adjust to this whole crazy idea?

Stephen took the question out of his hands.

Although, this time when he leaned forward to kiss Elliot, Elliot met him halfway.

And he tasted like coffee and sheer exhilaration as Stephen licked his way further into Elliot's mouth, and Elliot pulled him close, closer, his hands against Stephen's back, against his neck— his long, graceful, artist's fingers in his hair.

It was better than any dream, better than he'd ever imagined, and he wanted . . . He *needed* . . .

He let Elliot push him back onto the sofa, his thigh between Stephen's legs, his body pressed against him. And it felt so freaking great—not just what he was feeling, but what Elliot was feeling, as well. He not only felt Elliot's hands—in his hair, on his neck, on his chest—but he felt every sensation Elliot was experiencing, too, their accelerated heartbeats now pounding in sync.

The implications of that left him breathless.

But then Elliot pulled out of their kiss to look down at him, breathing hard. He spoke aloud. "God, I'm afraid of messing this up. We've got this meeting with Dr. Bach in just a few hours, and part of me is saying—"

"Go for it," Stephen filled in. He could feel Elliot's erection against his leg, and he could feel his own against Elliot. Hot *damn.* "I know. But the other part—"

"Wants it to be perfect. I feel like I should, I don't know, maybe make you dinner first?" He was touching Stephen's hair again, and God, that felt so good . . .

"I didn't know you liked to cook," Stephen said, closing his eyes. There was nothing in any of Elliot's memories about cooking, although the man *did* like good food—good restaurants. His favorite was a place in the South End and . . . To hell with that. *Kiss me again.*

Elliot laughed as he did just that. *I don't like to cook—in fact, I hate it. I think part of me thinks this shouldn't be so easy. I should have to suffer and, I don't know, earn it. Earn you. You're unbelievably delicious, by the way.*

Stephen laughed as he kissed Elliot longer, deeper, one hand slipping up beneath the back of his T-shirt, his palm against the smooth warmth of the other man's skin. He felt it and he *felt* it. God . . . *You are, too.*

Yeah, this is beyond great—to be able to feel what you're feeling . . .

Stephen pushed himself up against Elliot, and they both groaned. And Elliot laughed. *Oh my God. To hell with everything.* He started unbuttoning Stephen's shirt, even as Stephen yanked Elliot's T-shirt up and over his head, as he kicked off his sandals and half-sat up to try to help Elliot by shaking his shirt down his arms.

He saw what Elliot saw—the clearly defined muscles of his chest and abs. He knew he was attractive, but through Elliot's eyes, he was a god. It was almost embarrassing.

It is *embarrassing.* Elliot was viewing himself through Stephen's filter, too, as Stephen kissed him again, pulling the other man's head down toward his mouth with one hand while he went for his belt with the other. *I'm just not that hot.*

Yes, you are, Stephen thought back at him, as he continued to kiss the hell out of him and unfasten his buckle.

No, really, I'm not.

Stephen wasn't wearing a belt, and he felt Elliot pop open the metal button of his jeans, felt his fingers against Stephen's zipper, trying to force it down—no easy task, considering how tightly his arousal was pressing against it. And he let go of Elliot for just long enough to help him get that zipper down, to push both his pants and his shorts just far enough down his thighs to free himself from their confines. He stopped kissing the man long enough to tell him, "This is what you do to me. You—and only you," as he took Elliot's hand and wrapped those elegant fingers, hard, around himself.

The sensation nearly blew off the top of his head—it had been *so* long since he'd been touched by anyone, let alone someone for whom he had such deep feelings. He'd wondered over the past years, every now and then, if his body would remember how to do this, should he ever decide to return to a life where he embraced rather than shut out his sexuality.

But Elliot's deft touch, stroking him—not roughly but by no means gentle—made him moan, and God, he wanted . . .

Elliot knew exactly what he wanted, because Elliot was inside of his head, the same way he was inside of Elliot's, the same way he knew what Elliot wanted—which was to let Stephen come, just fast and furious, with almost no finesse, and no reciprocation.

Come on . . .

Elliot stroked him faster now, harder, as Stephen reached for the other man, wanting at least to give as good as he was getting, but Elliot slid out of his grasp, slipped down between Stephen's legs, off the couch, and onto the floor, pushing Stephen's jeans down farther. And Stephen sat up to try to tell him that *wasn't* what he wanted, except God, then it *was* as the other man took him into his mouth.

And that was that. It was over. Stephen surrendered, lying back against the cushions of the sofa, his fingers in Elliot's hair, allowing himself, for the first time in close to forever, to just *feel.*

But it wasn't just the sensation of the warmth and wetness of Elliot's mouth, or the softness of his lips, the insistent pressure of his tongue. It was the pleasure Elliot was feeling, too. The happiness. The optimism. The joy . . .

The love.

Stephen's wasn't the only one whose world had changed in a heartbeat. Elliot's had, too. And the way Elliot saw it, the promise of the future was hanging out there for them both, gleaming and beautiful and bright.

Come on, Stephen, just let go . . .

And Stephen came in a rush that was so intense, it made him cry out. It raced and roared through him and tore him apart, yet despite the sensation of shattering into a million pieces, Elliot was right there with him; connected. Always connected.

I'm here, right here, I've got you . . . Breathe, just breathe—you're okay.

Stephen felt Elliot move, carefully touching him the entire time, so as not to break their bond. He felt the sofa cushion compress as Elliot sat back beside him, and when he opened his eyes, Elliot *was* right there, smiling at him.

He spoke aloud. "You okay?"

I'm not hiding anything from you, Stephen told him. *I'm never going to hide anything from you.* "I'm very much okay."

Elliot pulled the computer closer. "You're . . . Only at sixty-one. Funny, I'd thought we'd gotten you up to a hundred with that."

Sixty-one's not an only.

"No, I know that," Elliot said. He didn't form the full thought, but it was clear that he thought it was interesting. That maybe it wasn't so much the sex that had elevated Stephen's integration levels, as it was the intimate connection—and that had begun long before their clothes had started coming off. He felt Stephen's awareness following his thoughts, and added, "And that's not to say it's *not* the sex." He glanced back at Stephen. "I feel the need to point out, that in order to be scientifically accurate—to get a true comparison to your history of celibacy—we really should get it on, nonstop, for the next fifteen years."

Stephen laughed. And he pushed himself up off of the couch as he kicked his jeans and shorts off from where they'd settled around his ankles. Even though he'd broken their connection, he could see the heat in Elliot's eyes as the other man looked up at him.

"Then what are we waiting for?" Stephen asked.

And although he could've moved Elliot purely with his mind, he instead picked the other man up in a fireman's hold, and, laughing, carried him to his bed.

FIFTEEN

Nika awoke with a gasp, immediately aware that she was no longer strapped down.

She was out of bed and on her feet before she realized that wasn't the only thing that had changed. Her bed was no longer a hospital bed, and she was no longer in that workhouse-infirmary-style room with all of those other girls.

In fact, she was in what looked to be a very fancy hotel room, and she was quite alone.

She could hear herself breathing—raggedly and almost as if she were crying—as she hurried over to the door.

But it was securely locked, with the hinges on the outside.

She hadn't expected to be able to just walk away, except maybe she had, because now she *was* crying because, God, she wanted to go home!

Okay. Okay. Think.

Why had they moved her? What were they going to do to her now?

She had no idea how she'd gotten here. She'd finally fallen asleep and . . .

As Nika tried to stanch her tears, she looked down at her arm and saw that the port that the man with the scars had implanted there had been replaced by something far more modern looking. There was some kind of drug attached to it now. It looked like the insulin pump her mother's friend Misha had had. She was afraid to poke at it, for fear it would trigger some kind of sedative—and she wanted to stay awake as long as she possibly could.

Her skin around this new port had been neatly stitched.

She was, she realized, completely clean—even her hair had been washed. Her soiled hospital gown had been swapped for a long white nightgown of the softest cotton. As she peed in the pristine bathroom, though, she realized that her panties were gone—which was both drafty and creepy. She didn't want to think about the scar-faced man seeing her naked—or worse that man named Devon Caine, who'd helped to kidnap her.

But it was unlikely either of them had been responsible for her new de-grimed condition. She looked at her stitches again as she flushed and washed her hands. Yeah, it was likely a real nurse or doctor had been involved.

There was no phone in the bathroom—or in the main room, on the bedside table, either. Nika hurried over to the curtains and drew them back to reveal a carefully sealed plate-glass window—there was no way to open it, and she doubted she could break it.

Besides, even if she did, she was up on a very high floor. God, the street was tiny below, the cars like toys, the people walking on the sidewalks even smaller.

She looked out at the horizon and . . . Wherever she was, the window overlooked a part of the city that she didn't recognize. Of course, for all she knew, she wasn't even in Boston anymore.

She leaned against the glass, trying not to cry again, as she attempted to get a glimpse of the type of building she was in. It was all steel and glass—again, nothing she recognized.

There was a CoffeeBoy way down below, on the corner across the street, but that didn't mean a thing. She could've been in *any* skyscraper in any city in America and there probably would've been a CoffeeBoy on a nearby corner. A Burger Deelite was next door to the C-Boy on the street below, and her stomach rumbled—until she realized there was a tray with food—still hot and delicious-smelling—on the desk there, near the window.

She lifted the metal covers to find a bowl of creamy New England fish chowder, a rather wan-looking salad, a thick cut of steak and french fries, complete with a miniature bottle of catsup and tiny salt and pepper shakers.

She had no idea how long this was going to last, or whether she'd ever get food again, so she dug in, turning to face that window, thinking about the other, somewhat distant skyscrapers she could see, and wondering if anyone would care—let alone see and be able to read it—if she wrote a big SOS on the glass.

Probably not.

Still, Nika opened the catsup and got to work.

———

"So how old were *you*, when you were recruited?" Shane asked.

Mac glanced over at him as she drove. They'd made it out of OI, past the gate, and were halfway to the hospital before he'd so much as cleared his throat.

"I guess it was too much to hope that we could make it all the way there without forcing the small talk," she said, meeting his eyes only briefly before she turned her attention back to the road.

He took up too much space in the compact car with his broad shoulders and snug-fitting T-shirt, with his blue eyes and his too-handsome face—that perfect, straight nose, his Boy Scout haircut, that mouth that managed to be sexy even when it wasn't quirking up into a smile, even when, like now, it was tight with determination and resolve.

If it looks like a hero and quacks like a hero . . .

Even the stubble on Shane's chin glinted with a really heroic shade of reddish gold.

"That wasn't small talk," he countered. "That was—and is—me, genuinely interested in finding out where you come from."

And Mac knew that. She could feel it, along with his equally sincere desire that she'd no doubt re-sparked when she'd suggested she go up to his room with him.

That had been stupid of her. Her effect on him was never going to wear off if she kept using it to try to manipulate him. Of course, maybe that was what her deviously selfish subconscious wanted.

"Juvie," she told him flatly. "I was in solitary detention, for fighting, and one day the door finally opened, I was taken down the hall to one of the counseling rooms, and Dr. Bach was standing there."

It had been just like that hokey old saying—the first day of the rest of her life. But no way was she telling Shane that, not when there were still days she couldn't quite believe it herself.

"I was fifteen," Mac continued. "And I was in for manslaughter. I figure those are the questions you're going to ask next. His name was Tyler Cooper. The dead kid. He and one of his dickhead friends—Tim, who also happened to be my own loving stepbrother—roofied me. My metabolism has always been fast, and the drug went through my system more quickly than they expected. I woke up to find myself naked, with the pair of them fighting over who was gonna go first—with the gangbang—which wasn't okay with me. In that moment of disoriented panic, I discovered my previously undocumented telekinesis. The dickheads went flying and Ty, unfortunately, landed wrong and snapped his neck. His parents were rich, their lawyer was stellar, and I make a lousy victim, even dressed in a skirt and button-down white cardigan. There was no trace of the drug in my system, and I apparently hadn't been raped yet. Not that night, anyway. That plus Tim testified against me with some pretty damning video evidence that somehow managed to prove I was a slut, so . . . I was found guilty and got locked up."

Shane was silent.

Good. She was trying to shut him up.

But then he said, "You should let me drive. Before we pull into the hospital parking lot. In case there are cameras—and there will be. There are cameras everywhere these days. Why don't you stop up here at the Pharma-City. I'll drive, and you can . . . Do whatever you did to look like a kid, so that's not caught on video, either."

It was a good idea, but Mac didn't say a word. She just signaled to turn right, and went into the drugstore parking lot, pulling into a slot away from the doors.

It wasn't until they were both getting out to switch seats, that she asked over the top of the car, "You *do* have a valid driver's license?"

He laughed a little. "Yeah, they don't take that away when you're blacklisted, although they probably wish they could, right?"

They both went around the front of the little car, with Shane still smiling at her, which was almost as disconcerting as him not questioning her further about Ty and Tim and the horribleness of her home life that had resulted in her becoming a ward of Dr. Joseph Bach.

It was unbelievably refreshing that he hadn't pressed. He hadn't recoiled in horror, either, or even offered words of sympathy—or worse, pity.

And it wasn't until they got back in, seatbelts fastened, that he spoke. "I'm not afraid of you," he said matter-of-factly, as he adjusted the rearview window. "I know you think that you're some kind of . . . What's the word you used? Badass. And me, I'm a Boy Scout. You've made that pretty damn clear. But—aside from always being prepared—I don't scare easily." He met her gaze steadily. "And I'm actually kind of insulted that you think you could tell me what you just told me, and then believe I'd judge *you* harshly."

"Most people do."

"I'm not most people," he told her quietly. "It sucks that it happened to you. And I suspect there's more to it—that it was way worse than what you told me. I couldn't help but notice how you intentionally didn't mention your parents—"

"My father and his wife believed Tim's story. That I seduced him and Ty."

"And your mother?" Shane asked.

"Dead," Mac told him. "Just drive," she added, and turned herself into a thirteen-year-old, even as she looked back at him.

"Don't like to talk about her, huh? Fair enough," Shane said. "But damn, that *is* freaky." He finally looked away from her to put the car into gear and back out of the parking spot. "And stop it. I felt you ramp up the sex appeal voodoo, or whatever it is, just to prove . . . Well, I don't know what you want to prove, because I know that you've been at OI for twelve years, which makes you . . . twenty-seven, which is well above the age of consent, regardless of what you look like. Besides, it's still you in there that I'm attracted to. It's your brain, your mind. Your heart and soul."

"So what are you saying?" Mac mocked him, as they pulled back out onto the street. "That after one night of good sex, you actually think you *love* me?"

As soon as the word left her lips, she knew it was a mistake to use it. But as soon as she did, she knew why.

She wanted to remind herself that despite the sensitivity Shane had shown in talking about her fucked-up childhood, that as nice and as smart and as funny as he was, his intense attraction to her wasn't all that different from Ty's and from Tim's. Or from her own freaking father's.

But Shane didn't take her bait and profess his undying love. Instead, he glanced at her again. "*Great* sex, not merely good."

"*That's* what you quibble about?" she asked, as he signaled to go right, following the faded blue H-for-hospital sign. "Out of everything I just said . . . ?"

"It *was* great," he insisted. "And love? Well, it's hard to define, isn't it? And it's certainly subjective, so . . . I *can* tell you this: I was engaged once, and that wasn't a relationship I entered into casually. But I never wanted Ashley even remotely close to the way I want you. And I'm not just talking about sex. I want to get inside your head, too."

Close enough for jazz. "Hello," Mac said. "Crazy-talk alert. Are you listening to yourself? Can you hear what you're saying?"

"Yeah," he countered, "but I'm not sure *you* can. What's the harm in seeing where this thing goes, in taking the time to explore—"

"The *harm*," she shot back, "is that it's *not real*. Everything you're feeling—you only *think* you're feeling it. Laughlin. Seriously. Engage your big brain here. People don't fall in love with a stranger they pick up in a bar, after a single night of hot sex. And when they hear the words *found guilty of manslaughter,* they back away. They don't talk about *exploring*—"

"*Hot,* I'll agree with."

"My point," Mac stressed, "is that anything that you think you feel about my *brain, my mind, my heart and my soul*"—she threw his own words back at him—"is purely a result of my *voodoo.* Exactly like that chubby I just gave you."

Shane smiled at that, even as he kept his eyes carefully on the road, following the signs to the emergency room. "Wood," he said. "I prefer the euphemism *wood.* And it *is* interesting how quickly you can make that happen. Is it everyone in the room who's affected—is it a proximity thing?" He pointed out the windshield toward an old man on the sidewalk. "Is he experiencing a sudden physiological reaction—which could be disappointing if he's been suffering from erectile dysfunction. He's probably calling his wife right now. *Mildred, quick, put on that negligee, I'm on my way home! I've finally gotten it up!* But then whoops, we're out of range, and he's like, *Oh. Damn. Never mind.*"

Mac laughed despite herself as Shane turned up the driveway, and into a circular drop-off in front of the clearly marked ER doors. But this was good. Maybe the scientific details would make him understand.

"It depends on how sensitive he is. It's aimed, when I actively do it," she admitted as he braked to a stop. "But there's definitely overflow. And some people are more susceptible than others. I mean, when I walked into that bar, I must've had it turned on, at least a little bit, even though I didn't really know it. But you picked up on it. There're definitely degrees. I can ramp it way up, or dial it down. I can shut it off, entirely. Like right now. It's off."

"And yet its aftereffect lingers on," he murmured.

"But that's okay, because you're all about *exploring* where this *thing* is going to go," she mocked him again. It was that or start crying. She unlocked the car door. "I'm going in while you park. The story is I was climbing a tree in the backyard and I fell. I hit the back of my head and knocked myself out—very briefly. I say

I'm fine, but you're freaked. My mother's at work, you insisted on bringing me here for a med scan, so I'm pissed at you." She got out. "The car's equipped with theft-proof tracking devices, by the way."

Shane leaned over to look at her through the open door. "I'm not going to steal your car."

"Yeah," she said, "because it's got theft-proof—"

"That's not why," he said. "I'll be right behind you."

"Whatever," Mac said as she slammed the door with the proper amount of thirteen-year-old disdain to make the security guard glance over at her and then dismiss her immediately.

She turned away from the car and tromped toward the hospital, aware that Shane was watching her—she could feel his eyes on her back, along with his concern and his fucking un-real affection.

It was nearly as palpable a sensation as his still-lingering desire.

———

It was hard—now that the passion was spent, now Elliot was lying there in this bed that he'd been in so many times in his literally wildest dreams—to keep his mind from racing.

Specifically, it was hard not to think about his ex-husband Mark.

He'd cheated on Elliot—Mark had. More than once.

How often? Elliot didn't know, didn't want to know. It hurt him to know, even all these years later.

"I didn't realize that," Stephen murmured, there beside him in that big bed.

And Elliot knew—because they were still touching, still connected, with his back spooned against Stephen's broad chest, Stephen's enormous arms around him, his presence heavy and so beautifully warm in Elliot's mind—that the Greater-Than hadn't heard any of the details of the divorce when it had happened.

At the time, Elliot had hidden behind wiping his glasses as he'd muttered something about Mark finding another job down in Atlanta, and Stephen hadn't pressed. He *had*, however, been simultaneously dismayed and elated at the fact that Elliot was coming to live, full-time, at OI. Two doors down from him in the barracks, on the very same floor . . .

How many times in the past three years had Stephen walked past Elliot's door and been tempted to stop, to knock . . . ?

For a struggling celibate, a happily married man had been the perfect love interest. Stephen had worshipped Elliot from afar, knowing that his own strict code of honor would never allow either of them to get any closer, but then—

"Worshipped?" Elliot said, shifting onto his back, turning to face Stephen.

Stephen smiled back at him, his green eyes lit with amusement. *It's kind of crazy, isn't it? I start out following your thoughts, and suddenly we're inside of* my *head. But, man, he hurt you badly, didn't he?* He leaned forward and kissed Elliot. *I would never hurt you like that.*

Elliot closed his eyes, losing himself in the softness of this incredible man's mouth, except, shit, that was exactly what Mark had promised, too and—

I AM NOT MARK.

Holy crap. Elliot pulled back, far enough away from Stephen to break their connection. "*That* was adamant."

Stephen looked as surprised as Elliot felt as he, too, sat up. "Sorry," he said. "I'm just . . . I'm *not* Mark. I won't lie to you."

"You kind of can't," Elliot pointed out. Every time they touched . . . So much for keeping secrets.

Stephen's eyes were now somber in his almost too-handsome face. He ran a hand through his dark hair. "It makes it twice as frustrating that you don't believe me."

"People change over time," Elliot tried to explain. "Or, you know, maybe they *think* they know you, and . . . It's only later that they find out they're in love with some fantasy version of you that you can't possibly live up to."

Stephen smiled at that. "I know you think I don't, but I *do* know you," he said.

"Oh, yeah? Quick, what's my favorite color?"

"Blue."

"Okay," Elliot said, "so maybe you read my mind while we were, you know . . ."

"Making love?" Stephen finished for him. He laughed. "First time in fifteen years and I figure, *yeah, I'm just not that into this. Maybe I'll surf around Elliot's head and find something more entertaining to distract me. I know, let's find out his favorite color. Oh look, it's blue.*"

Elliot had to laugh, too—it was hard not to. Stephen's amusement was just so contagious. "Okay, you win that argument, but . . . I don't know yours. Your favorite color. I don't know—"

Stephen reached for him, his hand against Elliot's face. The connection, as always, was quick—and hot. *My favorite color is you.*

Before Elliot could respond or react to what was, undeniably, the most romantic thing anyone had ever said to him, Stephen pulled Elliot with him, back into his mind, through a whirlwind of what must've been memories—seven years of them.

All focused on Elliot, his dirty-blond hair a mess, his glasses crooked, his clothing disheveled, his lab coat hanging open—and yet through Stephen's eyes, he managed to be gleamingly attractive.

Elliot saw flashes of himself smiling, laughing, talking—either in meetings with the full staff, or to Bach or Mac or one of the Forties or trainees, all while Stephen quietly stood off to the side . . .

And listened.

It was mind-blowing, particularly since Elliot had never even realized that Stephen Diaz had been paying all that much attention to the things he'd done and said.

There was one memory of an event that had happened just a few weeks ago, and Stephen slowed it down, so they both could look at it. Relive it together.

Elliott, Bach, Mac, and Stephen had been down in one of the classrooms, working with one of their promising young Thirties—a very serious girl named Ahlam.

She had notable telekinetic power, but like Mac, she struggled to control it. On that day, she had been doing an exercise in teleki-netic delicacy—involving several dozen raw eggs. She'd started out with promise, moving one egg at a time carefully across the room, taking it from one bowl and setting it gently into another.

But then, suddenly, an egg that was in mid-air exploded—almost as if it had been crushed by an invisible hand. The scram-bled contents sprayed in all directions. And it went downhill from there. All of the eggs launched out of both bowls and went flying around the room, exploding wildly, like miniature, single-color fireworks.

It happened so quickly, there was no time for the Greater-Thans to shield. And of course Elliot, who was the only fraction in the room, didn't have that ability.

Except, when it finally ended, Elliot and Stephen were the only ones in that classroom who were dripping with raw egg. Elliot used his fingers to try to clear the slime from his glasses, and Ste-phen wiped his dark hair and his face with his hands, as Ahlam turned toward them with tears welling in her big brown eyes.

"I couldn't shield everyone," she told them apologetically in her delightful, lilting accent. She looked at Stephen. "You're just too large." She turned to Elliot. "And you? I figured . . ." She shrugged. "You're probably used to it."

"I'm fine, and you're right, on both counts," Elliot reassured her even as he worked to keep a straight face, unwilling to give in to his laughter. There were times when laughing at mistakes helped provide the necessary levity for some of the younger trainees, but for others it was detrimental. And with this particular girl, the language barrier combined with her fear of men made what would seem to be his laughing in her face a big giant *no*.

But Elliot was on the verge of losing it. He started to cough to cover it, as Bach and Mac jumped all over what Ahlam had just said—*she'd* shielded herself and the two of them? Multiple shield-ing was a talent even the maestro hadn't yet mastered.

Stephen, meanwhile, saved the day, using his mind to open the lab door as he gestured to Elliot, who took it for the escape route that it was. He made a dash for the hall, with Stephen on his heels.

It was only when Stephen closed the door tightly behind them both that Elliot allowed himself to let go. *"You're used to it,"* he hooted as he completely cracked up. "She has *no* idea how true that is. And yet, every time it happens? I'm still completely caught off guard."

Stephen laughed, too, catching Elliot's eye and holding it as he grinned. "Come on," he said. "We should clean up and get back in there."

Elliot straightened, his laughter fading as he looked at Stephen. He paused the memory and said, "Wait a minute. This isn't what happened. I mean, yeah, that's what you said to me, but you didn't say it *that* way. You weren't laughing, and you didn't . . . You didn't even look at me."

"I wanted to," Stephen admitted, starting the memory up again as they went down the hall toward the locker room, as he caught Elliot's hand in his, sticky fingers interlocked as they walked together like the lovers they now were. "But I couldn't." He opened *that* door with his mind, too, and went in first, pulling Elliot behind him.

He used his telekinesis to take his cell phone out of his pocket, no doubt so that he wouldn't have to touch it with his eggy hands. He set it gently on the little metal shelf above the row of sinks.

If it were an egg, it would not have broken.

Elliot didn't have the no-hands option, so he let go of Stephen and went to the sink to rinse—same as he'd done on that day. He glanced at the Greater-Than questioningly as he turned on the water. "You didn't do *this*, either," he pointed out as he dried his hands, then set his phone and scanner down near Stephen's. "You opened the door for me, and essentially dropped me off and then went down the hall to another bathroom." He gestured around them to the multiple shower stalls. "As if this one weren't big enough for both of us."

"I know what I did and didn't do," Stephen told him quietly. "This isn't a complete memory. It's more of a daydream I had, a fantasy version. It's what I wished I could've done. Just . . . stuck around and talked to you, you know? Just . . . be your friend.

But . . . You kill me, you know, every time you laugh. It's so beautiful, and joyful, and . . . I wanted you, in every way, Elliot. I always had to walk away. But not anymore." He took Elliot's hand again, and just like that, they were back in his bed—right where they'd always been.

I've got plenty of time, Stephen told him. *You can take as long as you need to learn to trust me.* He kissed Elliot again. "We should get something to eat. And shower."

The big meeting was in just less than an hour.

"We should maybe go in to talk to Dr. Bach a little early," Elliot suggested. "In private, so that—"

"I don't need to do that," Stephen said. "But you know what we should do, before we go into that meeting?" He smiled at what Elliot was thinking. *Besides that.*

But Elliot *did* know. "We should see where your integration levels are—and see how long they take to drop, without physical contact."

He let Stephen pull him up and out of bed, and together they went back to the sofa.

Stephen positioned himself in front of the laptop's sensor, as Elliot grabbed his glasses from where he'd left them on the table and leaned in to look at the screen. The program had managed to continue scanning Stephen, even from across the room, and he had been steadily at sixty-one for the past busy hour—with no dips and no peaks.

The program had automatically scanned Elliot, too, and he had remained a dull and consistent Fifteen. It was disappointing, but not surprising.

Stephen glanced at him, surprised. *I never realized . . .*

That I'm envious of you and Mac and Dr. Bach and Ahlam and all of the others . . . ? "I am," Elliot spoke aloud as he broke their connection, moving slightly away from Stephen's warmth. "But I'm also grateful that despite my lack of aptitude, I'm still able to contribute in my own way. And okay, you're still a healthy sixty-one without contact. But there will be decay—we know this from experience. I scanned you after you left Shane and me in the examination room, and it wasn't long before . . ." He frowned at the screen and Stephen's unchanging numbers. "Although proximity might play into it. So I think I'm going to . . ." He stood up, pointing toward the bathroom. "You stay here, keep that sensor on you and watch the . . ."

"I got it," Stephen said, instead watching Elliot pick up his now-empty coffee mug and carry it to the kitchen counter on his way toward the only room in the apartment that was separated from the rest of the place by a door.

Elliot turned on the light, illuminating the pristine bathroom, and closed the door tightly behind him.

The entire wall was a mirror, just like in his apartment's bathroom, and he looked at himself as he stood at the toilet. He had a serious case of the bedheads—and surreal-itis, at the idea that he was taking a naked leak in Stephen Diaz's bathroom after having spent the morning in the man's bed.

"I'm dropping," Stephen called from the living room.

"Already? That was fast," Elliot called back, raising his voice to be heard through the closed door.

"I'm at sixty."

"A jot scan's imprecise," Elliot reminded him. "With a jot, sixty means you could be anywhere from an actual sixty to sixty-point-nine-nine-nine. Hang on, I'll be out in a sec—I thought I'd be in here longer."

"Take your time."

Elliot flushed and washed his hands, drying them on one of Stephen's plush towels. There was no point in trying to tame his hair. He'd need to get into the shower to do that and . . .

Yeah, he wanted to get into the shower to *fix his hair*. Right. Like he wasn't *really* thinking about getting Stephen into the shower with him and . . . Great. Now he was going to walk out of here with a very healthy hard-on—except there was a thick, white robe hanging on a hook on the back of the door. He took it down and put it on.

It smelled like Stephen, which only served to make him even more aroused, but the robe was thick and heavy enough to—

"Whoa, hang on," Stephen called from the living room. "I'm back to sixty-one."

Elliot opened the door and came out of the bathroom. "You went down, then back up—while I was out of the room? That doesn't make sense." He came over to look at the computer—not easy to do while Stephen was sitting there all distractingly tall, dark, and naked. But sure enough, he could see the graph dip down and then back. "Crap, I wish the reading was more precise. Did you . . . do anything different?"

Stephen spread his hands. "Just sitting here."

"Okay, then . . . What were you thinking about?"

Stephen looked up at him. "You."

"Me, like . . . fucking you blind?"

"Both romantic *and* poetic." Stephen laughed as he reached up to take Elliot's arm and pull him so that he was sitting beside him, close enough that their legs were touching. And just as it had done all along, their connection clicked back on.

And the Greater-Than replayed everything he'd been thinking, starting with watching Elliot walk naked across his apartment. *Jesus, he's hot, is this really happening? God, I'm happy. There's probably enough time before the meeting to . . . Wow, after all that, I still want more. I wonder if he also wants to . . . If not now, then later . . . Except I can't assume he's just going to want to spend tonight—Okay, integration levels dropping, gotta tell Elliot. Yeah, good point about the imprecision of a jot scan. Huh, look at my reflection in the computer screen—I'm sitting here, grinning inanely. Jesus, I've got warm fuzzies simply from having a conversation through a closed bathroom door. And okay, maybe that's not inane. Living alone for far more than fifteen years, isolated . . . But now . . .*

Stephen had gone into a full-blown fantasy then, imagining Elliot coming out of the bathroom and helping himself to more coffee, completely at home in Stephen's kitchen—which morphed into Elliot in the kitchen in the morning, in Stephen's bathrobe, bedhead and all, as Stephen kissed him good-bye as he left on an early A.M. assignment. He went out the door, but then he came back in, to kiss Elliot far more thoroughly before leaving for good.

God, as far as fantasies went, that was ridiculously G-rated, but it was also beyond sweet. Elliot's heart was actually in his throat.

And Stephen was a little embarrassed. "Apologies for appearing to want to move too fast," he murmured. "It was really just a fantasy. You know, a *someday* thing."

Elliot nodded and used the bathrobe to wipe his glasses. "For what it's worth, it's safe for you to assume that I . . . want more, too. But just so you don't have to assume . . . I can state, unequivocally, that I want to have many, many more conversations with you through the bathroom door. Hell, next time, I'll just leave it open."

Stephen smiled. "Good."

"Good." Elliot put his glasses back on and focused again on the computer and the numbers displayed there. *Okay, so it doesn't appear to be purely sex or sexual attraction that creates your surges of integration. Still, we should re-test. Maybe see what happens with greater distance between us. I should leave—see if you can't keep your integration levels up. Simply by thinking—what did you call them? Warm fuzzies.*

Maybe we were right earlier, and it is *the intimacy,* Stephen suggested, interlacing their fingers again. *Sex is just one part of an intimate connection. And for some people, it's the easy part.*

Like Mac, Elliot thought.

Very much like Mac.

They were both well aware that, after Dr. Bach's meeting, Mac was going to be chomping at the bit to get out there to find Nika Taylor. And as long as Shane Laughlin wasn't around to dangerously rev up her integration levels, she could safely hit the streets as a Fifty.

She'll want to go, Elliot concluded. *Immediately. And you'll want to go with her.*

"You know what they're doing to this girl," Stephen reminded him.

"I do." Elliot took a deep breath and stood up, cutting their connection. He turned to face Stephen. "But if your integration levels don't drop back down to fifty, we need to test you before I can clear you to go out. We need to see how many volts of energy you command—and whether you have control of it. I'd also like to know what other talents—besides this nifty telepathic connection— that you've added to your list. And we should test that, too. The telepathy." He headed back toward the bathroom. "See if that's something you can do with everyone, or exclusively with me. Come on, we should shower and grab some food, go find an open lab so we can get some of this work done."

"Uh-oh," Stephen said, and Elliot turned back to look at him.

"You just got an alert," Stephen told him, his eyes on the computer monitor, "that says you were e-mailed a med scan report on Michelle Mackenzie." He looked up at Elliot. "It just came in, but with the communications delay . . . Yeah, it was sent about an hour ago."

"Open it," Elliot told him, and Stephen clicked open the message.

"She's back down to fifty percent," Stephen informed him. "And that means—"

They weren't touching, but neither of them needed to say it aloud. They both knew exactly what it meant.

Mac had left the compound.

SIXTEEN

This was the same hospital where the missing girl, Nika Taylor, had been scanned, prior to her disappearance.

It was hard for Shane not to think about that—particularly when he went to the ER's front desk, where a harried-looking medical assistant was performing a financial triage on the injured or ill people who'd staggered in. What type of insurance did they have—if any—and what form of treatment—if any—would be covered under their plan.

Mac wasn't sitting out in the waiting area with the rest of the masses, which was odd. But maybe a potential head injury was taken before a broken ankle or the flu or even a cooking-knife accident.

But when Shane finally made it to the front of the line and said, "I'm with Michelle—the thirteen-year-old girl who just came in," he got a blank stare.

"She fell out of a tree and hit her head," he tried.

The man—*Bob* was on his name tag—shook his head. "I'm sorry, sir—"

"I just dropped her off," Shane said. "She came in while I was parking . . . ? Short hair, pretty eyes, nasty attitude . . . ?"

Nothing. No lights went on. Zero recognition.

And yeah, the first thought Shane had was that whoever had

taken Nika had—somehow—taken Mac, too. But that was crazy. She hadn't even been scanned yet. They—whoever the *they* were who made up the mysterious "Organization" that he'd been warned about—had no reason to believe she was anything special and thus worth taking.

Shane's second thought was far more likely: Mac had never intended to come here to get a med scan. That was just what she'd told him, and he'd played right into it—allowing her to lose him so that she could do whatever it was she'd really intended to do outside of OI's grounds.

Something probably far more dangerous.

Son of a bitch.

"Maybe she's in the bathroom," Bob suggested, pointing down the hall, already looking past Shane to the next person in line.

His pulse-rate rising with a righteous mix of anger and worry, Shane went back out to the entrance, to the circular driveway where he'd left Mac. He was well aware that, with her ability to change her appearance—plus she'd said she had a different shirt with her—he could have walked right past her while she was coming out of the ER, and he never would have known it. Especially since he was an idiot and hadn't been watching for it. Shit. *Shit.*

Of course, the only person out there now was the guard, who was eyeing him suspiciously.

Shane closed his eyes and . . . He'd hustled in from the parking lot, eager to prove himself indispensable and . . . He'd definitely walked past a group of three women leaving the hospital.

They'd clearly been together—two middle-aged women supporting an elderly relative. He knew Mac could make herself look younger, but could she also make herself look older? He had no clue. Although he was pretty sure none of the women he'd seen had been wearing olive drab cargo pants and sneakers. And truth be told, he really hadn't given them more than a glance, because he'd been so fucking eager to find Mac.

Shane turned abruptly and went back through the automatic sliding doors into the ER waiting room. But even before he started scanning for Mac's brand of sneakers among the crowd, he knew that she wasn't there. He couldn't feel her—not the way he'd felt her presence in the garden, from up on his balcony.

Unless she could somehow turn *that* off, too.

With Mac, Shane realized suddenly, anything was possible.

It was possible that everything she'd told him had been a lie. Everything—including that heartbreaking story about finding her powers upon awakening, drugged and naked . . . *I hadn't been raped yet. Not that night, anyway.*

Except . . . He'd believed her.

Shane wasn't a telepath, nor did he have empathic powers anywhere close to Mac's but . . .

She'd been telling the truth.

It was all he could do, not to overreact, when she'd told him what had happened to her when she was still just a girl. And, like he'd told her, he was pretty sure she'd left out the worst of it.

Still, his instinct had been to play it cool, to not pull her into his arms or even to say much of anything at all.

Shane knew she would read his response as pity, or—worse, in her eyes—possessiveness. But both the tragedy that she'd survived—including the accidental death of that boy on top of the trauma of abuse—and Shane's realization that she completely rejected any and all emotional connection to him despite their night together, had made his heart ache.

He wanted . . . He wasn't sure what he wanted. Regardless of that, he knew for damn sure that he wasn't going to quit.

So he stood there. Glaring as he looked out at the entire room, his message to her clear: *I will find you.* But no one made a break for the door or shifted guiltily in their seat.

He went to the door of the ladies' head, and keeping one eye on the crowded waiting room, he pushed it open. "Michelle, are you in there?"

But she wasn't. It was empty.

So Shane began his person-by-person search—looking hard at each of the women and girls sitting or lying on the uncomfortable benches. He didn't just look at their sneakers and pants, because for all he knew she'd already traded hers for something else.

Of course, then he realized that *she* was the one who'd told him about her appearance-changing talents. For all he knew, she'd lied about her ability to become male—at least outwardly so.

And forget trading her sneakers and pants. For all he knew, she had the capability of appearing—at least to others—as if she were wearing completely different clothing.

Which meant that he was about to be really rude and go through the ER waiting room touching everyone—because there was only one thing he was certain of. And that was that he'd know Mac when he touched her.

A stack of magazines had spilled off the top of a nearby table along with a piece of paper on which a child had drawn what might've been a dog. Maybe a horse, no . . . A dog. Shane bent to pick it up, turning to touch a large black man on the shoulder. "I'm sorry, did you drop this?"

And he could tell right away that no, Mac hadn't made herself nearly a foot and a half taller and eighty pounds heavier. And a man. And African American. Which, when he thought about it, really didn't seem possible—even in this crazy world in which he now found himself.

And speaking of impossible, the idea of parading down an entire row of people, touching them and asking if this drawing was theirs . . . *That* was going to raise some eyebrows or even get him smacked. He might as well just run down the crowded rows of seats, touching the tops of the peoples' heads and saying, *Duck, duck, duck, duck, duck, duck* . . .

"Shane!"

Goose.

Yeah, that *was* Mac's voice, and it was coming from behind him, from the double doors that led into the actual ER, and he spun around as she added, "Sweetheart! There you are! I'm over here!"

And there Mac was—she was actually waving—and Shane definitely felt her as well as saw her. He also felt a rush of relief, and that now-familiar heat.

She'd changed back to an adult, but she looked slightly different. Her hair was longer—crazy how she could grow it in a matter of minutes—and she'd pulled it back into a tight ponytail that made her seem older—or maybe she'd somehow adjusted her face to create that effect. She'd also changed her shirt. She was wearing a red blouse over a very non-thirteen-year-old body, and held her leather jacket over one arm.

Still, he would have recognized her, no problem, even without the wave. She may have changed her face and hair, but those were still Mac's eyes.

It was the words she spoke next that were the puzzler.

"I've found him," she told him as he headed over to her. "I found Grandpa!"

What the . . . ? Had he heard her right? *"Grandpa."*

"Yes, he's here. My missing grandfather. He must've had another episode while he was at the mall," she said, adding, "Play along," under her breath as he got close enough.

So he just barreled into her personal space and threw his arms around her. "Praise God! Grandpa's here. Grandma and Aunt Betty were so worried."

"What are you doing?" she hissed, her face against his chest as she simultaneously attempted both to not touch him and to look as if she were returning his embrace. She was thinner in places—more fragile-seeming. Less muscular. Which was strange. He liked her better when she was herself. Except maybe *this* was her real self.

Either way, he was hit with some pretty X-rated images upon contact, and he was certain she was experiencing the same. Were they his memories or hers?

It almost didn't matter.

"I'm playing along," Shane whispered back, adding in his regular voice, "Oh, *sweetheart,* this is *such* good news." He pulled her chin up to kiss her because, damn it, he wasn't likely to have this chance again, but she stepped on his foot. Hard enough for him to let her go. "Ow! Is he? How is he?"

She shot him a darkly exasperated look even as she motioned for him to follow, so he did just that as she led the way back into the ER, dodging several nurses and a doctor or two. "He's not doing well. I need to call, um, Aunt Betty, to arrange for a private ambulance to pick him up so we can get him the care he needs." She took his arm and pulled him closer, but only to whisper, "Did you *really* think that I ditched you?"

She let go of him again, a little too fast.

Obviously Mac knew what he'd been thinking—or more likely what he'd been feeling, since empathy was her strength. So he didn't try to bullshit her as they swiftly walked past a dozen curtained-off rooms, the beds filled with people in need of medical help. "Yeah. You were gone. I thought—"

"While you were parking," she told him, her voice still low, "an ambulance brought in an elderly man I met just this morning in a parking lot and—" She cut herself off. "It doesn't matter where or how I met him. I just did. He was living out of his car and it had just broken down and he was going to work for JLG— a drug-testing lab. I told him not to—I gave him some money—but I think he went anyway. Shit, I know he went, and I know they tested Destiny on him, because he's accessed some powers that he didn't have before."

Shane stopped short. "Did he *joker?*"

"I don't think so, but I don't know." Mac shook her head, her face grim as she refused to stop walking—to the point of taking him by his sleeve and dragging him with her. Despite her fragile appearance, she was still quite strong. "He's unconscious. The paramedics told me they answered a call about a man lying in the street, so the drug-lab motherfuckers must've dumped him—they do that. His med scan shows that he's had a massive heart attack. I'm pretty sure most of the powers he acquired have been shut down as his body focuses on repairing itself."

"*Most* of the powers?" Shane repeated.

"Yeah, he can still throw a kind of feeble mental bitchslap," she told him. "But even that's fading fast. When he first came in, it was like an ice pick in my sinuses—like, damn. But then I realized that the guy at the triage desk felt it, too. He goes, *Ooh, weird, an ice cream headache—where'd that come from?* And I turned around, and they were wheeling this guy in and . . . I recognized him. And I knew. So I went into the bathroom to change"—she said it so casually, but Shane knew she meant more than simply to change her shirt—"so I could come back out and be his worried grand-daughter. If we have any hope of saving him, we've got to get him to OI. Immediately."

She pulled Shane with her behind the curtain down at the very end of the entire row, where a very old man was strapped into a bed and hooked up to an IV, oxygen tubing beneath his nose. His eyes were closed. He didn't look dangerous, but Rickie Littleton hadn't looked very menacing when he wasn't flying around and breathing fire.

Still, Shane turned to Mac, and said, "What can I do to help make that happen?"

She exhaled, as if she'd been holding her breath for a long time, and said, "Stay with him. Make sure no one gives him anything—no medication, nothing. Don't let them move him and don't let any-one get too close. I didn't want to bind his hands"—she handed him several standard issue plastic restraints that she'd apparently been carrying in her pocket—"but if you can figure out a way to do it without killing him, go wild. I honestly don't know if he jokered, or if he's just under the influence of the drug. I can't use my cell phone in here, so I'm going out to the lobby to call Elliot and arrange for the medevac chopper to come pick him up. I'll be fast."

"I'll be here," Shane told her.

"Thanks," Mac said, adding, "If he comes to, and you believe that he *has* jokered? Don't wait for him to start flying around the room. Kill him."

And with that she was gone.

———

Bach was, as he'd written in his note, out in Anna's living room.

He was asleep on the sofa, only slightly sprawled so that his head was against the back of the thing, but both of his feet were still firmly on the floor.

He slept as he did nearly everything—quietly. Carefully. Formally—much like the way he'd signed that note with his full name. *Joseph Bach.*

He'd asked Anna to wake him, but there was still about twenty-five minutes before he was due at that meeting he'd mentioned in that note.

Besides, she could see, from across the room, that the comm-station over near the window was active, so she moved quietly toward it. Bach didn't stir, and as she sat in the chair in front of it, she glanced back at him. . . .

He was still asleep.

So Anna typed the name *Devon Caine* into the search engine.

The first link that appeared took her—oh, dear God—to the Commonwealth of Massachusetts sex offender database, where sure enough, there was a picture—a younger version—of the bigger of the two men who'd abducted her sister. Caine's address was also listed, and she leaned in closer to read the small font.

"He's no longer at that address."

Anna jumped and sure enough, Bach had awakened and was watching her from the sofa.

"We already checked," he continued as he stretched and smoothed down his hair, even though it wasn't messy. At least not compared to her own unruly curls. "We've also discovered that his driver's license was revoked five years ago—and he's not at *that* address, either. He's got a long list of priors, including some DUIs, and he's also no longer at the address he filed with his parole officer—whom he's failed to visit for nearly two years. There's an eighteen-month-old warrant out for his arrest—which doesn't nec-essarily mean that he's going to be hard to find, but rather that the police haven't been actively looking for him. But we are."

His message was clear. The team from OI wasn't going to take eighteen months to find Caine—or Nika.

Or so they hoped.

"I didn't mean to disturb you," she said.

"It was time to wake up."

Despite the sleep he'd gotten, Bach still looked tired—in fact, there seemed to be new lines of strain on his face. And at some point in the night or the very early morning, he'd changed out of his blue sweater and into an almost identical green one. It looked good on him, too.

"Any luck with the projections from Nika?" she asked, not daring to hope. She'd had no dreams of any kind—not about Nika, not about anything—so she didn't expect much.

He closed his eyes for a moment, as if checking his memory, but then shook his head. "No."

She'd been holding her breath. Despite her denial, she *had* been hoping. And she was more disappointed and frustrated than she'd expected to be.

"I'm sorry," Bach said.

"It was worth a try," Anna said. "And even worth trying again. Maybe you could sleep over again tonight?" She felt her face flushing slightly at her own words. There were sleepovers and there were *sleepovers,* and she didn't want him to think she was being at all suggestive.

But Bach didn't seem to notice. He just nodded. "I'm going to talk to Elliot—Dr. Zerkowski—see if we can't figure out exactly what happened that first time. If you're open to even more testing—"

"I am," she said. They'd only had time for some preliminary tests earlier, before Bach had been called away. "Whatever it takes."

He nodded again. Pushed himself to his feet. "I should go. I'll have someone pick you up—escort you down to my office. That's where we're meeting. Although it's going to be awhile. We have some other things to discuss before we get to Nika."

"I wanted to ask you, what were those sirens?" Anna asked him, standing up, too. "From before?"

"We had an event." His answer was as vague as she'd expected. But then he surprised her by adding, "An unfortunate one. The man that Mac identified from the satellite images . . ."

"Rickie Littleton," Anna supplied the name. She glanced back at the computer. That was the next name she'd been planning to search for.

Bach nodded. "He's a low-level dealer," he told her. "Specializing in Destiny. Mac and Diaz found him and brought him in for me to take a little walk through his mind, see if we couldn't find out what he did with your sister. But the security team didn't realize—none of us did—that Destiny is now being packaged and sold as something that looks rather disturbingly like an Epi Pen."

"A what?"

"People with severe allergies—to bee stings or peanut butter. They carry them around. It's a device that administers medication through an easy injection. You punch it into your thigh." He smiled grimly. "And yes, our lives just got a whole lot harder. Most people are put off by the idea of a recreational drug that they need to inject into a vein with a needle and syringe. But using one of those injection devices . . . ? Significantly less of a big deal."

"And Littleton had some and took it?" she asked.

Bach nodded. "He was a walking pharmacy, and nearly all of his supply was confiscated. One of the guards who searched him has a kid with a shellfish allergy, and she thought the Epi Pens—he had two—were for Littleton's own health. So she left them in his pocket, and he used them both. I'm certain he was hoping it would give him the powers he needed to break free. Instead, he jokered."

Oh God. "Was anyone hurt?" Anna asked.

Bach nodded. "*He* was. He was killed in our attempt to subdue him."

"So we're down to Devon Caine," she surmised, her stomach clenching.

"We are," he agreed.

Anna glanced back at the computer monitor and that sex offender registry listing—which Bach had no doubt intended for her to find. He was not a man who would allow a comm-station to be just carelessly left active.

"What can I do to help?" she asked. "Instead of just sitting here waiting, may I use the computer, and try to identify that man from Nika's projection—the one with the scars on his face?"

Bach smiled, and she got the sense that he'd expected her to ask just that.

"Please," he said. "Analysis is overworked and . . . You've seen things they haven't."

She'd already turned back to the computer, sitting in front of it, already typing the words "victims of facially disfiguring accidents" into the search engine.

"See you in a bit," Bach said and she heard the click of the door as he let himself out.

———

Elliot picked up on the first ring. "What the *fuck*, Mac? Where the hell are you?"

"St. Elizabeth's Medical Center," she told him from the waiting room, as she moved out of earshot of a mother holding a child with a horrible cough. "*What the fuck* I'm doing here is moot—"

"To *you*, maybe," he interrupted. "But it's sure not going to be to Dr. Bach and—"

Bach was going to be disappointed in her yet again, blah blah blah. Mac loved Elliot, she did, but *shit*. She spoke over him. "There's an eighty-year-old male in the ER and I'm ninety-nine percent certain that he's been a recent crash-test-dummy for JLG's drug lab. And I'm ninety-nine-point-nine percent certain that the drug they tested on him earlier today was Destiny. I don't know if he jokered or what, but I do know this: If he has any chance of survival, it'll be because you stop what-the-fucking and instead call for a helicopter pickup, so we can get him over to OI, stat—where the doctors actually know what-the-fuck they're doing."

"Patient's name?" Elliot asked, which was more like it.

"Edward O'Keefe," Mac told him. "He's in bed thirty-four, in the ER's red wing." Which meant they expected him to die within hours. They were just keeping him comfortable. And *that* meant they'd be more than happy to send him over to another facility, ASAP.

Where he'd be someone else's problem, and someone else's body to dispose of.

"Get him ready to go. Chopper's on its way," Elliot said and hung up on her.

Mac pocketed her phone and headed back into the ER as quickly as she could move without raising eyebrows.

Shane was standing at the curtain partition, waiting for her, and she could feel his relief when he spotted her.

She felt his desire, too—and that was her fault, entirely, for ramping up her powers while they were in the car.

Still, he kept it all business and respect—pure officer-and-gentleman—and as she approached, he gave her a sit-rep: "No change, no movement—and no one's been in to see him, either."

Mac nodded, keeping it all business, too. The hook holding the old man's saline bag was already attached to the bed, as was his oxygen tank. "Help me figure out how to get this bed ready to roll," she ordered, and Shane jumped to assist.

"I'm going to tell the truth, you know," he informed her as he bent down to look at the mechanism. "After we get back to OI. How I forced you to take me with you—"

"You didn't *force* me," Mac said. Ah, *that* was how the bed's brakes unlocked. She did the same thing on her side that Shane had done on his. "Don't be melodramatic, Navy. And don't worry, they're not going to kick you out of the program. They haven't kicked *me* out yet."

"The bed's designed to roll with the patient backward—the head goes first," Shane told her—apparently he knew that just from looking at the wheels. "So we essentially back him out of this area—"

"Got it," Mac said. "The chopper bay is up on the seventh floor, this wing. I'm going to go find a nurse or a doctor, so we don't get stopped on our way to the elevators. Hang tight."

But she was in luck and a doctor—late twenties, male, and radiating both exhaustion and annoyance—was out in the hall. It was a double win, of sorts, because she knew that Shane still didn't quite believe in her power. This way, he could watch it work on someone besides himself. He'd already followed her to the edge of the curtain.

"Excuse me, Doctor," she called, and as the man turned to her and caught a whiff of her skills, his body language changed so drastically, it was almost laughable.

"Wow," Shane said under his breath as the doctor nearly ran toward her.

Of course, Shane didn't know that stress and fatigue made a target particularly susceptible to her charms. And it was a well-known fact that ER doctors often went for forty-eight hours without sleep, making them extra malleable.

And it wasn't just sex appeal that she used. Mac tapped into the very elements of her target's psyche—in this case the very parts of his personality that had made him want to become a physician—his desire to help people, to save lives, to make a difference.

Too often, locked in as a cog in the workings of the current screwed-up medical system, doctors *weren't* able to help people. But the message she was currently sending out was heavy with *you are my hero.* And this man liked that.

"Dr. Samuels," she said, reading his name tag, "I know you can help me." She explained about the helicopter that was coming from OI and couldn't he bend the rules just this once for her dying grandfather?

He could, and he did.

Shane stayed silent, just watching, as the doctor escorted them all the way up to the seventh floor, chatting with Mac the entire way—not just about the fictional hospice program Grandpa was going to be put into, but also personal stuff, like the fact that he'd gone out to Arizona to get his medical degree, but now here he was, back in Boston, living not far from where he'd grown up, didn't it figure.

Mac maintained eye contact and smiled. And she may have leaned a bit too hard on her ability to be attractive, sending out

God-only-knew what kind of pheromones, because as they were wheeling the old man toward the door that led out to the helicopter deck, Dr. Samuels said, "I know we've only just met, and I don't usually do this, but . . ."

Here it came. He was going to ask her out or request her phone number, and Mac glanced at Shane to make sure he was paying attention—and he was.

"Will you marry me?"

"I'm sorry, what?" Mac turned back to look at the doctor.

"I know." The man was laughing, but at the same time he was deadly serious. "It's crazy, but . . . I don't think I've ever had such an immediate rapport with anyone, in my entire life. It's as if you . . . I don't know, as if you were created specifically for me. I'm afraid if I just let you leave, I'll miss out on the chance of a lifetime."

This guy had balls, Mac had to give him that. He saw something he thought he wanted, and he went for it.

Kind of like Shane.

Who was still watching closely, looking from her to the doctor and back, waiting to see what she was going to say or do.

What she did was dial it down. *Way* down. Still, she knew her effect on the man would take a few hours to wear off, so she said—as gently as possible—"Thank you so much. I'm flattered. I am. A woman doesn't get that kind of compliment every day, but . . . I'm already taken. I'm in a relationship, but if it ever ends, I promise I'll give you a call."

And now she was sending out serious *believe me* vibes despite her lie, and she could feel his acceptance. Thank God. Her targets didn't always take rejection gracefully.

He was embarrassed though—it was radiating off of him—and he quickly made his excuses and left them there at the nurses' station, to await the chopper.

It was only after the elevator closed behind the man that Shane finally spoke. "That was pretty intense."

"That's the way it works," Mac told him. "And with a little distance, in just a few hours, he won't remember why he was so attracted. He'll forget what he was feeling, completely. And he'll be like, *wow, that was weird. Good thing she didn't say* yes."

"I didn't forget," Shane pointed out as her cell phone buzzed with a text from Elliot. *Chopper ETA: ten minutes.*

Although when she checked—yeah. Elliot had sent that message ten minutes ago. And there, through the windows, was the approaching OI helicopter, its thrumming sound growing louder and louder. She unlocked the brakes on the hospital bed as she looked across the old man and into Shane's eyes.

"That's because I slept with you," Mac told him.

"Yeah, I remember that, too," he said with that smile that could melt her insides—if she let him. "Very clearly."

"Maybe what we need to do," she told him, "is ask Dr. Bach to go into your head, and block those memories."

Shane was taken aback. "He can do that?" he asked, then added, "What if I don't want him to?"

Mac didn't answer. She just pushed the button that opened the doors. And even if she'd answered with the *tough shit* that she was thinking, Shane wouldn't have heard her over the noise and the wind from the chopper's blades as they rushed to get Edward O'Keefe safely to Obermeyer Institute.

Nika had just finished the O she was painting on the window in catsup, when she heard the sound of the door being unlocked.

She quickly pulled the curtains closed and licked her finger clean, even as she braced to defend herself from whomever might be coming in.

It was a woman, and at first glance, she looked so much like Anna, Nika's heart soared. But it wasn't her sister. Whoever this woman was, she was much heavier than Anna. Her face was rounder, fuller. But then Nika saw that she wasn't quite a woman— she was still a girl. A teenager. And she wasn't fat, she was pregnant. And even though her skin, like Anna's and Nika's, was mocha-colored and her hair was dark and curly, her eyes were a brilliant shade of green instead of brown.

They were also hard and cold, and with her tightly pinched mouth, she looked dangerous, despite her swollen body and her drab-colored, loose-fitting dress.

She stopped about ten feet away from Nika and said, "This is your safe room. Learn to use it to recover, replenish, recuperate, and you'll survive. Waste your time in here on things you cannot control, and you will not."

"Where am I?" Nika asked.

The girl shook her head, her mouth tight again. "Listen to what I'm saying. I've been where you are—I'm trying to help you, girl."

"Then *help* me," Nika pleaded. "I need to get out of here—"

"There's no way out."

"There must be," Nika argued. "If you've been where I am, and you're walking around now, free . . ."

The girl laughed, but the sound was harsh. "I'm not free."

"But you can open the door," Nika pointed out. "Let's get out of here. If we go, together, maybe—"

"What?" the girl was disdainful now. "You think you can save *me?*"

"I think we should try!"

"Yeah, that's not going to happen."

"At least call my sister, tell her where I am—"

"So she can be taken, too? Of course, if she's not like you, they'll kill her. They'll bleed her, use her, work her until she's dead, like Zooey and the others. They don't get a safe room like this, you know. Only the special girls do. But if you stop being special—and you will, if you don't keep your strength up—you won't come back here. And then they'll just use you up."

"Use me for what?" Nika asked, trying not to cry. "I don't understand—"

"Try," the girl said, her arms now wrapped protectively around her belly. "To understand this: That *all* you need to know is that when you are in this room, you must eat and you must sleep. You must focus on your health." She pointed to the bed. "Lie down."

Nika lifted her chin defiantly as she refused to move from in front of the closed curtains that blocked the window where she'd written two-thirds of that SOS. Still, her voice came out with a definite wobble. "I'm not tired."

"Do you honestly think they're not watching and listening, that they don't know what you were doing in here? Lie *down* on the bed, girl, so I can clean off the window, and if you're lucky, they won't send a sedative through your system, because you *can't* recharge the way you need to if you're drugged."

But Nika shook her head.

And the girl's voice got tighter. "Your time in here is running out. They need you back in the line within eight hours, so you eat the food they bring you, and you soak in the tub, and you stretch and exercise your muscles—and you sleep as much as you possibly can and— There, did you hear that?"

Nika had heard something, a hissing sound from the contraption in her left arm and she looked at it as the pregnant girl continued, "You don't want to sleep? Too bad—they'll make you sleep, only it won't help you the way that it could. You best get on that bed, child, before you fall on your face."

But it was too late. The world blurred and the girl's voice faded and the lights dimmed and Nika felt her legs give out beneath her as she crumpled to the floor.

The last thing that she saw before the world went black was the pregnant girl looking down at her, one hand pressed against her belly as she grimly shook her head and said, as if from a great distance away, "You think you're special, but you're not. Not really. There are always more girls. That's one thing this goddamned world will *never* run out of."

SEVENTEEN

"This is frigging nuts," Mac said, breaking the silence that had fallen over Dr. Bach's office, after Dr. Zerkowski—Elliot—had given his report.

Shane was sitting there, trying to absorb all he'd just learned, and even though he wouldn't have phrased it as bluntly in a roomful of people he didn't know all that well, it *was* mind-blowing.

Apparently, *he* wasn't responsible for Stephen Diaz's sudden burst of new powers.

Apparently, *Elliot* was.

The two men were sitting side by side, and they both looked pretty damn at ease, considering that they'd just confessed not only to getting it on all morning long, but to the fact that they were in love. Of course, they'd couched it all in more scientific-sounding terms. Intimate physical contact and intense emotional connection.

Still, Shane couldn't imagine being that nonchalant about the total surrender of *his* privacy.

And he was still freaked out by the very graphic illustration of Mac's power, back at the hospital. He hadn't really believed her capable of casting such a spell over a stranger until he saw it in action. And now he was reviewing everything he'd ever said to her, every conversation, every moment of contact—wondering if he'd come across as annoyingly single-minded as Dr. "Marry Me" had.

Shane also understood Mac's reluctance to embrace Elliot's going theory—which was that the hormones and proteins, created not just by sexual desire but also by intense emotional connection, could cause a marked increase in a Greater-Than's integration.

If Mac accepted that, *and* it was also true that Shane was as responsible for Mac's enhanced power as Elliot was for Diaz's . . . *That* meant Mac was into Shane for more than just his usefulness in bed.

Which made Shane pretty freaking happy—although how much of that happiness was the residue from the voodoo she'd hit him with repeatedly over the past few days, he had no clue.

Although to hell with *that*. Happy was happy and Shane hadn't been anywhere close to happy, not like this, for far too long.

Mac, however, was decidedly *not* happy.

"I'm down with part of the theory," she said now. "I've been using sex for years to accelerate my ability to heal," she pointed out. "And I realize what I'm about to say is going to make you touchie-feelies recoil in horror, but most of the time, there was absolutely zero emotional connection."

She purposely wouldn't meet Shane's eyes, even though he was steadily watching her. So he murmured, "Ouch," which made her glance over.

Her eyes were intentionally unapologetic as she shrugged. "Sorry," she said, sounding not at all sorry. "It was sex. It was intense, true, but—"

She was lying, and they both knew it. "We made plans," Shane reminded her. "To meet again. Next week."

"And if I was in town," she told him, glancing around at the other men in the room, clearly uncomfortable with the personal nature of their conversation. "I might've shown up. Or I might not've."

Her body language dismissed him, but he wasn't ready to be dismissed. "You would've shown," Shane told her. There were few things in life he was absolutely sure of, but that was one of them.

"If I did, it would've meant the opposite: that I *didn't* give a shit about you. Get over yourself, Laughlin—"

"It's entirely possible," Elliot interjected, "that just like every talent or skill we've encountered with Greater-Thans, it varies according to each individual. Obviously, I haven't run any tests with you and Shane, Mac, but I *can* tell you that Stephen's been at sixty-one for the past several hours—including a thirty-minute stretch when I was in the ER with Edward O'Keefe and he was over in security. The computer's been running a continuous jot scan on him—Stephen, I mean—and he didn't dip, didn't drop, not even a decimal point. Not after we had a conversation, um," he cleared his throat as he glanced at Stephen, "in which we sorted a few things out. He's been holding steady at sixty-one, despite the separation, without any additional intimate physical contact."

"You might as well say *sex,*" Mac shot at him. "We all know you mean sex, so you should cut the bullshit."

"This conversation isn't easy for any of us," Bach spoke up for the first time in a while. "I don't think it's asking too much to allow Elliot to use whatever terminology he prefers."

"Fine," Mac said, heavy on the attitude. "But just because Diaz jumped to sixty-one doesn't mean that it's *not* purely about the *intimate physical contact.* Maybe, for him, it's enough to know he's gettin' some tonight. It's been fifteen years, right? I'd be horny, too."

"It's not just about the sex," Diaz said quietly.

Elliot glanced at him again, and the smile the two men exchanged echoed Diaz's sentiment plenty.

Shane knew that Mac saw the exact same thing that he did, and she looked even less happy. In fact, the muscle in her jaw tensed as she clenched her teeth.

Elliot accessed the comm-station. "Mac, you've been bouncing between fifty and fifty-five ever since you got back to OI. Have you been—"

"You've been probing me?" she interrupted the doctor, her voice loaded with outrage.

"No," Elliot countered evenly, "but we have been jot scanning you."

"It's called probing if it's done without the subject's knowledge or permission—"

"And you waived your permission the minute you disobeyed direct orders and left OI, with Shane Laughlin in tow. So quit wasting time with the indignant crap and answer the questions. Have you been in Shane's company the entire time you've been back in the compound?"

"Yes," Mac said, even as Shane answered, "No."

She looked at him and he reminded her, "We both used the head—the bathroom. We were apart for that. You also had a conversation with Elliot about Mr. O'Keefe. In the ER."

"I wasn't *that* far away from you," she pointed out. "Even in the bathroom."

"Maybe, for *you*," Shane said, since she seemed to like the theory that all Greater-Thans responded differently, uniquely, to intimacy, "it was enough of a separation."

"Wait," Elliot said, his eyes on the computer monitor as he stopped scrolling through data, "here's a spike that brought you up to fifty-seven. It was about ten minutes after you came in on the helicopter with O'Keefe."

"You grabbed my arm," Shane remembered, "to keep me out of the ER."

"You're currently a high Fifty-five," Elliot told Mac as he finally looked up. "Let's see what happens when you touch him."

Shane looked at Mac, who turned to look at him, and for a fraction of a second he saw sheer misery in her eyes. But it happened so fast and then it was gone—and she was holding out her hand to him.

He took it, and just as it always had done, heat surged between them—instant and powerful.

"Bang," Elliot reported. He laughed. "Fifty-seven—just like that."

Mac yanked her hand free, and when she spoke, her voice was tight. "Now don't you want to see what happens if he feels me up?" She was obviously angry—Shane didn't need any empathic skills to know that. She turned to Bach. "I'm *not* having sex with him in a lab."

Bach shook his head. "No one's asking you to do that."

"Well, actually, I kind of was," Elliot admitted as he rubbed the back of his neck and made a rueful face. "Although the experiment wouldn't actually take place *in* the lab. I'd set up a continuous jot scan, and you'd just go about your day, as it were. You'll keep a log of your—ahem—activities, and—"

"No." Bach was absolute. "It's one thing to volunteer to share personal information, but another entirely to make that kind of a request—not just of a Greater-Than, but of a Potential . . . ?" He shook his head, and said it again. "No."

"For the record," Shane chimed in, even though he knew that doing so would needle Mac. Still, if she could play the it's-just-sex game, he could, too. For now, anyway. "I'm okay with it. I'm happy to, um, experiment."

"Great," Mac snapped. "Let's see what happens when you fuck Diaz."

As Shane laughed his surprise, Elliot said, "Yeah, *that's* not going to happen, and you know it, Mackenzie. Now you're just being an asshole."

"*You're* an asshole," she shot at the doctor. "Oh, and thanks so much for being such a good *friend*, by the way."

"I *am* being a good friend," he fired back. "I'm just calling you out on your bullcrap. If sex really were just a biological function for you, no emotions involved . . . ? You'd have no problem with this test."

"Okay, fine," she said. She stood up. Looked at Shane. "Let's do it. Because *I'm* not the one with the problem."

Shane looked over at Bach, who—just as he'd expected—sighed heavily. "Mac, that's not—"

"No, Elliot's right," she spoke over him. "It's not a big deal." She looked back at Shane. "*You*, however, will need to sign a release that says you've been told that you're not functioning under your own free will and that despite being informed of this, you're still willing to participate in this *experiment*." She added air quotes.

"I'll sign whatever you want me to sign," Shane said, pushing himself to his feet.

"Really? And this doesn't raise even the smallest red flag for you?" Mac asked him hotly. "You don't think it's troublesome or . . . weird? That you're willing to stand here, in front of virtual strangers, and negotiate a chance to get with me again?"

"Honey, I've long resigned myself to the fact that ever since I've met you, I've been submerged in a world of weird. For all I know, this is just another average day at the Obermeyer Institute."

"Both of you, sit down." Although Bach still spoke quietly, he didn't look or sound happy. And that was definitely an order, not a request.

And while Shane was used to working within a chain of command that included higher ranking officers who were far less physically intimidating than he was, he didn't expect Mac to S-square so quickly.

But she sat down and she shut up—which said a lot about the man who was their leader. So Shane put his ass back into his seat, too.

And then they all just sat there, waiting for Bach to speak. Like a good leader, he knew just how long to extend the silence to convey both his disapproval and his authority.

"This is well outside of my comfort zone," he finally said, looking over to include Diaz and Elliot in his statement. "But I agree that further testing is warranted. But only—*only*—if all parties are in complete agreement." He looked pointedly at Mac. "What's right for Dr. Diaz isn't necessarily going to be right for me. Or for you. I hope you'll always keep that in mind, Dr. Mackenzie."

"Yes, sir," she murmured.

"While Diaz's increase to sixty-one is a huge breakthrough—assuming it lasts," Bach continued, "we've also got other important issues to deal with today. Nika Taylor is still missing. However, we're moving forward. We've ID'd Rickie Littleton's co-conspirator—"

"We have?" Mac sat up. "Who is he? I'll go, right now, to bring him in and—"

"You aren't going anywhere."

Because Bach said it in almost exact unison with Elliot, Mac wasn't sure where to aim her disbelief. "Why not?" she asked, looking from one to the other and back again. But then she answered her own question. "My fluctuating integration levels." She turned and spoke to Bach. "Sir, that's not an issue. Just keep Laughlin away from me and I'll be fine."

"I disagree," Elliot said. "You've yet to return to your normal levels. For the record, I wouldn't have let you leave OI even as a Fifty."

"The alternative," she said sharply, "is to let whoever's got Nika Taylor just bleed her dry."

Stephen Diaz spoke up. "Michelle, with all due respect, you turned Rickie Littleton's brain into pudding."

That shut her up.

"What Elliot's saying," Diaz continued, "is that he needs to test you, thoroughly, to find out exactly what your skills are. I'll be doing the same thing for my new integration levels, before I go out there—before I put anyone at risk."

"We've already got a team of Forties on the street, looking for Devon Caine—that's Littleton's partner's name," Bach told them.

"Sir, I've had a taste of this guy Caine's emotional grid," Mac said. "Because of that, I can find him faster."

"You know him?" Shane asked her. "Caine?"

"No," Mac said. "But I know what he's capable of."

Diaz saw that Shane didn't understand and added, "We're pretty sure that Devon Caine raped and murdered a girl in the same South Boston garage where Nika Taylor was originally brought after her abduction. Mac was able to read the past emotional disturbance—both from the dead girl and from the killer. Who we believe is Caine."

"Jesus," Shane breathed, looking hard at Mac.

Who wouldn't meet his eyes more than briefly. "Yeah," she

said. "That sucked. But at least now I can use it to help us locate him."

"How does *that* work?" he asked. "I mean, do you just drive through the streets, hoping you get a hit? Or can you feel him from here and . . ."

"I have to be in close enough range," Mac explained. "But randomly driving through the streets?" She shook her head. "That's too inefficient. Although, if we hadn't gotten this lead, I would have started doing that. But now that we know his name, we can dig through his file and get a sense of the neighborhoods where he's lived, the places he hangs out . . . And then I drive through *those* neighborhoods, trying to get a whiff of him." She looked back at Bach, who was nodding.

"Let's get Mac stabilized and tested as one of our highest priorities, so we can send her out there," he said.

"And if she doesn't stabilize?" Elliot posited. He turned to look at Mac. "I know you don't want to hear this, but what if you can use your connection with Shane to elevate to a whole new integration level that you *can* control? What if part of the power he opens up for you is an ability, absolutely, to find Devon Caine? What if, with Shane's help, you can just close your eyes and tell us where the bastard is?"

"That's expecting a lot, Dr. Zerkowski," Bach pointed out somewhat sternly, "from something that you have no idea is truly linked."

"It *is* linked," Elliot insisted as Shane watched Mac, who was clearly still thinking about what Elliot had just said. *What if . . . ?*

"I understand that you *want* it to be linked," Bach said.

"And that doesn't mean that it's not, sir," Elliot countered as Mac turned to look at Shane—and the look she gave him was so similar to the way she'd looked at him in the bar in Kenmore Square, right before she'd stood up and brought him home, that he momentarily stopped breathing. Was she really considering . . . ?

Jesus, she *was*.

"You're right," Bach conceded. "But I urge caution." He, too, had made note of the way Mac was looking at Shane, and he re-peated, "Dr. Mackenzie. Caution."

She looked at Bach and even nodded, but Shane knew that this was a woman who was rarely cautious. "If this meeting's over," she announced, "I'll walk Laughlin back to his room."

Bach was sighing as he shook his head, and Shane stood up, fully expecting to be dismissed. But he had a question he wanted answered before he left. "What's the status on Edward O'Keefe—the old man?"

"He's still in ICU," Elliot reported. "He suffered a massive cor-onary, and he should be dead, but he's not. The medical team's doing their best to keep him that way."

"This meeting's not over. There's more to discuss," Bach said, and waited until Shane sat back down. "It's possible that Nika Taylor is the most talented Potential we've ever encountered." He got their full attention with that, but then added, "Even though we've never come across anything like this before, I'm virtually certain she's reaching out to her sister. Making contact via projec-tion into Anna's dreams."

As ridiculously whoo-whoo as that sounded to Shane, it was obvious that neither of the other Greater-Thans nor Elliot were on the verge of laughing. In fact, Diaz and Elliot exchanged an almost-startled glance.

Mac, too, was intrigued. "Anna's been *dreaming* about Nika?"

"Vividly." Bach said.

"Are you sure it wasn't just a nightmare?" Elliot asked. "She's under a lot of stress."

"I'm aware of that," Bach said with a nod. "But whatever she experienced, there was projection involved. Even though Anna re-ceived the images while she was asleep, it wasn't a dream. It was too chronological. Too linear. The theory I'm leaning toward is that these projections are unconscious—that Nika is unaware of what she's doing. And I don't think it's by mistake that Anna was asleep when she received the projections, either. I think the two sisters have a connection that's more easily accessible when Anna's experiencing REM sleep. FYI, that's where we came up with the name Devon Caine. And it was a positive hit—Devon Caine *was* the larger man who abducted Nika."

"Seriously?" Mac asked, her skepticism apparent. "Anna had a *dream,* and suddenly we've ID'd Nika's kidnapper? That sounds pretty freaking fishy to me, boss. Did you take her word for it or—"

Bach cut her off. "Anna's definitely not working for the Organization. You've met her."

"Or she's an Eighty-Nine or Ninety and has us all duped," Mac said.

"No." Bach was absolute. "I ran additional tests on her. She's integrated at only ten percent. She's who she says she is. Also there's . . . more. About the projection from Nika." He cleared his throat. "It wasn't just Anna who experienced it. I had the exact same dream—this was before we found Littleton. I was out in Newton and I was burning out, so I took a combat nap."

"While Anna was all the way back at OI?" Elliot confirmed and Bach nodded.

"My best guess," Bach said, "is that Nika subconsciously picked up on my earlier telepathic connection with her sister and somehow managed to send the same images—the same cry for help—to me."

"*Damn,*" Mac said. "A double projection, across dozens of miles . . . Who *is* this girl?"

Across the room, Diaz and Elliot were exchanging another long look, and Diaz nodded.

"Sir," Elliot said to Bach. "It's possible Stephen can help. We haven't had time to run tests, so I left it out of our report, but . . . We just found out that Stephen's been, um, sharing his dreams with me for several months now. He's able to project images from a dream state—from his apartment to mine. True, it's not as far as OI is to Newton, but . . . He's also been practicing a form of wake-initiated lucid dreaming that he calls *controlled dreaming.*"

"I can choose what I'm going to dream about before I fall asleep," Diaz explained. "I've learned to retain some degree of control over my unconscious mind."

Bach was nodding as Elliot continued, "If Nika really is as powerful as she appears to be, and her connection with her sister is so strong . . . It's entirely possible that, with Stephen's help, through this type of projected and controlled dreaming—"

"We can use Anna's unconscious mind to reach out and make contact with Nika," Bach finished for Elliot. He stood up. And this time the meeting *was* over. "Let's do it," he said. But then, as if he'd just made note of the time, he reached for the comm-station on his desk and typed in a quick message. "Anna was going to meet us for the end of this meeting—I'll have Ahlam bring her over to the sleep lab instead." He sent the message, then looked pointedly at Mac as he headed for the door. "Maybe we won't need you to find Devon Caine."

Mac nodded, glanced at Shane. "But having a Plan B," she said, "is always useful, sir. Until we find the girl, I'm going to do whatever it takes to be ready."

Bach stopped and looked back at her, even as the door opened, seemingly of its own volition. "At least be honest with yourself," he told her quietly. "That's all I've ever asked of you."

Mac's chin went up. "I always am."

Bach didn't look convinced as he went out the door with Elliot and Diaz behind him.

Which left Mac and Shane alone in Bách's office.

She looked at him. "Come on, Laughlin. I'll walk you to your room."

————

Anna followed her escort—a dark-haired teenage girl who'd quietly introduced herself as Ahlam—into a room in the R&D building that bore a sign saying "Laboratory Seven."

It looked more like a hospital room than a lab, with a door leading to a small bathroom off to one side, and an array of equipment on the wall around a bed. Although the bed was not your standard, narrow hospital-issue, but rather a generously proportioned and comfortable-looking queen-sized, complete with a sturdy wooden frame, thick blue comforter, and big, fluffy pillows.

A small sitting area nearby added to the obvious attempt to make the room more homey.

A curtain could be pulled around both the bed and the sitting area, in an attempt to cocoon it from the scanners and IV tubing and various wires.

Anna doubted that would help. Particularly since there was an obvious mirrored one-way observation window on the wall that couldn't be blocked by the curtain.

"Please wait here, Miss Anna," Ahlam told her, in her charming British-tinged accent. "Dr. Bach is on his way."

The girl quietly closed the door behind her, leaving Anna alone in the room.

She wasn't quite sure why she'd been brought here instead of over to Bach's office, where he and his Fifties were holding that meeting. But on the walk from the barracks, Ahlam had not been forthcoming.

The comm-station in the room was locked, so Anna couldn't resume her research while she waited—not that she'd had any luck so far. Or maybe she'd had too much luck. She'd already compiled a list of thirteen men, about the same age as the knife-wielding man she'd seen in her dream, who'd had disfiguring accidents sometime in the past thirty years—and a lack of funds to pay for corrective surgery. But she'd only just scratched the surface of Google hits. There were plenty more news articles to search.

Not to mention the fact that she'd focused on injuries received here in the Boston area. It was entirely possible that their man had received his scars in Miami. Or even Baghdad or Mumbai— a thought that led her to search for the records of former military personnel from the Boston area, who'd been injured in one of the past decades' many wars. The current corporate government was particularly lax in providing veterans care. Plastic surgery wasn't considered essential treatment.

Nor was mental health care—and it had seemed obvious that the scar-faced man had needed *that* as well.

Anna had just re-aimed her search in that direction when Ahlam had knocked on her door.

Now she sat on the edge of the bed and considered tapping on the mirrored glass and asking whoever was watching her to contact Bach and get his permission to turn on the computer.

But then she heard voices in the hall, and as she got to her feet, the door opened.

". . . biggest possible problem," the big, darkly handsome man named Stephen Diaz was saying with great intensity as he and Joseph Bach and Elliot came into the room, "is my limitation when it comes to telepathy. I've got a connection with Elliot, it's true, but it's also really new and I haven't tried establishing a similar link with any other non-Greater-Thans." He noticed Anna standing there. "Ms. Taylor."

Bach was already smiling a greeting. "I hope you haven't been waiting long," he said.

She shook her head and murmured, "No," and Bach glanced at Diaz and said, "We'll all just do our best." He looked back at Anna, gesturing toward the grouping of chairs, indicating that they should sit. "Please. And . . . may I?"

As she sat, she felt that now-familiar bump at the edge of her mind and she nodded, even as he added, "It'll be faster and easier to explain what we intend to do, if I can just . . ."

And just like that, Bach's warmth was back, and Anna understood almost instantaneously that Stephen Diaz had had experience with something called *controlled dreaming,* and that he was going to attempt to enter Anna's mind and use those techniques to try to establish a long-distance telepathic connection with Nika.

Diaz had never done anything like this before, but Nika's ability to project what she was seeing and feeling into Anna and Bach's dreams was new territory, too.

And even though Anna was what Bach called a Less-Than or a ten-percenter, he believed that her bond with her sister was unusually strong. He also believed that Nika's fledgling powers—even untrained—were massive.

So Diaz would use this controlled dreaming to implant within Anna's mind a dream in which she'd explain all she'd learned about Greater-Thans and the Obermeyer Institute to Nika, with the intention of this dream being ready and in place should Nika reach out to Anna again while she was sleeping.

In this dream, Anna would at least reassure Nika that help was on its way.

At best, maybe—through Anna—Diaz and Bach could help Nika learn to control and develop her powers so that she could help them locate and rescue her.

It was a long shot, but Anna was already nodding her consent. *Let's do it. Let's try it.*

But Bach's explanation wasn't over.

In order to do this, you'll need to be asleep, because the unconscious mind is always more . . . Bach paused. *Adaptable:*

And malleable? Anna asked.

Yes.

And wasn't *this* going to be fun? She was going to be incredibly vulnerable during this procedure. Stephen Diaz would have complete access to her unconscious brain. Her every fantasy, her every petty thought, her every fear, hope, desire . . . Her worst nightmares and memories . . . This stranger would have access to them all.

I'll be in the room, too, Bach told her. *Along with Elliot.*

Anna nodded. As hard as it would be, she was going to do this. If it would help them find Nika, she'd do anything. But . . . *I'm not sure I'll be able to fall asleep in front of a crowd.*

We'll give you a drug to assist—if we get that far.

The very first thing they had to test was whether or not Diaz had the ability to enter Anna's mind. He could, apparently, initiate a telepathic connection with a fellow Greater-Than. And he'd recently established a mental link with Elliot, but the two men were lovers—information that surprised her. She'd honestly had no clue.

Across the room, as Elliot was activating the computer he spoke quietly to Diaz. "You know, it's okay if you call me a fraction."

"Yeah, well, I don't want to call you that," Diaz countered just as quietly.

"But it's true. It's a fact."

"It's derogatory. Besides, it's actually a fact that we're *all* fractions. No one's a hundred percent integrated."

"Still," Elliot said, "I prefer it to Less-Than."

"Yeah, but you're not that, either," Diaz said as he moved closer and put his hand on Elliot's shoulder.

Anna must've simply missed it earlier, but now their connection seemed so obvious. Elliot glanced up and Diaz smiled down into his eyes—as if they were sharing some unspoken joke.

She turned back to Bach, who'd gently withdrawn his presence from her mind.

It was good that he had, because Anna found herself wishing that *he* was the one who'd have full access to the inside of her head. Taking a deep breath, she turned to Diaz and Elliot. "What do I need to do?"

Diaz straightened up and crossed the room toward her. "It's more about what I need to do," he told her. "I'm nowhere near as skilled in telepathy as Dr. Bach, so I apologize in advance for that. It's also possible—likely—that I'll need some kind of physical contact to bolster the telepathic connection, so . . ."

He held out his hand to her as he sat down beside her, even as Elliot swiveled in the comm-station seat, so he could watch.

Anna found herself glancing at Bach, who nodded his reassurance, and again she found herself wishing . . .

But Stephen Diaz had already closed his eyes, and he didn't open them as she put her hand in his. His hand was large and warm and slightly damp—he was nervous.

"It's okay," she told him quietly, as she braced herself for . . . What? She wasn't quite sure, but she suspected the nothing she was feeling wasn't right.

Still, she waited.

And waited.

"Stephen, don't try so hard," Elliot said quietly from across the room. "Your integration levels are dropping. Just try to relax."

Diaz opened his eyes then, and they were filled with both anguish and longing as he looked directly at Anna and said, "God, I want to help find Nika, but I'm sorry. I don't think I'm capable of doing this."

"Let's see if you can't augment him," Bach suggested—and he was talking to Elliot, who quickly pushed his chair and rolled across the room to put his hand gently on the back of Diaz's neck.

The Greater-Than closed his eyes at Elliot's contact and . . .

Anna felt it—just a whisper of movement—as if someone were mentally brushing past her, not quite touching, just stirring the air between them. Still, she said, "I can sense you, Stephen," hoping that information would help him.

"Keep breathing," Elliot murmured, moving in closer to wrap both of his arms around Diaz in an embrace, his head tipped against the bigger man's. "You can do this—I know you can."

And there it was again, that ghost of a whisper of a sensation. But even if Elliot was somehow augmenting Diaz's power, it apparently wasn't enough.

Anna turned to Bach. "Can you help? Is there any way you could combine your power with Stephen's?"

"It's never been done."

"But we're experimenting," she reminded him. "So let's experiment."

Bach looked at Elliot—Diaz's eyes were still tightly closed.

"We've tried—and succeeded—with the equivalent of a mental conference call with a group of Greater-Thans," Elliot pointed out. "The biggest problem I could imagine comes from Anna's inability to shield her thoughts. Her privacy will be compromised with both of you inside of her head. But as long as she's willing—"

"I am," she said, even as she inwardly cringed.

Stephen's eyes were still closed. "Stephen, are you all right with this?" Bach asked, reaching out to touch the bigger man on his arm.

It was then that it happened. Just, boom.

Bach was inside of her head—no asking permission, no nudge, no greeting, no etiquette. It was as if he were just suddenly there—mentally knocking her over and lying on top of her, completely covering her with his telepathic presence.

He was astonished, too. *What the hell . . . ?*

Just as quickly as he'd appeared, he was gone, and Anna realized that she'd been thrown back in her seat, and the movement had made her lose her grip on Stephen's hand.

Stephen opened his eyes at the break in their contact, but it was clear that neither he nor Elliot had a clue as to what had just happened.

Bach, though, was a different story. "What the . . . heck was that?" he asked. He'd used a different word inside of her head, and he knew it, too, because he actually looked abashed and added, "I beg your pardon." Or maybe he was apologizing for the unrestrained burst of emotion she'd felt from him—which was a first, even with all the times he'd traipsed through her head.

Joseph Bach was on fire from his absolute commitment to finding Nika. Anna knew that now, without a doubt.

He liked her, too—Anna knew that as well. He thought she was courageous and smart and extremely beautiful, and that made her feel embarrassingly pleased—especially considering how insignificant that was compared to her need to rescue her sister.

"What was what?" Stephen asked, looking from Anna to Bach and back again. "What happened?"

"Elliot, step back," Bach ordered, and Elliot let go of Stephen and rolled his chair away just a bit. "Let's try that again."

Anna knew what Bach wanted and she held out her hand to Stephen, who took it, even as he looked quizzically at Bach. Who met Anna's eyes and nodded before reaching out again, and putting his hand solidly down on Stephen's shoulder.

And just as quickly—although far less awkwardly this time around—Bach was again inside of her head. Now, however, because he'd been ready for it, everything he was thinking and feeling was back to being cool and restrained and completely under control.

Stephen? she felt Bach ask.

I don't think he's with us. Anna closed her eyes, but . . . *No.* She couldn't feel the other Greater-Than at all.

In fact, "What's going on?" Stephen asked.

"Apparently, you're a conduit," Bach told him. "I've achieved a telepathic connection with Anna, merely through physical contact with you."

"Really?" Stephen asked. He looked from Bach to Anna and back. "Is it related to my ability to deliver an electrical current, do you think? I mean, could it be physiological? Do you have an automatic telepathic connection with Anna when you touch her?"

"No," Bach answered. "I've never experienced telepathy triggered by physical contact. Not with anyone."

Actually, Anna told him, *there is something that happens when we touch. I can feel you. It's not the same as when you're inside of my head like this, but . . .*

"Wow," Elliot said, unaware that he was speaking over Anna's thoughts to Bach. "So this thing with Stephen is new."

"But totally useless," Stephen pointed out, his frustration obvious. "Dr. Bach doesn't need me to establish a connection with anyone."

"Maybe we'll find that you're a conduit for other powers as well," Elliot suggested. "Until we run some tests—"

"It still seems pretty useless."

Bach tested the conduit theory, taking his hand away from Stephen, and sure enough, he was instantly gone from Anna's mind. Holding her gaze, he reached out and put his hand on her knee. And there it was—that tingling sensation she'd felt before—that sense of feeling his presence, his power, his passion. But it *was* vastly different from a telepathic link. And, really, maybe part of it was the simple unsteadiness that came from gazing back into this man's ridiculously pretty eyes.

"I feel waves of your concern for your sister," Bach murmured, "but I feel that from you regardless of physical contact."

He moved his hand back to Stephen's shoulder and . . .

"Whoa," Anna said, because—again—the sudden rush of Bach being inside of her head was nothing like his usual, gentle, almost-gradual entrance.

Sorry.

I knew it was coming—it's just very different.

I have less control, Bach told her. *It's not unlike going into freefall and experiencing the pull of gravity. Once the connection's made, I'm going to end up in your mind, whether either of us likes it or not.*

"I don't feel anything," Stephen said. "I'm trying, but . . ." He shook his head.

"Augment," Bach ordered, looking over at Elliot even as he shot Anna a *Hold on.*

I'm ready, she reassured him.

But when Elliot, too, put his hand on Stephen's other shoulder . . .

Nothing changed.

"I've got a telepathic connection to Elliot," Stephen reported. "But that's it."

"And I'm still only in Anna's mind," Bach confirmed.

Stephen shook his head in disgust, as Elliot said, "Passive skills can be very useful."

"Not for this," Stephen said, his frustration ringing in his voice. "If we're going to use controlled dreaming to find Nika, I need to get inside of Anna's head."

"Still, this is a talent we haven't seen before." Elliot could put a positive spin on anything. "It's very cool."

"I don't have the power to establish a telepathic connection to more than a single ten-percenter at a time," Bach said. "Not even with another Greater-Than. But let's see what happens—" He broke his connection with Anna by letting go of Stephen. "—if I first establish a telepathic connection with Dr. Diaz, and then we use him in this conduit function to bring me over to Anna. Maybe, that way, he'll come, too."

"That could work," Elliot said. He smiled at Stephen. "See, maybe not so useless after all. Just give me a sec to get back to the comm-station . . ." He rolled back across the room.

"Ready?" Bach asked Stephen, who closed his eyes and nodded, despite the muscle that was jumping in his jaw. They must've connected swiftly because Bach added, "And now . . ."

Stephen held out his hand to Anna, his eyes still tightly closed, teeth still clenched.

Anna looked at Bach, who again held her gaze and nodded as she reached for the other man and . . .

"Whoa, hey, wait a minute," Elliot said from over at the computer—and that was the last thing Anna heard before the world seemed to split in half.

The pain was incredible as she was engulfed by a brilliant, blinding light and surrounded by an invasive, high-pitched squeal that was so loud that she felt it in her stomach and her spine, as her head almost seemed to explode.

She heard the sound of someone shouting—wow, that was *her* voice—as she felt herself flung back, as her head hit the wall behind the chair. But even that was okay, because compared to that original razor-sharp burst of pain, the duller thud was an improvement, and now it was fading, thank God. Her vision, too, was slowly starting to return from the darkness into which she'd been plunged after the fireworks went off in her brain.

Still, things were blurry as she felt herself lifted up, as she felt herself moving, and then felt the softness of what had to be the sleep-lab bed beneath her. It was then that her vision cleared enough to see Joseph Bach gazing down at her, concern written on his too-handsome face.

He was already inside of her head—she suddenly became aware of the warmth of his presence.

"She's okay," he was saying, talking not to her, which confused her until the clouds in her mind cleared enough for her to remember that both Stephen and Elliot were in the room with them.

Anna tried to sit up, but Bach held her in place even as he shook his head and spoke aloud, even as he mentally told her the exact same thing. "Don't move. Not yet. Elliot's med scanning you."

So she stayed still, but she had to ask, "Is Stephen okay?"

"I'm fine." The Greater-Than stepped forward so that she could see him, too.

You're the only one who had a negative reaction, Bach told her. He then spoke aloud, turning to include the two other men in the conversation. "We should have done more tests before trying that."

"Maybe it was my fault," Anna said. "Maybe I should have been better prepared."

"Whatever the case, whatever happened," Elliot said, coming over to look down at Anna, too, "it lowered and then raised your blood pressure dramatically." Bach turned to look up at him, and Anna could feel both his concern and dismay as the doctor nodded. "Dangerously. It's back to normal now. She's okay, but . . ."

"We're not trying that again." Bach was already shaking his head.

Anna pushed herself up so that she was sitting. "Maybe if I can somehow brace for it—"

Bach cut her off. "No."

"But if it's the fastest way to find Nika—"

"*No.*"

Joe, please . . .

He gently extracted himself from her mind as he said, "I want to find her, too, and doing it quickly is important—but not enough to risk your life."

"I'm fine now," she told him as he continued to shake his head. "Maybe it was only a fluke . . ."

Stephen cleared his throat. "Maybe I can show Dr. Bach exactly what it is that I do," he said, looking at Elliot as if for support. "With the controlled dreaming. Give him, I don't know, a road map or recipe . . . ?"

Elliot nodded. "It's worth a try, Maestro, because . . . I'm with you. Anna, we're lucky you didn't have a stroke." Back to Stephen. "Your integration levels were suddenly in flux. You were all over the place. That's why I shouted to hold up."

Bach was not happy at that news—nor was Stephen.

"I'm so sorry," he said. "I didn't hear you."

"I want a jot scan running on Dr. Diaz," Bach ordered Elliot. "Twenty-four/seven."

"He's stabilized now," Elliot reported. "He's steady again at sixty-one."

"But obviously his integration levels *aren't* steady, despite what you previously believed."

"I *have* been jot scanning him continuously," Elliot replied. "This was the only blip since his levels first went up."

"But it happened when it mattered," Bach said. "And Anna could have been badly hurt. This is why we advocate slow and steady advances—controlled increases in integration."

"But I wasn't badly hurt," Anna said as Elliot bristled at Bach's words.

"Everyone spikes at some point," Elliot said. "With an eleven-point increase, there's going to be an adjustment period."

"That's contrary to what you said earlier," Bach pointed out.

"He's solidly sixty-one, sir," Elliot said. "*Most* of the time. And even though you might have preferred for him to stay celibate—"

"Dr. Zerkowski, I've never said that," Bach said.

"You didn't have to say it," Elliot countered.

"El, stop," Stephen interrupted him. "Dr. Bach is right. We thought I was stable, but obviously I'm not—which means we need to be more cautious."

"More cautious," Elliot repeated.

"In dealing with my enhanced abilities," Stephen said. He reached out and touched Elliot—it was barely noticeable, just one finger pressed lightly against the other man's back. But whatever he said via their telepathic connection, it made Elliot exhale forcefully, as if he'd been holding his breath, and then nod.

And apologize. Both to Stephen and Bach. "Sorry, Stephen. Sir, I'm . . . sorry. I'm . . . guilty of whatever you think I'm guilty of. But then again, we're all way more emotionally involved in this situation than usual. And isn't *that* saying something, considering Mac's not even in the room."

Bach was back to shaking his head and laughing, but not as if he found anything particularly funny. He took a deep breath and turned to Stephen. "Let's see if you can't show me how you do your controlled dreaming, but let's go to my office to do it." He looked at Elliot. "I want a complete medical exam for Ms. Taylor—including another full med scan."

"You got it," Elliot said. He went to the comm-station. "I need a nurse in sleep lab seven."

"Excuse me, Dr. Bach," Stephen spoke up. "Would you mind giving me a minute with Elliot?"

"Of course not," Bach said, and the two men slipped out the door, into the hall.

Leaving Anna alone with Bach.

"So now the plan is for you to learn—from Stephen—how to do this controlled dreaming thing," she confirmed, "which means it's going to be you inside my head while I'm asleep . . . ?"

He nodded as he went to the comm-station to check whatever readout was on the screen. "Yeah."

"I'm relieved," she said. "I mean, Dr. Diaz seems great, but . . ."

Bach looked up, meeting her gaze, as if he knew that she had something important to tell him.

"The idea of him having access to all of my thoughts was disconcerting," Anna admitted, and then said it in a rush: "I've done some things I'm not proud of. Things Nika doesn't know about. I realize that, as we try to make this connection with her, it might not be possible, but if it is . . . ? I'd very much like to keep it that way. Keep her from . . . knowing about . . . Things. I guess I just feel like I have a better chance of that with you."

"I'll do my best," he said.

"Thanks," she said.

"For the record," Bach said quietly. "I'm not going to judge you. You know, I'm human, too. I've done plenty of things I'm not proud of. With that said, I'll try—as best I can—to respect your privacy. And if I can't, I'll keep your secrets."

"Just help me get my sister back," Anna told him.

"That," he said, "I promise you I'll do."

EIGHTEEN

Shane didn't say anything. He just followed Mac out of Dr. Bach's office and toward the bank of elevators that would take them down to the tunnels.

Even though it was a nice day, walking outside meant they'd have to go through a security checkpoint to get into the barracks. And if Mac was really going to do this, she wanted to get it over with.

Yeah. Right.

That's why she was in such a big honking hurry to get to Shane's quarters.

As Mac pushed the button for the elevator, she glanced at Shane, who met her gaze only briefly before returning his attention to the numbers counting down above the door. The lift finally landed on their floor and opened with a *ding*, and he waited, always the officer and gentleman, letting her go in first.

She knew he had something to say—when *didn't* he?—but that he'd been waiting for the semi-privacy of the elevator to say it, so she didn't give him a chance to speak. Instead, as they went down, she went over to the comm-station that was in the elevator. "Computer, access MM-one. Initiate a jot scan focusing on integration levels of myself and newly processed Potential Shane Laughlin. Continue scanning constantly for an as-of-yet undetermined amount of time into the future." Her stomach growled, loudly, but she ignored it. "Also activate the comm-station, including the printer, in the living quarters of newly processed Potential Shane Laughlin."

"Computer, access SL-five. Send the two meals that Dr. Mackenzie orders most often to the room of *newly processed* Potential Shane Laughlin," Shane added, giving her a look that told her he got her message about the fact that he was the outsider here, "with room-service setups for two."

"What?" Mac laughed her scornful disbelief as the elevator doors opened into the tunnels with a *ding*. "Computer, cancel that last request," she said, reaching to shut off the computer.

But right before she hit the switch, Shane said, "Computer, belay the cancellation of that last order."

She would have had to power the computer back up to belay his belaying of her cancellation, but that would have meant standing there, holding the elevator doors open, and inconveniencing a group of twelve-year-old girls who were no doubt heading for class. Instead, she just got off, shaking her head as she led Shane down the tunnel to the barracks.

"This isn't a four-star hotel," she told him, letting her annoyance ring in her voice, "with room service."

"I was told I could use my computer access code to order food that would be delivered to my rooms, so . . ."

"Yeah, because you're locked in, Navy," Mac pointed out. "So it's more like prison-cell service. But you can call it room service if that makes you feel better."

Shane laughed as he hustled to keep up with her through the tunnel as she double-timed it. "Are you really pissed off because I figured you were hungry, too, and might want something to eat?"

"This isn't a date, Laughlin," she said shortly, grateful that the tunnel was empty, so that she could be direct and not mince words. "It's an experiment."

"Even scientists have to eat," he pointed out. "I thought I'd order something you like."

"Yeah, well, I *like* to eat alone."

"Yeah, well, *I'm* hungry, so . . ."

"Then you should have ordered something *you* like to eat," she said. "Trust me, Laughlin, you don't have to work for this. All you have to do is shut up and walk."

"Has it occurred to you that maybe I ordered what I ordered because it's the only way I'm ever going to find out more about you?" he asked.

They'd reached the elevators that would take them up into the barracks, and Mac savagely punched the call button. "You already know all you need to know."

"I disagree."

The elevator opened and more twelve-year-olds spilled out. Shane held the door and then waited for Mac to go first before following her in.

She pushed the button for his floor—the third—and as the doors slid shut, she turned to him.

He was watching her with those eyes and a hit-me-with-your-best-shot expression on his face, clearly waiting for her to continue the argument, no doubt planning his rebuttal to whatever she had to say. So she didn't say anything.

She just stepped toward him, closing the space between them and then pushing him back so that he bumped the elevator wall, even as she pulled his head down so she could kiss him.

She could feel his surprise even though he didn't hesitate to kiss her back. But then he definitely faltered as she reached between them for a junk-grab and stroked him right through his pants. He was already packing wood—his euphemism of choice—but of course she'd been aware of that starting back in Bach's office.

She'd practically smelled his desire for her during that meeting.

Here in the elevator, he was both incredibly turned on and horrified by her PDA, but not horrified enough to push her out of grab range. In fact, he himself took some serious double-handed possession of her ass as he continued to encourage her to lick his tonsils while he tried to do the same to hers.

And the knowledge that if she'd unfastened his jeans and somehow magically adiosed her own pants, he would've screwed her right then and there, regardless of the security cameras that he *had* to know were broadcasting their images down into Security, made her want to both laugh and cry.

He was that far gone.

As the elevator doors dinged open, she roughly jerked herself out of his grasp and went out into the hall, saying, "*That?* Is all you need to know."

It would've been the perfect tough-bitch line, tossed carelessly over her shoulder—if her voice hadn't wobbled. But maybe she was lucky and he'd missed that.

"Whoa," he was saying, "*whoa,*" as he staggered out after her into the hall, his eyes a tad out of focus. He was breathing as if he'd just sprinted a 5K, which would have made her smile—if any of this shit had been real. "I'm sorry, but . . . Hello? Cameras?"

Mac was already beelining it for his apartment door. "Grab a clue, Boy Scout," she said. "There's no one in OI who couldn't guess what we're doing here—not after the report that Elliot submitted on my enhanced ability to heal. They don't need video down in Analysis. They're probably making popcorn and getting ready to huddle around a read-out of our vital signs from our on-going jot scans. Hope you don't get performance anxiety."

She unlocked his apartment with her passkey and went straight to the comm-station. "Computer, access MM-one. Type and print a legal document for Potential Laughlin to sign," she ordered, "stating that he's been given a full explanation of my power and correlating skills, and despite my recommendation otherwise, that he's willing to participate in today's experiment. Use whatever legalese is necessary to make the document binding immediately upon his signature."

"Computer, access SL-five. Please adjust the language in the agreement to include any and all experiments," Shane raised his voice to add, "starting today but continuing into the future, as needed."

Mac looked at him. "As *needed?*"

He shrugged. "Hey, we might need to do more. In the name of science. And I'd prefer not to have to take the time to sign additional documents. Assuming, of course, that today's *tests*"—he made air quotes—"don't kill me. Hmm, maybe I better handwrite an addendum stating that, should I not survive, that's okay with me, too, because if what we're going to do here is even half as good as what just happened in that elevator, I'll die smiling."

Mac just looked at him as the printer whirred to life and spat out the document she'd requested.

"Uh-oh," he said. "No laughter. Not even an eye-roll." He crossed the room to take the document from the printer tray. He glanced at it, glanced at Mac. "Is a pen okay, or you want this signed in blood?" He didn't wait for her to answer. He took it over to the kitchen counter and picked up the pen that was atop a pad by the phone. The ballpoint scratched against the paper before he recapped the pen and set it down with a very solid-sounding thunk. And turned back to Mac. "It's official. I'm all yours."

The stupid thing was that he meant it. Or he thought he meant it. He was standing there with that heat simmering in his pretty eyes and on his too-handsome face, with that lean, hard-muscled body with his naval officer attitude, and Mac wanted to cry—or hit something—because she didn't want just another impersonal sexual encounter with this man.

She wanted something that she could never have.

But Shane was just like Justin, and Robby, and all of the other guys she'd used, and who'd used her in return, all the way back . . . To Tim.

Who'd been so handsome and funny and smart and sweet when she'd first moved in with her father and Janice, after her mother and little brother had died.

He'd been the only one to offer her any comfort—if you could call what he'd offered that.

And Shane . . . ? He was doing the very same thing, responding in the very same way.

Not to her, but to her power.

God, Mac hated her power.

She wished she were telepathic instead of empathic. Being telepathic would have been easier to manage. It was far more straight-forward than her stupid abilities, and it wasn't fair.

Of course, fair had nothing to do with it.

Powers and talents were not fair. And Greater-Thans were not equal.

They were individual. Your strengths were your strengths, and you were born with them—the same way that Shane had been born with those pretty reddish hues in his hair.

And Mac could only hope that that same unique individuality held when it came to being enhanced—that even though Diaz's boost in integration levels had come from his having formed an intimate emotional attachment to Elliot, Mac's shift upward would be found to come purely from steaming hot sex.

Because the idea that she was skyrocketing up around sixty because of her *feelings* for Shane . . .

It was unbearable, even to consider.

But it was then, as Shane was standing there gazing at her, obviously watching and waiting to see what she was going to do now that he was *all hers,* that his eyes narrowed. "Shit," he said.

And now the heat was replaced with something else. His eyes were still warm, but it was less about sex and more about . . . kindness?

"Jesus," Shane said, "I can't believe I'm saying this, but . . ." He exhaled hard, and shook his head. "Let's not do this, Michelle. Not like this."

She couldn't believe he'd said it either. In fact, she was so surprised, she didn't know what to say, so she reamed him for the fact that he'd used her given name. "It's Mac," she told him sharply. "Or Dr. Mackenzie. Or just Mackenzie."

"I kinda like Michelle," he said. "It suits you."

"Fuck you."

"Yes please," Shane said. "In my wildest dreams. But right now? No. I honestly don't think that's smart. I don't think . . . Look, I don't know why I scare you so badly, but—"

"*Fuck* you!"

"Not like, *Grrrr,*" he said, making bear claws of his hands. "That's not what I'm talking about, so don't get all defensive. That's not what I mean when I say *scare*. I think there's a good chance that you could kick my ass if you wanted to."

"Not a *chance,*" she said. "I *could.*"

Mac could see—clearly—that he doubted it would be that absolute, but he let her win. "I've been in battlefield situations," he told her. "I've studied the psychology of what fear can do, and I know that it comes out as anger, and ever since we walked out of Dr. Bach's office, you've been angry as hell at me and—"

She started to sputter. "If you seriously think—"

But he held up his hands. "Will you just let me finish?"

"No," Mac said. "Because you *are* finished. You don't know me. How do you know what's angry and what's just . . . *bored.*"

He laughed at that, his amusement genuine. "You expect me to believe that I *bore* you?"

She shrugged expansively. "You really don't know me. A few hours of sex and a coupla conversations . . . ? You have no idea who I am."

"*Fuck you* is bored? Because where I come from, *fuck you* is angry. It's upset. It's . . . fuck you! I don't bore you, *Michelle.* I scare you shitless."

"Sorry, but you really don't." She shot him a blast of sincerity and he should have believed her and backed down.

Instead, Shane raised his voice. "Computer, confirm ongoing jot scan of Dr. Michelle Mackenzie."

"Jot scan confirmed," the computer responded.

"Computer, provide the audio of Dr. Mackenzie's heart rate please," Shane ordered.

"What?" Mac said as a low-pitched throbbing came through the overhead speakers. "What gives you the right—"

"Sounds a little accelerated," Shane said. "Of course, I'm not a doctor. Computer, comparison of Dr. Mackenzie's current pulse to her average resting heart rate."

The computer complied, reporting that she had the average

resting heart rate of an athlete, but it was much higher than that now—as Mac shook her head.

"Hmm," Shane said. "Maybe all Greater-Thans' heart rates increase when they're *bored.*"

"Computer, terminate," she ordered, and the sound cut out.

"I scare you because you like me," Shane insisted. "And I know you think the only reason I'm into you is because of your voodoo, but that's not true."

"Isn't it?" she asked. And she let him have a blast of that very same *voodoo,* which made him take a step toward her. And then another.

"I've told you things that I've never told anyone," Shane said, clearly determined to keep the conversation going even though the body language she was giving him now was pure *shut up and kiss me.*

"About cage fighting?" Mac said, trying to be flip and irreverent.

He took another step toward her, even though he was clearly fighting it. "About the blacklist. I know you probably think it's bullshit, but the shame I feel when I think about that is . . . I'm a Navy SEAL, Mac. I'm used to winning, and I'm used to receiving respect—hard-earned respect. Being blacklisted is . . . It makes me sick."

She wanted to ask him about it—what had gone so terribly wrong—but she didn't dare, for fear he'd realize she gave a shit.

Because she did. Despite everything she'd learned from Tim, and from every other man who'd come after him, Mac *did* care about Shane. Too much.

"We were assigned to take out a high-ranking terrorist," he told her quietly, even though she hadn't asked. "I was leading an eight-man team—my very best men. The risks were incredible, but they all volunteered to go.

"We inserted just over the border of a country that our military wasn't supposed to be in, with the understanding that if we were caught by our so-called allies, we were on our own." He sighed, a heavy exhale of air. "But we weren't apprehended. The entire op went like clockwork. We easily found and ID'd our target and we were literally moments from transmitting the coordinates for a stealth missile attack, when one of my men—I won't tell you who, and it really doesn't matter. But he realized that our target wasn't a terrorist, but was instead the sole surviving witness to a political assassination that certain of our corporate government's CEOs had spent months insisting they hadn't carried out. And here we were, about to eliminate that only witness . . . ?"

"Shit," Mac said.

"Shit plus," Shane corrected her. "I didn't want my men faced with that kind of moral dilemma," he continued, "so I ordered them back over the border and I called in the coordinates for a deserted farmhouse. As things were blowing up down the road, I helped the witness disappear. Forever, but in a much nicer her-heart's-still-beating way." He paused. "Problem was, there was a second search team sent after her—a team of mercenaries that I wasn't told about. And they'd set up a more accurate mortar attack, which made it . . . kinda dangerous. But I got her out. She won't be found unless she wants to be—and she doesn't want to be. She was pretty invested in seeing her children grow up."

"You did it all by yourself?" Mac had to ask.

"I had help from the locals," Shane said.

And wasn't it interesting, the way he'd worded that. It wasn't an absolute yes or no. So she pushed. "You sent your team of eight SEALs—"

"Seven," he corrected her. "I was the eighth."

"They didn't help you. At all."

"Nope." He popped the P, and again all she got from him was a wave of honesty and truth.

And Mac realized . . . She grabbed a piece of paper and wrote it down, because the computer was listening in. Her handwriting was shitty, but as Shane came to look over her shoulder, it was clear he had no trouble reading it. *You fooled the lie detectors because of the language that you're using. You* ordered *your men over the border. But they didn't go. And they didn't help you, you helped* <u>*them*</u> *hide the witness. Because you were injured. Your ankle, that you told me about, back in the bar???*

She looked up into his somber eyes and he nodded as he gazed back at her.

He'd intentionally taken the fall, protecting his men. And pissing off a lot of people high up in the corporate government, no doubt.

She didn't say it or even write it, but it was obvious that he knew what she was thinking. "I did what I had to do," he told her quietly. "And as much as I'd like to tell you more . . ." He'd already said too much.

I won't tell anyone, she promised him, writing it on the note and then, after he'd read it, tearing it up into small pieces that she took over to the sink, soaked into a sodden mass, and then ground up in the disposal.

"Thanks," he said, as she turned the grinder back off.

"You're a freaking idiot," she said.

He smiled at that. "I did the right thing."

Again, Mac was struck by the intensity of his convictions. It radiated off of him in waves of honor and sincerity that she felt in the pit of her stomach. It practically made him glow.

Even at his most deceptive, he was pure and golden and true.

He was so wrong for her—for someone who lived and breathed trickery and illusion.

Still, she wanted him, more than she'd ever wanted anyone . . .

He looked away from her first, turning and gesturing toward the door. "Look, as much as I want you to stay, I really do think you should go. Or stay to have lunch with me, but—"

"No," Mac said, forcing her feet to move past him. "You're right. I'll go. There are other ways to test this theory. I shouldn't do this with you."

But before she opened the door, he caught her arm and pulled her back toward him. "Other ways? What other ways?"

And now Mac was standing so close to him, she could feel his body heat. She had to tilt her head back to look up into his eyes as he frowned down at her.

It should have pissed her off—his proprietary attitude combined with the manhandling, except he wasn't really manhandling her. Yes, he was still holding her wrist, but he was being careful not to hurt her. Still, she was glad she'd ordered the computer to shut off the sound of her heart, because it was now undeniably racing.

She shook her head. "Just . . . other ways that don't involve you."

"Do you mean with other *people*?" he asked. He was jealous—she could feel it. "Other test subjects—other *men*?"

"Or women," Mac said. "Sex is sex, right?"

He blinked. "Are you . . . really bisexual?"

"No," she said. "Just an asshole. Who likes jerking your chain."

He laughed at that—a low chuckle. But the warmth of his breath brushed her face and she found herself looking at his mouth. It was just a glance, she looked away almost immediately, but he didn't miss it, and he pulled her even closer so that his leg touched hers, and her breasts brushed his chest.

"No way," Shane murmured, "am I going to let you *experiment* with anyone else. That's not gonna happen."

"*Let* me?" she asked. "I don't think you get to *let me* do anything."

"Oh, yeah?" he said. "Because right now, I'm going to let you kiss me." Now he was watching her mouth, and she fully expected him to lower his just a few scant inches. But he didn't.

And he didn't.

Because he was waiting for her to kiss him.

"Take your time," Shane murmured. "I've got all day."

Despite the fact that Mac held the power, he was somehow able to resist her. And she was the one who surrendered—she couldn't stand it anymore. She went up on her toes even as she pulled his head down and kissed him—knowing that she was making a huge mistake, but unable to stop herself.

The right thing to do would be to walk out that door and find some other unattached Potential willing to sign her permission slip and participate in this test of her expanding integration levels. Because sex *was* sex. It was better to keep it purely physical—to keep her emotions out of it, because no matter how she played it, it wasn't going to be an emotional encounter for whomever she hooked up with. It couldn't be.

Everyone wanted her. Guaranteed. That was her power. Everyone wanted her—which meant no one really did. Because they didn't really want *her.*

Who she was had nothing to do with it. It was all about manipulation and control and biology.

Although the bitch of it was that the emotion that her victims experienced read, to her, like real love. But it wasn't real—it was purely a reaction. It was no different than someone who was allergic to strawberries eating some and getting hives.

Still, Mac heard herself moan as Shane angled his head to kiss her harder, deeper, as he massaged her breast, his hand already up beneath her shirt.

"I know I should make you leave, but . . . Damn," Shane breathed before he kissed her again.

And Mac knew she wasn't going to stop them either. She wanted this too badly. Even though she knew it was going to come back and kick her in the head.

She wanted . . .

God, she wanted to feel good, to erase all of the ugliness that the world had dumped on her in the past few hellish hours.

And she wanted her integration levels to jump right to sixty. Shit, she'd take fifty-five. But she wanted it to come from no-strings sex. She wanted proof that it wasn't Shane alone who enhanced her—that she could have sex with anyone and get the same results.

But most of all, she didn't want to wonder if—maybe—Shane really did like her, too. She didn't want to spend any time at all wondering if maybe his wanting to screw her was a natural and honest response to genuine attraction. Like, maybe he honestly had a thing for short women with round faces, shitty hair, and small boobs. Maybe he thought she was funny or smart or interesting, and his wanting to fuck her sideways had nothing to do with her power to make everyone want to fuck her sideways.

She didn't want to wonder that, so she purposely took all wondering off the table by letting him have a nuclear blast of her power.

"Holy shit," he breathed as he could no longer resist her. He tried to unfasten her pants with one hand as he unbuckled his belt with his other. "I gotta . . ."

Mac knew exactly what he needed and she helped him by kicking off her sneakers and pushing her pants down her legs, as he wrestled with his zipper, still kissing her all the while.

Then, God, her pants were off, and he'd freed himself enough to pick her up—still kissing her—and wrap her legs around his waist.

And just like that he was inside of her, which felt unbelievably good, but there just wasn't enough resistance even though he desperately tried to get deeper by pulling her closer. And she thought, then, that he was going to carry her into the bedroom, because he headed in that direction, but she was wrong, he was going for the wall.

She felt it hit her back and then, God, they both got what they wanted—what she'd wanted since the last time they'd done this—and they both cried out because it was that damn good, except now Shane was laughing, too, as he moved against her, inside her, as he broke away from kissing her to look into her eyes.

"You're unbelievable, you know that?" he breathed. "You kill me—you're just so freaking great . . ."

And Mac roughly pulled his mouth down to hers and kissed him again, because, no, she really didn't want to know.

———

This wasn't going to be fun.

Bach's back was twingeing—which happened when he pushed himself too hard, or for too long without significant rest.

Or when he was under significant stress.

And yes, his session with Stephen Diaz, learning all about controlled dreaming, had been a tad stressful. Bach had been exposed to a serious amount of TMI about the other Greater-Than's fledgling relationship with Elliot Zerkowski.

Diaz had been embarrassed by the content of the dreams he'd programmed himself to have—dreams he'd managed to project, while sleeping, into the mind of a Less-Than.

Which truly was remarkable.

And while Diaz had been successful in showing Bach exactly what he believed he'd done both to control and project his dreams, there was no guarantee that Bach would be able to access those same neural pathways and open a connection, via Anna, to Nika.

Still, he was going to try.

His back twinged again, but it was nothing, however, compared to the pain of the crash, or of the horrible sensation of no-pain that had followed for so long, all those years ago.

So he ignored it as he looked at Anna, who'd taken off her shoes and positioned herself somewhat stiffly atop the comforter on the bed. With an IV in her arm, the sleep aid that dripped into her bloodstream had quickly kicked in.

Bach's discomfort was nothing, too, compared to the sacrifices Anna was willing to make to find her little sister.

The lab tech, an older woman named Haley, was sitting at the computer, monitoring both Anna's and Bach's vitals, and watching to make sure nothing improper happened—outside of Anna's head, at least. Her eyebrows went up as Bach took a fleece blanket from the cabinet and opened it, spreading it out over Anna, even though she'd refused it while awake.

"It gets cold in here," he told the tech, not wanting to admit that the relaxed abandon with which Anna now slept seemed too private for either of them to witness.

"Do you need one, too, sir?" Haley asked him.

"I'm fine," Bach said tersely, as he pulled up a chair and got to work.

Even though he knew he had Anna's full permission to enter her mind, he still felt awkward about doing so. The unconscious mind *was* more malleable. He could, quite easily, plant ideas and suggestions in her head—as simple as *the sky is green.*

After which, Anna would wake up and be convinced that that was a truth—until she went outside and saw the sky for herself.

Although, even after a visual, she *still* might not believe her own eyes. Some people were naturally programmed to reject easily proven truths that challenged ideas and beliefs that had been deeply planted in their psyches. If Anna were in that subset, he'd have to go back into her head to correct this absolute "fact" that he'd put there.

With a related technique, given just slightly more time, he could have taught her Farsi. Or advanced calculus.

Or—if he were immoral and twisted—instead of saying that the sky was green, he could implant within her the belief that, in order to find Nika more quickly, she should have sex with him as often as possible.

And the truth was that Anna couldn't possibly know that Bach would never, ever do something as heinous as that.

And yet here she was, willing to lay herself open and vulnerable to him, anyway.

It was sobering and awesome, and it shook him a little, even as it helped maintain his faith in humanity.

Of course, he was still shaken by his foray into Diaz's mind—and not by Diaz's unbridled sexual attraction to another man, but by the sheer force and enormity of the Greater-Than's feelings for Elliot.

Love.

It had stirred Bach to be surrounded by that certainty, that absolute and passionate conviction.

It made him remember . . .

What it felt like, what it was, what he had once been, what he could no longer be . . .

Bach took a deep breath and exhaled and then slipped into Anna slowly, carefully, aware that the drug in her system could provide some incoherence or added mental chaos. But he'd waded through some very convoluted minds before. The key was in staying alert, and in retreating back into his own self with some regularity, as if swimming underwater and coming up for air.

Bach closed his eyes as he sank into the warmth that was uniquely Anna Taylor, and he forced himself to focus on sensing any trail or train of half-formed thoughts or contemplation that might lead him to memories of Nika.

That was the first thing he had to do—find and learn to recognize Anna's little sister—before he could attempt to create a dream message for Anna to send to the girl.

He immediately found a powerful memory, still deeply linked to Anna's emotional core—of Nika, needing comfort after their mother died. Anna had stayed strong as the much younger girl sobbed in her arms, even though she was close to overwhelmed herself—not merely with grief from the loss, but with fear of this new and impossibly heavy responsibility of caring for her little sister. *We'll be okay,* she'd told Nika. *We're gonna be okay. . . .*

Her thoughts skittered and jumped then—like an old-fashioned LP recording onto a completely different track—to the image of a man, tall and dark-haired, imposing in a business suit, red power tie, his handsome face stern with anger. He swung his arm and delivered a resounding openhanded blow that knocked Bach to the ground.

What the hell . . . ?

But then Bach realized he was seeing and feeling this from Anna's perspective. He'd slipped, deeply, into this new memory—or maybe it was a dream.

You think that gives you the right to steal *from me?* the man shouted at him—at Anna. *You owe me, bitch! You get back here!*

But Anna fled the room, sobbing and frightened. She made it out into a hallway, but the man was chasing her. He caught her by the wrist, his fingers bruising her as he jerked her to a stop, as he dragged her through another set of doors and across a plush maroon carpet, where he threw her onto a king-sized bed. She scrambled to get away from him, but she couldn't because he was on top of her, suffocatingly heavy, pinning her down even though she fought him, kicking and hitting and shrieking—*No! No! Don't do this! Don't!*—as the dark-haired man slapped her again, hard enough to rattle her brain, as he tore at her clothes, and—*No!*—shoved himself roughly, painfully inside of her—

Jesus!

Bach pulled himself up and out, opening his eyes and gulping for air as he nearly fell out of his seat.

Haley was on her feet across the room, her eyes wide. "Are you all right, Doctor?"

"Yes," he gasped. "Shh!" He closed his eyes as he bent almost completely in two, back of his hand pressed to his forehead as he held up one finger, hoping the tech would understand that he needed her to be silent, to stay back, because as awful and as violent as that nightmare had been, there was something about it, something that he'd recognized or seen before or maybe something that *Anna* had seen before . . .

But—*damn it!*—it was too elusive, too awful, and it was gone.

Still breathing hard, Bach straightened up and his back tweaked, but this time he ignored it because it didn't hurt him even a fraction as much as knowing that he was going to have to go back there, into the thick of Anna's nightmare.

Or memory—he couldn't tell which it was. Nightmare, memory, or a nightmare of a memory?

He had no idea why he felt it was so important—what it was that he hadn't seen, what he needed to learn. But he knew, unequivocally, that he had to go back.

So he did, but only after he'd taken several deep breaths and forced his pounding heart to slow. Only then, as gently as possible, did he retrace his tracks.

Anna with Nika. *We'll be okay. We're gonna be okay. . . .*

The dark-haired angry man. *You owe me, bitch! You get back here!*

This time as Anna ran down the hall, Bach was ready for it. He separated from her, moving slightly back so that he wasn't reliving this as Anna.

But Anna didn't see him. Nor did the angry, violent man take note of Bach as he pushed Anna onto the bed and threw himself atop her even as he worked to free himself from his pants.

And that meant . . .

This was a memory.

If it were a dream, Bach could have stopped it, changed it. But even he wasn't powerful enough to change the past.

Feeling sick, he turned away.

And there in the misty shadows at the edge of this memory, he saw another version of Anna. She was watching him watch her assault—with such sadness in her eyes. Her hair was down around her shoulders, a mass of curls, free from the ponytail that she'd worn into the sleep lab. She was also dressed differently, in a simple white tunic that flowed around her, contrasting perfectly with her flawless brown skin. It seemed—at times—diaphanous, revealing brief glimpses of the soft curves of her breasts and the trimness of her legs beneath.

She was beautiful—breathtakingly so.

Which of them had chosen that outfit, here inside of her mind? But then Bach looked down to find that he was wearing clothing that he didn't recognize, clothing that seemed like a costume. Camel-colored knee britches, with a wide, buttoned-shut flap in the front instead of a traditional zipper enclosure. His shirt was as white as her dress, with long, loose sleeves. It was completely open in the front, revealing his bare chest. He tried to close it, but there was nothing to fasten. No buttons, no zipper, no Velcro.

So he held it together, but Anna didn't seem to notice or care as she said, "I haven't thought about this in a while."

"I'm sorry that I brought you back," Bach said. "But I have to ask you . . . Who is he? I think he might be important."

Anna shook her head. "You won't find Nika here. She never knew what he did."

"But she . . . knew him?"

"Yes." She looked over Bach's shoulder, at the man on the bed. "He was . . . once . . . a friend."

"Did Nika maybe, I don't know, did she know at least that you had nightmares about him?" Bach asked.

"Why does your back hurt so much? I thought you said you were in perfect health?" Anna asked, concern for him in her eyes. But then, abruptly, she vanished.

In her place was the angry dark-haired man, as if Bach were once again caught in her memory.

And *shit,* sure enough, he was Anna again, combined with her, entangled with her, as the man grabbed their wrist and threw them onto the bed, pushing himself between their legs.

And try as he might, this time Bach couldn't get away—had the drug in her system somehow trapped him?—and he felt her anguish on top of her physical pain. *I loved you! How could I have loved you?*

"Stop, David, please, *stop!*" She herself stopped fighting to get away. Instead, she tried clinging to the angry man, holding him close. "Please, David, if you *ever* loved me—"

But her words didn't stop him from slamming himself into her again and again and again. And even though she'd stopped fighting him, he now pulled her hair so hard that her head jerked back and she cried out in pain, until finally he came with a shudder and a shout.

And then she was crying, soundlessly, tears just spilling down her cheeks. The man—David—lay there, on top of her, his breath hot and foul in her face, and she turned her head away, once again pushing at him and trying to get free.

This time he let her go, releasing her hair and rolling off of her to sit on the edge of the bed as she scrambled away and off the mattress, hitting the carpeted floor with a thump. She'd lost a shoe, but she didn't care. She pushed herself to her feet and ran for the door.

As she ran down the hall, heading for the stairs that led to the foyer and the front door of his house, David called after her. "I never loved you. But we're even now, don't you think?"

It was only then, as Anna flung open the door that led to the street, that Bach was able to pull away from her—to pull out of both her memory and her mind.

But before he left her, he saw with dismay that instead of reaching the freedom outside of that house, she was thrown back into a loop of that same awful memory, where, once again, David hit her, where it was all going to happen, over and over and *over* again.

This time Bach couldn't catch himself as he fell out of his chair. He hit the floor hard, but even that wasn't enough to help him identify where he was or even *who* he was.

And when someone, a woman, came to help him—"Dr. Bach, are you all right?"—he pushed himself away from her, on his butt and his elbows, much the same way that Anna had finally gotten out from under David, on that bed.

Bach was out of there—he realized with a gasp. He was free.

But, God, *she* was reliving it again—and again.

"Assistance needed—STAT—in lab seven!"

And with that, Bach was back—enough, at least, to identify the lab technician who'd called for help—Haley. He also recognized that, for some reason, the drug that had been coursing through Anna's system, to help her stay asleep, seemed to be impacting him still. He was disoriented and nauseous and his legs didn't work right.

Although he was definitely doing better than Anna—she was curled tightly into a fetal position on the bed, visibly shaking beneath that blanket he'd used to cover her.

"This is *not* okay," he tried to tell Haley, pointing toward Anna.

"Sir, I swear, she *just* did that—right when you hit the floor! I think she's having some kind of negative reaction, either to the drug or to your intervention."

He was closer than Haley was, so he crawled to Anna's IV tube and swiftly disconnected it.

It would take a few minutes for the drug to leave her system and for her to awaken—and when she did, he knew that he was the last person she'd want to see.

Okay, maybe not *last*. This man, David, whoever he was, whoever he'd been to her, probably still held that dubious honor.

Despite that, Bach knew Anna wasn't going to be thrilled to see him.

And that was too bad, since he wasn't just leaving her here, alone. "Scanning both Dr. Bach and the subject," Haley announced to the doctor who'd burst into the lab, as Bach dragged himself up onto the bed, beside Anna.

As another doctor came in, and then yet another, Bach pulled Anna's still-tightly-clenched body into his arms. He was so dizzy himself that he couldn't sit up, so he sagged back, but he still managed to wrap himself around her.

"The subject is having a negative reaction to the drug," Haley reported.

One of the doctors—it was Elliot, thank God—spoke up. "Joseph, it's going to be ten minutes before Anna comes out of this state. I have to recommend that you—"

"Do *not* interfere," Bach ordered, working hard to make sure his words came out clearly. "As long as the scan shows I'm within normal range, just *stay back*."

They all spoke at the same time—Haley and Elliot and all of the other doctors—but Bach didn't wait to hear what they said. He just closed his eyes and plunged back into Anna's mind.

Because even one minute was too long for her to have to relive that bullshit, all by herself.

NINETEEN

Mac was using her voodoo on him.

It was freaking great, because it heightened and amplified every-thing Shane was feeling, making this moment—without a doubt—one of the best of his life.

He tried to remember if the sex they'd shared back in her Ken-more Square apartment had been this incredible, but then he stopped thinking about anything but Mac, moving against him and with him.

He'd stopped kissing her to position her at a better angle to receive him, and her eyes were closed, her lips slightly parted. Each breath she took, each ragged inhale and exhale was part-gasp, part-sigh, and he found himself wanting to stay here like this, for-ever, just watching her face. This woman in his arms was a master at hiding her feelings—except when she had sex. Her pleasure—pure and unfettered—turned her into an open book, and God, how he loved that.

"Hey," Shane breathed, but it wasn't until he slowed their near-frantic pace to an almost-stop that she opened eyes that were lumi-nous with desire to look at him.

"Don't," she whispered back as she closed her eyes again. But then she caught her lower lip between her teeth and swallowed a moan as he pushed himself home.

Shane kissed her—how could he not?—before he breathed, "Don't what?" into her eager mouth.

"Stop," she gasped.

"I haven't stopped," he pointed out even though he redefined the word *slowly* as he withdrew from her softness and heat.

"Don't be a dick," she said as she tried to follow him, tried to keep him from pulling out, tightening her legs around his waist. But he moved her away from the wall, and lifted her off of him so there was nowhere for her to go. She dug her fingers into his back. "Come on, Navy, you *know* what I like."

If she'd used his real name, he might've given her exactly what she wanted.

"I am pretty certain, *Dr. Mackenzie,*" Shane murmured instead, as he lowered her onto him just as slowly, as he pressed her again back against the wall, as she again tried—but this time failed—to keep herself from moaning, "that you like *this,* too."

"Oh, God," she gasped, as he began another long, slow retreat, as she again tried to keep him from leaving her, "oh, please, oh, don't, Shane, *don't!*"

She opened her eyes again then, and this time they were luminous with tears. He was so surprised that he froze. But just like that, it was gone and maybe he'd imagined it, but he didn't think so because now she was angry, and she said, "Don't try to make this something that it's not! And god *damn* you! Don't look at me like that!"

"Like what?" he said. "I'm just . . . looking at you."

"With those eyes!" she said.

"Well, yeah," he said. "Because I kinda use my eyes to *see,* so—"

"Just don't look at me!" she said. "Just . . . I want . . ." She pulled his head toward her and kissed him so hard, it was almost as if she were trying to suck his soul from his body.

Somehow she pulled him back, and Shane felt her shoulders hit the wall with way more force than he would have liked, but he couldn't stop her. And Jesus, she'd cranked her voodoo up to ten, and when she began to move against him—hard and fast, the way they'd started, the way she said she liked it—his body strained to respond.

What she was doing to him was crazy and literally out of control, because he had no power to stop or slow what was happening. He was done. Just like that. It was over. He just came in a hot rush as she, too, unraveled around him.

And, God, he wasn't the only one who'd exploded—all around them lightbulbs were flaring and popping, and the electrical outlet on the wall by his legs was buzzing and sparking.

The comm-station printer must've had a power overload, because it whirred and rattled and celebrated by printing out a full page that was probably an alignment test sheet. It probably didn't say *Fuck yeah!* interspersed with *Hoo-yah!*, but it should have.

Because right now, Shane's personal alignment was fucking perfect.

"Computer, report integration level." Mac spoke with her face still pressed against Shane's neck, her legs still locked around him, and for a moment he thought she was maybe speaking another language because he couldn't figure out what she was asking him over the slowly fading roar in his ears.

But when the computer answered her—"Sixty-three percent integration"—through a heavy stream of static, he finally understood.

Sex—with him—had increased Mac's integration level enormously. Higher even than Stephen Diaz, which was unbelievable.

"Computer, report any changes," Mac said. "Any at all. Audio response open and ongoing."

"Sixty-two-point-nine-nine-eight," the computer immediately responded, the static clearing a little.

"*Shit.*"

"Sixty-two-point-five-nine-seven."

"Computer, only report whole number changes," Mac ordered.

Shane lifted his head—he'd ended up with his face pressed against the wall, his hands still filled with Mac's incredible ass, his arms guilty of some definite wobble from the workout, his legs decidedly weakened but happy nonetheless.

But when he started to shift, to try to give her as graceful and elegant a dismount as possible, considering that she was still half-dressed and his pants were flapping around his boots, hobbling him, she tightened her grip on him and again said, "Don't!"

So he didn't. He didn't move. He didn't even speak, but maybe she knew he was going to, because she added, "Shhh! Just, *shhh*!"

Okay. She was clearly doing something—he had no idea what, but it was obvious she felt it was vitally important.

"Sixty," the computer reported then, "Fifty-eight. Fifty-seven."

"What the *fuck* . . . ?" Mac lifted her head and opened her eyes, and there they were nose to nose. "Why am I dropping so fast?"

Before Shane could respond, she added, "Computer, explain," and the computer answered for him. "Answer unknown. Fifty-five."

"How can I help?" Shane asked Mac, even though the exertion from continuing to hold her there like that was making him sweat.

"I thought I'd have more time," she said and the despair on her face was so honest and raw, just looking into her eyes made his heart lodge in his throat.

"I don't know what you're doing," Shane told her as he held her gaze, as he willed her to believe him, as he forced his arms not to shake. "But if there's anything—at all—that you think I can do . . ."

She didn't answer. She just looked at him.

So he pushed. "At least tell me what you're trying—is it that emotional grid thing? Are you searching for that man, Caine?"

Mac closed her eyes as she nodded. "For a second I thought . . . I thought maybe I felt him . . ."

"But that's *great*," Shane enthused. "Mac, that's amazing. Hey, come on, don't look so disappointed. We got you up to sixty-three, right? I'm pretty confident we can do it again—hell, I'm certain. Just aim a little more of your voodoo at me, and I'm ready to go, right now. And if you can't do that—for whatever reason—the room service guy can bring some Viagra with lunch. Wait—I keep forgetting—he's the *prison-cell service guy*. Although right about now, with the prospect of an immediate replay in my exceedingly bright future, I'm just not feeling all that terrible about being locked up."

Mac opened her eyes to look at him, but the despair hadn't left her face—if anything, it had gotten worse. Shane felt his heart lurch and he knew saying, *Please, please, please don't shut me out,* would make her do just that. So instead he said, "Smiley face emoticon?" and he made a face that was half-anxious, half-smile, which did what he hoped it would.

It made her roll her eyes and exhale a laugh.

So he pushed even harder and, all kidding aside, he quietly told her, "I know you're used to solving problems on your own, and sometimes the hardest thing in the world can be accepting help, but . . . Let me help."

"Fifty-seven," the computer announced. "Fifty-eight."

"Whoa," Shane said. Mac's integration levels were . . . going back up?

But she didn't look happy. In fact, she looked stunned and then horrified as the computer continued. "Sixty. Sixty-one. Sixty-two."

"Oh, *shit,*" she whispered, as tears filled her eyes. And this time, Shane knew that he wasn't imagining it, because this time two very fat tears escaped and rolled unchecked down her face, followed by more as—Jesus—Mac started to cry.

Anna wasn't alone.

She'd been caught in this nightmare—and even though it seemed and felt more real than any dream she'd ever had, she knew it *had* to be a nightmare, because it was happening to her over and over and over again.

Plus, there was something even worse that was happening, something that had to do with Nika, but what exactly it was remained elusively out of her grasp as David slapped her and she fell, then tried to scramble away.

She failed, as she'd failed before and before that.

But this time, as David drove his fingers into the tangle of her hair and savagely pulled, as she cried out in pain and disbelief, as she felt him slam himself into her with enough force to bruise and tear, she heard a voice in her head that wasn't there before.

Low and calm, with the diction and elocution of a 1940s-era movie star: *We're going to stop looping now, okay? Don't move. He's almost done and I know we're going to want to move, to do what we did, to get away, to get out of here, but we can't or the loop won't break. Think of quicksand. I know you've never been trapped, but you've seen movies, read stories. . . . Struggling makes you sink. We have to float, spread out, stay still. It goes against every instinct, I know, but if we do this, now, David will vanish and we'll be . . . Where do we want to be?*

And just like that, the voice was right, and David was gone, only now Anna *was* trapped in a pit of quicksand, gluey and yellowish and stinking of rot. And in that first second as her weight took her down, as her feet scrambled for a toehold and found nothing to support her, the muddy slime went over her head and she felt a flare of panic.

I've got you. You're safe.

And she felt herself lifted up and pulled out as she coughed and spat and wiped the muck from her face and eyes.

And there was Joseph Bach, standing on solid ground, dressed like a Disney prince. And she realized that *his* had been the voice in her head, that he had been with her. He hadn't left her there, alone. And she didn't know whether to feel grateful or mortified as she moved through the air like some kind of nasty version of Tinker Bell. As her feet gently touched the ground, she realized—of course—that she was naked. But Joseph—also of course—was there with a blanket to cover her as she sank down to the ground, her legs pulled in tightly against her chest. She let him wrap that blanket around her, holding on to both it and herself to try to keep from shaking.

"What does it say about me," she asked him, "that I actually prefer being trapped in quicksand than thinking about . . . ?"

But God, the nothingness around them seemed almost to quiver and change back into the walls of David's house.

Joseph grabbed her. *Don't think about that!*

To her complete surprise, he kissed her, but then she realized that he wasn't kissing *her*, he'd just pulled her back with him, somewhere she didn't recognize, somewhere she'd never been before. And she realized that she was now inside of his head, and that this was *his* memory.

And he wasn't kissing *her*—well, he *was* kissing her, but she wasn't Anna Taylor. She was someone else. Someone with much paler skin and reddish blond hair. Someone who was closer to Nika's age than her own.

And then she was laughing softly as she joined him beneath the covers of what Anna somehow knew was Joseph's bed, in Joseph's room. But this was clearly a memory from years ago, when he was barely older than this girl himself.

"Annie, my God, what are you doing?" His voice cracked.

"What I want to do before you go," the girl told him. "What you want, too." She laughed. "Or you wouldn't have left your window open so I could climb in."

"Ah, God," he breathed as she pulled off the T-shirt and dungarees she'd put on to make the journey across the fields in the dark, as she pressed herself against his warmth.

"We should be married right now," she whispered. "This should have been our wedding night—and I say we *are* married in the eyes of God. To hell with what my parents say."

"They only want what's best for you."

"*You're* what's best for me," she said and kissed him.

This is the place I always ran to, whenever I needed to run. To lose myself. To save myself. To punish myself. It's an equal opportunity memory. Not as awful as yours—not for the same reasons, anyway.

Anna turned, suddenly apart from and outside of the two young lovers, suddenly aware that she was watching them from the darkness in the corner of the room. Joseph was beside her, and she could feel his longing and sorrow, his regret and grief—and she knew that this girl, whoever she was, was no longer alive.

I'm sorry, she told him.

I am, too.

He opened the door for her, relentlessly polite, and she went through it and into a narrow, dark hallway, suspecting that they could have passed through the walls if they'd wanted to.

It was then that Anna realized they were dressed as they were before—he in his princely get-up, she with only that blanket wrapped tightly around her. She still had mud from the quicksand on her, caked in her hair and beneath her fingernails, and she knew that he'd saved her yet again, by pulling her into this memory that he'd just as soon not have to relive.

He looked back one last time at the golden-haired girl in the bed before following Anna out of the room. He closed the door gently behind him, then led the way along the dark, narrow hall to a flight of stairs that went downward.

"This is the house where I grew up," he said, glancing back at her. "I haven't been back here in a long time."

"What happened to her?" Anna asked as she followed him into a quaint-looking living room, filled with antiques. It was dark in there, with no lights turned on, but somehow she could see. "Annie."

"She took her own life," Joseph told her.

She stopped short. "Oh, God. You shouldn't have brought me here—"

"I didn't have a lot of time to pick and choose our destination." He sat down on a rather stiff-looking sofa that had a straight and barely padded back.

"And you couldn't have picked, I don't know, a frat party at your college or—"

"I didn't go to parties at college," he said. "Please sit. Or don't sit. But listen, okay? We have just a minute—seconds now—before you're going to wake up, and you need to know that you shouldn't be afraid. I'm on the bed with you, I'm holding you, but there's nothing . . ." He stopped himself, started again. "It's not *meant* to be sexual. You were shaking and . . . Plus it helps for me to be as close as possible while I maintain telepathic contact. Bottom line,

I didn't want you to be alone, especially when I realized what was happening."

"The loop," she said.

He nodded. But then sighed. "If you ever want to talk about it—"

"I don't." She shook her head. "This shouldn't be about me. We were trying to reach Nika. Did you connect with her?"

He shook his head no. "You had a negative reaction to the sleep aid."

"Shit."

He smiled at that, but only briefly. "Look, if you change your mind about—"

"Thank you," Anna said. "But no. I went to counseling. I'm over it."

He didn't call her on it, but she could tell that he didn't believe her.

Instead, he said, "Time's up. Your eyes are going to open now. And it's not going to be awkward. For either of us. It's just going to . . . be. On three . . . two . . ."

One.

Anna opened her eyes to find herself nose to nose with Joseph Bach, his arms tightly around her as they lay together on top of that bed in lab seven. From this proximity, his eyes were very brown and his lashes ridiculously thick and long.

Her hair had come out of her ponytail, and some of it was in his face. She was glad to see that the quicksand had stayed safely back in the caverns of their minds.

And even though he had to spit some of her hair out of his mouth, his being there *wasn't* awkward—despite everything they'd just shared. And Anna knew that he'd probably done some sort of hypnosis on her back in his childhood living room, similar to the way he'd gotten her into his car, out in front of her apartment.

But with Nika still missing, she didn't want to waste time on the inconsequential, so she cut to the chase.

"Can we try this again," she asked him, "*without* the drugs?"

It was only then, as Bach released her and sat up, pushing his own hair back out of his face, that she noticed his hands were shaking. Still, he didn't hesitate to nod. "Absolutely," he said. "Let's just let Elliot check you out first."

———

"Sixty," the computer in Shane's apartment reported. "Sixty-two. Fifty-seven. Sixty-one. Fifty-six. Sixty-two."

Mac's integration levels were erratic. She was flopping all over the place like a fish on a dock.

She was also royally screwed.

This was Tim, all over again. Except Shane was no mere Tim. He was Tim times a thousand. He was a *million* times the man Tim could only ever hope to be.

And Mac? She had no one to blame but herself. Fool that she was, she'd been playing with fire. And now that she'd gotten this far, she couldn't turn back. Not while the very real possibility of finding Devon Caine hung out there, almost within grasp.

Worse thing yet, she couldn't stop her tears—she was crying like a little girl who'd lost her puppy. And Shane didn't fuck-up his current standing as the world's nicest guy by saying something dickish, like, *Hey, it'll be okay,* or *Don't cry, baby, it's not that bad,* or even, *I'm sorry,* when he had no real clue why she was crying.

Instead, he gallantly provided her with an acceptable excuse for her emotional outburst as he looked at her with those eyes and said, "I want to find Nika, too."

"Sixty-one. Sixty-two. Sixty-one . . ."

And then Shane leaned in and kissed her so sweetly that if she hadn't already been crying, she would've started.

As Mac closed her eyes and kissed him back, she knew what she had to do. She had to let go of her fear and accept what she was feeling.

She wanted to have lunch with this man.

And dinner. And breakfast.

For the next sixty years.

She wanted the heat in his eyes to be real. She wanted the sex they'd just shared to have meaning beyond immediate gratification. She wanted this kiss . . .

She wanted this kiss to last forever.

God, god, god help her . . .

"Sixty-two," the computer said, and then fell silent.

With her eyes tightly closed, through the sweetness of that kiss, Mac had done what she vowed she'd never do.

She'd given this man—who could never truly love her—her heart.

"Can't you make me fall asleep?" Anna asked. "Just by telling me to?"

"We could try that," Bach said. "But it's not always easy to do. Although first, I'd like to take advantage of your conscious mind." He smiled to try to soften his request—she was sitting across from him in his office, his desk between them, and she was so serious. So somber and subdued. "I'd like to ask you a few questions. If that's okay."

She nodded, but now her eyes were guarded, as if she knew what was coming, and she not only didn't like it, but she didn't see what it had to do with making contact with Nika.

"First I want to show you something that I found, purely by accident," Bach told her, and instead of giving her a mental push—his usual way of asking for access to another's mind—he did the equivalent of gently laying his hand on her head, which he hoped came across as less aggressive. He tried to make it far less of a command and more of a request.

Anna closed her eyes and sighed her displeasure as she granted him entry. "Great, I can't *wait* to see what you . . ."

But her voice trailed off, because Bach didn't waste any time. He led her directly to it—to the dream she'd been having before Nika hijacked it with the violent images they believed were projections from the girl's captivity.

The hospital. Nika on the table, sitting up after getting scanned for those sinus infections, giving Anna that baleful look. The doctor in his white coat, standing with his back to them both as he looked at the results from that scan . . .

Bach stepped directly into the dream, gently taking Anna's arm and leading her around the man, so that she could see his face and—

Anna's eyes flew open as she gasped, as Bach let her push him all the way out of her head.

"That was David," she said now. "In the lab coat. In my dream."

Bach nodded.

"He's not a doctor," she said.

"And yet your subconscious assigned him that role—and made him turn his back to you."

"Why? What does that mean?" Anna asked him.

"What do *you* think it means?" he countered.

She shook her head as she held his gaze, but he waited, and she finally spoke. "That . . . I'm still not completely over what he did? That despite moving hundreds of miles away, I still think of him as a threat? Or maybe it's that I blame the hospital and the doctors for letting the Organization hack their records and kidnap Nika. Those doctors must suck, and *David* definitely sucks, so in my dream he's playing the doctor . . . ? It could be anything. Including the fact that the doctor reminded me—in some way—of David, and I just didn't notice it at the time. Except wait, I'm pretty sure the doctor we saw was a woman and . . . I don't know. I give up. What do *you* think it means?"

"I think David's presence in your dream is significant," Bach told her. "And I think you probably dream about him more often than you remember. You've been working—successfully—to overcome the trauma of his attack, and I think that's symbolized by his facing away from you. If I were counseling you, I'd recommend that you learn to recognize his presence in your thoughts—both conscious and subconscious, and try to make him smaller whenever he appears. Shrink him or push him away, into the distance. What he did to you is never going to go away—it's a part of you, yes—but it doesn't have to define you. And it already doesn't. You've done good work."

Anna smiled at that—just a brief twisting of her lips—before, as always, she brought them back to her single-minded purpose. "But what does any of this have to do with Nika?"

"I don't really know," Bach admitted honestly. "Not for sure. It's all just theory."

"You asked," Anna remembered, "before, if Nika knew I had nightmares about David. And yes, I'm pretty sure she does know that."

"That was one of my theories," Bach said. "If I had to make an educated guess, I would say that Nika is aware that something traumatic, something even nightmarish, happened between you and David. I believe it's possible she's subconsciously using him as a link, as she reaches out to your unconscious mind." He smiled. "Of course, maybe it's just coincidence. Maybe we're digging too deep, and the link is that you were having a nightmare—and Nika's currently living one. Still, my gut says that David didn't show up in your dream by accident."

Anna nodded, still so somber. "So . . . what do we do now? Do you think that if you can brainwash me into falling asleep," she said, and he inwardly winced at the use of that word *brainwash,* "and use Dr. Diaz's controlled dreaming techniques to make sure that I dream about David—oh joy—we might somehow . . . ? Activate that same link and reach Nika?"

She was amazingly bright. "It's a shaky theory," Bach said. "But . . . Yes. That's what I think."

Anna exhaled hard. "Okay, then. Let's do it."

She was also amazingly courageous.

Bach cleared his throat. "May I ask you some questions first?"

She sighed again, even more heavily this time. "About David." It wasn't a question.

He answered it anyway. "Yes," he said.

"What don't you already know," she asked, leaning forward in her seat, "simply from spending time in my head?"

"I don't know all that much," he admitted. "I was focused on getting you out of that memory loop."

She sat back again and just looked at him. Again, he waited.

"You asked me—before—if I wanted to talk about it," Anna said. "I should have asked you the same thing. I could feel you. With me. It made it worse at first, because I could tell that was the first time something like that had ever happened to you. It brought me back even more thoroughly into the experience. What you were feeling. The disbelief and powerlessness."

The idea that he might have made the memory worse for her was sickening. "God, I'm so sorry."

"*You're* apologizing to *me*? Are you kidding? You came *back*. You didn't have to, but you did. My point, however, is that even though it didn't actually happen to you, it kind of did, and you haven't had two years to come to terms with it. I should have warned you, going in—"

"And I should have been able to pull you out of that loop," Bach cut her off. "Immediately. But I couldn't. And, yes, I *do* want to talk about it with you, because it . . ." He stopped himself. Took a breath. "It *did* impact me. But let's plan to do that after we get Nika back, okay?"

Anna nodded, looking down at her hands, clasped tightly in her lap.

"Let's start with the basics," Bach said quietly. "David. Who was he?"

"He was my boss, at least at the beginning," Anna told him. "It was . . . complicated." She looked up at him. "Actually, it wasn't, but that's what I told myself. *It's complicated.* But, really, it was very simple. He was married. I knew that, and . . . I let him get too close." She closed her eyes. "God, I was stupid. I don't know what I was thinking, but he was so . . ."

She forced herself to look at Bach, and he could see the shame in her eyes. "He was persuasive," she continued, "and I was . . ." She shook her head. "Wrong. It was wrong, and I did it anyway. And then one day, I woke up and I finally did what I should have done right from the start, and I put in a request to be transferred. But by then, it was too late. The damage was done. And he went a little crazy. Coming by the apartment. Begging me to come back. Leaving messages about how much he loved me. Creating a scene in the corporate cafeteria . . . Of course, Jessica, his wife—she found out about the affair. And even though it was over, even though it was after-the-fact . . . It must've been her. But someone set it up to look like I'd been stealing from him, from David—as if I'd sold important documents to a competitor. He was the president of the R and D division of a company that . . . It doesn't matter. Or maybe it does, because it's so stupid. One of the things we were working on was a way to develop condiments—like catsup and mustard—that not only didn't spoil, but had no calories or nutritional value. Kind of like—I don't know—flavored paint? It was as disgusting as it sounds and when it was consumer-tested, it failed miserably—*no* one wanted it. The entire project was going to be dropped, everyone knew it, but . . . I should have stayed away from him after we broke up, but he called and said he'd found an earring that I'd lost months before—it was my mother's and I wanted it back. I hadn't yet heard about the missing documents, so I went to his townhouse to get the earring and, I don't know, apologize again? But he didn't have the earring—or if he did, he didn't give it to me. Instead, he ambushed me. He accused me of corporate espionage. He said that I'd used him from the start to get those chemical breakdowns. And then he hit me. I tried to leave and . . . You know the rest."

Bach did know. "How long were you together?"

"Two weeks," Anna said, tears suddenly brimming in her eyes, and he knew she was almost unbearably ashamed. "It started while we were on a business trip to Phoenix. And then it kept going, even after we got back and . . ." She shook her head, forcing back her tears.

"Two weeks is not very long."

"Yeah, well, it was two weeks *too* long," she countered.

"You said he came to your apartment," Bach prompted her. "After it was over . . ."

She knew where he was going and she nodded. "Yes. Once. And he only came over one time during those two weeks we were"—she cleared her throat—"sleeping together. In fact, it was seeing him with Nika . . . I remember thinking, God, I couldn't let her fall in love with him, too. The next day, I did it. I ended it. I put in for the transfer—I was in the secretarial pool—isn't that such a cliché? The secretary and the boss . . . ? Anyway, I took an immediate leave of absence, and Nika and I went out of town. When we came back, I was in a different department. Not that that kept him from calling me night and day."

"Tell me about when he came over, after you broke up," Bach said.

"He was drunk," Anna said. "And he started crying and swearing and . . . He just went to pieces. Nika was scared. I was, too. I asked her to go into her room, and she did, and then I got David out of there. I got him a taxi and . . . When I went back inside, Nika didn't want to talk about it, so . . . We both pretended it never happened."

"After the rape," Bach said. "What did you do? Did you go home?"

Anna nodded. "I showered and . . . Made dinner for Nika. The next morning I got a message from the personnel office telling me not to come in—that I'd been fired. I didn't fight it. I didn't want to."

"You didn't press charges?" he asked.

She just looked at him.

"Are you sure he only came to your apartment that one time?" Bach asked. "That he didn't come by after the rape? Maybe while Nika was home alone?"

"If he did, she never told me." She shook her head. "And I never thought to ask."

"Of course not," Bach said. "That's not something you would ask. *What happened today that you're not telling me about?*"

"I *do* ask her that," Anna said with a fleeting smile. "Now. But this was almost two years ago. When she was eleven and she still volunteered information about her day."

"But if David *did* confront her in some way," Bach pointed out, "Nika might not have wanted to tell you. And even if he didn't approach her again, she still might have recognized that he was a danger or threat. What I want to do to test our theory is to bring him front and center in your dreams; use him as a kind of a lightning rod, to see if we can't connect you to Nika, nightmare to nightmare."

"Fantastic," Anna said, even though it was anything but. Still, it was obvious that she was willing to set aside her own fears and discomfort to try to help her sister. "Let's try it." She paused. "Unless you need to take a break . . . ?"

"What?" he said. "No." He stood up. "Let's head back to the sleep lab."

"Are you sure?" she asked. "How's your back?"

"My back's fine," he reassured her, and of course, right then, it twinged. Still, a twinge now and then was nothing.

"Then why not just do it right here?" Anna pointed to the sofa where Bach had taken his share of naps through the years. "I'd actually be more comfortable without a bunch of people watching, if that's okay."

He nodded. Without the use of the sleep aid, there was no need for medical monitoring. What he'd be doing was not all that different from what he'd done to Anna to get her to climb into his car. Still . . . "It's for your safety," he told her. "The lab techs who watch. They make sure you're not exploited or taken advantage of."

"You would never take advantage of me. You want Nika to attend your school. You're not going to jeopardize that." Anna lay down on the sofa, her hair fanned out across one of the throw pillows as she looked up at him expectantly. "And yes, that was me being a jerk. I think it's kind of obvious that I trust you by now, Joseph. So let's find her."

Bach smiled and reached out with his mind—and this time she was ready and waiting for him.

Thank you, he told her. *I'm glad. Now, sleep.*

TWENTY

"Hey, babe, how is he?"

Elliot looked up from his conversation with the nursing team to see Stephen standing in the door of Edward O'Keefe's room in OI's critical care unit.

"Hi, Kyle, Lynda," Stephen quickly added. "Sorry, I didn't see you there." The look he shot Elliot was pure apology, even as his cheeks tinged with his embarrassment.

"Ted's a fighter," Elliot answered Stephen's question, even though the old man was dying. He believed firmly in the power of mind over body, and as long as O'Keefe was willing to fight on, he wasn't going to provide—even to the guy's subconscious—the suggestion that he should surrender.

"Um . . . mind if I borrow Dr. Zerkowski?" Stephen asked the nurses, as he gestured with his head for Elliot to come out into the hall.

Elliot did, murmuring some nonsense to the wide-eyed nurses, who muttered some nonsense back, closing the door tightly behind him.

"Sorry," Stephen said, wincing. "Sorry! I honestly didn't see them. I think I was dazzled by the sight of you."

That would've been lovely to hear, if . . . "Are we on the down-low with the Less-Than staff?" Elliot asked. He'd filed a report on the theory that sexual and emotional intimacy could enhance integration levels, but he hadn't used any names. Just subjects A, B, C, and D. "Because I don't think I knew that."

But Stephen was already shaking his head. "I just didn't know how you want to play this, since we work together. Things like, what I should call you when other people are around—not *babe* obviously. I just . . ." He laughed, still ruefully embarrassed. "Props to me for not just grabbing and frenching you."

Holy crap. "That would work for me, quite nicely, in my office, with the door closed," Elliot said. "And I'd like to point out that you are welcome to drop by any time you want."

Stephen's smile was less embarrassed and more genuine now. "Good to know."

"As far as outside of my office goes," Elliot added, "I think we can start by finding the middle ground between *babe* and *Dr. Zerkowski*. Elliot seems just about right. Although despite not being a big fan of terms of endearment, I do find *babe* oddly appealing."

And there they stood, foolishly grinning at each other.

But then Stephen got serious again and asked, "So how did it go with Dr. Bach and Anna? I went down to lab seven, but they were already gone."

"It wasn't successful," Elliot told him.

Stephen didn't drop the f-bomb very often, but he did so now, under his breath. And then he said. "Do they need me to try again? I could try again. God, I really don't want to try again . . ."

"Anna had a negative reaction to the sleep aid," Elliot explained. "But Joseph hasn't given up. He seemed pretty confident that he could use what you showed him about controlled dreaming. And Anna's okay. They were both just a little shaken and they needed a break."

Stephen nodded. "Good. I mean, not good that they were shaken, but . . . I mean, I'm not going to say that I *won't* try again. I would just . . . prefer not. To."

"Yeah, I'm getting that," Elliot said, looking at him hard. "What aren't you telling me? You said it wasn't painful when you

tried to connect with Anna, when her blood pressure flipped out—
that you didn't feel anything at all."

"I didn't," Stephen said. "And maybe, in part, that was because
I actively didn't *want* to make that connection. I've been thinking
about this—about why my integration levels suddenly started to
bounce."

Elliot just stood there, waiting for him to explain.

"Telepathy is new for me," Stephen finally said. "And yes, I've
had some experience going into the heads of other Greater-Thans.
And sometimes—like with Mac, who's even less experienced than
I am—it can get messy. But most of the time, at least with Dr. Bach,
he's completely in control. He shields his thoughts and stays away
from my shields, even though I know he could break through
them. I can trust him to stay separate."

He paused, and because Elliot knew where he was going, he
continued for him. "But going into the head of a fraction . . . ?"

"A non-Greater-Than," Stephen chided him gently, then sighed.
"And you're right, that's the problem. I panicked, which made my
levels do a dance. I knew I didn't have the ability to shield myself
from Anna's private and personal thoughts. And *she* certainly
doesn't have the ability to create a block to keep me out. And I
know she said it was okay with her—she wants to find her sister so
badly—but the idea of it just feels too personal. It *is* too personal.
I know this because being inside of *your* mind . . . ? With your inability to block your thoughts . . . ?" Stephen shook his head. "It's
a deeply intimate experience, El. As intimate as sex. And, well, I'm
just going to say it, okay? I don't want to do that with anyone but
you."

Elliot didn't know what to say, which was fine because even if
he had the perfect rejoinder, he wouldn't have been able to get his
mouth and vocal cords moving to say it.

Stephen took Elliot's silence for a need to change the subject
and did so, glancing back at Edward O'Keefe's door. "So how is he
really?"

Elliot went with it. *This* he could talk about. "A few hours ago, his organs were shutting down," he informed Stephen, "and I would have told you he had only a few more hours left. But now . . ." He shook his head. "He's not getting better, but he's not getting worse, either. We just hooked him up to the massager, because Analysis just sent an alert—"

"Yeah, I saw that, too," Stephen said.

Analysis's team of scientists had just finished examining a high-level complex brain scan that had been done on the elderly man, and had discovered that part of his brain was active.

It was the same smallish area of real estate that lit up for the Greater-Thans like Mac who had self-healing skills. So Elliot had come to hook O'Keefe up to the device lovingly nicknamed the brain massager. He'd programmed it to stimulate that same specific region of the old man's brain.

"Do we still think he jokered?" Stephen asked, still unable to do more than glance into Elliot's eyes, embarrassed again—this time no doubt because he feared he'd given too much away with that *anyone but you* proclamation.

"I'm not sure," Elliot admitted. "He had traces of oxyclepta di-estraphen in his blood. What I've yet to find out is how much Destiny he was given and when. We're hacking into JLG's system right now."

"Keep me posted," Stephen said, and it was exactly what he might've said to Elliot in the past. So much so, that Elliot half-expected the Greater-Than to finish the sentence with *Dr. Z.*

Elliot reached for him without fully thinking, his intention to put his hand on Stephen's arm and spark their instant connection so he could bring their conversation back to the *anyone but you* thing, but right before he touched Stephen, he remembered the words the other man had said about that connection being as intimate as sex. And it suddenly occurred to him that Stephen might not want to experience that intimacy in the hallway of the med unit, so he froze with his fingers mere inches from Stephen. And of course, Stephen being Stephen, he understood exactly what Elliot had been thinking, and he shifted closer, close enough to close the gap.

It's okay. It's private, simply by nature of being what it is, he told Elliot. He also knew exactly what Elliot wanted to discuss. *I'm sorry if I freaked you out.*

You didn't. I love that you don't want to mind-fuck anyone else.

Stephen laughed. *It's not—*

I know, I'm teasing, Elliot told him. *Although I do apologize for having such a messy mind, and for being unable to control—*

It's not messy, Stephen interrupted. *It's beautiful—as is the trust that you show me by letting me in. I love feeling what you're feeling. And that connected circle . . . ? When I'm feeling what you're feeling, which is what I'm feeling . . . That's intimate on a scale that I've never experienced before. And I probably couldn't do it with anyone else, but . . . The truth is, I don't even want to try.*

Elliot nodded, and he knew that Stephen could feel his sudden burst of complete happiness. *We should talk to Bach, set some parameters that you're comfortable with, in terms of your new telepathic skills. He's the king of setting boundaries. He'll understand, completely.*

Stephen nodded, too, but he didn't look convinced. And he didn't try to put his thoughts into words, he just unleashed it, and as Elliot absorbed it all, he knew that Stephen felt guilty about setting any restrictions. If his going into Anna's head could help them find Nika, he felt that he should man up and do it.

Yeah, but you wouldn't feel compelled to have sex with Anna in order to find Nika, Elliot pointed out. *Would you?*

Mac is, Stephen said. *Not with Anna, but . . .*

Mac is engaging in what she thinks is a win/win with Shane Laughlin, Elliot told Stephen. *She can pretend it's all about finding Nika through finding Devon Caine, but it's not.*

Stephen nodded. He knew.

You know I love her dearly, but I would never judge any of my *own decisions based on what Mac would or wouldn't do,* Elliot told him, and then, as he broke their connection because his phone was buzzing in his pants, he added aloud, "Let's give Bach a chance to work his magic with Anna. I have faith in the maestro." He glanced at his phone. "Ooh, I'm getting a message from Analysis. They just hacked JLG's records. They've got a slew of information about Mr. O'Keefe. *Yes*. I'm going to go into my office and review it."

He looked up at Stephen, and before he could ask, *Wanna come?* Stephen said, "Yes," adding, "Didn't need the telepathy for that one."

Elliot laughed.

And Stephen said, "For the record? My answer's pretty much universally *yes*."

"Good to know," Elliot echoed Stephen's earlier words as they headed for his office.

——————

Something had happened.

Shane had no idea what. All he knew was that after proclaiming that Mac had hit an integration level of sixty-two, the computer was no longer reciting numbers.

And that Mac had stopped crying.

He was ready and willing to just stand there, holding her until he dropped, but she broke away, finally ending their kiss.

Her face was somber and pale, but she opened her eyes and met his gaze as she quietly said, "I have to call Diaz and Bach. I know where Devon Caine is."

"It worked?" Shane couldn't keep from smiling even though she was still looking grim. "How did you—"

"I don't know," she cut him off, clearly frustrated with herself despite her success. "I don't have to do anything. I just have to think about him and I can *feel* him. He's out there. And I know I can find him. I mean, I couldn't pinpoint him on a map, but I know I can lead a team to him. I'm certain of that." She paused. "I'm sorry, but you'll have to come, too. I can't risk my integration levels dropping."

"I'm ready," Shane said. "Let's do it. Just point the way."

The *don't be stupid* look she gave him was far more like the irreverent Mac that he knew and loved. "I think you can probably put me down now."

"And risk your integration levels dropping?" He shook his head. "Hmm, I'm not sure that's wise."

"But walking the streets of Boston with our bare asses hanging out, engaged in public fornication *is* wise?" she countered, even more color returning to her cheeks.

"You're right," he said. "It's much smarter to drive. A van, I think. That way we won't bother Diaz if we need to jump into the back for a little integration enhancement. Chicka-chicka-bow-bow . . ."

She rolled her eyes. "Just put me down, Laughlin."

"Yeah," Shane said, drawing the word out. "I'm pretty sure my muscles locked about fifteen minutes ago." It wasn't quite true, but it was close, and he didn't want to drop her.

"Oh, shit," she said, genuinely contrite. "I'm sorry!"

"Don't be," he told her. His legs were fine. Aside from the post-release wobble, he could've stood there for days, and he now managed a knee-bend to get her closer to the floor as she slid off of him. That freed up his arms and he shook them out and rolled his shoulders and stretched his back. "I'm not."

She'd already turned away, searching for her panties as he reached to pull up his own pants. She found her clothing and escaped into the bathroom, closing the door behind her.

It was then that Shane noticed that the wall was dented. The drywall had been pushed in just a little bit—in the shape of Mac's back. The paint was chipping along the edges of the indentation and as he ran his fingers across it some of it flaked off onto the floor.

"Hey, are you all right?" he called, but his words were obscured by the sound of the toilet flushing and the water running in the sink.

The door opened pretty quickly after that, and she came back out, drying her hands on the thighs of her cargo pants.

"Is your back okay?" Shane asked.

Mac said, "What?" so he tapped the wall and she moved closer to look. "Whoa."

"This time we didn't just overload the electrical system," he said.

Mac swore. "I had no idea . . ." She looked at him hard. "Did I hurt you?"

"I'm not the one who hit the wall hard enough to do that. Let me see your back."

She shook her head. "I'm fine."

"Humor me."

He must've been radiating determination because she rolled her eyes and pulled off her tank top, turning around to let him see—her body language broadcasting her impatience.

She was wearing another of her sports bras, this one blue—a good color for her. Her shoulders were unmarked. Still, Shane took a moment to make sure, slipping his hand up beneath the tight racerback. Her skin was smooth and soft and, as always, touching her increased his heart rate.

And he was struck again by her total lack of art. He couldn't remember the last time he'd met a woman who didn't at least have a rose on her ankle.

"Even if I got bruised or scratched when it happened, you won't see it. I heal really quickly," she reminded him. "Little things, like this? I don't even have to think about."

And suddenly, it made sense. "That's why you don't have any tattoos," he realized.

"Correct for ten," Mac said, pulling away from him and putting her shirt back on. "My body reads them as wounds, and heals them. I absorb the ink, and they're gone in about twenty-four hours. Total waste of cash. One of these days, I'll figure out how *not* to do that. Maybe sixty-two's the magic number."

She crossed to the chair where she'd thrown her jacket as Shane looked over at the comm-station. Despite the power surge it was still active even though the computer's voice was silent. Which meant . . .

"You seem to be holding pretty steady now, at sixty-two," Shane said.

She glanced up from digging in her jacket pockets. "Yeah."

"How exactly did you—?"

"I don't really know." Mac cut him off as she found what she was looking for—her phone. "I guess I focused. Whatever I did, it worked. Obviously."

"Well, that's . . . good," Shane said.

"Yup," she said, devoid of all emotion—neither positive or negative. She was just remarkably flat as she scrolled through her contacts list and dialed, no doubt calling Diaz. "It's great."

"So how are we going to do this?" Shane asked. "Devon Caine. A simple locate and grab? Similar to the way you brought in Rickie Littleton?"

"*We* are not going to do anything." She put her phone to her ear. "You're going to stay in the van."

Shane felt a flash of frustration, but bit back his words as Mac turned slightly away from him to speak into her phone. "Yeah, D, it's me," she said. "It worked. I'm picking up Caine's emotional grid. I don't know how I'm doing it—you're just going to have to trust me. Also? I don't know how long it's going to last, so we should move quickly." She paused, nodding slightly as she listened, and then ended the conversation with, "Thanks. We'll meet you down there."

When she turned back to Shane, there was a clear challenge in her eyes, and one eyebrow was slightly raised, as if she could sense his irritation and was expecting or even daring him to argue.

And while he completely believed that, despite being a lowly fraction, his skills as a former SEAL would benefit any team looking to make a 270-pound sociopathic serial killer vanish off a city street in broad daylight, he knew that this was not the time to have that debate. They were in a hurry. A little girl's life depended on their getting this done.

"Let's go," he said instead.

"I don't know how you do that," Mac said as she unlocked his door and led the way out into the hall. "Because as we're driving into Boston, Diaz is going to go *blah blah blah don't want to risk you turning Devon Caine's brain into pudding, Mac,* and he's going to make me stay in the van, too. Or worse—once we locate Caine, he's going to make us drive away, just flat-out vacate as the rest of the team goes to work. And I am not going to be able to keep from bitching."

"Yeah, you will," Shane told her as they double-timed it toward the elevators. "Because you'll have something else impor-tant to do. You know, it occurred to me that if you can find Caine this way, then maybe you can find Nika directly. She was abducted off the sidewalk by her school, right? After we point Diaz at Caine, we can go there and—"

Mac was already shaking her head. "I already tried that," she said. "It's harder to do, if the emotional event occurred outside. It—I don't know—dissipates or something. The emotions. I thought that, too—that she must've been terrified when she was kidnapped—they hit her really hard, but . . ." She shook her head. "I couldn't feel her. I was there for over an hour. I tried."

And failed—and suffered for it, blaming her own inadequacies, even though she was attempting the virtually impossible. Shane knew Mac well enough now to be certain of that.

"Sixty-two," he reminded her as they approached the bank of elevators. "Maybe you could feel her now. We could go over there. You know. After. Just to give it a try."

She clearly liked that idea and she nodded. "Yeah. That's a good plan."

"Yes," Shane celebrated as he reached the down button first and leaned on it. "Proving myself valuable as more than just an extremely well-educated sex toy."

Jackpot. She finally laughed. True, it was more of an expression of exasperation or disgust than genuine amusement. Still, she was about to say something, when the doors opened with a *ding.*

The elevator wasn't empty. Robert from Hospitality was stand-ing behind a cart that was loaded down with metal-covered plates of food. It was the lunch Shane had requested from the computer. Had to be.

"Damn," Shane said. "You are one hungry woman."

Mac laughed again, pulling him to the side, but then holding the doors open with her foot, so that Robert could wheel the cart out. "This is for the entire floor."

"Thank you, Dr. Mackenzie. Oh, don't forget this," Robert said, reaching down to the lower shelf of the cart to pull out . . . A brown paper sack and a cardboard holder filled with two fairly small coffee cups, their lids securely attached.

Shane took the bag as Mac took the coffee.

"Thanks, Bob," Mac said as she and Shane got into the elevator.

As the doors closed, Shane opened the bag to look inside, even though he'd already realized what was in there, from its size and weight.

"You asked for it. Two energy bars and a cup of coffee," Mac confirmed. "Times two."

"Always to go." He didn't need to make it a question. He knew. The coffee was a small enough cup so that she could probably finish it before she reached the lot where her bike was parked. The energy bars—filling and far quicker to consume than a sandwich—would go into her pockets.

But Mac answered anyway. "Nika's not the only missing girl in this city," she told him quietly. "There're a lot of them out there, being bled dry every single fucking day. I'll eat when I'm old and I'll sleep when I'm dead."

Shane nodded. And here he'd thought the most he'd learn from her dining habits was whether she had a secret love for junk food or was a strict vegan.

Instead he'd gotten a glimpse inside of her head.

———

Anna was dreaming that she was back in David's townhouse, in the expansive entryway.

She wasn't surprised to be here—she'd more than half expected it.

What she didn't expect was Joseph—he was with her. And he

was dressed the same way he'd been in the dream she'd had while drugged—like a Disney prince.

"This is still you, you know," he told her, gesturing to his outfit.

"Sorry," she said. She herself was dressed in jeans and a T-shirt, clunky boots on her feet. "I don't know why I do that."

"I'll live," he said. "You know, this *has* to start as a nightmare. I'm sorry about that."

Anna did know. She nodded and turned, and there he was— David—at the top of the stairs, on the second-floor landing. Just the sight of him there, looming and angry, made her heart pound.

"Easy," Joseph murmured, and she felt his hand, warm on her shoulder. "That's good, but don't wake up. She's out there, I feel her—Nika."

Anna blinked and David moved closer—he was now standing halfway down the flight of stairs. And it was then that Anna didn't simply feel Nika, she *saw* her—a flash of movement out of the corner of her eye—but her little sister vanished the moment that Anna turned. Of course, when she turned back to David, he'd reached the bottom of the stairs. He stood there, just staring at her, his eyes lit with anger, the same way he'd looked at her on that awful, awful day.

But this wasn't a memory, it was a dream—albeit a bad one— except, Joseph was still beside her. "Don't wake up," he told her again, but God, she couldn't help but remember the nightmare of David's weight on top of her, keeping her from getting away even though she struggled and fought and kicked and hit.

And there was her little sister again, another flash of movement or maybe it was just smoke, closer now, but with a ghostly echo of Nika's voice shouting, *"Annaaaah!"* as if from a long way off.

"Neek!" Anna shouted back, turning to look in the direction of that ethereal apparition that she just *knew* was her sister, wherever she was . . .

You think that gives you the right to steal *from me?* Anna turned back to see David, raising his arm to hit her with his open palm—not quite a punch, but still with far more force than a mere slap. She saw it coming and she could taste the blood in her mouth from where her teeth were going to cut her cheek, she could hear her ears ring, feel her very brain rattle in her skull.

Except before it happened, before he made contact, she raised her arm to block the blow, even as she spun like a dancer—no, like a black belt in karate delivering a roundhouse kick—and hit him square in the face with her boot.

David went down—hard—and Anna stood there, stunned. She looked around for Joseph—he was driving this dream, wasn't he? Except he was gone.

And her first thought was one of absolute terror—how could he have left her alone like this? As she looked down, she saw she was dressed once again in the skirt and blouse that she'd been wearing that awful day. She was wearing those same stupid shoes in which she couldn't possibly run.

And as David pushed himself off from the floor, wiping the blood from his mouth with the back of his hand, Anna knew what was coming and she heard herself scream.

But in that instant, as David took one step and then another toward her, she realized that whatever happened here, in this nightmare, didn't matter. What mattered was Joseph Bach finding Nika, and if he wasn't standing there next to Anna, didn't that mean—please God—that he'd found her?

And Anna kicked off her shoes and instead of running away, she ran *toward* David. And she used her hands, fingers formed like bird's beaks, to go for his eyes even as she stepped close enough to knee him—with all of her might—in the groin.

She didn't know how she knew to do that. She didn't know how, as he kept coming, that she knew to hit him with her elbow; to kick him again—her boots were back—so that he couldn't get close to her. He couldn't grab her and pull her down.

Although she knew that even if he did, she could still fight him off, because she knew how to do it, how to protect herself from anyone who might try to hurt her—as if someone had dropped that knowledge directly into her mind and . . .

Someone had. Joseph had.

Stay asleep . . .

Anna laughed as David kept coming.

Because this was *his* nightmare now.

———

Nikaaahhh . . .

Nika heard her name being called through the sound of two dozen girls sloppily eating—shoveling handful upon handful of some kind of bland tasting rice into their starving mouths.

She was back *on the line,* which was what the pregnant girl had called the horrible hospital-dorm-at-an-orphanage room where she and the other girls were strapped into their beds.

Nika had woken up here. The last thing she'd remembered was the pregnant girl looking down at her in that hotel-like room after the machine on Nika's arm had hissed and sent a sedative into her system.

The day had already been a nightmare.

She'd awakened to the piercing sound of screaming, and had witnessed a brutal attack on one of the littlest girls—a girl whose name she hadn't yet learned.

The worst of the screams came from the girls around her. Like her, they couldn't get free and were forced to watch as the scar-faced man beat the girl senseless with his fists.

At least he wasn't using his knife, but the fear that coursed through Nika at the thought that he might made her heart pound so loudly she could barely hear the screaming.

When it was over and the girl lay unconscious, the scar-faced man stopped at the end of Nika's bed and she shook with her fear and anger.

"Should we give this one to Devon?" he asked her, and at first she didn't understand his words.

But then she *did* understand. He was asking her—her!—if he should *give* the girl he'd just nearly killed to the awful man who'd grabbed her from the sidewalk. And she couldn't answer—she wouldn't.

Except then he said, "Silence implies consent."

And that meant unless she said no, she'd be telling him yes, so she said it, loudly, *"No!"* And if she'd been any less afraid, she would have spat at him. But she didn't.

He laughed his awful laugh and said, "Soon you must choose," and he bent and picked up the girl and tossed her back onto her empty bed and strapped her in before he left.

But the girl didn't wake up and she didn't wake up, and the man came back in and bled them, and the girl *still* didn't wake up.

And when the doors opened again, Nika expected the worst— that the man had come back to bleed the little girl dry—but instead it was a woman who came in. She was older, pale and heavyset, with washed-out, colorless hair, wearing a bloodstained white uniform. She didn't speak, didn't say a single word even though Nika begged her to help them.

She just dragged in a cart and then kept her eyes downcast as she delivered to each of the girls a cardboard plate upon which was heaped a small mountain of a pasty white food. Nika wasn't sure what it was at first, until the woman plopped her plate onto her lap, and she saw the gluey grains of rice.

"If they unlock us, eat quickly," one of the girls—Leah— warned her. "Sometimes when they bring food, they take it right away again. And sometimes they bring it and they don't unlock us, so we can't eat." Her voice shook. "Oh, please, let them unlock us," she repeated to herself, over and over and over.

As she was whispering that, the lady set the last plate down and slowly turned and headed back toward the door.

With a click, the strap that held Nika's left arm in place was released—they all were similarly released. And without another word, they all dug in—eating like animals with their fingers, scooping as much food as possible into their mouths. ·

All, that is, except the little girl who'd been beaten. She still lay unmoving and silent.

Nika, too, pretended to grab for her food and shove it into her mouth. She was hungry again, so it wasn't hard to pretend—when in truth she was watching as the woman shuffled slowly out the door. She waited for it to close behind her. And as soon as it did, she went for her other restraints, trying to unfasten them.

Nikaaahhh . . .

Trying and failing.

She couldn't get free. Of course she couldn't get free. The people who held her here wouldn't have unlocked her if there'd been even the slightest chance that she could get free.

Still the disappointment was almost too much to bear, and she started to cry.

Nikaaahhh, be strong. Take heart.

"I can't," she sobbed. "I can't do this anymore, I can't!"

Nikaaahhh, I'm a friend of your sister Annaaaahhh's, and we're coming to find you, we're coming to get you out of there.

Great. Now she was going mad.

Hearing voices in her head.

Schizophrenia. She'd read that people under a huge amount of stress often surrendered to any mental illnesses they may have successfully warded off under normal circumstances.

It's not schizophreniaaahhh. My name is Joseph Bach, and I'm a friend of Annaaahhh's.

Multiple personality disorder then. She'd read about that, too. But maybe that was a good thing. Maybe part of her brain thought she was someone called Joseph Bach, who could unlock her restraints and kick both the old lady's and the scar-faced man's asses and lead the entire room of girls to freedom.

Although, wait. She/he would have to kick Devon Caine's ass, too. He was probably here, somewhere in the building, just waiting for her to try to get free.

Devon Caine is there? the voice asked. *You know this for a fact?*

"I don't," she admitted. "I only think so."

Ah, I see, the voice said. *The man with the scar mentioned Caine again after . . .*

"I should have told him *yes,*" Nika said, starting to cry in earnest again. "She's going to die anyway and I should have told him yes."

Nika, the voice said, and it was far less echo-y and distant now, which was simultaneously better and weirder. *You did the right thing. No one should ever be asked to make those kinds of choices.*

"But she's dying—she's probably already dead! And now he's going to make me pick one of the other girls, and they're going to die, too!"

Those very same other girls were eyeing her warily as they finished up their food, and the voice in her head said, *Breathe. I need you to breathe for me, Neek. Calm blue ocean. I know it's hokey, but it works. Clear your mind of all other thoughts but calm blue ocean and breathe. . . .*

And maybe it was the quiet serenity of the voice, or the fact that Anna was the only person who ever called Nika *Neek,* and he said he was Anna's friend . . . But Nika breathed. Breath in, breath out.

That's good, the voice continued, *keep breathing, don't say anything. If you can, try to eat. I don't want anyone to know that I'm here, and I don't want the other girls to be afraid of you, so it's important that you don't speak aloud to me. If you have something to say, all you have to do is think it, and I'll know.*

Whoever he was, he didn't want Nika to look or sound crazy— which was kind of ironic.

And it was weird, because whoever he was, she could feel him smile. *I know, it seems a little crazy. But I'm real, Nika. My name's Joseph. And I'm working with your sister to find you and bring you home.*

Is Anna all right? Nika thought with a flare of anxiety. The pregnant girl had told her that whoever was holding Nika prisoner might try to find and capture Anna, too.

What pregnant girl? Joseph asked.

I don't know. I don't know her name—

Shhh, he said. *Breathe. It's okay, Nika. I need you to be as calm as you can be. Can you try to do that for me? I know you're scared, but you're not alone anymore.*

They come in, and they kill them, she told him, *the girls. They just kill them. I know they won't kill me, not yet anyway, but I'm just so afraid that they're going to kill them.*

Do you know why they took you? Joseph asked her.

They said I'm special, she told him. *They said I'm a* fountain. *There's something in my blood, I think it's in my blood. But I don't know what, and I don't know why, and I want them to stop.* And she couldn't help herself, she started to cry again. "I'm sorry," she sobbed. "I'm sorry!"

Just breathe, he said again. *You're doing great, Neek. You're doing unbelievably great. Just breathe and relax—I know it's not easy, but try your best to relax. That's all you can ever do—your best, right? And you're giving me your best, and it's great, you're doing great.*

He just kept saying that, over and over and over, until she had to believe him, and her tears slowed, and her breathing became less ragged. And she realized he was telling her something else, too.

You are *special—more special than they can imagine. They have no idea who you really are. They have no idea the mistake they made by taking you. That's right—just keep your eyes closed and breathe. You're doing great. You're doing* great. *And if you can relax, just a little bit more, just breathe it out, I'm going to tell you what, and I'm going to tell you why. The how-we're-going-to-get-you-out I'm still working on, but know this. Believe this, Nika. Breathe this. Be* this. *Because you and me? Together, we* are *going to make them stop.*

And with Joseph Bach's voice warm and intimate inside of her head, Nika could believe it.

TWENTY-ONE

This was unbelievably hard.

Mac could feel Devon Caine out there—not because she'd had raw, hard-core sex with Shane. No, her integration levels were high enough for her to locate Caine because Shane was sitting close and holding her hand.

She was breathing in his calm resolve, his steady determination, his quiet respect, and yes, his adoration. She didn't have to drag him into the back of the van for a quickie. She just had to meet his eyes and let his smile warm her.

She just had to shut her own eyes to the truth.

Shane didn't love Mac any more than the hookers on Boylston Street loved the tricks that they went down on.

Still, she had to let herself care about him—for the sake of that missing little girl.

But as soon as they found Caine, who would lead them to Nika, Mac was going to end this game.

Because it wasn't fair to Shane. And it sure as shit wasn't fair to *her.*

And really, if it was just about what was and wasn't fair to her, she might've been able to go with it.

But she hated—*hated*—the fact that she was deceiving Shane.

"You okay?" he murmured, and she lied and nodded.

"Left up here," she told the Thirty who was driving, an earnest twenty-something named Charlie Nguyen who'd been given the inglorious task of making sure that—after she led Diaz to Devon Caine—Mac and Shane made it safely back to OI.

Their impending side-trip to the sidewalk where Nika had been grabbed had been approved by Diaz, since Dr. Bach had had his do-not-disturb sign up on his office door. But Charlie was only to drive them over there, and—again—see them safely home.

"Left again, here, sorry," Mac told Charlie, and they wound their way deeper into Charlestown with Diaz and a team of Thirties in the van directly behind them, hugging their bumper as they made the abrupt turn.

Diaz had actually kissed Elliot good-bye, leaving the doctor in his office, working on the mystery that was the elderly Edward O'Keefe. Mac had only seen their PDA because the door had been open a crack, and she'd been on the verge of poking her head in to see what was keeping D.

So it really wasn't a PDA, unless the P in that display of affection stood for private.

"Eyes open out there," Mac had overheard Elliot saying quietly, and Diaz had smiled.

"You know it," the Greater-Than had said, and the genuine love and trust that the two men shared came at her in a wave that was so powerful, Mac had nearly lost her balance.

Of course, Shane had been there to keep her from falling.

Damn him.

"Slow it down," Mac ordered Charlie now as she eyed a dilapidated triple-decker with peeling brown paint that sat beside a vacant lot. And sure enough, as they approached, she felt an unmistakable tug, and she knew Caine was inside. "Pull over. I think I might need to get out of the car to be sure—"

"*That's* not gonna happen," Charlie said.

Mac nodded. "I know, but I had to try. Brown house. Caine's in there." She closed her eyes and reached again for Shane's hand, which he gave her immediately.

He wanted her again. She could feel that, along with his hope that, with his help, she was going to be able to get a read on Nika's emotional grid from the sidewalk where the girl had been abducted. At which point picking up Devon Caine would be moot, because with Mac a Sixty-two, she'd then be able to find Nika as easily as she'd just zeroed in on Caine.

Shane was gazing out the window at the brown triple-decker, and Mac knew he was strategizing the best way to get inside and take down Caine. She felt his rush of both adrenaline and envy, and she also knew that even without a more detailed analysis, his first instinct was probably in line with hers. They'd use the Thirties to watch all of the entrances and exits from the building—windows included—while they kicked down the door.

Of course, first they'd use the high tech spy-gear that Diaz had in the van to verify that Caine wasn't using his apartment as a munitions dump, or that he didn't have an entire army in there to protect him. But if the man was alone, his capture would be relatively easy.

"Third floor," Mac reported, again not sure how she knew this, but certain just the same. "Back of the house."

Charlie relayed that information to Diaz, then pulled away from the curb, away from the house, away from the action.

Fuck.

Shane squeezed her hand, and she looked over to meet his sympathetic gaze.

"Don't go too far," Shane ordered Charlie. "If Caine squirts, Diaz is going to need Mac to track him."

"Yes, sir," Charlie responded.

Every now and then, despite their care in watching all of the known exits from a building, their target would escape—squirting out through a leak they didn't know about. It was unlikely to happen with this shithole of a house in this shithole of a neighborhood, but Mac knew through Analysis's extensive research that some of the upper-level members of the Organization had elaborate escape routes—tunnels or even camouflaged helicopter hangars.

If Caine had been given access to a company safe house with tunnels or a corporate chopper . . . That would be really bad.

"It's just as a precaution," Shane told Mac. "From what we know about Caine, I doubt he'll squirt."

"Always be prepared," Mac said, and when his smile turned rueful, she quickly added, "I mean that as a good thing. What, did you think it was some kind of insulting Boy Scout reference? You *are* touchy about that, Navy."

He looked down at their hands, still clasped, before he met her gaze again. "I would like, very much, for you to take me seriously."

"You think I don't take you seriously?"

"My empathic skills are only average." He glanced at Charlie, who had pulled into a CoffeeBoy parking lot and was checking text messages on his phone. The driver had put in an earphone, so as not to disturb them as he listened to his messages. Still, Shane lowered his voice even more. "But, right now? I can practically smell your fear."

"Oh, please," she said, pulling free from his grasp. "Not this again."

"Hey," he said. "I'm not the one making it be *this again*. You are. What's the problem with just going with it? This you-and-me thing. Relax into it. See where it takes us . . . ?"

"I don't have time to relax," she reminded him.

"Well, you should make time. When was the last time you took a vacation?"

She looked at him.

"Was it absolutely never?" he asked. "Or abso-fucking-lutely never?"

She refused to laugh. "You have no idea," she started.

Shane cut her off. "Yeah, I actually do, Mac. Because I was you. When I was in the teams. Everything was life or death, now or never, fight or fight harder. And it burned me out. You know, I should've seen that lose/lose situation coming. The one I told you about? I should have done the research in advance, and gotten my guys lost in the mountains. Or, I could have manufactured a helo malfunction—it happened all the time, no one would've blinked.

Instead, I got caught in a clusterfuck that I could have avoided if I hadn't pushed myself that hard for so many years. I was doing a lot of good out there, taking a lot of very bad people out of commission. But I went from being just like you, to . . . being nowhere. Blacklisted."

"Yeah, well, I don't belong to a team that's going to kick me out," she said. "And even if they do? Fuck them. I'll work on my own."

"Until you work yourself stupid from exhaustion, and you make a fatal mistake. You want to save these girls? Gotta be alive to do it, Michelle."

"Fuck you!" Shane said it with her—it was clear he knew it was coming.

"Why do you hate your name?" he asked her.

She made an outraged sound as she gazed at him. "I thought you were supposed to be helping me maintain my integration levels, not pissing me off and send me bouncing all over the place."

"I know I'm not going to get what I want by sitting quietly in the backseat," he motioned around them, "waiting for you to need me. Instead, I'm going to do what I do best. And a big part of that is identifying the problems that I see."

"And my choice not to use the name that some asshole gave me when I was an infant is a *problem*?"

"Yes it is," he told her. "Because you think you're not Michelle anymore."

"I'm not," she agreed. "I left her behind a long time ago."

"But it doesn't work that way," Shane said. "We drag everything we've done and said and been with us, always and forever, Mac. Michelle's not gone, she's just hidden behind the giant curtain that you pretend not to see. You might want to bring her out and make friends with her, because she's *always* going to be there. And maybe if you stopped running from her, you could find some inner peace. And look, I'm not saying this because I want to change you. I happen to like you, very much, exactly the way you are. But I believe—absolutely—that achieving an inner balance will give you strength and help you grow. I *know* you take what you do very seriously, and I honestly think this is something that can help move you to the next level as a warrior."

He was sitting there with his conviction and his admiration swirled together with his desire and affection for her—she refused to think of it as love—having just called her . . .

A warrior.

And he meant it.

Mac couldn't help herself. She grabbed Shane by the shirt and kissed him.

Which, of course, was exactly when Charlie took out his earphone and turned around. "Hey, Dr. M., I just got a text from Brian—whoops, sorry, ma'am and sir!"

They immediately sprang apart and Mac was flustered, but Shane, as always, kept his cool, morphing smoothly into officer mode. "The Brian who's driving Dr. Diaz's van?" he asked.

"Yes, sir," Charlie said, peeking at them cautiously in the rearview mirror. "He reports that they successfully apprehended and contained Devon Caine. They're bringing him back to OI."

"That's great." Mac found her voice, even as her cell phone buzzed. It was Diaz. She picked it up. "Yo. I just heard. Good job."

He didn't say hello or otherwise respond. In a voice that was clipped and tight, he just asked, "Have you spoken to Elliot since we left OI?"

"No," she said. "Why?"

"I can't—" he started, then cut himself off. "Please, if you hear from him, just tell him to call me."

Mac sat up. "D, what's going on? Do you need us to get back to OI?" She looked at Charlie, who was watching her cautiously in the rearview. She nodded at him and mouthed the word, *Drive,* and he put the car into gear. Shane, too, was on high alert, watching her.

"No," Diaz said. "I just . . . Michelle, I had—I don't know what it was—a vision? And it was . . . Bad. And now I can't get through to El to . . . I don't know, warn him?" He drew in a ragged breath. "Although, it's typical for him, you know? He gets into something and he turns off his phone. I know he's safe—he's in OI. He's gotta be safe. Just do what you were doing. Try to pick up Nika's grid. I'll call you if I need you." And with that, he cut the connection.

Mac closed her phone, more disturbed by that than she was willing to let on to Shane and Charlie. "Diaz had some kind of crazy-ass freak-out vision," she reported, "but he still wants us to go to the crime scene."

Charlie nodded and did a youie right there in the street, heading back toward Cambridge.

Shane was watching her as she opened her phone again, as she scrolled down to Elliot's number, and called him. But it went right to his voice mail, so she left a message. "El," she said, "D wants to ask you to the prom, so get off your butt and call him back, asshole."

She snapped her phone shut and pocketed it. And glanced over to find Shane still watching her.

"Diaz doesn't usually freak out," she told him, but again tried to make light of it. "But then again, he's never been in love before."

Shane nodded. And whatever he was thinking, for once he kept it to himself.

It left Mac wondering, in the silence as the car moved into the left lane, why she had no problem with it at all when Diaz called her *Michelle*.

———

Elliot woke up surrounded by a security team.

"We've got him, team leader," an earnest young security officer named Patricia Gilbert was saying into her radio. "He's in the lounge. He was sleeping on the bench in the southwest corner of the room."

Louise had delivered his soup and sandwich, and it sat now on the table in front of him. As Elliot sat up, he stuck his finger into the soup and yes, it was cold. And that meant his five-minute nap had gone on a little longer than he'd planned. He looked at the crowd around him. Yeah, make that a *lot* longer. "What's going on?" he asked.

"You were missing, sir. Dr. Diaz was quite concerned."

"Crap." Elliot started to stand up, but quickly sat back down. He'd been having an awesome dream—one of his own this time, but no less erotic than Stephen's had been. "Is he back?"

Stephen *was* back. In fact, here he came, striding into the lounge with his kick-down-the-door walk and his intensity showing in the tightness of his shoulders and on his stunningly handsome face. "Computer, access SD. Immediate medical scan of Dr. Zerkowski," he ordered. "Text the results to my phone—STAT."

"I'm fine," Elliot told him. "I fell asleep."

"Hold still," Stephen commanded, then nodded to the young woman who'd woken Elliot up. "Thank you, Ms. Gilbert."

"No problem, sir. Just doing our job." She herded her team toward the door.

Stephen was left standing there, looking down at Elliot with his teeth still clenched and his heart in his eyes. "That really scared me," he admitted.

"I'm sorry," Elliot responded, even though Stephen had been careful to say *that* not *you.*

His phone beeped at the same moment Stephen's did—it was the result of the med scan. Elliot had his alerts set to notify him any time he was scanned, and to provide him with a copy of the results.

As expected, he was in very good health. His heart rate was slightly elevated and his blood pressure was a tad higher than his usual readings, but yes. The reason was right there for them both to see. He was aroused. And Stephen's super-hot he-man posture and attitude wasn't helping.

Or rather it was helping too much.

Before he pocketed his phone, he saw the whole string of missed calls—not just from Stephen, but from Mac, too. And he also saw the text that announced the good news that Devon Caine had been apprehended.

Nika Taylor's surviving kidnapper was safely ensconced in Security's holding cell, after having been stripped of all of his possessions and dressed in a bright orange jumpsuit. No doubt about it, this one was not getting away.

As Stephen sat down heavily next to him—but far enough away to not accidentally touch—he saw the text that Elliot was reading and nodded. "As soon as Dr. Bach can, he'll take a walk through Caine's mind. He's been given the message that Caine is here, but he implied that it might take him another hour to break free from trying to contact Nika."

Elliot looked at him. "You gonna tell me what's going on?"

The muscle in Stephen's jaw was still jumping as he nodded again. "The takedown went like clockwork. We did a quick sneak and peek into Caine's apartment, verified he was alone. He was in the shower, which made it even easier."

Elliot understood. All Stephen had to do in order to shock the man into unconsciousness was to send a jolt of energy through the pipes with the water.

"I knocked him out, we went in, shot him full of sedatives as insurance, and popped him into the van. The entire operation took three minutes. We were in and out. Or we would have been," Stephen told him. "I was doing a quick look-around in his place— collecting his cell phone and wallet and anything else that seemed to stand out, and . . . That's when it happened." Tears actually filled his eyes and he closed them, taking a deep breath, and exhaling hard.

Elliot would have reached for him, taken his hand, touched his leg, but the distance Stephen had put between them was not accidental, and he didn't want to cross that boundary. So instead, he clasped his own hands and waited.

Stephen took another deep breath, exhaled again, and finally opened his eyes. "I'm sorry."

"I'm a little scared," Elliot admitted.

Stephen nodded. "Me, too. And I *know* what I'm going to say. I think it's bad, El."

"Please tell me." Elliot was now as aware as hell of the fact that

Stephen wasn't reaching for him. Still he had to . . . He held out his hand. "Or show me, if it'll be easier?"

But Stephen shook his head, vehement in his *no*. "I don't want to freak you out."

"Too late?"

"I had a vision," Stephen told him. "While I was in Devon Caine's apartment. It was a really awful place, babe. It was filthy and . . . I'm pretty sure, just from the feel of the room, that he'd brought some of his victims there. God, I wanted to leave. It was oppressive and I couldn't breathe. And it got worse, like I was being smothered. And then I was both hot and cold and I had to sit down, because my vision was tunneling. And *then*—bang— I was outside, except I wasn't. I could see the sky even though I knew I was sitting on that disgusting carpet in that disgusting room. I could still smell Caine's feet and his dirty laundry and his . . . general stank."

"But you saw the sky," Elliot confirmed.

"Like I was really there." Stephen nodded. "It was bright blue, with these big, puffy, beautiful clouds. I was watching this bird flying—a big black hawk. And it should have been beautiful, wheeling in circles way up there, but as I watched it, I was afraid. It made me feel this . . . foreboding. And then I saw that Anna and Mac were both there, only Anna had incredible power, and she started to fly, too. Not as high as the hawk, not at first, but I knew she was going up there. And she was carrying Mac with her, and at first Mac was angry and she was fighting her, but then she screamed and pointed at something behind me, and I turned and . . ." His voice broke. "You were lying there, in the grass—it was so green—and you were bleeding. You'd been shot in the chest and in the throat and . . . There was no way I could save you. No way. And it was so fucking *real*."

To hell with boundaries—Elliot reached for him. And God, at the contact, he saw it, too. Stephen's vision or dream or whatever it was. And the power of Stephen's grief as he knelt beside Elliot— and there was so much blood in that green, green grass—hit him with such force that for a moment, he couldn't breathe, either.

He felt Stephen's fear, too. It was there, outside of the vision. *What if I'm prescient?* Stephen asked. *What if one of my new powers, as a Sixty-one, is foreseeing the future?*

Holy crap. *What if,* indeed.

Elliot had worked with a powerful prescient, once—a young woman named Tilda, whose time at OI had been relatively short. She'd walked through the halls with haunted eyes. She'd left, right after correctly predicting the death of her younger sister.

I'll find my notes, Elliot told him, *see if we managed to locate the part of Tilda's brain that she accessed in order to—*

I didn't mean what if I'm prescient and how will that affect me? Stephen interrupted. *I meant,* what if I'm prescient, and you're going to die?

I'm not dead yet, Elliot pointed out. *Prescients don't see* the *future, Stephen, they see* a *future. If you're really prescient, then we'll learn how to use your talent for the warning system that it is. And we'll take a different path.*

Stephen nodded, his relief palpable. He wiped his face with his hands as he took a series of deep breaths.

Unless, of course, Elliot added, *you foresee us winning the lottery. Then we'll proceed as planned.*

Stephen laughed, and he turned and he kissed Elliot, right on the mouth, right there in the lounge. And then he made Elliot completely forget that they were sitting there, kissing in public. *I love you madly. Marry me.*

Elliot pulled back, laughing his surprise. "What?"

"Too soon?" Stephen asked.

"Yeah," Elliot said, but then he lost himself in Stephen's gorgeous eyes. "Holy crap, you're not kidding are you?" He reached out to touch the other man's arm. As always, the connection was instantaneous and . . .

Stephen was dead serious. *Was that a* yeah, too soon *or a* yeah, you'll marry me? he asked.

It was absolutely a *yeah, too soon,* but it was also the other. Elliot didn't have to put the thought into words. He knew that Stephen could feel his *yes.*

The Greater-Than smiled, but it faded far too quickly. *Life's too short,* Stephen told him. *And I don't want to waste a minute of time that I could be spending with you.*

"I love you, too," Elliot said the words aloud—words that, after the fiasco with Mark, he'd never thought he'd say again, certainly not that easily. But he didn't hesitate, not one bit. In fact it was so easy to say, he said it again. "I love you completely. And I'll make it a point," he promised, "over the next few days or weeks—or however long you think it'll take—forever, if you need me to—to stay completely off the lawn."

"Thank you," Stephen said, and kissed Elliot again.

———

David was gone.

After she'd seriously kicked his ass, Anna was left wandering through her former boss's palatial townhouse, all by herself.

It was impressive that she could be here, and not feel the fear and revulsion.

Well, maybe some of the revulsion was still lingering. His "man cave" decorating—the dark stained wood and lack of brilliant color, the King-of-the-Jungle design in the master bath—was slightly stomach-turning. But she most definitely wasn't afraid.

Thanks to Joseph Bach. He'd implanted some terrific and very powerful self-defense skills into her mind, which was a little weird—but only a little.

Anna liked knowing that she could defend herself.

She went into a kitchen that was black, white, and red, with pictures of WWII-era pinup girls in frames on the walls. And it was only then—looking into a refrigerator filled with food she couldn't eat because she was asleep and neither the food nor the fridge was really there—she realized that since this was her dream, she could go anywhere she wanted to. Anywhere in the world . . .

So she left David's house, not really knowing where she wanted to be, but ending up in the living room of Joseph's childhood home.

That was interesting. What did it say about her that she sub-consciously wanted to come back here?

She liked Joseph Bach. A lot.

Anna couldn't deny that.

It was night in his living room—just as it had been when she'd been here before. Also just like before, she didn't need to turn on the lights to see—which was a good thing, because she wouldn't have been able to manipulate the switches.

The furniture was beautiful—all antiques, all astonishingly well cared for. Joseph's parents had had money—that was for sure. She browsed the titles of the books on the built-in bookshelf and discovered that they were all antiques as well. In fact, everything in here—the phone on an ornate little side table, the lamps, the light switches on the walls, the electrical outlets, even the magazines that were out on an end table—was an antique. There was a pristine copy of *Life* magazine, dating from February 1942.

She couldn't pick it up and read it—she couldn't move or alter anything—but she *could* see a piece of mail on the table beneath it that was addressed to Dr. and Mrs. Frederick Bach. . . .

"Hey."

Anna spun around to find Joseph sitting on the sofa, same as he'd done the last time they were here. He was dressed in what he called his "Disney prince" clothes, his flowing pirate shirt hanging open to reveal his well-defined chest.

"You're back," she said, somewhat inanely.

"I found Nika," he told her with a beautiful smile, and the relief that filled her was so sudden and overwhelming, she felt herself sway.

Joseph was on his feet immediately, keeping her from falling as he led her over to sit on the couch.

"Oh, my God," she said, as she started to cry, "oh, thank God. She's alive! Is she all right?"

"She's fine," Joseph told her, one arm still around her as he used his other hand to push her hair back from her face, and to catch the tears that were now rolling in earnest down her face. "She's safe."

"Safe?" Anna asked, hardly daring to believe.

"She escaped," he told her. "I showed her the way to one of our safe houses, downtown. A team of Greater-Thans is already on their way to meet her. They'll bring her back to OI."

Anna couldn't believe what she was hearing. "Oh, thank God," she said again. "We should go, too. We should be there—"

He was already shaking his head. "It's not safe. Once they realize she's gone, they're going to come looking for you."

"Why me?" Anna asked. She didn't understand.

"Because you're special, too," he told her. *God, you're so beautiful . . .*

He was inside of her head—of course he was. This entire encounter was taking place in her mind. Or maybe they were in *his* mind—she couldn't be sure.

And then Anna didn't particularly care as he leaned in, just a little, and brushed his lips across hers.

She'd kissed him before, although not as herself. She'd been part of his memory of his long-dead girlfriend.

But this, now, was him kissing her. Specifically. Intentionally. Longer this time. Deeper. But no less sweetly. She closed her eyes and let herself be filled with happiness even as she let herself be thoroughly, deliciously kissed.

Nika was coming home, and this incredible, magical man thought Anna was special—and when he kissed her like that, she could believe that she was.

She was strong, she was smart—and she was no longer completely on her own. The relief was powerful.

"Come on," Joseph whispered, and Anna opened her eyes as he pulled her up and off of the couch, and then up the stairs and . . .

They didn't use the door this time. She must've blinked as he pulled her through the wall, because they were suddenly in his childhood bedroom.

He must've seen her hesitation, because he said, "This is okay, right?"

And it was okay. It was very okay. Except . . . "It's been a while for me," she admitted.

"Me, too," he told her. "It's been a very long time. You're the first woman I've ever brought here. The only woman I've wanted in this way . . ."

He put his arms around her, pulling her hair back to kiss her neck, her throat, and she could feel his arousal, and it *was* okay. It was more than okay as she pressed herself back against him.

He pulled her T-shirt up and over her head and she laughed, but then there was that oddness again—a sensation of time slipping. Or maybe she'd just blinked again, but now she was completely naked, and he was, too. And God, he was gorgeous—tall and lean, all hard muscles and smooth, pale skin . . . His body was beautiful, and he smiled at her with equal admiration in his eyes, and she crawled across the bed to kiss him.

And that weird time slip happened again—just a heartbeat or a blink—and Anna was astride him, riding him, with his body already buried deep inside of her. And she heard herself cry out—dear God, it felt so good—but despite that, she found herself wanting to stop, to go back, rewind. She'd missed that first moment of joining, that sensation of ultimate trust, of unbearable, unstoppable passion, as he'd first pushed himself home, as she'd first taken him within. And she wanted to feel that, to remember it always, but it was already gone. She'd missed it.

But then she forgot her regret as he sat up to wrap his arms around her, to kiss her, to rock himself inside of her. And she heard herself cry out as she felt herself start to come, and he was right with her. "Oh, my God," he said as he pulled her back with him onto the bed, as he bucked against her, as he covered her mouth again with his, and kissed her.

Except he said it again, "Oh, my God." And even through the exploding pleasure and haze of her orgasm, Anna realized that he couldn't have said those words that clearly with his tongue in her mouth. And as he went limp with his own release, she turned her head and . . .

Joseph Bach, fully dressed in the jeans and sweater he'd been wearing back in his office, was standing in the far corner of the room.

His eyes were wide, and the look of horrified disbelief on his face would've been funny, if it wasn't so utterly un-funny.

And just like that, Anna woke up.

One second she was naked, in a bedroom with two Joseph Bachs, one fully dressed and the other as naked as she was and smiling up at her from between her still-trembling thighs.

The next, she was lying on the leather couch in his office, and he was sitting as far back as he possibly could in a chair that was beside her, looking at her with that very same expression of horror that the fully clad Bach had had on his handsome face.

She blinked up at him, disoriented and uncertain of what had just happened.

"Um," he said, turning slightly away from her, and reaching up to scratch the back of his head. "That was . . . not a nightmare. So, that's good, at least."

"Oh, shit," she said. "That was a *dream*? I was having a dream?"

"Yeah," he said. "That was . . . Yeah."

She sat up. "*All* of it?"

He nodded.

"So, you *didn't* find Nika?" Her disappointment at that news choked her.

"No, I found her," he reported, still looking shell-shocked.

"But you told me that you found her and that she's escaped and . . . She hasn't escaped," Anna concluded. "Shit. *Shit*. That was *really* just a dream?"

Joseph nodded again. "She's alive," he told her, which would have been far better news if her dream version of him hadn't already told her that her sister had *escaped*. "And we're definitely moving closer to getting her out. It's not going to be easy though. She's incredibly powerful—that's true, which is great on the one hand. On the other, she's completely raw—untrained—and she's got so many shields in place, that when I'm in her head, I can't simply read her memories."

The way he could do with Anna. The way he'd no doubt done with her memories of that *dream she'd had about having sex with him.* Oh, God . . . "I'm *so* sorry," she said. "It seemed so real. God, what is wrong with me?"

"Nothing," he said quickly. "You're human, so you dream about . . . all kinds of things."

"Obviously, I want to have sex with you," she said. "And for the record, you're not the only one who's surprised by that little revelation. I'm kind of stunned, too. In my dream, you seduced me, by the way. It was your idea to go upstairs."

"Sorry," he said.

"No! *Shit!*" she said again. "I'm not trying to blame you. I'm just trying to figure out what's going on in my mind that I should—obviously—want you to do . . . that. I mean, you've been great. You're amazing, you are. And I really do like you. A lot. Apparently more than I thought."

"Dreams aren't necessarily reflections of things that we want," he pointed out.

"Nice attempt at a save," Anna said. "We can certainly play it that way, if you like."

He laughed at that, but she could tell he was still extremely embarrassed.

"Just for the record," he said. "Under other circumstances—"

"Oh, God," she said, closing her eyes. "Please don't."

"But considering the current circumstances, I can't," Bach told her, "ever be more to you than a friend."

Oh, good. Her humiliation was now complete.

"Right now, though, I, um, have to go," he told her. "Stephen Diaz brought in Devon Caine. I need to go down to Security and attempt to get inside of his head, see if we can't locate Nika that way. And just so you know, I made sure she was sleeping before I left her, because she grabbed onto me as a lifeline pretty quickly. I want to get back to her as soon as possible. It helps her to not be alone."

Anna nodded, her heart sinking. "Does that mean I'll need to go to sleep again?"

"Yes. When I get back," he told her. "I'm sorry."

"No, that's okay," she said. "Maybe this time I can dream that we do a little S&M, B&D, whips-and-chains thing. And yes, I'm kidding."

He laughed, but it was a shade nervously. "I'm glad you see the humor of the situation."

"It's a laugh riot," she agreed.

"As soon as I can get Nika to lower her shields," Bach tried to reassure her, "I can teach her a few things that . . . With luck and her natural talent, I'll be able to establish direct contact with her—and keep that contact open twenty-four/seven. At that point, I'll no longer need your help."

And somehow, hearing that news—which should have been great—instead disappointed her. What was *wrong* with her? Anna nodded. "May I come with you? Down to Security?"

A great big, giant *no* was in his eyes, but he said, "If you like."

"I'm sorry," she apologized. "I know that the last thing you probably want right now is the nympho following you around—"

"I *don't* think *that*," he said. "And you shouldn't either. People dream about sex all the time—I think it's the third most common dream. Right after flying and teeth falling out. And there are definitely reasons—quite a few, in fact—that would make you . . . form an attachment. To me. It's not that surprising, Anna. And it's not that big of a deal."

"Okay, then," she told him. "I'd like."

TWENTY-TWO

Mac stood with her eyes closed on the sidewalk where Nika Taylor had been abducted.

It wasn't going well—Shane could tell that just from watching her, just from the way she was standing.

Shoulders hunched as if against a cold wind, even though the early evening was still quite warm, she was clenching her teeth—along with every cell in her body.

Shane moved closer. Spoke quietly. "How can I help?"

Mac opened her eyes and looked at him, and she didn't even bother trying to hide her bitter disappointment. "You can't," she said, as she headed back to the car, where Charlie was idling at the side of the busy street. "I got nothing."

"You said that might happen," he reminded her as he followed. "That these kinds of emotional disturbances are more likely to dissipate in the open."

"Please don't try to make me feel better," she said. "I'm pissed. I thought this would work, now that I'm a Sixty-two, and I really don't want your gee-gosh-and-golly optimism right now. So just . . . go help some old lady cross the street."

"Wow," Shane said. "*That* was pretty bitchy."

"Get used to it," she said shortly, climbing into the backseat. "Or better yet, get lost."

He climbed in after her. "Look, I know you're really upset," he started.

"Let's get the hell back to OI," Mac told Charlie.

"Yes, ma'am." He met Shane's eyes briefly and sympathetically in the rearview mirror before he pulled away from the curb.

"Mac," Shane said, and she turned to him.

"Please, I need to close my eyes. Just for a few minutes. I need . . . silence."

Shane nodded. Fair enough.

So they rode in silence through the busy city streets, finally pulling onto the Mass Pike, where Charlie kicked it into high gear.

They'd traveled nearly the entire way back to OI before Mac spoke again.

"You know, if this had worked?" she said with her eyes still closed. "If I'd've been able to find Nika that easily? I was actually going to do it. I was going to sacrifice us both for the greater good of mankind. But it didn't, so congratulations. We're done. I'm cutting you free."

"What?" Shane said.

"You heard me." She opened her eyes and looked at him, and great, the icy stranger was back.

But he'd come to know Mac pretty damn well over the past few days, and he knew that the ice was just a front to hide her inner terror.

"The experiment, part one, is officially over," Mac told him. "Thank you very much. On to part two."

"Part two," he repeated warily.

Mac raised her voice slightly. "Charlie, you wanna hook up? Be my little lab partner, see if you can't raise my integration levels sufficiently, via the exchange of some bodily fluids?"

"Mac, come on," Shane said. "Don't embarrass the kid. Charlie, ignore her, she's not serious."

"Yes, sir." Charlie turned on the radio and kicked their speed higher, even as he pulled onto the off-ramp that meant they were nearly home.

Home. Funny how Shane had come to think of OI as *home* after such a short amount of time.

"I'm dead serious," Mac was saying. "How do I know that you're the only person who can raise my integration levels until I try raising them with someone else?"

"I'm pretty sure I'm not the first man you've slept with," Shane pointed out, trying to keep his voice even.

"But you're the first man I've slept with while checking my levels," she countered. "If I want to be thorough, and as a scientist, I do—"

"How about as a human being?" Shane asked, because he was starting to believe that she wasn't just being an asshole. He was starting to believe she might actually do it—that her fear had pushed her over the edge and was making her actively try to ditch him. And what better way to do it, than this? "How about as a woman?"

"I'm a Greater-Than," she said as if that were a counterargument. "Don't worry, Charlie. One of the new Potentials will be happy to participate."

"So you're just going to have sex with a stranger," Shane said, as they pulled up to OI's gates.

"You were a stranger when I first had sex with you," she pointed out, as up front Charlie desperately started singing along with the song that was playing on the radio.

"But I'm not a stranger anymore," Shane argued.

"Yeah, because now I've known you all of . . . what is it? Two days. You know, I think I'll set it up like speed dating. Put the interested Potentials around the edges of a room. I can sit on their laps, one at a time, have a little conversation, see who makes my levels rise just from the body contact—"

"Okay, now you're just being cruel," Shane said, as the gate finally opened and Charlie raced up the hill. "Knock it the fuck off."

"It was an experiment," she reminded him. "And I'm telling you that your part of it ended. If it means my levels drop back to fifty, so be it."

"I know I signed that paper," he told her, "and maybe that makes you think that it's just about the sex for me, but it's not."

"What," she said, leaning hard on her sarcasm and tough bitch attitude. "You're going to sit there and try to make me believe that you *love* me?"

"Why not?" Shane said. "You're sitting there and trying to make *me* believe that you *don't.*"

Mac laughed, but it came out sounding far more like a sob. "This isn't about me, it's about you. You say it doesn't matter, but it does."

"What doesn't matter?" he asked. "When did I say—"

"My talent," she cut him off. "You're not sitting in this car with me because you *want* to."

They were back to this.

Okay.

At least now Shane knew the source of her fear. "We've had this conversation before, and I respectfully disagree."

"And I *respectfully* point out that I'm sitting here, treating you like *shit,* yet you have absolutely no desire to run away."

Charlie, however, did just that after pulling into the parking lot and slamming the car into park. He was out of there.

"That's just fucked up," Mac continued.

"No, it's not," Shane said, as he watched Charlie run for his life toward the main OI building, "because I happen to think you're worth fighting for. Because I know you don't mean what you're saying. I know you."

"No, you don't!"

"Yeah, I do," he said.

"Oh!" she said shouting so loud that Charlie glanced back at them before he pulled open OI's door. "Damn it! You're not going to walk away, you fool, regardless of how badly I treat you, because of what I *do* to you with my stupid fucking powers!"

"I'm not going to walk away, because I like what you do to me," Shane said.

"Do you?" she shouted. "You do, huh? That's because you're thinking with this." She reached over and grabbed him right through his pants, and okay, yeah, he was already aroused. He couldn't ride in a car with this woman without getting turned on. So sue him.

And God, he loved her touch, but he caught her wrist and pulled her hand away. "I'm sorry, you're not allowed to touch me like that if you really do intend to ditch me."

"But that's my point," she said, breaking. "I don't need to *touch* you. You know what I can do without even *touching* you . . . ?"

She hit him with a wave of her voodoo that was so incredibly strong, it was all he could do not to reach for her. And Jesus, he'd thought he'd been hard before, but now he was a rock.

"Okay," he ground out between clenched teeth, "I get your point."

"No, you don't," Mac said, and even though he would never have believed it possible, she ramped her power up even higher.

"Oh, *shit*," Shane said, as he came, just suddenly, just right there, in the car, in his pants, without her even looking at him, let alone touching him. "*Shiiit. Holy shit . . .*"

It was mind-blowing just how good it felt. In length and intensity, it was, without a doubt, the big one, and it left him gasping and spent.

"Okay," he said, when he could once again finally speak. And wow, now he was a total mess. And awesome—in order to get inside, he was going to have to go through security, take off his jacket, and get wanded. That was going to be awkward. "All right. Now I know, for an absolute fact, that I love you."

"Oh, fuck you," Mac said and opened the car door, obviously intending to bolt.

Shane caught her arm. "I'm not done."

"Yeah," she said, struggling to break free. "You are. You're really that shallow—"

"I know that I love you," he told her, speaking loudly over her, "because as great as that was, with your voodoo cranked to eleven? It didn't come *close* to what I feel when we're together, when we make love. Frankly, it doesn't even rate, *Michelle,* compared to what I feel when you get your head out of your ass long enough to smile at me."

Her eyes filled with tears and her face was filled with anguish and pain that she didn't hide. "But it's *not. Real.*"

"I've said it before, I'll say it again. I. Don't. Care."

"You don't understand," she said, pulling her arm free. "You may think you don't care. You may even really not care. You might honestly think you like it, but . . . *I don't!* I fucking *hate* it, all right? I hate it because I could love you. I really could. But I can't. I can't do it. I can't do this. I can't."

"Wait," he said, as she got out of the car, as he scrambled after her. "Mac. Wait. Why? You're right—I *don't* understand."

She stopped, but she didn't face him. "You don't love me, Shane—you *can't* love me. You can say the words, you can say them constantly if you want to, but that won't make them true."

"But if it's what I feel—"

Mac turned to face him, and the sadness in her eyes nearly did him in.

"I was ten years old," she said, "when my powers first made an impact on my life. My father, who was an asshole and a drunk, beat the shit out of me, and then told my mother that he *had* to do it—to keep himself from having sex with me. Apparently, I was irresistible."

"Jesus," Shane said.

"Yeah," Mac said. "I've never told anyone that before, because it was just too awful. She kicked him out, but we didn't press charges, because she needed the child support. My brother, Billy, had special needs, and . . . I spent the next four years dodging creepy old guys who would follow me around at the state fair, or at the mall. It got so that I just stayed home, because it was worse after I hit puberty. Except then, when I was fourteen, Billy and my mom were killed when the brakes in the car failed. There was a lawsuit that the lawyer was sure we were going to win, and she was right, but it made my father petition for custody, and he won, so I went to live with the asshole instead of my aunt."

"Oh, shit," Shane said.

"I won't leave you in suspense," Mac said. "He didn't touch me. Although what *did* happen was worse. I would have preferred . . ." She cut herself off and got back to her story. *"Dad* was onto his third wife by then. Janice—she was a piece of work. He'd married her for her money, but blew through that really fast.

"When I moved in, they had just downsized to a really shitty two-bedroom apartment. I had to sleep under the dining room table. I used sheets to make walls, for privacy, but I knew they wouldn't keep me safe. You and I both know that the asshole didn't touch me, but back then, I had no idea what was going to happen. Needless to say, I didn't get much sleep. Not until he got a job overseas. See, Janice didn't like the way he looked at me, so he went to work as a contractor in Libya, which paid really well, but somehow made her hate me even more.

"The only one who seemed to notice that I was grieving and in shock," Mac continued, "was Janice's son. Tim."

She paused. And met Shane's eyes.

"I fell in love with Tim," she told him. "He was almost eighteen, and I was only fourteen, but he was so nice and handsome and . . . nice. He really was. And that first summer, we were both living in a new city and we didn't know anybody else, so we spent every day together and . . . He said he loved me, and I believed him. And I gave him everything. We made all these plans for the future. He was going to graduate and get a scholarship to college, and I was going to go with him, and work to help pay the bills. And then I was going to go to college, too, and when I got old enough, we'd get married." She paused again. "He always used protection—I suppose I should be thankful for that . . ."

Shane found his voice, but it cracked just a little as he asked, "Do you still love him?"

Mac gave him a look that said *Please.* "He and a friend tried to gang-bang me."

"So, he was playing you."

"No," she said, and her conviction rang in her voice. "That's the really awful part. He meant everything he said—as long as I was in the room. As long as he was with me. See, my power—it was even more erratic back then. I honestly didn't even know that I was doing anything. I didn't . . . But my power made him *think* that he loved me. I mean, God, I was jailbait. He risked a lot to be with me. We had to hide our relationship from his bitch of a mother and . . . And I didn't know it at the time, but I was manipulating him with my talent—the exact same way I manipulated you."

"Mac," Shane started, but she stopped him.

"No, let me finish. Because maybe you'll understand, at least as much as you can." She took a deep breath. "School finally started, and Tim was going to this private academy, and I was jammed into the local bullshit public school, but we still saw each other every night. I mean, I slept with him. Every night.

"And one day, I don't really remember what happened, but I got the brilliant idea to go meet him at his school, instead of waiting for him to get home from basketball practice and . . . I saw him with this girl. She was beautiful. She looked like she belonged with a boy like Tim, and . . . I saw him kiss her."

Mac paused, and in that moment, her fatigue and her sadness overpowered the current of attitude and anger that always lurked just below her surface. "The next two months were hell—a lot of fights, a lot of begging my forgiveness, a lot of e-mails and texts and phone calls where, because he wasn't with me, he'd break up with me. But then he'd come home and I'd be there and he'd cry and . . . We had a lot of makeup sex, too. But then, the next day, it would start all over again with the texts and calls.

"See, when I wasn't with him, he *didn't* love me. And he knew at those times that he shouldn't be screwing his fourteen-year-old stepsister, and it really messed him up. On top of that, he really was in love with this other girl, Heather. It wasn't until years later, until I learned more about my power, that I really understood. It wasn't his fault. He wasn't lying to me. When he was with me he thought he loved me."

Shane felt sick—not just that this had happened to her, but because he now, absolutely, understood. "I'm not a seventeen-year-old boy," he told her.

But Mac ignored him. She just kept going. There was more to the story—it apparently wasn't over yet. "Finally, I had enough, and *I* broke up with *him*. And he kinda went crazy. Being around me all night, every night, was . . . My powers made him want me, right? *Really* want me. And since I didn't know what I was doing, I certainly didn't know how to dial it down.

"One night, Tim's friend Ty came over, and Janice was out." Mac paused. "And shit happened. At the trial, Tim provided video of me coming to his room at night. Willingly. Eagerly. I had no idea that he'd taped us, probably with his webcam. But the lawyer used it at the trial as proof that I was giving it away."

"Proof of statutory rape," Shane pointed out, unable to keep silent.

Mac smiled, but it was sad. "We're so different, Navy. You live in a world of right and wrong, black and white. The world I live in's not like that. Tim's not to blame for what he did to me. If it was anyone's fault, it was mine."

"No," Shane said. "Nuh-uh. You can't blame yourself. He should have stayed away from you. You were *fourteen*. Besides, you had no idea—"

"But I do now," Mac interrupted him. "Now? I know exactly how my power affects men. When I aim it, and turn it up? I know. I knew in the bar, when you sat down next to me. And I should've stayed away from you."

"No," Shane said again.

"Yes," Mac countered. "Just like Tim, you don't love me. Just like Tim, it's not real."

"I'm sorry that happened to you," Shane told her, talking fast because she was glancing now toward Old Main, and he knew she was going to walk away. "I'm sorry that Tim was a dick—"

"But he wasn't," Mac said. "I mean, yeah, but not at first."

"Yes, at first," Shane insisted. "If he didn't really see how incredibly special you are—"

Mac closed her eyes. "Please don't," she said. "God, Shane, if you only knew how many men have told me just how *special* I am . . ."

"I'm not like them," Shane said, and even as the words left his lips, he knew that Mac had probably heard *that* before, too. And he felt tears of frustration and anger and God, desperation fill his eyes, and he forced them back, because he was not defeated yet. "Mac, I honestly don't care—"

"But I do," she said again. "Shane, please, listen to yourself. And tell me how is it okay for me to continue to manipulate you? What does that say about me if I'd be willing to do that?"

He had no answer for her, and she nodded.

"Yeah," Mac said. "Try, if you can, to put yourself in my shoes. Try to understand how *I* feel—how awful, really awful, it would be to let myself love you." She was crying now. "I'm not going to do it. I don't want this. I don't want *you*."

There was nothing he could say to that.

"Just stay away from me," she said, wiping her eyes and her face on her sleeve. "Go back to the barracks and leave me alone."

And with that, she walked away.

———

Bach's carefully ordered world was falling apart.

Not only was Stephen Diaz showing signs of prescient ability, but the man that Bach thought of as the most thoughtful and steady member of his team had announced simultaneously that he was gay and that he was in love with Bach's Research and Support Department Head. Oh, and now? After a seven-minute courtship, Stephen and Elliot had decided to get married.

Speaking of prescient ability or lack thereof, Bach hadn't seen *that* one coming.

And then there was Anna Taylor. With her ultimate trust and strength of will, she'd done everything Bach had asked of her, in order to help him make that connection with Nika.

Everything he'd asked—including everything that his dream self had asked, which was to have sex with her.

He'd returned from the incredible strain and difficulty of navigating through Nika's unbelievably complex and barrier-filled mind, anticipating the quiet comfort and warmth that he felt with

Anna. It was similar to the way he looked forward to a hot bowl of chicken soup and a soft bed at the end of a hard day.

At first he couldn't find her.

And then?

He found her.

The fact that she was having a sex dream about him shouldn't have surprised him. He'd felt her attraction. He knew that she admired him.

But it *did* surprise him.

What surprised him even more was his reaction. He'd had a lot of options to choose from besides standing there, watching, with his mouth hanging open.

He could have immediately withdrawn from her head. He could have backed away and then clouded her memory, so that when she awoke she'd remember little more than the fact that she'd had a vague but lovely dream.

Instead, he stood there watching for far longer than he should have, not just because she was beautiful—although that played into it, too—but because he knew that she was on the verge of orgasm.

And he wanted to let her come.

Although okay, yeah, watching her do that—and watching his shiny and extra-buff dream self do the same—that had been freaking weird.

Was that really how she saw him? Did he really smile at her like that? And yeah, okay, the fact that Anna was naked and in his arms would warrant a smile of that magnitude from any man, to be sure.

But . . . *Oh, my God.*

He'd been so stunned by both the experience and his lack of judgment, that he made the mistake of speaking aloud, which made her turn and see him.

And even then, if he'd been thinking clearly, he *still* could have backed away and clouded her memory.

Instead he'd yanked himself out of her mind, which brought them face-to-face in his office.

And hadn't *that* been awkward.

Anna was sitting now—fully clothed—beside him in the OI Security lobby. She was waiting, just as he was, for Mac to appear.

Bach's initial trip inside of Devon Caine's ugly-ass mind had been even less successful than his visit to Nika's. He was really striking out all over the place, today, and he needed Mac's help.

He needed her empathic skills to navigate the murky depths of the serial killer's mind. He needed her to help him feel his way past the delusions and fantasies to the real memories.

They'd gotten word that Mac was finally in the building, but she'd no doubt stopped in the ladies' water closet to freshen up.

The door opened, but it was only Elliot. "Got a sec?" he asked Bach.

"Until Mac gets here," Bach said. "Sure."

"Stephen thought it was important that I fill you in on what's happening with Edward O'Keefe," Elliot said. "And I agree. This is big. We're keeping him alive."

"That's good news," Bach said. He could use a little more news of the good variety today.

But Elliot tempered his positive words. "Although, before we get *too* excited, we still may lose him—he was in terrible health to begin with. But the important thing you need to know is that he no longer has any trace of oxyclepta di-estraphen in his system."

"Oh, my God, that's huge," Anna said, and Bach glanced over to find her paying close attention.

He looked back at Elliot. "*No* trace of the drug?"

"None whatsoever," Elliot confirmed. "Now, to be fair, we don't know whether or not he jokered. I suspect he didn't. We *do* know, from JLG—the drug testing lab's records—that he was given a significantly large dose of Destiny about an hour before he went into cardiac arrest. So he has the drug, right? And that makes him instantly addicted. But then he has a massive coronary, to the point that his heart actually stops. The clowns at JLG use a defibrillator to jump-start him again. And somehow—I still don't understand why it happened—those two events, his heart stopping and then being restarted, while under the influence of this drug, stimulated the self-healing centers of his brain. He's currently in a coma, and most of his organs appear to be in some kind of stasis. But that small part of his brain is, as far as we can tell, not only working overtime on repairing his heart, but it's burned up all traces of the drug, detoxing him and put him in a place where his body no longer requires more Destiny to stay alive."

"So he's been essentially cured of his addiction—at least the physical side of it," Bach said. Anna was right—this *was* huge. Provided it worked on anyone besides Edward O'Keefe. Provided O'Keefe came out of his coma. Provided his heart hadn't been irrevocably damaged. Provided his body was able to get his other organs working again. Provided there wasn't a lingering psychological need for the drug.

"Problem is," Elliot said, "his self-healing abilities are slowing down, and his heart's still not repaired, not enough to function without some serious open-heart surgery—which *will* kill him in his current condition. I'd like your permission, Maestro, to give him small doses of Destiny as we continue to stimulate his brain's healing center—with hope that it, too, will burn out of his system as he continues to self-repair."

"And if it doesn't?" Bach asked.

"Then we stop and start his heart, all over again—and rinse and repeat if we have to."

Bach was silent. "I don't know, Doctor," he finally started.

Anna spoke up again. "If I were dying," she said, "I'd want you to try it. And if that were Nika? I'd say do it."

"Definitely do it."

Bach looked up to see Mac standing just inside the door. It was odd that he hadn't felt her come in. He was nowhere near the empath that she was, but he could usually sense and find her anywhere in the building, because she used her anger as a fuel. She reminded him of that character, Pig Pen, from *Peanuts*. All he had to do was find the black cloud of rage, and there she'd be.

But right now, she had some significant emotional shields up and in place, and all he felt from her was . . .

Sorrow.

"Please," she said to Bach. "I liked him. O'Keefe. He really loved his dead wife. I think you'd like him, too. A lot in common, right?"

She was trying to be her usual irreverent self, but it came out forced.

Bach turned to Elliot. "Try it."

"Thank you, sir," Elliot said and turned to go, but then stopped to look hard at Mac. "You okay?"

"I'm *great*," she said. "I'm *so* ready to go spelunking inside the horror-filled head of a psychopath—because my day just hasn't been shitty enough."

"You don't have to do this," Bach told her.

"Oh, yes," Mac said, "I do. We're going to find this girl." She turned back to Elliot. "I understand congrats are in order. Good for you, bagging Diaz, and okay, that came out wrong, I didn't mean it that way. Although, good for you, too, if *that* happened because, shit, life's too short, right?" She looked from Elliot to Bach and then over to Anna, then back to Bach, then to Anna, then Bach.

And Bach knew that Mac had picked up on the extra-charged emotional vibe that was still connecting him to Nika's older sister.

It was only dream sex, he had the urge to say. Fortunately, he had control over his urges. Most of them, anyway.

And, wisely, Mac didn't comment. What she *did* say was, "Let's do this thing, shall we?" But then she looked at Anna again. "I'll bring him right back."

———

"So . . ." Mac looked at Bach as the door to the cell that held Devon Caine was unlocked. "You've been busy."

Bach didn't beat around the proverbial bush. "I like her," he said, and yes, he was talking about the very lovely Anna Taylor. "She's quickly become a good friend."

"Your *friend* wants to screw you blue."

Don't.

Okay, she'd hit a nerve, if he was making the kind of mental proclamation he usually reserved for his communications with jokering drug addicts.

Sorry, she sent back to him.

Bach didn't respond. He just looked down at Caine, who was strapped to a hospital bed, still unconscious from whatever drugs Diaz's team had shot into his bloodstream.

If they could have, Mac would've gone with Bach, directly into Caine's head. But not even Bach was capable of doing that. So what he was going to have to do was reach into Caine's odious mind and pull out a series of images. He'd hold them in his own head, and pull Mac in. She'd be able to sift through and identify, hopefully easily, if they were fantasy or true memory.

Yeah, this was going to suck ass.

"More than you can know," Bach murmured his agreement. He looked at her. *I'm going to keep you close. I won't let you go.*

Mac nodded. *I'd appreciate that, sir. And I am sorry. Not just about what I said, but . . . There's a lot of bullshit in my own head that you're probably going to run into.*

Bach smiled at that. *When is there ever not?*

"Ha," she said. "Ha."

He glanced at her as he held out his hand—which was a giant hint and a half that this was going to be worse than she could imagine, since her relationship with Bach usually involved as little touching as possible.

Still, she took hold of him. She felt him say *Brace.* And just like that, she fell into the violent and horrific nightmare that was Devon Caine, knowing that, whatever she experienced . . . ?

Bach was getting it supersized, and dozens of times worse.

TWENTY-THREE

Mac was sitting alone in the otherwise empty bar.

Stephen sat down next to her, but she didn't look up. She'd lined a row of drinks—it looked like whiskey—in front of her and was downing them one after the other, with the rather clear intention of self-anesthetization.

She'd obviously helped herself. Louise wasn't behind the bar. In fact, she was nowhere in sight, which was good. It would allow the two Greater-Thans to talk freely.

"We'll find Nika another way," Stephen said, and only then did Mac look at him.

"I should have been able to do it," she said. "But I couldn't."

"That wasn't about you," Stephen told her. "That was about Caine. The guy's insane. If he honestly can't tell the difference between fantasy and reality, his daydreams are going to read as memories. It wasn't you, Michelle."

Mac nodded, but he knew she didn't believe him.

"Dr. Bach couldn't do it either," he pointed out.

She nodded again, toying with her glass.

"It must be twice as hard," he said gently, "knowing that you sifted through that horror-show without a positive outcome. Like you need more nightmares than you already have."

"They'd been using him," Mac told Stephen. "Caine. He was

working for them—and not just by helping them move their product."

Stephen nodded. When it came to acquisitions—the Organization's intentionally bland term for the kidnapping and exploitation of little girls—Caine would be an asset. "He has the talents they need—targeting and trolling . . ."

"Not just that." Her voice was tight. "They pay him—they fucking *pay* him—to go into their holding rooms and play the bogeyman."

"Oh, God." He closed his eyes. The Organization imprisoned the girls they *acquired* in rooms where they were kept in constant terror. He could only imagine what a man like Caine would do. But then he didn't have to imagine, because Mac told him.

"He's allowed to pick one—just one. One's all it takes. And one's enough for him, because he knows he'll be back, probably the next day," she said. "And it's like the best shopping spree ever. For Caine, it's like being a kid in a candy shop with a hundred-dollar gift card. So it takes him awhile, but he finally makes his choice." Mac's voice got even harder. "And he rapes her. In front of the others."

And the fear the girls felt would increase their adrenaline and trigger the hormones and proteins that made their blood more potent, so the Organization could use it to make their drug.

"I'm sorry you had to see that," Stephen murmured.

"But when they *really* want to shake things up? The bastards who run these places?" Mac said, her voice shaking. "They let him kill the girl he's raped. Again—right there. It goes in stages. The girls who've just been brought in are terrified to start with. So it doesn't take much to set them off. A guy with a scarred face comes into the room. And everyone screams because he's so scary looking. Then he comes in with a knife and starts randomly slashing. And then, after they get immune to that, he kills one of them. And it goes like that for a while. Maybe he'll kill one of them, maybe he won't. But then they get tired—they've been bled so often—their energy drops. And some of them probably start to think that death wouldn't be that bad. A flash of the knife—it'll be over nice and quick. So the fear levels just aren't the same. Which is when management calls for Caine, and he comes in and shows those girls just how bad it *could* get, because he doesn't kill his victims quickly. He likes to hear them scream."

Dear God . . .

Mac's face twisted again. "If Bach hadn't been in there with me?" she said. "I would've killed him."

"Devon Caine's not going to hurt anybody ever again," Stephen promised her.

"But they'll find someone else to hurt them," she said. "D, we've *got* to get those girls out of that nightmare."

"We're working on it. You know that."

Mac nodded again, struggling to control her emotions. She drained another glass. Pulled the last one closer as she exhaled hard. "Listen to me, bitching and moaning to you, while you have your own nasty-ass nightmare to deal with."

"Yeah," Stephen said, drawing the word out. "And then there's that."

She glanced at him. "Wasn't it you who once told me that the last skill you wanted—the dead last—was the ability to see the future?"

He smiled tightly. "That would be me."

"You could lose that talent," Mac told him. "I've dropped back down to fifty-one."

She said it so nonchalantly, but Stephen wasn't fooled. He knew exactly what she meant—that she and Shane were history. "I'm sorry to hear that."

She shrugged and tossed back her last drink—the row of which suddenly made even more sense.

"Doesn't it bother you," she asked him, "knowing that you're using Elliot the way you are? I mean, really, D. Would you have hooked up with him if he didn't raise your integration levels?"

"Eventually," Stephen said. "I've been working my way toward him for a while."

Mac looked at him and laughed. "Yeah, right, *eventually*, like when you both turned eighty?"

"Probably before that."

Mac nodded. "You know, I felt you before. When you and El were in his office. There was so much love in the room, I kinda threw up in my mouth."

Stephen smiled. "Jealousy'll do that."

She sat back on the stool. "I don't get how you're just suddenly *okay* with it. I mean, you just accept the fact that Elliot loves you? He suddenly genuinely *loves* you. And it's not at all because you look the way you look . . . ?"

"I'm sure that plays into it," Stephen told her. "It plays into my attraction for him—it always has." He shifted toward her. "I know it seems fast, but . . . To answer your question, yes. I accept the fact that he genuinely loves me. The telepathic connection was key, though, in convincing me. Spending time in his head is . . . It's like an hour together is the same as if we spent three weeks just talking. It's crazy how comfortable and right it feels. And El's so open and . . . Trusting. He's so ready to be loved. If you want to know the truth, I'm exactly what he's been waiting for, all his life. And we're both very much okay with that."

"He loves you because you're special," she persisted.

"Damn right, I'm special." Stephen smiled. "He is, too. Michelle, I know it's scary to let someone like Shane get that close," he told her quietly, but she cut him off with a laugh and a disbelieving look.

"You have *no* idea. With your fairy-tale, happily-ever-after, found-your-soul-mate bullshit? Yeah, it must've been real *scary* falling into Elliot's perfect arms."

"How about knowing that it ends with him taking bullets in his chest and throat, and bleeding out?" Stephen asked her. "Is that *scary* enough for you?"

She was silent.

"You know, whether my *vision*—or whatever the hell it was—was real or just a result of low blood sugar and lack of sleep," he told her, "the truth is, it could end that way at any time—for either of us. For *any* of us." If they weren't already on the Organization's hit list, they'd all be there soon enough. "For me, it's scary to think that I used to believe it was better to be alone. How could that be better? It's safer, yeah. But it's not better."

"You have no idea," she said again, as if her life was hard while his was easy.

And that pissed him off a little, which made him throw her some snark. "And then there's the fact that maybe if you weren't down to fifty-one," he pointed out, "you might've been able to see the truth in Devon Caine."

That got him a deservedly dark look. "You really think I haven't thought of that?"

"I was just rubbing it in," he said. "Pouring salt onto your foolishness."

"I'm foolish?" she asked, shaking her head. "Foolish would be . . ." Her voice broke, and for one heartbreaking moment, her face twisted, and Stephen thought she actually might to start to cry.

But her face morphed immediately into her standard semi-bored half-scowl, and she said, "I'm being practical."

"You say practical, I say foolish."

"Shouldn't you be prying Elliot from his office, and throwing him over your shoulder, forcing him to stop working and come home?" she asked. "Or is the sex going to be a once-every-fifteen-years thing?"

Stephen smiled at that absurdity.

"I'll take that as a no," she said. And her tough-bitch mask broke again. "Seriously, D, I'm really happy for you. I am. Elliot's amazing. I've loved him right from the first day he came in for that job interview."

"Me, too," he told her. He gently nudged her leg with his boot. "I'm going to need your help to keep him safe."

"You got it," she told him, zero hesitation. "You know it."

"Good." He knocked on the bar. "I gotta go. But oh. My reason for looking for you. I took Caine's cell from his apartment, and Analysis was able to track his wanderings via his phone's GPS. I don't think he knew how it works, because he didn't shut it off. He's never even wiped the memory. As a result—"

Mac was already sitting up straighter on the barstool. "We know where he's been—and where he's gone! Do we have the route he took after grabbing Nika Taylor?"

"We do." Stephen held up one hand. "We've got a surveillance team not only tracing his footsteps, but also staking out any location where he spent any time at all. But we do know, unfortunately, that he went to his apartment from Rickie Littleton's garage. Littleton—or someone else—may have taken Nika in. Or it might've been a handoff, right in the street. You know, here's the girl, here's your cash."

"Or Caine was in charge of taking Nika in, but he took a little unauthorized side trip home with her first." Mac's face was tight. "I want to see that list."

"It's in your e-mail," Stephen said. "You were cc'd a copy. It came in about fifteen minutes ago—along with Analysis's list of locations. You know, the list that they compiled after they tracked all twenty-three vehicles that left Littleton's South Boston garage? It took them awhile. Of course, there's nothing on there that pops . . ."

Mac had taken her phone out and was scrolling through her e-mail. She clicked the message from Analysis open, and scrolled down . . . "Shit!"

"What?"

"I know this address." Mac looked up at Stephen, and the darkness in her eyes made a chill go down his back. "According to this, Caine was only home for two hours after leaving Littleton's garage, and then he went to Western Ave. Number two-ten. Littleton used to go there all the time, to get paid. We never found absolute proof that it's an official Org building, but it is."

"It's not on our list," he told her. "Not even of suspected Organization holdings."

"It will be," she said, sliding down off her stool. "It should be. Now that Littleton's dead, those reports should've been filed."

"Analysis has been a little busy," Stephen pointed out. "Have you filed *your* report on Littleton?"

That should have made Mac laugh, or at least smile. Her allergies to paperwork were legendary. Instead she only looked grim. "Nika's there. She's gotta be."

"If she's there, we'll find her," Stephen tried to reassure her. "There's nothing you can do that we're not already doing."

"Yeah there is," Mac said as she took her jacket off the stool's back and slipped it on. "I can blow the fricking roof off the place and get her out!"

Stephen stood up, too, intending to block her, or at least slow her down, saying, "That's not the plan—"

"Fuck the plan!"

Behind the bar—one at a time—the bottles broke, exploding with a spray of liquor and glass.

"What the hell, Michelle?" Stephen said, ducking for cover, and pulling his jacket up over his head to shield himself.

But she'd already turned away, as if she didn't even notice. She just headed for the door, pulling her gloves out of her pocket and slipping them on, even as she kicked her speed up to a jog and then a run.

Stephen scrambled after her, skidding on the gin- and tequila-soused tile as the lights in the room continued to pop and spark. By the time he reached the lounge door, he could see through the glass panel that she was nearly at the end of the hall and still picking up speed.

He yanked the door handle, and nearly dislocated his shoulder. What the . . . ? He tried the other door, but it, too, was locked. He focused, trying to use his power to flip the lock, but it didn't budge. He couldn't open the damn thing—she was somehow jamming it.

"Shit! Mac!" He pounded on the door.

One last bottle exploded from behind the bar, and he jumped, and when he turned to look back down the hall, Mac was gone.

He reached for his phone, dialing Elliot even as he went to the nearest comm-station and activated it. "Computer, access SL. Link me to Security."

Elliot picked up his phone. "I'm so sorry, but I'm still not done—"

Stephen interrupted him. "I need you to authorize a jot scan for Mac—immediately."

Elliot didn't hesitate. He raised his voice. "Computer, jot scan Dr. Michelle Mackenzie, STAT." Back into his phone, "What's going on?"

"I don't know. Mac is . . . Shit, El, is it possible for a Greater-Than to joker?"

"What?" Elliot said. "No." But then he switched it to, "I don't know. Jesus, your guess is as good as mine. I mean, I suppose anything's possible."

The comm-station beeped as Patty Gilbert from Security appeared on the computer screen, via webcam. "Sir, is there an issue with which you need assistance?"

"Hang on, El." Stephen opened the connection to Security. "Affirmative, Ms. Gilbert," he said. "Send an immediate message to all personnel. If they see or encounter Dr. Mackenzie, they *must* keep their distance. I have reason to believe she's leaving the building—just let her go."

"Yes, sir." Gilbert had to be curious, but she knew him well enough not to ask questions.

He shut the connection and went back to Elliot. "Do me a favor," he said.

"Anything."

"Go to the barracks and get Shane Laughlin. Meet me in the south lobby."

"Consider it done."

"El, wait," Stephen said before Elliot hung up. "Don't go outside."

"I'm going to kind of need to," Elliot pointed out, "if we're going after Mac."

"Shane and I are going," Stephen told him as he went back to the door. This time, with Mac long out of range, he got it open. He went out, moving swiftly toward the elevators that would take him to Bach's office. "With Dr. Bach."

On the other end of the phone, Elliot was silent and his subtext was clear. This was going to get old, fast.

But Stephen had his own subtext to his answering silence: *Too bad.*

"I'll get Laughlin and meet you in the south lobby," Elliot finally said.

"Thank you," Stephen said, and hanging up, he started to run.

———

They'd returned to the scene of the crime.

It was a ridiculous thing to be thinking, but Anna couldn't help herself as she sat on the sofa in Bach's office.

Besides, it wasn't even true. Bach's childhood bedroom had been the *real* scene of the crime—except no crime had been committed. Nothing illegal, anyway.

Anna heard the toilet flush and the water running in the sink in Bach's private bathroom—the water closet, he called it in his quaintly old-fashioned way—and she braced herself.

Whatever had happened with the "spelunking" of Devon Caine's savagely twisted mind had been ugly, and Elliot had been called in to help Mac and Joseph, who'd both experienced some rather extreme physical distress.

Apparently, Caine was a monster, with an impenetrable mind that was filled with darkness. Finding him was a good thing, because it got him off the streets. But it brought them no closer to locating Nika.

And Anna realized that it was down to Bach—and the connection he'd established with Nika, via Anna's dreams.

Bach had ended up isolating himself for about fifteen minutes of what he called balancing meditation, while Mac, looking a little dazed after having lost her dinner in the security lobby's trash can, waved off Elliot and staggered away.

Bach had finally emerged, looking pale and ill—similar to the way he still looked as he now came out of his bathroom.

"Sorry," he said.

Anna stood up. "I think you need to take more time."

"We don't have time."

"Just another fifteen minutes," she suggested. "I can wait outside."

"Lie down," he told her. "Please. Nika's going to wake up soon—if she hasn't already. While I didn't promise her I wouldn't leave, I did say that if I had to go, I would try to get back as quickly as possible."

Anna sighed and sat on the edge of the sofa. "You won't be able to help her if you make yourself sick."

"I'm fine," he said, meeting her gaze steadily. He even managed to force a smile. "Believe me, this is nothing. I've felt far worse. Now, please, lie down."

Anna was about to sit back, when someone knocked on the door. Knocked and then pushed it open and peeked in.

"I'm so sorry, sir." It was Stephen Diaz. "But it's urgent. It's Mac. Her integration's fluctuating wildly with spikes up to seventy. She seems to have . . . I don't know, snapped."

———

Mac pulled onto the Mass Pike and pushed her bike as fast as it would go, only vaguely aware of the streetlights burning out with a flash or even a surge of sparks as she passed them.

It wasn't as hard as she'd imagined not to think about Shane. True, she'd back-burnered him, and she could feel her awareness of her loss, and the deeply gnawing heartache, but it wasn't front and center.

Right now, she had one and only one thing front and center in her mind: walking into those rooms where Nika and all those girls were being held, and setting them free.

She focused on it, because if she didn't, then even with the roar of her Harley's engine, even with the whine of her tires against the pavement, she could still hear the horrible sounds that Caine made as he raped and murdered that nameless little brown-eyed girl that he'd chosen after walking around the room filled with girls strapped to hospital beds.

He grunted and he gasped and he giggled and he moaned and

he clicked his teeth and smacked his lips. And sometimes he sang little bits and pieces of songs. And he liked it when the girl he was abusing screamed, but not half as much as he liked it when all of the other girls joined in. He was a showman and the screams were his applause. And he reveled in the power it gave him, and he got off on their fear.

And when he was in that place, in that time of abandon, his enjoyment was so . . . pure. It was absolute and practically child-like.

He had no sense of wrong or right, no concept of morality, no idea of empathy or compassion.

He did what he did because he liked doing it. He liked the way it made him feel.

But the people who hired him? The people who knew that he was so terribly broken, who were not only aware of what he did, but allowed him—no, *paid* him—to do it?

They were pure evil.

And Mac was going to find them. She was going to go through that entire list of places that Caine had visited, and she was going to find not just the girls who were locked in those rooms, but the people who'd locked them there and hired motherfuckers like Devon Caine solely for the purpose of keeping the girls' adrenaline flowing.

Mac was going to find them, and she was going to rip their hearts from their chests.

And she wasn't going to sing any songs while she did it, but it was going to feel fucking *great*.

———

Nika awoke with a gasp and a sense of emptiness.

Joseph?

No answer.

She tried again. *Joseph, where are you? Are you still there?*

But there was nothing. She closed her eyes and searched her mind, but the odd warmth and strange sensation of having some-one else inside of her head was gone.

She'd been abandoned.

Nika panicked. And even though Joseph had been adamant that she never speak to him aloud, she started to cry, and as she cried, she called for him: "Joseph! Joseph, please, *please* don't leave me here! Where are you? Please be real! Please, please be real!"

And the other girls in the room started crying and screaming, too—shouting at her, "Stop that! They'll hear you, and they'll send someone in!"

But Nika didn't care—she just wanted Joseph back, even if he was just a figment of her disturbed mind. Maybe, if she kept shouting, he'd appear—if only to chastise her for breaking his rules.

But no matter how loudly she screamed, it was soon clear that he wasn't coming back. And then Nika railed at herself for falling asleep—for letting him soothe her to a place where she *could* sleep, where she felt safe enough to close her eyes.

If she'd stayed awake, he would still be here, and she would be in that warm, hopeful place that included the possibility of her escape.

She would still be in that amazing place where she was something special called a Greater-Than, where she would be rescued from this nightmare and go to a special school called the Obermeyer Institute, and she would learn—with Joseph's help—to move objects with her mind. She would learn to read people's thoughts and to use telepathy to put her own thoughts into people's minds, even across great distances—the way Joseph told her he was doing even as they thought-spoke. She would learn to heal her body from all injuries and diseases. She might find out that she could predict the future, or develop exceptional strength, have amazing athletic ability . . .

But the first step, he'd told her, was for her to learn how to embrace a place of complete and total calm. She had to seek serenity and inner peace—and only then could Joseph help her unlock the mysteries of her powerful mind.

So now she tried to stop crying, and even though she couldn't still her sobs or the tears that ran down her face, she pushed them away and focused, instead, on the breathing exercises that Joseph had taught her.

Maybe if she did them and worked hard enough to be peaceful, she would demolish the blocks that Joseph said she'd erected in her mind. Maybe that's why he'd disappeared. Maybe—unconsciously—she'd pushed him away.

So she breathed. And breathed. *Calm blue ocean . . .*

She breathed as some of the younger girls continued to cry.

And even though Nika had started their noise with her own outburst, the despondent sound started to drive her crazy. It permeated, despite her attempts to shut it out, and it kept her from achieving even a remote sense of peace.

"Shut up! Shut up! Just shut up!" she screamed, and the surge of frustration and rage that gripped her shocked her with its power, and for an instant the lights flickered, and she froze.

Was that her? Had she done that?

None of the other girls seemed to have noticed, so she tried it again, only it wasn't all that easy to work up that kind of anger. Except maybe it was. She thought of Zooey—the little girl that the scar-faced man had killed. She thought of the nightmare of having to select her disgusting kidnapper's victim—although right now the little girl who was simultaneously crying and hiccupping was a good candidate for that. And now she aimed her anger and disgust at herself—and the people who'd locked her here and forced her to have such uncharitable thoughts.

Nika didn't know who they were, but one thing she knew for sure? If she ever did get out of here, she was going to devote her life to hunting them down—including that stupid cow of a pregnant girl who . . .

The world seemed to slip and stutter and skip, and suddenly Nika was no longer strapped into a hospital bed in that roomful of girls. Suddenly she was lying on her side, with her eyes closed, and when she opened them, she was back in a hotel room. But it was nothing like the room where she'd awakened and tried to write an SOS in catsup on the window.

This was no impersonal, generic room. Two of the walls were

covered with posters and colorful tapestries and the biggest flatscreen TV she'd ever seen in her life. Music was playing softly, and something that smelled vaguely soup-like was simmering on a stove—another entire wall was a kitchen filled with shiny appliances.

She sat up, because the fourth wall was covered by a curtain. And even though she knew the window probably couldn't open, she went over to it and pushed it aside.

It was dark out—it was night—and the city's light sparkled and danced, but that wasn't what made her stare. It was her reflection in the glass . . .

Her face was round and full and not her own. And her body . . . She looked down, and sure enough, her stomach poked out, round and smooth and hard and weird. And she felt something moving inside of her and it was the strangest thing she'd *ever* experienced.

As she looked back at the reflection of that face, she realized it belonged to the girl who hadn't told Nika her name—the pregnant girl, with the ocean-colored eyes.

And just as she realized what she had done—that she'd somehow managed to propel her mind into the body of this stranger—she felt the girl—Rayonna, somehow she knew that her name was Rayonna—wake up with a gasp of shock.

Nika pulled back—fast—and the world shifted and tilted and spun again, and she found herself back in the room with all of the other girls, still strapped to her bed.

She was breathing hard, as if she'd just run a mile, and she realized that, in her anger, she'd been thinking about that pregnant girl.

Maybe—just maybe—she had to get angry again, and this time think about Joseph. Maybe instead of bringing him to her, she could go to him.

And Nika closed her eyes and instead of breathing slowly and calmly, she breathed hard and fast. And she let her anger churn and burn and build.

———

Shane sat in the back of the car, as Stephen Diaz sped through the darkness of the crumbling Boston streets.

He could see the GPS screen on the dashboard, and he knew they were close.

Bach was riding shotgun, looking grim as he turned to glance back at Shane. "When we get there, stay in the car."

Shane considered just not answering but that seemed too disrespectful, so he said, "Sir, I will not."

Diaz spoke up. "We have no idea of the danger—"

"She won't hurt me," Shane said.

"She came very close to hurting me," Diaz reminded him. Shane had seen the Security tape of what Mac had done in the lounge—the exploding bottles and the sparking lights.

"*Very close* is not the same as hurting you," Shane pointed out. "In fact, I'd argue that if she'd wanted to hurt you, she wouldn't have missed."

In the front seat, the two men exchanged a look, and Bach said, "Jokers have no attachment to anyone or anything but the drug. Mothers murder children. Husbands kill wives."

Shane sat forward. "Are you fucking kidding me?" he asked, adding a belated, "Sir? Are you trying to tell me that Mac's been taking Destiny? Because I know for a fact that's just dead wrong."

"There's never been an instance of a Greater-Than jokering naturally," Diaz said. "But that doesn't mean it can't happen. Mac had a recent traumatic experience. By surrounding herself with Devon Caine's memories and fantasies—"

"Are you *fucking* kidding me?" Shane said again. "You *let* her do that . . . ?"

"Nobody *lets* Dr. Mackenzie do anything," Bach said quietly.

And then—shit—there she was. Standing beneath the streetlight in front of an industrial-looking building on a street that paralleled both the Mass Pike and the commuter rail, looking smaller than he'd remembered. Slighter. Shorter. And very female—but no less a warrior in the manner in which she stood.

But as Shane watched, the streetlight fizzled and popped and went out, plunging her into shadow.

Bach must've had some kind of hand scanner with him, because he announced, "She's still in serious flux. I'm picking up spikes of seventy-one now."

Shane unfastened his seatbelt and pushed himself forward, manuevering around Diaz's broad shoulders to lean on the horn in the middle of the steering wheel.

Mac turned at the sound and saw them, and held up one hand. And shit, even though Diaz was braking and they were no longer moving all that fast, it was as if they'd hit a wall. The front of the car crumpled and the airbags deployed. But Shane wasn't belted in, and by all rights he should've shot forward and gone right through the front windshield, headfirst.

Except he didn't. Something—or someone, namely Mac—held him safely in place.

Diaz and Bach, though, both got facefuls of the car's airbags, as the sound of an explosion ripped through the night.

Whatever that was, blowing up? It couldn't have been good.

The force that was holding Shane released him and he kicked the car door open and scrambled out onto the street—to see Mac crouching on the sidewalk, one hand down and bracing herself, as if making her body less of a target for the heat and force waves from the blast. Or maybe she was just surfing the damn thing.

She'd used her power and blown more than one hole through the front of the building. Flames were shooting up and out as smoke billowed and dust rained down, pinging on the hood of the car, and bouncing off the leather seat of her Harley.

"Is there anyone inside?" Diaz shouted, and Shane turned to see that both he and Bach had gotten out of the car, too.

His question was answered by a man with an ancient but clearly operable rifle, who leaned out of a second-floor window.

"Hey!" Shane shouted, trying to draw the man's fire, but he'd already aimed at Mac—who hadn't seen the gunman. His first shot connected, hitting her in what looked like her left shoulder and spinning her completely around.

Shane raced toward her, remembering what she'd told him— that her ability to shield herself from bullets was not advanced.

"Shield, Mac! Damnit, shield," he shouted. She'd told him that she had to focus—only—on protecting herself.

But as she blew another hole in the building, it was clear that she was still vulnerable. And God, the gunman fired again, and something must've happened. Bach or Diaz must've intervened, because instead of blasting a hole in her head, the bullet that was fired only grazed her temple. Still, she fell, hard, to the ground.

And Shane hit the sidewalk in a hell of a stealing-home move that was going to hurt later, as he used his body to try to shield Mac, as Bach and Diaz approached the building with as much stealth as the Redcoats marching on Lexington. They were front and center, just walking right up in full view of any potential adversaries, and drawing the gunman's fire.

Jesus, there was a frightening amount of blood on Mac's clothes and pooling beneath her on the sidewalk. Along with that glancing head wound, she'd been hit in her left shoulder, but Shane didn't have time to check exactly where—he could only pray that that bullet hadn't come too close to her heart.

She was unconscious, which wasn't helping as far as the scaring-the-shit-out-of-him went.

He had no idea how many gunmen were inside that building, or how long Bach and Diaz could keep them distracted, so he picked Mac up and carried her back toward Diaz's crumpled car, as up on the second floor, the rifleman's weapon jammed. He threw the thing aside, then pulled a sidearm from his pants, and Shane shifted his pace into triple-time, aware as hell that his back made a very large target. But the handgun misfired into the gunman's face—obviously not by accident—and he went down.

As Shane gently lowered Mac onto the street behind the car, he glanced up and saw that a second shooter had just appeared in another window. He shouted a warning, but Diaz had already seen the guy. Diaz pointed to the gunman and made a pulling motion with his arm, and both weapon—it looked like some kind of modified Kalashnikov—and man came flying out of the window, and hit the pavement hard.

God, Mac was bleeding badly. But only now could Shane dig

beneath her leather jacket to search for the wound—which, thank God, was far enough from her heart that he could cross her imminent and instant death off his things-to-worry-about list. She had an exit wound, too, which—good news—meant the round wasn't still inside of her.

The bad news was that an exit wound meant she had *two* places to bleed from. Shane pulled off his jacket and his T-shirt beneath, in order to use the soft cotton as a pad to stanch the flow.

"This is going to hurt," he told her even though she still hadn't roused, as he held his shirt in place and, wincing for her, applied pressure.

That got her attention, and her eyelids fluttered and her mouth moved, and she whispered, "Shane."

And yes, she said his name, but it probably didn't mean anything. It certainly didn't provide significant cause for celebration, and yet he found he *was* celebrating, because . . . she'd said his name.

"I'm here," he said through a throat that suddenly felt thick with emotion. "Honey, I'm right here. What do you need, Mac? Tell me what you need."

But then she grabbed him, and her eyes—those incredible eyes—opened, and she said, "It's a drug lab. I can smell it. You've gotta tell Bach and D to get out—it's gonna blow."

He was staring at her stupidly, he knew that he was, but he was hypnotized. And she said, "Go. Tell them!"

But then she pulled his head down and kissed him, and God, it was sweet.

And he thought it was a test, so he pulled away despite the fact that he wanted to stay right there, kissing her, for-fucking-ever. He said, "Hold that thought," and he went screaming out from behind the car, telling Diaz and Bach to *get down, get down, get down, the place is going to blow!*

They weren't moving fast enough, so he tried *Mac says it's a drug lab and it's going to blow!*

And as he watched, Diaz looked at Bach and Bach looked at Diaz, and then they both looked at something over Shane's left shoulder, and he turned to see the taillights of Mac's bike vanishing into the distance, accompanied by the roar of her bike. He couldn't believe what he'd just seen, couldn't believe it was possible, so he ran back behind the car and . . .

Mac was definitely gone.

"Destiny labs don't explode," Diaz told him, as a van from OI pulled up, driven by none other than Charlie Nguyen. "Meth lab's'll blow, but . . . Not this one."

"I think I just passed Mac, driving like a bat out of hell," Charlie said, as he lowered the driver's-side window.

"We need teams," Bach said grimly, "to move into place at all of the other locations on Devon Caine's GPS list. Mac's injured, but she's still dangerous. Give the order to trank her, if we have to."

"I'll relay that to Security, sir," Charlie told him.

"Let's clean this place out," Bach continued, as more Thirties and Forties poured out of another van that pulled up. "We've got two prisoners who need medical aid. Let's get them back to OI first."

"Search the building," Diaz ordered loudly. "Confiscate both the product and equipment. There were only two guards on the premises, but I'm sure they hit the alarm so more will be on their way." He raised his voice even more. "And I need a team to sterilize the damaged OI car. Let's move it, let's go!"

And as Shane stood there, feeling out of place and in the way, he realized that the kiss Mac had given him had been to heal herself enough to get on her bike and ride away.

"*Fuck*," he said, and then he shoved his arms back into his jacket and he walked away, fading into the shadows of the night.

Because he knew *exactly* where Mac had gone.

And he was going to find her and bring her back.

TWENTY-FOUR

Bach was driving the van that was transporting the Organization's injured security guards to the medical center at OI when it hit him.

At first he had no idea what was going on—only that, whatever it was, it knocked him back in his seat and made him swerve across the highway because his body was no longer his own.

Charlie was sitting beside him and he grabbed for the steering wheel as Bach heard himself scream, high-pitched and shrill, "Oh, my God, oh, my God!"

"I got it!" Charlie shouted over him. "Just slow down, slow down—let up on the accelerator!"

"The what?" Bach heard himself scream again—just like a little girl.

"The pedal, the pedal!" Charlie was shouting. "Lift your right foot, sir! Lift it, lift it!"

He lifted his foot—or rather Nika did and it *had* to be Nika, but how could it be? How could she have harnessed this much power this quickly—enough to knock him completely aside and gain full possession of his body? Forget about the fact that she'd located him across such distances.

It didn't make sense. But of course, it didn't have to make sense. Bach had learned long ago, when training both himself and other Greater-Thans, to not spend too much time on the question *How did that happen*, but rather to focus on *How can we control this?*

With his foot off the accelerator, the van slowed as Charlie steered it to the side of the turnpike, as Bach heard himself continue to breathe heavily, as for the first time in decades, unrestrained adrenaline coursed through a body he could no longer control.

"Are you Joseph?" Bach heard his voice say as he looked at Charlie. It was beyond odd. He could see what Nika was seeing, hear what she was saying, but he couldn't read her thoughts. It was as if she'd somehow managed to enter his mind completely shielded, while somehow managing to block off his own ability to communicate or otherwise respond.

"Okay, now you're *really* scaring me, sir." Charlie called into the back of the van. "I need some medical help up here." He also used the van's phone to call OI.

"Am *I* Joseph?" She used Bach's hand to pull the rearview mirror over to look into it and said, "Whoa, I'm kinda hot. Is Joseph asleep, too? But that's stupid, he was driving, of course he wasn't asleep." She closed his eyes and focused. *Joseph? Where did you go?*

I'm here, he tried to tell her, even as he realized that, from this place where she'd pushed him—from the outside looking in—he had the power to sense where she was in his brain, which was . . . fascinating. With a little time and concerted effort, he could learn to do this, too. And that meant . . .

"Yeah, hi, Elliot," Bach heard Charlie say. "I need some immediate assistance. I think it's possible that Dr. Bach just had a stroke—"

"I'm not Joseph Bach," Nika told Charlie and the other Forties who'd come from the back of the van to try to help. She struggled to stay strong, to not cry, but her voice shook and tears filled her eyes. *His* eyes. "My name's Nika Taylor, and I'm here because I needed to find Joseph. But he's still not here."

If Bach could learn to do this in reverse—to gain full possession of Nika? Then they wouldn't have to break into whatever facility in which she was being held.

All he'd have to do was find her—and then break her *out*.

Mac was in the bathroom, lying on the floor in only her under-pants, when Shane showed up.

He made it into the apartment without a key, which wasn't that big of a surprise. He'd already proven himself to be handier than she was when it came to locked doors.

She heard him coming, heard his familiar footsteps in the living room and then in the hall, and as he stopped in the doorway, in that fraction of a second before he dropped to his knees to help her, she looked up and told him, "I'm okay, I'm just taking a little break."

He was large and warm and totally rocking the bare-chest-beneath-the-jacket look, particularly in the candlelight. As he knelt beside her he managed to keep all of the recrimination and re-proach she knew he was feeling completely out of his eyes and off his face.

Which would have been awesome, if she weren't an empath.

"The head wound's already healed. The other is . . . I just fin-ished cleaning it out," she told him as he helped her sit up. "And I was going to take a shower, but apparently I needed a nap first."

Shane lifted the candle she'd put on the sink counter—she still didn't have new bulbs to replace the ones they'd burned out last time he was here—and held it up, projecting the dim light into the corners of the room. He was looking for something that he could give her to cover herself—other than the pile of bloody clothes in the corner or the blood-streaked washcloth that was in the sink.

"There's a clean towel in the hall closet," she told him. She could feel his reluctance to go even that far away from her, so she shrugged and added, "But it's not as if you haven't seen me naked. Or like I'm some overly modest and blushing virginal miss."

He didn't smile. He was busy looking at her bullet wound in the candlelight, both the entry and exit points. It was healing fast—even without his assistance.

Although they both knew it would heal far more quickly and painlessly if he took his clothes off and joined her in the shower.

In fact, he put the candle down as he met her gaze and spoke, saying, "If you want, I can, um . . . It doesn't have to mean any-thing. Just me wanting to help you."

"A purely selfless act," Mac said.

And Shane finally smiled, but it was more than rueful. It was sad. "No. I get what I get. I'll make it last until the next time you need me."

"What if there is no next time?" she asked as she looked into his eyes. "I'm not going to lie to you. If I can find someone else who can . . . help me this way? I won't need you again. Not ever."

His response was a kiss. And as he licked his way into her mouth, Mac knew that he didn't believe her. Or maybe he didn't believe she'd find a substitute, even if she looked.

And most of all, he didn't believe she'd look.

She couldn't help thinking that he was going to be sorely disappointed.

But then? She stopped thinking and just let herself heal.

———————

Joseph Bach saw her and started to run. "Anna!" he cried and burst into tears, as he threw himself into her arms.

Anna hadn't quite believed it when Elliot had called, telling her he was going to send Ahlam over to escort her down to Security, to await the arrival of the team—because Bach's body had apparently been possessed by her little sister.

Talk about strange.

Wherever Bach was, they hadn't been able to contact him. Not even Nika could find him. Plus the girl wasn't quite sure what she'd done to get where she currently was. She'd said she'd gotten angry—and tried to reach out and connect with Joseph Bach.

And suddenly here she was.

"Does she have Bach's abilities?" Anna asked Elliot now, as she sank to the floor in order to hold her sobbing sister—who was inhabiting the body of this man whom Anna had a mad crush on. *Talk* about strange.

"Not that we know of," he told her as Anna stroked Bach's hair and tried her best to comfort him. Her. "No."

She looked up at Elliot. "Is there another Greater-Than, a telepath, who can go into Bach's mind—Nika's mind—" Which was it? But Elliot clearly understood what she was asking, because he was nodding.

"We've already tried that," he told her, now shaking his head. "He got nothing. He couldn't access Nika's mind. She has too many blocks in place."

"Is it possible Dr. Bach is . . . inhabiting Nika's body?" she asked. "Could they have somehow . . . ?"

"Done a full *Freaky Friday*?" Elliot finished for her. "I guess that's possible." But he didn't sound convinced.

"Neek," Anna said as this odd hybrid of her sister and Bach tried to gain control. Their breathing was ragged and they reached up and tried to scrub away the tears that were still rolling down their face. "I need you to talk to us. Since we don't know how long this is going to last, we need to use this opportunity to ask you some questions about where you are. Can you do that?"

"Yeah. Okay." Nika nodded and pulled back from the soggy mess she'd made of Anna's shoulder. She wiped her nose on her sleeve. But then, as she looked into Anna's eyes, she lowered her voice and said, "There's something really weird going on with my man-parts. I mean, I've never had man-parts before so maybe it's not weird at all. But maybe I . . . I think I need to pee . . . ?"

Elliot started to cough.

"Oh," Anna said, as she gazed back into what looked like Bach's eyes. "Wow." But before she could comment further or even come up with a solution or suggestion for how her little sister could take Bach's body into the bathroom to relieve themselves, something changed in Bach.

Not just in his face, but in his body as well. Everything sharpened and hardened—and okay, maybe that was the wrong word, considering their current problem, but even before he spoke, Anna knew that Joseph Bach was back.

"I'll take care of that," he said briskly. "Too much adrenaline in my system, makes things, uh . . ."

His face changed again, and he asked, "Joseph?"

"I'm back, Neek," he answered himself, as he looked from Anna to Elliot. "It took me awhile to figure out how to return.

When Nika entered my mind, she kind of blasted me aside, and at first I couldn't get back, but then I didn't want to—until I figured out exactly what she'd done."

"It was an accident," Nika said, through Bach's mouth.

"Yeah, I know that, sweetheart."

His face started to crumple. "I'm so sorry."

"Don't apologize. You're amazing. I've never met anyone with your power and abilities. We're going to get you out of there. I just . . . I still need you to lower more of the blocks you've erected, so I can mine your memories and see if there's something there that'll clue us in to where you're being held." Bach looked up at Elliot. "I want to get her—me—into a lab. And ask Dr. Diaz to join us, as soon as he's back."

"Yes, sir." Elliot helped Bach to his feet, who then turned and held out a hand to help Anna up.

It was Nika, though, who clung to her and wouldn't let go. "I want Anna there, too."

Anna answered in unison with Bach: "Of course."

And they walked hand in hand down the hall toward the elevator that would take them to the labs, as Elliot ran ahead to get the room ready.

———

Mac was pretending to be asleep.

After their shower, Shane had dried her off and carried her into the bedroom, where she didn't complain when he climbed into bed with her and spooned—with her back against his chest, his arms tightly around her.

She'd slept for a little while—he could tell she was exhausted—but now she was awake again. He could sense her checking to see if he was asleep, no doubt to gauge whether or not she'd be able to slip away without waking him.

So he spoke—both to let her know he was conscious, and because he wanted to know the answer to his question. "Feeling any better?"

She stiffened only slightly before he felt her nod. "Yeah.

Thanks." She pulled away from him and sat up. And Shane knew she was still feeling at least a little wobbly, because she took a moment before standing and crossing to the closet.

He sat up, too, to watch her in the moonlight that was sliding into the room between the slats in the blinds. He could see that, where the bullet had exited her body, she had only the slightest of scars. Before long, it, too, would be gone.

His own scars, from seeing her take those bullets, weren't going to vanish that fast.

As he watched, she found some clothes—a pair of cargo pants that she pulled on commando, and one of her trademark black tanks that she put on without a bra. Apparently this apartment was underwear free. He could relate—doing his laundry often got bumped by higher priorities.

Her boots were out in the living room—he'd seen them when he'd first come in. She turned to head in that direction, and he knew that she wasn't going to slow down. She was going to jam her feet into her boots and walk them right out the door, leaving him to eat her dust again.

So he rolled out of bed and just stood there, blocking her path.

Mac closed her eyes and sighed, but then looked up at him—careful to keep her gaze only on his face because yes, he was very naked.

"We have to talk," Shane broke the news to her.

Mac shook her head. "I said thank you. There's nothing else to say."

"Not about that," Shane corrected her. "I meant it when I said that it didn't have to mean anything. I got what I wanted. And it's completely on me that I happen to keep wanting more. I know that. You don't owe me anything."

"And yet you won't let me pass."

"Because I know where you're going," Shane said gently, "and it's not going to help, Mac. It's going to make things worse." He laid it on the line. "It's bad enough that you did what you did, with your one-man assault tonight. Forget the fact that if we hadn't shown up you would've been killed. Although, to be honest, I'm having a little trouble pushing that into the *doesn't matter* column."

"Someone had to do something," she said.

"Not that way," Shane told her. "And you know it. Truth is, you may have really fucked things up by going there and blasting the shit out of the place. The Organization's probably already been alerted to the fact that both Littleton and Caine are AWOL. If you go down Analysis's GPS list for Caine, just one address after another, leaving death and destruction in your wake? Someone's going to figure out what's happening and they'll move Nika so far and so deep underground, we'll never find her. Bach has surveillance teams in place at all those locations—keeping their heads down and gathering information. And ready to intercept you, by the way. Because what you were doing was making things worse."

He could see from her face that his words were getting through. She'd no doubt gotten dressed on the residuals of her anger, but she now seemed exhausted, defeated, subdued.

"You probably would've figured it out for yourself," he continued, "before you got too far. I just wanted to make sure you'd thought it through. I know that sometimes the noise in my head can drown out the reason, so . . ."

She laughed her disbelief at that. "Yeah, right. You've never acted impulsively in your entire life."

Shane smiled, too. "I don't know about *never*." He willed her to look back into his eyes instead of down at the floor, and when she finally did, he said, "I do know I've never spent any time in the head of a pedophile serial killer."

Mac closed her eyes again, shook her head slightly.

"If you want to talk about it . . ." he said.

"Don't be so fucking nice."

"What, you want me to be like you, and pretend to be a bitch so people keep their distance?"

She laughed at that. "I'm not pretending. Not entirely."

"And I'm not entirely being nice," Shane pointed out. "There's plenty of totally selfish ulterior motive in my getting you to stay a little longer. As well as the practical. You're exhausted. You need more sleep if you want to be worth anything to Bach and Diaz—or Nika. And you know damn well that if you let me, I can help you sleep. Just by being a warm body next to you—if that's what you need."

And it was then that her eyes slowly filled with tears. She fought them valiantly, but lost as one and then another escaped. And she turned and sat heavily on the bed. "Don't do this to me," she said.

"What," he asked her. "Try to get you to sleep some more?"

She shook her head. "Don't act like you love me, when we both know that you don't," she said.

"I thought you didn't want to talk about that." He sat down next to her. "But as long as you brought it up . . . You don't have to love me, Mac, but . . . You're not allowed to decide what it is that I feel."

"Oh, God, I'm too tired for this shit," she said. "Because I *do* get to decide. Weren't you listening to what I told you . . . ?"

"Then make it stop," Shane said. "If I'm so much like Tim, then make me stop wanting you."

"It doesn't work that way. Not anymore. My power's grown. It doesn't wear off as quickly as it did back then. If I could shut it down, I would. God . . ." She lay back on the bed, just flopped back, her arm up over her eyes, elbow to the ceiling.

"Look, I know you don't want to get into this," Shane said quietly, "but I've been thinking about it ever since you told me about Tim and . . . We don't have to make this a conversation, but I would appreciate it if you could just listen to what I have to say."

She didn't speak, didn't move, didn't run screaming from the room.

He took that as an affirmative. "Every time my heart beats," he told her quietly, "it's like I'm just marking time until I can be with you again." He laughed softly. "It's crazy, that kind of wanting, you know?"

Mac didn't move.

"And I get how it must be beyond annoying for you. After hearing what happened when you were a kid, after seeing Dr.

Marry-Me in action back at the hospital . . . ? I get how upsetting it must be to believe that you're wanted not for who you are but for what you are. For reasons that, to you, don't feel real. But can I tell you something?" he said. "Can I tell you what it feels like from this end? Because, to me, it feels fucking real. It feels like . . . Connection, to the nth. It feels like joy, like truth. It feels like I belong somewhere again."

She laughed at that—or maybe it was a sob, but she still didn't move, so he kept going.

"Maybe that's too *touchie-feelie* for you. And maybe you won't be satisfied until you lock me up and keep me away from you for a week or a month—or however long it's going to take for you to believe your voodoo's worn off. But I can tell you this right now. You can lock me away without food or water, but the first thing I'm going to ask for when they open the door? Is you. Because even if I stop feeling this? I *am* going to remember what it feels like. And I'm going to want it back."

She finally pulled her arm away from her face and spoke. "But it's not *about* me," she argued. "Whatever it is that you're feeling. You could feel this way about anyone. Don't you get it? It doesn't *have* to be *me*!"

"Are you kidding me?" he said. "It *completely* has to be you. You're one of a kind, Mac. And Jesus, maybe I gave away the fact that I love you too soon. Maybe I skipped over the part that you really wanted to hear, which is *I like you.* I like you, Mackenzie. I really do. I like being with you. You're smart, you're funny, you're beautiful—you're *the* most amazing woman I've ever met. You want to shut down the sex and be friends with me for a year or five years or however the fuck long it takes for you to understand that? Let's do it. I'm ready."

It was then that she reached for him, pulling him down toward her for a kiss.

And his first reaction was a joyful leap of his heart—she believed him! But reality came crashing in as he realized, in those split seconds before his mouth covered hers, before he completely lost himself in the sweetness of her kiss, that he was being tested.

So he kissed her only briefly—just a brush of his lips across her soft mouth before he pulled away.

Which shocked the hell out of her, but just for a moment. She covered her surprise with a laugh and more of that attitude that both pissed him off and turned him on. "So what are you going to do?" she asked. "*Sing* me to sleep?"

Shane laughed, too, and felt his body responding as she slapped him with her power. Which was completely unnecessary.

"I don't need that to want you," he told her as he pulled one of the pillows onto his lap, because, damn. "And I don't need sex to want to be with you. You want to test or even torture me? Go for it."

"But I'm not doing it on purpose. I can't always control it," she admitted miserably. "It happens because . . . God, I think it's instinctive. Like using body language or releasing pheromones. It just *happens*."

Shane knew that was true. Human beings instinctively responded to a person whom they believed would be a good biological match—a good mate.

So in other words, Mac had instinctively chosen Shane, right from the get-go. And it also meant that her body's effort to make him succumb to her charms was not going to let up any time soon. In fact, it was likely to get worse before it got better.

"Well, okay," he said, standing up, still holding that pillow in front of him. "This is going to be . . . interesting."

Mac actually laughed. "Ah, shit," she said. "Just . . . come here. Just . . ." As she looked up at him, she let herself want him, and she let him see it in her eyes.

It was the moment of truth. And Shane hesitated, because he was only human. But he was in this not to win the battle, but to win the war. So he shook his head. Sadly and with deep regret. But he shook it.

"Nope." Shane popped the P. "I'm just gonna go get my pants. Pants are gonna help."

But she was looking at him with those beautiful eyes, and he found himself leaning over to kiss her. Just one kiss . . .

Just . . .

One . . .

Kiss . . .

He maybe could've done it—kissed her once and walked into the bathroom to pull on his pants, but she whispered, "You're always asking me how you can help . . ."

And it was true. He wanted to help. He desperately wanted to help . . .

So he kissed her again, and his pants stayed off, and she came undone in his arms, and he lost himself, too.

And he lost.

He knew, even while she was gasping her pleasure, as she was shuddering her release that he'd . . .

Lost.

"Sleep now," she told Shane.

And he did, even as he tried to hold on to her, as he wrapped his arms around her.

Even though he knew that when he woke up?

She'd be gone.

————

Elliot glanced up as Stephen came into lab one's observation room. "Hey."

"Hey." Stephen stood beside him at the window, a solid presence looking out at the research and testing area that was set up as a living room with several big comfy couches and a lot of pillows. Bach was sitting on one couch, with his feet up and his eyes closed. Anna was nearby, watching him anxiously. "How's it going?"

"Weird," Elliot admitted. "But a little less so now that Bach's back. When it was just Nika, broadcasting out of Bach's body . . ." He glanced at Stephen again. "Do you know how powerful that little girl has got to be to gain access to Bach's mind the way she did? With complete physical control of his body? That's crazy. And yet, she's still struggling to lower the blocks she's got in place in her own mind. Until she can do that, not even Bach can get access to her memories—he's working it hard, right now, just to get back into her head. He hasn't managed to do that yet—which is scary for everyone. If something pulls Nika away, we're not sure we'll be able to regain contact, even with Anna's help."

"Shouldn't we be talking to her?" Stephen asked. "Getting as much information as possible?"

"Already done. She doesn't remember anything between the abduction and waking up in the holding room, except for a brief moment of consciousness when she was with Littleton and Caine. She remembers being afraid of Caine," Elliot told him. "Other than that, she said she's seen only three different people while she's been a prisoner—not including the other girls. An older woman, a man with a badly scarred face, and a girl in her late teens who's—you're going to love this—pregnant."

"Oh, God," Stephen murmured.

"Yeah," Elliot agreed. "It looks like they're trying to breed 'em now. Nika said the girl appears to be a prisoner, too—at least to some degree. But the man and the woman work there, from what Nika's described. The plan is for Bach to essentially make her memories his own, and then pass them along to someone who can draw, like *moi*. I can draw as realistic a sketch as I can manage of their faces, and we'll then try to get a computer match. If we can identify these people, and they live outside the Org building so we can track them as they go to work . . ."

"Those are some very big *ifs*," Stephen said.

Elliot nodded. "I'm with you on that. Any word from Mac?"

Stephen shook his head. "No, but Shane's gone missing, too. Since he's been to her apartment before—I feel pretty confident he'll find her. If she needs help, he'll call in."

Elliot took a deep breath and just said it. "Is there any chance that the vision you saw—your premonition—"

"No," Stephen said.

"Okay, was that supposed to be funny, like you're prescient now so I never have to finish any of my sentences again or—"

"No," Stephen said again, but then winced. "Sorry. I didn't mean to . . . I just knew what you were asking—not because I'm prescient, but because I know the way your brain works. So no, the vision I had wasn't about Mac getting shot—"

"Well, I know *that*," Elliot said. "But visions can be cryptic. Maybe you knew *some*one was going to be shot, but you didn't know who, so your mind made it be me because you love me so ardently—"

"No. I mean, yes, but . . . No."

"That's too bad." Elliot sighed.

Stephen sighed, too, and reached for him, holding out his hand first, silently asking permission. They were alone in the room, and Bach and Anna remained silent and unmoving in the lab, so Elliot interlaced their fingers.

I would know if the threat is past, Stephen told him as their connection immediately snapped on. *I don't know how I know that, but I do. And I know the vision was cryptic because Anna was flying away with Mac, and unless she jokers from taking Destiny, that's not going to happen the way I saw it. But, really, it's beside the point, because when I had the vision, I experienced this . . . god-awful sense of foreboding. And it's still back there, El. You're still in danger.*

Then I'll continue to be careful, Elliot reassured him.

"Calm blue ocean, calm blue ocean—it's just *not* working."

They both jumped and even sprang apart as Bach's voice came through the speakers, higher pitched and odd sounding.

But then he answered himself, his voice more normal. "Give it time."

"I've given it time." That was Nika again, speaking through him.

Stephen glanced at Elliot. "You were right. That's very weird."

Anna spoke. "Give it a little bit more, Neek."

They fell silent again, and after a moment, Stephen asked, "How's Edward O'Keefe?"

"Astonishingly still not dead," Elliot answered. The old man was clinging to life. "He's responded to the low levels of oxyclepta di-estraphen we've given him. The self-healing centers of his brain have reactivated. We're continuing stimulation, and the damage to his heart is continuing to be repaired. His improvement is pretty miraculous."

"That's great news, babe," Stephen said, managing a smile.

"It's good," Elliot told him. "It doesn't get to be *great* until he comes out of the coma, which may not happen for some time. If it happens at all. But my fingers are definitely crossed."

"Still not working." In the lab, Bach was now up on his feet. Or rather, Nika was on Bach's feet. "I can't *do* this anymore!"

Anna stood, too. "Neek . . ."

"No, Anna, I tried it. Joseph, I tried it your way! I've *calm blue oceaned* ten thousand times. Now I wanna try it my way."

Bach reclaimed his body and said, "Anger isn't the answer. The powers it sparks are impossible to control. Yes, it may provide surges—"

"But maybe that's all I need," he appeared to argue with himself. "One good surge!"

Anna, too, appealed to Bach. "What can it hurt to try?" she asked. "We have no idea what's happening to Nika's physical self while she's here. We need to find her, and, I'm sorry, but it does feel like we're wasting time."

"Nika's certain that she got here by channeling her anger," Elliot told Stephen, as Bach just shook his head. "She wants to try doing that again."

Dr. Bach, of course, believed that harnessing anger—or other passions—was never productive.

"Bach would hate trying that," Stephen agreed with a nod. "Maybe I can help." He leaned forward and hit the on switch for the microphone that would allow him to be heard in lab one. "Excuse me, Dr. Bach? How about you sit back for this one—let me come down and run the experiment."

Bach looked up toward the mirrored window as if his powers allowed him to see through it. Maybe they did. He finally nodded. "Thank you, Dr. Diaz," he said, as always remarkably polite. "That would be most appreciated."

Bach sat on the sofa in lab one, and let Nika have total control of his body.

Right now, she wasn't using more than his vocal cords.

"It started as fear," she told Dr. Diaz, who'd pulled a straight-backed chair across from them, and was sitting there, giving Nika his full attention. "I woke up and Joseph was gone, and . . . I was really scared."

I'm so sorry, Nika.

It's okay, she responded silently. *I'm sorry, too—sorry that I'm disappointing you this way.*

Sweetheart, you're not. Just . . . Listen to Dr. Diaz.

"And then what happened?" Diaz asked, obviously repeating his question.

"And then some of the girls were crying, and I got angry at them," Nika said. "And I stayed angry and I thought about this girl they killed, right in front of us—"

"Oh, God," Bach heard Anna say, as she reached over and took his hand.

"And then I got even more angry, because the man with the scar said he was going to make *me* pick one of the other girls, and *she's* going to be killed." Nika was breathing harder now, faster, as she let herself get upset all over again.

Or maybe Bach was the one breathing harder, outraged by the sheer evil of Nika's captors.

After spending far too much time digging around in Devon Caine's disgusting head, he was well aware of the ways the Organization kept their girls terrified. But this was particularly awful, especially for a sensitive girl like Nika. If such a terrible thing were to happen, even if Bach and his team found Nika and got her to safety, she would be irrevocably changed. She'd be scarred for life.

But they weren't going to let it happen. They were going to find her and they were going to get her out of there and—

"I'm sorry," Nika said aloud to Diaz. "I need to . . . I just need . . . Joseph is, um . . ." *You've got to stop that,* she thought at

Bach. *At any other time, it would be great, but . . . It's not helping. And it's particularly not helping because unless I learn to do this . . . this . . .* impossible *thing, to lower these blocks that I can't even* feel, *you're not going to find me, and you're never going to get me out of there. And I don't know why I'm blocked—I don't even know what it means—*blocked. *It's not something I did, not intentionally, so I don't know how to fix it. And you say I'm special, but I don't* feel *special and—*

Wait. Bach stopped her. "Holy shit."

"That was him, not me," he heard Nika say to Anna.

"It's not something *you* did," Bach repeated to Nika, saying it aloud, looking to Diaz to see if he was following. He wasn't. "The blocks. Nika's blocks. If *she* didn't erect them . . ."

Diaz got it. "Then someone else did," he finished for him.

"I've been looking in the wrong place," Bach said, laughing his amazement. He spoke aloud so that Diaz and Anna could follow. "Neek, I assumed you erected those blocks unconsciously, but there *is* another option entirely. And that's if someone else entered your mind and created these obstacles."

"Someone else?" She was confused. "Who else?"

"I don't know," Bach told her. "But whoever it was, they surely knew you were a Greater-Than." And if *that* wasn't a big enough bomb, he dropped another, "It's possible they created those blocks in an attempt to protect you—to hide you from people who might try to exploit you."

"That's absurd," Anna said.

"No, it's not." Bach turned to look at her. "With those blocks in place, Nika has access to only a small fraction of her power. And yet she *still* scanned at twenty." A fact that was amazing. "Whoever did this knew that her integration was going to explode off the charts when she hit puberty."

"And actually," Diaz broke in, "*who* did it is secondary. A mystery for a rainy day. Our primary goal right now is to knock the blocks down. ASAP, Maestro."

"I'm on it," Bach said. "Nika, I know we tried this before, but we didn't really try *this* before."

She knew what he wanted. *You want me to breathe. And think about a perfect, still ocean. A cloudless blue sky. A drop of water flowing into the—*

And just like that, approaching from the outside, instead of trying to unblock her from the inside out, Bach was in.

"Whoa!" If he'd thought Anna's mind was chaos . . . Being in the unfettered middle of Nika's mind was like being caught in a paint store when a tornado hit.

It caught him off guard and he didn't know where to look first, and for a moment he just spun.

From the corner of his eye—although it really wasn't his literal eye, it was more his own mind's perspective—he caught the shape of a woman, a shadow, a shade, as she leapt and faded away. He almost followed, intrigued, certain it was a memory of Anna and Nika's mother, long dead.

But he needed to focus on this mission, which was hard enough as it was.

Because Nika was emotion personified. She was a thirteen-year-old girl, and her thoughts and observations and memories swirled and skipped and sparked and danced around him in age-appropriate madness, as he took another moment just to get his bearings.

He spoke aloud, though, for the benefit of everyone—including Nika. "I'm in."

And Bach saw it all now—her vivid memories of everything she'd lived through in the past few days: the abduction, her waking up in the room with the other girls, the visit by the scar-faced man, the dying girls, the port in Nika's arm, her awakening in the safe room, the steak and french fries, the view out the window . . .

The window.

The window!

"Nika tried to write SOS on the window in ketchup," Bach said.

"Tried and failed," she said. "I only got as far as an S and an O, before Rayonna came in and wiped it off."

"But it was up there for at least five minutes," Bach confirmed, replaying her memory. "Rayonna is the pregnant girl," he added for Anna and Diaz's benefit.

He jumped back in time, into Nika's memory of the view out that window, the way she'd looked to see what type of building she was in, the glass and steel. As she looked down to the ground, he slowed the memory wa-a-ay down, and counted forty floors below them. She'd then looked up—again just a glance—and he counted, as best he could, fifteen above.

"She's in a building with about fifty-five floors," he reported, "across the street from both a CoffeeBoy and a Burger Deluxe and a former Burlington Coat Factory, which was next to what looks like a now-defunct florist—called Maxie's Best."

Although Nika hadn't paid any attention at the time, Bach now made note of the angle of the sun in the sky. It was either morning or afternoon, which meant the window was facing either southeast or northwest and . . . He focused his attention on the horizon, where—there it was—a shimmer of water. It was morning, and southeast, because that was the harbor.

"There was a Maxie's Best on Washington Street," Diaz reported from the comm-station. "And . . . up until about four years ago, a Burlington Coat Factory."

"Have Analysis check satellite footage," Bach ordered, "from the past few days, from six to ten in the morning. I want to find and verify the building in which an S and an O appears on one of the windows, somewhere around the fortieth floor."

"I've already sent out the request," Elliot said, after clicking on the speaker from the observation room, where he was watching.

Bach turned to Anna, who was wide-eyed and nearly breathless with hope.

"We found her," he said, and she launched herself into his arms.

Or maybe it was Nika she was hugging.

You're only going to have to hang on a little bit longer, he told Nika, as he felt the girl use his arms to hug her sister back, enthusiastically. *As soon as we verify your location, we're coming to get you out.*

TWENTY-FIVE

Shane woke up, alone in the bed. Mac wasn't just out of the room—she'd left the apartment.

It was possible that the near-silent click of the closing door had awakened him, so he rolled out of bed and ran to the door and opened it and . . .

No one was out there. She'd been gone for a while.

Shane retraced his steps into the bedroom, scanning the dining table and the kitchen counter for any sign of a note. *Just stepped out for coffee* or *Went to get doughnuts . . .*

As unlikely as that was, it wasn't until he checked the bed and the pillow she'd been sleeping on that he gave up hope.

No note.

Not that big of a surprise, considering how totally he'd failed.

Shane took a leak and a quick shower, got dressed, pulling on an extra-extra-large T-shirt that he'd found in the closet advertising the long-dead *Grateful Dead*—no doubt the ghost of some giant fuck-buddy past.

He made the bed and let himself out of the apartment, locking the door behind him.

Shane stood on the building's front steps in the pre-dawn of what was going to be a beautiful fresh spring day, and it occurred to him that now might be a good time to just cut his losses and walk away. He had forty dollars in his debit account—he'd already been paid, in advance, for his first week.

He could take the T, not back out to the burbs and OI, but rather farther into Boston. To South Station where he could catch a train down to New York City. Maybe get another under-the-table job, driving a truck to Atlanta or Miami.

Except now he'd wonder what the truck was carrying. He'd wonder if its cargo was Destiny.

Shane stepped down to the sidewalk and headed into Kenmore Square, pretty certain that, whatever choice he made, he was going to lose.

———

Joseph helped Nika find her way back to her physical self—to her body.

She had no clue how he did it, but by now, her faith in him was so strong, she wouldn't have been surprised if he'd been able to bring her to the moon.

Still, as she felt herself return, felt the gnawing hunger and the restraints holding her in place, she was gripped by fear.

Easy, Joseph said. *Breathe. Keep breathing.*

The room she was in was dark, regardless of the fact that, outside, it was morning. And even though Nika kept breathing, she was still afraid. *Please don't leave me.*

I'm not going anywhere. Joseph's promise filled her, warmed her, even before she'd gotten out most of her plea.

Because she was no longer inside of Joseph's head, she couldn't see what he saw. But she could—somehow—hear what he heard. She wasn't sure why or how, and he wasn't able to explain it either.

She was just glad that he was with her, despite those limits.

He and hunky Stephen Diaz and the cute doctor—Elliot—had had an argument when they'd learned, from something called Analysis, the address of the building where Nika was being held.

Elliot had called it *impenetrable* and Diaz had gotten grim, using words like *fortress* and *army of guards*. But Joseph? He'd insisted *impenetrable* only meant that they hadn't yet figured out a way in—or out. He reminded them that all they had to do was break out.

Joseph had told them to get working on a solution, and he'd pulled Nika away as she caught a whiff of thoughts he was trying to hide—something about keeping her far from that negative energy bullshit.

Coming from the King of Zen, that was a clue that her *easy rescue* wasn't going to be as easy as Joseph had hoped.

Still, if anyone could get her free, it was Joseph and his team.

I'm glad you have faith.

Nika felt him, warm and solid in her mind, even as he turned to speak to Anna. "I'm staying with Nika until this is over," he reassured her sister. "And now that I'm in her head without your help . . ."

"You don't need me anymore," Anna said, and it was weird, the way Nika was lying there in the darkness, and yet able to hear Anna's voice through Joseph's ears. She sounded different. Her voice seemed richer. More melodic. But maybe that was just because Anna was tired.

And Joseph said as much, too. "You must be exhausted. Why don't you go get some sleep—or at least some breakfast."

Nika couldn't see Anna, yet she knew, through Joseph, that her sister smiled. But it was forced and it made her appear even more worn-out, and Nika felt his concern and his . . .

He felt . . . something, that she couldn't identify. It was . . . not exactly affection. It was . . .

"Isn't there something I can do?" Anna asked. "Some way I can help?"

"Yes, actually. Go remind Diaz and Elliot that they need to eat, too," Joseph told her. "Tell them I said to go to the lounge with you, get some breakfast, and while you're eating, I want them to explain to you—so that you understand clearly—the problem we're up against, the challenges of trying to breach this particular building. Sometimes that helps us find solutions."

"Breaking it down into simple language for the unwashed fractions," she said.

"That's not how I think of you."

"Sorry, I'm just tired. Can I bring you anything?"

"No," he said. "I'm good. But thank you. So much."

His words were super-polite, and with them came a hint—just a whisper—of a little extra reserve, as if he'd taken a step back, or was trying to verbalize the fact that he was keeping his distance, and with that Nika knew. *Oh, my God! You have a crush on my sister!*

She felt Joseph sigh.

You do! Oh, that's . . . kinda creepy.

It's not creepy, he told her, laughing slightly, *because it's not true. Yes, I admire her. But I admire a lot of women. I admire you.*

I'm not a woman, she reminded him.

Yeah, you are, he said. *After all you've endured with such courage? You are.*

But then Nika jumped and squeaked and was unable to suppress a surge of fear as the overhead lights smashed on, and the door to the room opened.

Oh, my God, she told Bach. *Here he comes. It's the man with the scar, and no, God, he's got that knife . . .*

I'm here, Joseph said, steady and warm and strong. *I'm right here.*

But he wasn't really there. He couldn't really help her.

Please, Nika begged him, *I know you don't want any negative energy bullshit, but if I don't get out of here, if you can't rescue me—*

Nika, we're going to.

I know, but if you don't, she asked, *will you promise me that you'll take care of Anna? Will you make sure that she's safe?*

I promise, he told her as the other girls in the room all started to scream, as the man with the scar came toward Nika and smiled.

———

Anna took a bite of her omelet even though her stomach was churning while Elliot and Diaz—as Bach had ordered—were explaining what Analysis had discovered when they'd checked out the building where they'd verified Nika was being held.

First of all, it was massive. And it was right in the city. It was, apparently, nothing like the little thousand-square-foot dilapidated semi-rural houses where Bach's team from OI had gone in to rescue girls or liberate Destiny-cooking equipment in the past. They'd never encountered anything like this before.

The fact that an illegal and underground group like the Organization should be in a location that was so blatantly aboveground and in-your-face was disturbing. Anna didn't even want to think about what that meant in terms of the city government or police, although the phrase *in their pocket* flashed to mind.

Second, part of the building was leased to innocent civilians. Thousands of tenants rented apartments on both the lower and higher floors, as did a number of nonprofits, including, ironically, the beleaguered international equal rights group, *Women Now.*

Or maybe their presence there *wasn't* ironic. Analysis had discovered that the building's owner, a corporation called The Brite Group had made an in-kind donation of ten years' rent to *Women Now.* Possibly in the spirit of *keep your friends close, but your enemies closer.* Of course, there was also the strategy of using both the nonprofit and the civilians as human shields.

"So blasting a hole in the building," Stephen Diaz told her as he dug into a bowl of fresh fruit, "isn't an option."

"If Analysis knows which floors the Brite Group occupies," Anna asked, tapping the schematic of the building's floor plan that Elliot had called up on the table's comm-station, "why not just walk in through the front door, grab Nika, and run?"

"It's not that easy," Stephen said. "They've got a legion of heavily armed security specialists—"

"Whose bullets will bounce off of you if you're shielded," Anna pointed out.

"But we can't shield Nika on their way back out," Elliot said. "Neither Bach nor Stephen can shield more than one person—

themselves. Also, that kind of protection is an energy-drain. Out of all of our Greater-Thans, *only* Bach and Stephen have the ability to access their other powers while they're shielding—and even that's limited—"

"Ahlam can multi-shield," Stephen said, looking at Elliot. "Maybe if we brought Ahlam . . ." He turned to Anna. "She's one of our Thirties."

"I've met her," Anna said.

"You really want to bring *Ahlam* into a place like that?" Elliot wasn't convinced. "Her abilities are erratic at best."

"I'm just thinking aloud," Stephen said. "And you're right, we shouldn't bring Ahlam anywhere near that place. But maybe if we went in with a big enough group—made this the biggest full-on assault that we've ever attempted—"

"Or if you came in from the outside, while Joseph shared possession of Nika's body from the inside," Anna said, "the way she did with him? Then he's not physically there. He can use his powers to shield her but won't have to shield himself."

"An intriguing idea," Elliot said, "but Stephen and his team won't even get past the lobby." He explained to Anna, "Analysis reports that the Brite Group uses probes—illegal medical and jot scanners—as a big part of their security monitoring. They take continuous scans of their lobby, their basement, their roof, and every hallway. They've got their scanner calibrated to provide information about integration levels—which is interesting, and not in a good way."

Stephen could see that Anna wasn't quite following, so he explained: "The study of integration levels isn't accepted by the corporate government, even though more and more members of the scientific community are validating OI's work. And the fact that a mega-corporation like the Brite Group has adjusted their scanners to include integration levels is both alarming and informative."

"See, they're using this equipment to get personal medical information on every man, woman, and child who walks into their building," Elliot broke it down for Anna even further. "They've got their equipment set not just to perform jot scans, but to automatically run *full* medical scans on everyone who stays still for long enough."

"That's a huge violation of privacy rights." Anna stated the obvious. "But . . . Why do they do it? What do they do with that information?"

"Good question," Elliot said. "We're wondering the same thing. Are they using this to identify more of these little girls that they call *fountains*?"

"Oh, my God," Anna said.

"Or are they using this information as security," Stephen suggested. "But think about what *that* means. Any Greater-Than who sets foot in this building will immediately be identified. Our mere presence will set off alarms. Before this, we weren't sure we were on the Organization's radar. Even though we've gone in and shut down a number of Destiny-cooking labs, and rescued dozens of girls from what they call their *farms* . . ."

"I think the fact that they scan for integration levels means that they know we're here, and that we're a threat to their operation," Elliot agreed. "And that's a little scary. That plus the size of this building where they're holding Nika. We really had no idea how big the Organization was. We're like a gnat trying to take out Godzilla."

Stephen nodded. "Personally, I prefer the Davy versus Goliath analogy." He smiled at Elliot. "Or Ewoks versus the Empire."

Elliot laughed, but he sobered quickly. "This is what we're up against," he told Anna. "As soon as we try to get into the building, alarms *will* go off."

"So sneaking Nika out of there isn't an option, either," Stephen surmised. "Analysis reports that they're not scanning in the holding rooms, but as soon as Dr. Bach walks Nika's body out into the hall? With their combined integration levels? Alarm bells."

"But if Joseph can protect her . . . ?"

"To a limit," Elliot said. "He's powerful, that's true, and the guards won't be able to shoot Nika, because Bach can shield her from their bullets. But enough of them could overwhelm her. Remember, Bach's going to be in *her* body, limited by her physical strength."

"She'll be the baddest, most kickass thirteen-year-old in the world," Stephen told Anna, "but not even Dr. Bach can make her invincible."

"So . . . that means we need to shut down their med scanners," Anna concluded.

"Analysis already rejected that," Elliot said. "The scanners work off a wireless self-contained system that's unhackable."

"Well, it's probably hackable," Stephen corrected him. "We just haven't figured out how to do it."

"Which, for the sake of this discussion," Elliot said, "makes it unhackable. I mean, we're looking to get Nika out ASAP, not after seven months of research and experimentation, right?"

"Then ignore the med scanners," Anna suggested. "And the alarms. Let's go back to the idea of sending in a big enough group of Greater-Thans to meet Bach and protect Nika."

"Just blow past 'em." Stephen answered his own question by shaking his head, no.

Elliot chimed in with, "Twenty-five Greater-Thans, marching up the Org's ass? In theory, it's beautiful. But the problem with *that* is we're back to these alarms. The bad guys have ample warning—and all kinds of escape routes that are not on these plans. We'll take out some of their guards and grunts, sure, and we'll rescue some of their prisoners. But they're going to take all of the girls like Nika—their *fountains*—and boogie out of Dodge."

"So we're back to figuring out a way to shut down their med scanners," Anna persisted.

"Which can only be done from the inside," Elliot said, making an adjustment to the computer screen, to show a mazelike layout of rooms and hallways. He pointed to one of the rooms. "Here's where their scanning system is housed—smack in the middle of the main security floor."

They sat in silence for a moment, as Anna tried not to be over-whelmed by the apparent impossibility of the situation. She thought about Nika, who was really only marginally safer now that Bach was with her. Because, as Stephen and Elliot had made clear, there *were* limits to his ability to protect her.

She closed her eyes and took a deep breath and then another, because she refused to accept that saving her sister was impossible. She thought of Bach's calm and she embraced the techniques he'd used to try to teach Nika to achieve the control she'd needed to unlock the powers of her mind.

And Anna could practically feel his warmth and power inside of her head again as, in a flash, she saw the answer.

"I'll go in," she said, opening her eyes to look across the table. Stephen didn't understand, but Elliot did—she could see both his surprise and then the glimmer of excited hope in his eyes, as she explained to Stephen, "I'm a fraction. I can go into the building, be scanned, and not set off a single alarm. Joseph can implant whatever knowledge I need directly into my head. He taught me self-defense that way. He can teach me how to breach their scanning system, the same way. He can teach me to climb up the elevator shaft if he has to." She said it again. "So I'll do it. *I'll* go."

———

Bach could feel Nika's heart racing as the scar-faced man repeated his question. "Which one will it be?"

Don't answer, Bach told her. *Burst into tears—can you do that?*

She could, and she did. Quite effectively.

"Touching," the man said, his words slightly slurred from his inability to move the badly scarred muscles on that one side of his face. "I feel similar grief for a missing friend. Of course, just because he's not here, doesn't mean the game won't be played."

Caine. He was talking about Devon Caine. That was his missing friend. It was all Bach could do not to recoil. He'd hoped, because Caine had disappeared, that Nika wouldn't be forced to do this terrible thing, but he'd been wrong.

"So the girl you pick won't get to . . . enjoy my friend's company before she shuffles off this mortal coil. But I'll do the killing in his name. Now, pick one—or I'll slaughter five."

Bach focused, finding his inner calm, despite Nika's sobs and the other girls' screams. He wasn't certain he could do this, considering he was using a large portion of his own power to possess Nika, but he tapped into her raw power, too, and . . .

It worked.

He reached out to the man, careful to leave Nika safely behind, as he pushed his way into the dark cavern of the scarred man's mind, planting ideas that he hoped would stick and grow.

She's frightened enough—just by this threat.

Her adrenaline levels are high enough.

There's no need to damage one of the other girls. They're all providing excellent product.

But they weren't, Bach saw, feeling his own adrenaline levels rise just from being privy to this man's hideous thoughts, his foul memories of his many years here. This creature—Cristopher was his name—loved his work a little too much.

And he'd recently found out, from blood samples taken, that three of the girls in this room—Stacy, Mandy, and Brianna—were performing miserably, their blood sub-satisfactory to the point of barely usable. Their usefulness was at an end. Brianna had been showing signs of dehydration and shock, and was at death's door. She was no longer worth keeping. She occupied a bed that should and would be filled by a newer girl. He'd been ordered to remove her today.

Not today, Bach suggested. *Today the threat is enough. Just take the blood and go.*

The girl is frightened enough.

She's frightened enough.

Her adrenaline levels are high enough.

The man turned away, and still Bach focused and would continue focusing until he was out that door. But then the man stopped—he moved with a peculiar shuffling gait—and he tipped his misshapen head to one side.

Bach leaned on the idea. *The girl is frightened enough. Time to go. Time to leave.*

"Are you trying to mind-control me?" the man said, turning

back to look at Nika, and Bach immediately pulled out. "What a clever girl. Perhaps too clever for your own good."

He came shuffling back, and Bach didn't dare try again. This time this man would be ready, he'd be expecting it. And this time, *if* Bach tried again, the man would know it wasn't Nika alone who'd put those thoughts into his mind.

And Bach couldn't risk him finding out that Nika was no longer alone.

"Pick. One," the man said again, his voice steely.

And Nika spoke up before Bach could stop her, her chin held high in defiance, even as she continued to cry. "Me," she said. "I pick *me*."

Nika, no.

Too late, she told Bach. *I can't do it—I won't do it. I won't pick someone else.*

"That's not acceptable," the scar-faced man said. "You're too valuable to your new owner."

Nika, I know this is hard to understand, but in a way, he's right. Your power is unprecedented—

"Well, that's too bad, because I picked," Nika answered them both.

"Pick again," the man said.

"No."

Nika, Joseph told her. *I'm going to push you away, push you far back into your mind, into a happy memory, where you won't see and you won't hear—*

Joseph, no, I won't do this!

Don't fight me. But she did fight him, her will sharp and strong, despite her days of abuse and captivity.

The man's knife came out. "Pick again, girl, or I'll kill five, right here, right now. And if you still don't pick, I'll kill five more."

He was going to do it. Bach knew that he would, just from the brief amount of time he'd spent in the man's ugly mind.

"I can't do this!" Nika cried, as Bach pushed her away from this nightmare.

Nika, go, and you won't have to, he told her, and in a rush, he could feel her understand what he was doing and why. But still she fought—this time for him.

Joseph, no, I can't let you do this for me!

Go. GO. He was stronger than she was—at least for now. In years to come, that would probably change—provided she survived the next few days. But here and now, Bach pushed her back, pushed her down, and then pushed her even further, even more deeply into her own unconscious mind, so she would not witness and therefore have no memory of the awfulness that was to come.

"I'm going to count to three," the scar-faced man told Nika, who was no longer there. It was all Bach now, in Nika's body. "One."

Bach closed his eyes. God help him.

"Two."

Nika wasn't going to do this, but *he* was. He looked up and he spoke in Nika's voice, because, really, that was the only voice he had access to, right before the man said, *Three.*

"Brianna," Bach said.

And it was harder to get the name out than he'd imagined, even knowing what he knew—that the little girl was already doomed to die.

He wanted to throw up, and it was possible that his true body did just that—back in the safety of OI.

But here, as Nika, he shut his mouth, and didn't say aloud, *Know this, now: If you hurt this girl? I will fucking kill you. I will follow you to the ends of the earth. I will personally hunt you down and end the toxic poison that is you.*

To Bach's horror and despair, the man didn't shuffle out the door. Instead, he turned and made his way toward one of the few girls who weren't screaming, one of the few whose eyes were glazed, whose voices were silent.

And he lifted his knife and slashed.

And Bach could have stopped it. He could have taken that knife from the man's hand. He could have forced the man to turn the knife on himself, to slash his own, scarred neck. Or he could have slammed the man against the wall, broken his back, broken his neck, crushed the life and the rotting evil out of him.

But then Nika's other captors would know. And they would kill Nika, or move her far away, or lock her in a room where, when the time came, Bach wouldn't be able to help her get free.

His team wasn't ready yet, and the Organization's defenses were too strong, so this little girl that he'd named had died.

Bach heard himself screaming, heard his voice, ragged and raw as her blood sprayed, as for the first time in decades his anger nearly owned him. For the first time in decades, he allowed himself to hate.

But for Nika's sake, and for Anna's sake, and for the sake of all of the other girls in this godforsaken hell of a place, he buried it all inside of himself. He locked it up—all except his grief.

That, he tried to release as he wept—but he knew it would never, ever leave him.

"Anna, thank you," Elliot said. "You're brilliant, you are. But it's not going to be you. It doesn't have to be you. It shouldn't be."

"But she's *my* sister," Anna pointed out, even as Elliot turned and looked at Stephen.

"Raise your hand if you know a former Navy SEAL, who also happens to be a fraction," Elliot said, lifting his hand.

"Shane Laughlin?" Anna said the man's name in unison with Stephen.

"Oh, that's good," Stephen added. "That's *really* good, El."

"But why would he do it?" Anna asked. "Going in there? It's a huge risk."

"Why do Navy SEALs do anything?" Elliot asked and then answered his own question, his voice lowered as if telling her a secret. "They're a little crazy."

"He'll probably enjoy the challenge," Stephen said.

"We can seal the deal—pun intended—by making Mac part of your assault team," Elliot told Stephen, who was nodding.

"I'm part of what assault team?"

They all looked up to see Mac standing there, a plate of scrambled eggs and a mug of coffee in her hands. "I got a text from Bach last night—he told me when I got here, I should come find Diaz. So, here I am. Mission accomplished—well, except for the accepting-my-punishment part."

"No one's going to punish you," Stephen said quietly. "I think you've probably already punished yourself enough."

Mac looked at him and although she didn't nod, it was clear she was in agreement. She appeared decidedly worse for the wear. Her pixie-short hair looked as if she'd showered and then slept on it. And still she managed to be one of the most beautiful women Anna had ever seen in her life.

She watched as Mac sat down and began shoveling the food into her mouth.

"Speaking of medical scans . . ." Elliot said, using the computer keyboard to enter some information.

"Were we speaking of med scans?" Mac asked, looking to Anna and Stephen for confirmation, her mouth full.

"It was back a bit, but yeah," Stephen told her.

"Hold still," Elliot said. "For a full scan—or at least the best we can do with your clothes on."

"I'm fine," Mac said, continuing to eat.

"Hold. Still."

Mac sighed and froze with her fork halfway to her mouth, while giving him a baleful glare.

"Look at that, you *are* fine," Elliot confirmed as Mac went back to her food. "Both bullet wounds are completely healed, and . . . Your integration levels are back to only minor wavering between fifty-three and fifty-four. Thank you, Shane Laughlin. Job well done."

"Do you know that you spiked to seventy-one?" Stephen asked her.

Mac was surprised. "Shit. Did I really?"

"After you eat," Elliot said, "I want to run more tests on you—and Shane, too. I want to see if there's anything we can do to keep this from happening again."

"Next time, just lock me up," Mac recommended, "after you send me into the head of a psychopath. FYI, it wasn't about Shane."

"Yeah, sorry, I'm not buying that," Elliot said.

"So . . . where is he?" Stephen asked, scanning the room. "Shane."

"He needed to sleep," Mac said, but her shrugged casualness seemed forced.

"Seriously?" Elliot asked. "*That's* how you thank him? By ditching him? Again?"

"I didn't ditch him," Mac said. "I just let him sleep."

Their conversation continued—Anna could see them talking, see their mouths moving, but their words faded, drowned out by the strangest buzzing sound.

She looked around, confused. Where was that coming from?

But no one else seemed to hear it. Their mouths were in motion as Stephen and Elliot used the computer as a visual aid and explained to Mac everything they'd discovered about the Organization building where Nika was being held—about the illegal medical scanners used by the Org's security team, and about the need for a non-Greater-Than to shut those scanners down from inside.

And still the noise continued, rattling her brain. Anna tried to take a sip of water, but her hand was shaking so she put the glass back down.

The conversation was still going on, but the words were distant and the colors of the room itself seemed odd and too bright, so she closed her eyes and breathed, again using Joseph Bach's peace-inducing techniques. *Calm blue ocean . . .*

At first the buzzing got louder and the dizziness increased, but then suddenly it just snapped off and there was silence. But it was a weird silence. A warm silence—as if she'd just stepped into the pitch-blackness of a small closet that was already occupied. And when a voice spoke, she wasn't completely surprised.

Anna? Whoever it was, it was a girl or maybe a young woman. And it was clear from Stephen, Elliot, and Mac's complete absorption in their conversation that this female voice was something only Anna could hear.

And even though she knew it wasn't her sister, Anna thought back, *Nika?*

No, the voice said. It was strained, whispered, urgent. *But I know her. I've seen her, spoken to her. Cristopher—the man in charge—he wants to kill her. She's become too much trouble. Too powerful for him to handle. He's talking to the board of directors right now. If they give their permission—and they will, they always do—he'll return and bleed her dry.*

Oh, God, no . . .

You must listen, the girl told her. *Very carefully. Because I'm going to do it. I'm going to help her. Together we'll try to escape— God help us. But you and your friends have got to help. You've got to meet us halfway—if you can. . . .*

We will, Anna told her. *We can. We're devising a plan right now, to break in.*

Really? There was a pause. *How soon?*

I don't know, Anna said. *It's complicated. It's going to take us awhile. Days, possibly.*

The girl was adamant. *That's not soon enough.*

We're just not prepared—

I'm not going to wait, the girl told her. *I'm going to take Nika and run, but you've got to meet me at—*

The buzzing was back, obscuring her words, and Anna stood. Stephen, Elliot, and Mac all looked curiously up at her.

"Excuse me," she said, and walked slightly away from the table, hoping that the buzzing was some sort of interference and if she moved a bit, the girl would come back.

And sure enough, as she headed toward the door to the lounge, the buzzing lessened. It was still back there, but she could hear the girl again. *Are you there? What happened? I almost lost you—oh, Lord, maybe they know . . .*

Tell me quickly before I lose you again—where should we meet you? Anna asked, jumping as Mac touched her arm.

"Anna, are you all right?"

Anna could see the concern in the other woman's eyes, as she shook her head, no, even as the girl's voice was again drowned out by the buzzing sound.

Tell me again, Anna said. *I'm losing you!*

She could only hear ragged bits and pieces of words now. *Maybe* and *connection* and *prove—improve—*and *outside.* And then she heard the girl's voice, crystal clearly, *Maybe if you go outside, and up onto a hill without any buildings or trees . . .*

Yes, yes—she could do that! Anna pulled away from Mac and went out of the lounge, running now through the hall toward the stairs that led to the ground-floor entrance.

There *was* a gently sloping tree-free hill between this main building and the fence that surrounded the compound. It was covered in the lush green grass of spring, thanks to all the rain they'd been having lately. Anna thundered down the stairs, aware that Mac was right behind her, with Stephen and Elliot bringing up the rear.

"Where are you going?" Mac asked, her voice nearly drowned out, too, by the buzzing in Anna's head. "Anna, what the *hell* . . . ?"

Stephen wasn't quite sure what was happening. All he knew was that Mac had taken off, chasing Anna down the hall, so he'd followed, curious as to what was going on, aware as hell that the feeling of foreboding that had been pressing down on his chest was back with a vengeance.

"There's a girl," he heard Anna shout back to Mac, even as she kept running, "who's a prisoner, with Nika, and she's sending me a message—she's *projecting* a message! She's going to escape with Nika, she's going to help! But there's this weird interference, this noise in my head, and I've *got* to get outside!"

"No," Mac said, "Anna—*no*!"

But Anna was already past the Security checkpoint, and bursting through the door. Mac was right on her heels, but Anna was surprisingly fast.

Stephen skidded to a stop and turned to Elliot, who was right behind him. "Stay inside."

Elliot didn't say a word, but his expression held a shade of *oh no, you dih-n't,* so Stephen added, "Please," and touched him briefly on the side of his face. *Thank you. Love you.*

He didn't wait for Elliot to respond, he just turned and raced after Anna and Mac.

He could hear Mac shouting as she followed Anna up the hill. "Don't make me tackle you—don't make me do it!"

He heard Anna's reply, "Be quiet—you've got to be quiet! I can't hear her over the noise!"

Shit—there *was* noise, and it wasn't just inside of Anna's head. It was a low sound, a thrumming sound, and Stephen looked up . . . And there it was, in the brilliant blue of the crisp spring morning sky—not a hawk circling overhead, but a pitch-black helicopter, diving toward them, fast, growing larger and larger.

And it wasn't just a helicopter, it was a gunship, with weapons bristling on either side of the fuselage.

Stephen heard himself shouting to Mac, "Get inside, get her back inside," but he knew there wasn't enough time. It was over. Anna was going to be taken, flying up into the sky and away from OI, just as she'd done in his vision.

And he focused all of his power on that helicopter, on telekinetically swatting it out of the sky. It jolted and jumped, but it didn't stop coming. Stephen tried again, and again he couldn't move it—which didn't make sense, unless it was somehow shielded . . .

So he changed tactics and he reached out with his mind and tried to find the minds of the men and women who were inside the gunship. Although this wasn't his strength, his new Elliot-enhanced powers were still being revealed, and this was certainly worth a try.

But he felt—nothing. Almost as if the gunship were a drone, or manned by robots. There was no warmth, no humanity—again as if the people within were completely shielded.

But he didn't give up—he couldn't—and he tried to find a way in, a weakness in the shield, perhaps a chink where he could squeeze through and jam the engine, make it stall, but that didn't work either.

Stephen could see the guards and some of the Thirties and Forties come out of Old Main as he kept running toward Anna and Mac, but there was nothing anyone besides Bach could possibly do to help.

But Bach wasn't there. Stephen couldn't feel him—wherever the Seventy-two was, he was far, far away.

And whoever was manning the weapons system on that gunship saw all those men and women spilling out of the building, and clearly had no idea that they were armed with little more than Tasers and trank guns. Or maybe they *did* know, and they were just motherfuckers, because Stephen knew with a hard, cold certainty that they were going to fire those machine guns. And he also knew with a sense of icy fear that those guns were—somehow—shielded, too. Still, he tried, with all of his might, to stop their bullets. He slowed one of the guns down, but he couldn't stop them both. And as he felt the other break through his defense, he threw all of his own shielding powers, all of his self-protection, back toward Elliot, to keep *him* safe, right before that burst of machine-gun fire cracked and pinged against the building, shattering the glass in the windows and front doors.

And as the gunship swung back around, like some kind of death-spewing monster, Stephen felt something hit him hard in the back, again, and then again, and his legs crumpled beneath him and he went down, even as he saw Mac throw herself on top of Anna, as a trail of bullets tore up the turf around them, sending bits of dirt exploding into the air.

As he tried—and failed—to pull himself back to his feet, he saw the spray of blood as Mac was hit, saw three dark figures fast-roping down from the helicopter, saw one of them pull Mac's life-less body off of Anna, who was kicking and screaming valiantly, but didn't stand a chance against three large men, particularly since Mac, before she was shot, had clipped her wrist to Anna's with one of the plastic restraints she always carried in her pockets.

Then one of the men hit Anna in the head with the butt of his rifle, and she slumped to the ground.

And as Stephen crawled toward them, still trying to reach them, as the gunship throbbed and thrummed overhead, the three dark-clothed men picked up both Anna and Mac. And all five of them were pulled up through the open door and into the cabin, even as it rocketed away.

Stephen rolled onto his side to watch it, a shrinking black shape, vanishing into the brilliant blue of the morning sky.

Only then, in defeat, did he allow himself to see the bright red of his own blood that was pooling around him, beneath him. He reached down to touch the sodden front of his shirt, to finger the hole in the fabric.

His stomach was bleeding—an exit wound from one of the bul-lets that had hit him in the back.

He was cold and his vision was tunneling, which couldn't be good, but still, his heart leapt as Elliot's face came into view. "You're alive," he said, but he couldn't hear his voice, so maybe he didn't get the words out.

Elliot was in full-medical-doctor mode, shouting for a stretcher and an IV, plasma extender, and something sterile to stop the flow of blood. He must've decided that sterile wasn't as big a priority as immediate, because he whipped off his shirt and used it to apply pressure to Stephen's back.

As always, their connection clicked on.

God damn it, god damn it, god damn it, don't you die on me, you son of a bitch! Work with me now, work it—keep your blood flow away from your wounds. You can do this, stay with me!

This would be easier, since Stephen didn't have to manipulate his throat and mouth to speak. And yet he couldn't seem to organize his thoughts. He just kept flashing back to his apartment, to the too-short time he'd spent with this amazing man, in each others' arms. *El. Love you.*

Don't you dare give me that kind of last word bullshit, you asshole! I was safe in there! I was safe! Why didn't you trust me? You should have trusted me to stay inside! You should have shielded yourself!

Afraid, Stephen told him as he felt himself picked up and put on a gurney, as he felt them both moving fast, then faster, back toward the building, *that bullets would go through. Walls. Windows. Hit you.*

Yeah, well, they didn't!

Did, too. He didn't know how he knew that, but he did. As they carried him through the front doors, moving double time, they passed the very spot where he knew, without a doubt, that Elliot would have died had Stephen not thrown his protection over him. *But I did it. I changed the future.* His heart ached as he remembered Anna and Mac, being taken away. *Part of it, anyway . . .*

He still wasn't quite sure what had happened, why Anna had run outside, but he remembered, vaguely, hearing something she'd said to Mac, and he pushed that memory at Elliot as hard as he could. It was something Bach would need to know.

"There's a girl," Anna had shouted, *"who's a prisoner, with Nika, and she's sending me a message—she's projecting a message! She's going to escape with Nika, she's going to help! But there's this weird interference, this noise in my head, and I've got to get outside!"*

Dear God, Elliot realized. *It was a trap. Whoever they were, they came to get Anna, and they tricked her into going outside.*

God, Stephen was tired and so very, very cold . . .

Enhance, Elliot told him, sharply. *Stephen, stay with me! I need you to focus on healing . . .*

But the darkness was pressing down on him, and the pain was starting to register and he was too weak to fight it. He just wanted to sink back into his memory of . . . was it just yesterday morning? When he first kissed Elliot, while sitting on his sofa . . .

Best coupla days of my life, he told Elliot. *Love you always.*

And he surrendered to the darkness.

———

"He's flat-lining!" Elliot was shouting as Stephen Diaz, covered in blood, was wheeled into OI's Medical Center.

Shane had started to run when he saw the gunship bearing down on the main OI building.

He'd taken the T out to Riverside, and then walked the rest of the way to the compound, uncertain as to his reception at the gate when he arrived.

But the guards didn't question his right to be there. They just searched him for weapons, and when he was cleared, they offered him a ride up the hill.

Which he'd declined because he hadn't wanted to get there too soon. He still hadn't figured out what he was going to say to Mac when he saw her again.

Or even if he should say anything aside from *Good morning.*

But the disappointment he'd felt upon waking up alone vanished when he saw the helicopter attack, and saw Mac get shot—again.

Shot and abducted, along with Anna Taylor.

He ran toward them, shouting, and got a hail of bullets for his trouble. But luck was with him and as he dove and rolled, he wasn't hit.

But Stephen Diaz had been, and Jesus, the man was a mess. Elliot was already kneeling beside him, silently working to stop the bleeding. Shane helped, too, tearing off his own borrowed T-shirt to try to stanch the flow.

He'd seen his share of mortal wounds on various battlefields around the world, and this was, without a doubt, a life-ender. If the hospital hadn't been so close, it would have unquestionably been time to administer the morphine and make the man's last moments on earth more comfortable. But the hospital was just inside, and Elliot clearly wasn't ready to give up and let go.

Shane could relate, because part of him was up in that helo, with Mac—please God, keep her alive until he could find her and bring her back . . .

He helped carry Diaz inside, helped race him into the Med Center, where the man promptly died.

But Elliot apparently wasn't going to accept that, either, because now he was shouting for the defibrillator and the paddles, and ten cc's of God only knew what.

And Shane stepped back, out of the way, to let the medical team work.

"Where's Bach?" he asked one of the guards, who was covered in almost as much blood as Shane was.

The man looked dazed, and just shook his head. There were other wounded, too, but all were superficial, at least compared to Diaz. And all of the Greater-Thans had managed to protect themselves. But right now, nobody seemed to know what to do.

With Elliot busy, Mac abducted, and Diaz out of commission, someone had to take command. So Shane stepped to the nearest comm-station and logged in.

"Computer, connect me with Analysis," he ordered. "I want all satellites tracking the gunship that just took Anna Taylor and Michelle Mackenzie. I want any new information on the location of Nika Taylor, and I want to find and alert Dr. Bach—immediately."

"Dr. Bach is in his office," the computer told him. "He is not to be disturbed."

"Disturb him anyway," Shane commanded.

"Dr. Bach is not to be disturbed."

Fuck that. Shane knew where Bach's office was, and he took off for it at a run.

TWENTY-SIX

They held the meeting in the hall outside of Stephen Diaz's room in the ICU.

Elliot had managed to get Diaz's heart beating again, and had brought him into surgery to clean out his wounds and try to help repair the damage done. During the course of that, the Greater-Than's heart had stopped twice more.

The doctor now looked a little shell-shocked, but Shane had to give the man credit. Whatever happened to Diaz—however this ended—it wasn't going to be because Elliot had given up.

Dr. Bach was looking extremely gray, too. He was, quite literally, in two places at once, and the strain on his physical body was intense. Shane had found him curled in a ball behind his desk, in an office that looked as if a hurricane had blasted through it.

The bookshelves had been knocked over, and artwork hung at odd angles. Books and files had been shredded and littered the floor. And about a dozen pens were stuck, point first, into the wall, as if they'd been flung there like darts, with enormous force.

And, to add just a little more fuck to the what, when Bach roused, he looked around with surprise, as if he didn't remember doing any of that. He'd immediately started cleaning up—until the words *Anna* and *Mac* and *helicopter abduction* hit his ears.

That had caught his complete attention. Complete, that is, except for the piece of him that was still locked in the Org's Washington Street building with Nika.

Together, Shane and Bach reviewed all the information that Analysis had compiled about the building and the Organization's security detail inside. They read the notes from the meeting that Diaz, Anna, and Mac had had with Elliot, and agreed that the plan to send Shane inside to shut down their illegal medical scanners was their only real option.

They also decided that Bach should and would gain full possession of Nika's body, so he could protect her with his shielding abilities as they attempted to break free.

Of course, now they had to add finding and freeing Anna and Mac to their to-do list.

Assuming that the Organization's leaders didn't just immediately kill Mac when they realized she was a Greater-Than, and therefore a threat.

But that kind of thinking didn't serve Shane.

"Maybe if we can figure out *why* they took Anna, we can narrow down the possibilities of where she and Mac are being held," Shane said now.

Elliot and Bach exchanged a glance. "We know why they took Anna," Bach said. "The lengths they went to with this abduction confirm what we already believed—that the Organization has never seen a girl with Nika's powers before, either."

Shane connected the dots. "So . . . They took Anna, hoping to gain access to another *fountain?*"

Bach nodded, his mouth tight.

"Except Anna's a fraction," Shane put voice to what they were all thinking, "and when they find that out, they're not going to be happy." So maybe this was going to be a rescue of only Nika, after all. It was looking more and more likely that for Mac and Anna, OI would do little more than recover their bodies.

He saw that grim truth echoed in Bach's eyes.

Elliot was not as pessimistic. "Mac's a fighter," he reminded them. "If she's allowed to stay with Anna, she'll figure out a way to keep them both alive."

That was a pretty huge *if*, considering that both she and Anna were unconscious when pulled aboard the helo.

But there were other aspects of the coming battle to focus on. "If you're inside, with Nika," Shane asked Bach, "and Diaz and Mac are obviously unavailable, who exactly is leading the Greater-Than assault team?"

"Jackie Schultz already volunteered to do it," Bach answered.

It was a name Shane had never heard before. "Who's Jackie Schultz?"

"She's not ready," Elliot said. "For something like this?"

"She's the best of the Forties," Bach countered grimly.

"Wait a minute," Shane said. "The best we've got is a *Forty*? Aren't there any other Fifties? Are you seriously telling me that you and Mac and Diaz are *it*?"

"Most Greater-Thans never integrate higher than thirty percent," Elliot told him, and yeah, Shane had heard that before, but it hadn't sunk in, not the way it was sinking now.

"There are several known Fifties in New York City," Bach said, "but it would take them too long to get here."

Several. The biggest city in America only had *several* Fifties. "I'm sorry," Shane said. "I'm certain I should have known this, but I'm . . ." He looked at Elliot. "So Mac is . . . ?"

"One of maybe a hundred people, around the world, who have elevated to that elite integration level," Elliot finished for him. "The number of Sixties is even lower. There're maybe a few dozen. Fewer still of the Seventies."

So Mac, who was already, literally, one in a billion, had the chance—by hooking up with Shane—to move her integration level from fifty to sixty, and yet . . . She'd turned it and him down.

"Huh," Shane said and then brought his brain back on-topic. "So this girl, this Jackie—"

Bach cut Shane off. "She's not a girl, she's a woman, and she's a Forty, which means she's significantly more integrated than you are. She'll lead a team of a dozen Forties and Thirties—"

"With all due respect, sir," Shane said as mildly as he could manage, "you could well be sending those Greater-Thans to their deaths. Or worse—if their blood proves to be a viable source of the drug—"

"You think I don't know that?" Bach asked, his voice tight.

"I *think*," Shane said, "that you have no idea just how bad this could get."

But Bach's face hardened. "And I think you should focus on your plan for getting inside the Brite Group's security area."

Shane glanced again at the schematic of the Washington Street building that was up on the computer screen. He'd already memorized the layout of the lobby, the basement, the roof, and the floors in question—as well as several surrounding them in either direction. He knew where the elevators were, and he'd mentally marked the stairs. He knew the locations of the fire alarms and the air ducts—and every public men's and ladies' room in the building.

Because sometimes the bathroom was the best place to hide.

"My plan is ready to go," Shane told Bach and Elliot, too. "I don't suppose you have any C4 in storage . . . ?" Yeah, and that was a great big no he was getting from Elliot, but just in case he was misreading a WTF look for a negative, he elaborated, "C4 plastic explosives . . . ?"

"Not a chance," Elliot said, and Shane looked toward Bach, who had on his poker face, and who managed to surprise them both.

"We actually do," Bach said as he looked at Elliot. "In a special lockup, beneath the old auditorium building. Last year, Dr. Diaz urged me to start acquiring supplies of a military nature. I think he's always been a bit prescient." Back to Shane. "How much do you need?"

"Not a lot," he said. This was an awesome break—now he wouldn't have to shop for black-market C4 before heading over to Washington Street. "I certainly won't be able to bring much in without detection. I'll take it in as sticks of gum. I'm not looking to bring down the building—just take out the scanners and the power source if I can."

"Why go to the trouble to disguise it as chewing gum," Elliot asked, "if you're going to sneak in?"

"Never said I was sneaking in," Shane told them. "And I didn't say I wasn't. I think I'm not going to reveal any further details to you, Dr. Bach, since you have direct access to Nika's head, and she's already under the Organization's control. It's better that she knows as little as possible."

Bach, despite his earlier testiness and his obvious fatigue, was a good enough leader not to take Shane's words personally. "I think that's wise."

"But how will you know when he's in?" Elliot asked, but then answered his own question. "Because the scanners will go down. Analysis will be watching via satellite."

"And the Thirties and Forties will be waiting, nearby, ready to enter." Bach nodded. "Meanwhile, I'll break Nika out from the inside."

Shane stood up. "Where do I go to get that C4?"

Bach rose, too, but stiffly, as if his back were aching. "I'll have someone get it for you."

"What should I be doing?" Elliot asked.

Bach stopped for a moment, briefly resting his hand on the other man's shoulder. "You're doing it," he told the doctor, who glanced back in to where machines were both breathing for Diaz and keeping his heart beating.

"Before we're dismissed," Shane said. "There's one more thing that we haven't discussed, that I believe is important to consider, sir. The girl—the young woman—who contacted Anna. She projected a message into the head of a fraction, across a great distance. Whoever she is? She's a pretty fucking powerful Greater-Than in her own right. And she's working for the enemy."

———

Anna woke up with her heart racing, her head pounding, and her mouth dry.

She was in a dark room—it was pitch-black. Even though she strained to see something—the tiny red light on a smoke alarm or the vague afterglow of a recently used computer monitor—there was nothing there.

She was strapped down—restraints held both her arms and

legs. As she struggled, she knew that her captors were serious. She was not going to get free until they released her.

Her feet were bare—she could feel the weight and texture of a light blanket that had been placed across her. It was then that she realized that her clothing was gone. As far as she could tell, from her limited ability to move her hands, she was dressed in some type of thigh-length cotton gown.

Anna.

Anna froze, recognizing the voice she'd heard in her head—projecting, Bach had called it.

Welcome to your new home.

Before, the voice had sounded urgent and convincingly frightened. But now—whoever she was—she was faintly mocking and contemptuous.

Who are you? Anna asked, avoiding the obvious and leaving *You tricked me, you bitch,* as a thought that was mostly unformed.

But present.

My name's unimportant. Almost as irrelevant as you'll be, when the board sees your blood test results. All that trouble, for nothing. She made tsking sounds.

If I'm irrelevant, Anna thought back at her, *then let us go.*

Hot tip, girlfriend. Never ask for that. We don't let people go. We turn them to ash, and toss them out with the trash. It's a daily ritual—don't let it be you.

Where's Nika? Anna tried. *I want to see my sister.*

Hello. Which one of us is lying in a dark room, strapped to a bed? That would be not me. And that makes you *the one who doesn't get to make the demands. So wake up your little friend and tell her to lower her mental blocks and shields so I can communicate directly with her. Oh, and tell her if she uses any of her super-secret-special powers against me or anyone else who comes into that room? In any way at all? You'll both immediately be killed. Over and out.*

And with that the girl was gone, leaving Anna listening to the sound of her own ragged breathing, as she still strained to see something, anything in the darkness.

She'd just been told that Mac was in here with her, but she couldn't hear the Greater-Than breathing. Why couldn't she hear her?

"Mac?"

Silence.

Anna had a flash of memory. The chopper, the men, the guns firing—Mac getting hit.

"Oh, my God, are you injured? Can you hear me? Mac? Mac! *Mac!*"

It was not the way she herself would have wanted to be awakened, but her panic made her louder and louder and she finally heard, from across the room, the sound of the Greater-Than stirring.

"What the hell . . . ?" she heard Mac say, heard her straining and pulling against the straps that held her. "What the *fuck* . . . ?"

"Mac, it's me," Anna said. "Anna. I'm locked in here with you. That girl—the one who contacted me at OI, who projected that message . . . She says to lower your mental shields so she can communicate with you. She says that if you use your powers to harm anyone, or fight back in any way—"

"Fuck. That." Anna heard popping sounds that were either Mac's restraints being unlocked, or just flat-out broken.

She heard a sound that had to be Mac, slipping off the hospital bed, her feet against the floor. She must've bumped something— another bed—because she swore, and then Anna heard slapping sounds, as Mac muttered, "Freaking light switch's gotta be around here somewhere."

And then the overhead lights came on—gloriously, brain-stabblingly bright—and Anna had to squint as she lifted her head to see Mac by the door.

And yes, she, like Anna, was wearing a hospital gown that tied in the back. She had blood caked in her hair, and as Anna watched, she reached up to touch her head, and winced. Her fingers came away red, wet with blood. She must've been grazed by a bullet back at OI.

"Mac, she was serious," Anna insisted. "They'll kill us. You've got to get back in that bed."

"I can't do that. If we just sit here, Shane'll come and try to save me, get his fraction-ass killed." Mac tried the door instead. But it wouldn't open. She looked at it. Looked at how it was hanging in the door frame, looked at the wall around it, and Anna knew she was intending to blast it right out of the wall.

"Mac," Anna said again, and the Greater-Than turned to glance back at her, and then to look around the room.

It was small and contained the four beds, two of them empty and one with broken restaints. The walls and ceiling were bare, and painted a dull shade of beige. The floor was industrial tile of the same color.

"Anna. We've got to get out of here," Mac told her. "Now— before they discover what powers I actually have. I kinda suck with the telekinetic stuff, so hold on while I . . ."

She focused and not only did the straps around Anna's arms and legs disintegrate, but the entire bed collapsed, too.

"Oh, shit, are you hurt?" Mac asked, running over to help her up.

"No, I'm okay," Anna said. "But—"

"I heard you," Mac said, as she gazed up at the cover to an air vent on the ceiling. It was, possibly, big enough for Mac to fit through, but not Anna. "You relayed the message. Threats of death. Me. You. And . . . What is that noise?"

It was a hissing sound. And then another hissing sound joined in. It was coming from . . .

Anna lifted the sleeve of her hospital gown to reveal a medical port sewn into her arm. It was more neatly done than the one she'd witnessed in Nika's projection.

Mac had one, too, beneath the sleeve of her hospital gown. "Shit! *Shit!*" She grabbed it, as if to pull it off, but then her legs gave way beneath her. "Drugged," she said as she hit the floor, her words slurred, "Bastards drugged us."

Anna, too, could feel it now, the numbness coursing through her, and she, too, hit the tile. She found herself looking directly into Mac's eyes as the Greater-Than apologized. "Sorry," Mac said. "F'I weren't gon' die, Bach'd prolly kill me—'cuz that's two for two . . ."

Anna didn't understand. "What?" she said, as Mac's eyes rolled back in her head, right before the world went black.

———

Stephen was dying.

Elliot sat at his bedside, holding Stephen's hand, knowing that he'd done everything he could possibly do—and it still wasn't going to be enough.

Stephen's integration level was steady at sixty-one, and had been right from the moment he was brought in. There was nothing Elliot could do to boost his levels—even though he'd tried some extremely risky procedures.

Just as he'd done with old Edward O'Keefe, Elliot had injected some oxyclepta di-estraphen directly into the self-healing areas of Stephen's brain. He'd used the massager to attempt to further manipulate and increase Stephen's ability to heal himself.

But even though the drug burned off—exactly as it had with O'Keefe—Stephen's self-healing capabilities *didn't* increase.

It was true that a mere fraction would have been long-dead by now, but all that meant was that Stephen's powers had brought him more hours of pain and suffering. In fact, more than one of the other doctors had stopped by and pulled Elliot out into the hall to suggest that, since Stephen was going to die anyway, maybe Elliot should just pull the plug.

It was all Elliot could do not to deck his esteemed colleagues.

"Fight harder," he told Stephen now. "I believe in you."

"Excuse me, Dr. Zerkowski . . . ?"

Elliot looked up to see Shane Laughlin standing in the doorway. He'd gone back to his apartment to shower and shave and put on clean clothes. He looked nice, like he was going on a date or . . .

Elliot somehow managed to laugh. "A job interview," he said. "Brilliant."

Shane glanced over his shoulder, looking both ways down the hall before nodding. "May I come in?" he asked, even as he did just that, shutting the door behind him.

Elliot glanced back at Stephen's slack face. "Maybe we should step into the hall."

"No, actually," Shane said, moving closer to the bed, "this is something that Dr. Diaz can hear. I mean, I know he's in a medical coma, but he can still hear, right?"

"I'm not sure how much he's able to listen to right now," Elliot admitted. His telepathic connection with Stephen had failed ever since the Greater-Than had flat-lined.

"I did a little research while I was upstairs," Shane said, "and I read your report on the old man—Ted O'Keefe—and how you believe you've found a possible cure to the addiction of Destiny."

Elliot sat down again next to Stephen. He was so freaking tired. "And . . . ?"

"And I want some," Shane said. "Epi Pens. I heard Destiny was available now in that format, which is more convenient than, you know, having to stop and shoot up. I'm pretty sure I'm going to be under a certain amount of duress and won't have the time."

Elliot's mouth was hanging open. He closed it. Opened it again. Finally he managed to access his rather large vocabulary. "Are you suggesting that—"

"I'm not suggesting, I'm requesting," Shane said. He pulled the other chair in the room up to the other side of Stephen's bed, and sat down. He was dead serious. "Look, I know I can get into the Brite Group's security center. They're going to take one look at me, at my online résumé—which includes that very important word, *blacklisted,* and hire me on the spot. Once I'm in, I can take out the illegal med scanners and even their entire power system. But that's where my plan gets a little sketchy. I'm going into an enclosed room to blow out the scanners, and there're gonna be a lot of angry men with guns waiting outside that door for me. After a very short while, they're not going to wait for me to come out. They're going to come in. And then they're going to kill me."

Shane looked from Elliot to Diaz and back, and said, "I know I don't have to explain my motivation when I tell you that I'm willing to do that—to die to make this rescue happen. But I'd prefer not to. And then there's the fact that simply shutting down the scanners doesn't mean the team of children—pardon me, the Thirties and the Forties—are going to find Mac and Anna. Bach's got Nika. Once the scanners are down, he'll connect with the team and we'll get her out. But I'm personally invested in making damn sure Mac doesn't spend the rest of her life bleeding into a plastic bag. If I take the drug, I'll access some powers and hopefully one of them will be to make myself bulletproof. At which point I have a chance to help search for Mac. Then, once I reach her, I'll enhance her."

He smiled at the expression that must've appeared on Elliot's face, and added, "Not like that. Just by being in the room with her. Just by touching her hand. And once that happens, odds of both of us getting out of there are that much greater."

Elliot looked down at Stephen's hand, at Stephen's lifeless fingers entwined with his own. Holy crap. Holy *crap* . . .

He looked up at Shane, who was waiting for him to say . . . something. So he spoke. "The key word in my report was *possible*," he told the former SEAL. "I've found a *possible* cure for this addiction. Edward O'Keefe is still in a coma—a real, non-medically-induced coma. We're unable to rouse him—believe me we've tried. His heart is in good condition again—he's now got the coronary health of a robust fifty-year-old, but . . . It's possible he was brain-damaged by the drug, and we just haven't discovered it yet. It's possible he'll just never wake up."

"But it's also possible that he will. And *that* possible provides better odds than the *absolutely dead* that I'm looking at," Shane said somberly.

"You understand," Elliot said, "that we're talking about a drug that will kill you. An addiction so crippling—"

"I understand."

"And that my so-called *cure* includes stopping and damaging your heart—enough so that the drug is burned out of your system by the healing centers of your brain as it attempts to fix that damage. And oh, by the way, as a fraction? We don't even know if you *have* a healing center!"

"I won't be a fraction anymore," Shane pointed out. "And again, I understand—completely—everything you included in your report. I read it thoroughly. I'll be in a coma. I may not come out. It's a risk."

"Maybe you should take more time," Elliot suggested. "Figure out a plan that actually includes your escape from—"

"We don't have time," Shane said. "Elliot, please. I'm ready to die if I have to. But like I said, I'd prefer at least a glimmer of your *possible.*"

———

Nika found Joseph Bach standing in a corner of her mind, within a small area he'd created to shield himself from her private thoughts—both for her sake and his.

Now that he'd managed to unlock her shields and various mental blocks, he was no longer just a voice and a sense of warmth. She could see him, completely, as he sensed her and turned—and then opened the shielded area to let her in.

It was weird. It was nicer in there than it was outside. It smelled good—not unlike the cologne that Anna's creepy ex-boyfriend David used to wear.

As Nika moved closer, Joseph didn't put on any fake *everything's okay* attitude. He didn't try to soften this little reunion with a smile. He didn't even try to hide the pain he was feeling from what he'd done—from what she imagined he'd done. She didn't know for sure.

So she braced herself and asked, *Did you . . . ?*

And Joseph didn't lie. *Yes.*

Oh, God. She didn't ask "How could you," because she didn't want to know how *any*one could make such a terrible choice, let alone this kind man.

We're safe for a while, he told her. *They took more blood.* And he'd done some work, stimulating the part of her brain that worked to quickly heal her, replenishing what they'd taken. Nika knew this because she didn't feel as weak as she usually felt after a bleeding.

Are you okay? she asked him.

Again, he answered truthfully. *No.*

Nika's heart broke for him, for having put him in this awful situation, for having brought him to this terrible, hellish place.

She'd come looking for Joseph, pulling herself out of a wonderful memory of a long-ago birthday morning when her mother and Anna had made pancakes, all ready to get up in his face for having treated her like a child.

But one look into the darkness in his eyes, and she was deeply grateful that he'd pushed her away.

And as far as treating her like a child went, he certainly wasn't doing that now, with his raw honesty.

I'm so sorry, she said.

I'm sorry, too. Nika, there's more bad news. They took Anna. What?

Again, he didn't try to sugarcoat it. He simply showed her a memory—not his, someone else's . . . Elliot's—of Anna running outside, of Anna and Mac being taken away in a helicopter.

Nika was shaking so hard she had to sit down. *Is Stephen Diaz dead?*

Not yet, Joseph told her, moving to sit heavily beside her. *But it doesn't look good.*

I'm so sorry, she said again.

It's not your fault.

Isn't it? She looked at him. *I think I know who projected that message to Anna. Her name is Rayonna.* And instead of attempting to explain, Nika just opened up her memory of the way she'd accidentally found herself in the pregnant girl's head when she'd been reaching out for Joseph.

I wish you'd told me about this sooner, Joseph said. *I would have been watching for her. I should have been, anyway, though . . . I mean, I thought that there'd been a mental breach when I heard that Anna had received a projection from a girl who claimed she was helping you escape. I wasn't sure how it had happened, but I thought it was likely that the girl that you'd mentioned coming into your safe room had somehow gotten access to your mind and . . . In hindsight, I'm pretty sure that I saw her—Rayonna— inside of your head, back when we were at OI—I thought it was a memory of your mother, but . . .* He sighed. *Damn it.*

So Rayonna did find Anna through me, Nika struggled, forcing herself not to cry. *Does she know about you?*

She must, Joseph told her. *But I've been discreet. Kept a very small footprint. Set up this shield*—he gestured around them—*so that if there are Greater-Thans here, working for the Organization, they won't be able to see me. And when you're in here with me, the read they'll get from you is that you're sleeping.*

Are you sure Rayonna can't see you? Nika asked. *Maybe . . . You should go. Until . . . You know.* Just in case Rayonna had access to her thoughts in a way that Joseph hadn't anticipated, Nika didn't want to think about the events that she hoped were still coming. Events that now included the rescue of Mac and her sister . . .

I'm as sure as I can be, Joseph told her. He leaned toward her slightly, to bump her with his shoulder. *Either way, I'm not leaving you.*

How powerful is she? Nika asked. *Rayonna.*

Very.

More powerful than you?

He looked at her. And answered honestly. *I don't know, Neek. But I think we've got a temporary advantage. I suspect she thought Anna provided the link that allowed us to communicate—the link between you and me. Otherwise, the Organization would have come after me directly. Instead, by taking Anna, they likely believe they've not only cut off your contact with me, but that they've obtained another fountain.*

What's going to happen, Nika asked, *when they find out Anna doesn't have any power at all?*

Joseph looked grim as he shook his head. *I don't know that either. But I do know that they're not just going to let her go.*

As Shane entered the Washington Street building, he was aware that he was being watched—both by the team of Thirties and Forties from OI, and by a half a dozen rent-a-cops who stood guard both outside and in the entrance to the building's vast lobby.

He was carrying nothing in his hands.

In his pockets, however, he had his wallet, the keys to one of the OI trucks, an open and half-empty pack of cigarettes, a lighter, the pack of "gum" he'd gotten from Bach's associate, along with a particularly thin detcord that he'd braided into a necklace that had two small silver blasting caps dangling at the end of it—both in rather unique shapes; one a Christian cross, the other a beatific-looking angel.

Oh yeah, and he also had two Epi Pens. To counter his brand-new allergy to assholes.

In truth, they held doses of Destiny.

After giving Shane his unenthusiastic blessing, Elliot had warned him of the dangers of jokering. It was possible—to the tune of a five-percent chance—that Shane would joker immediately upon injection. At which point he would no longer be an asset to either Bach or Mac.

He would, however, provide a hefty distraction for the Organization's security guards to deal with as the team from OI engineered the escape.

And if the three men Shane had seen fast-roping down from that gunship had been an accurate representation of the quality of people who made up the Organization's security team? They would have their unskilled and barely trained hands full.

Only one of the three had had any kind of military background—Shane had made note of that immediately.

Which was one of the reasons why he was now here. Because he couldn't believe that whoever was in charge of security for the Washington Street building would turn down the opportunity to add a former Navy SEAL to his ranks.

And, sure enough, as Shane approached the desk in the lobby

and announced that he'd heard from a friend that he'd met while serving with the *U.S. Navy SEALs* that the Brite Group's security head was hiring, the two men who'd gotten to their feet at his approach exchanged a message-laden glance.

Unlike with Mac, the word SEAL worked its magic with these two, and they were properly impressed.

"You were in the teams, huh?" the blond one with the goatee asked.

"An officer," Shane said, even though they hadn't asked. "But not quite a gentleman."

And yes, they laughed.

"May I have your name, sir?" Goatee asked.

Shane told him, spelling Laughlin as the man typed it into his computer.

"The name of your friend?" Goatee asked.

"Anonymous," Shane said. "He's still active duty."

"We get a lot of referrals from old Anonymous," the guard with the shaved head and the tattoo peeking up over the edge of his shirt collar said, and again, they all laughed. *Ho, ho, ho.*

Despite the tatt, the man was neatly dressed—jacket, shirt, and tie—and it was clear that, like his co-worker, he was carrying a weapon in a shoulder holster. As opposed to the uniformed guards out front, who wore their weapons visible at their hips. He gestured toward a bench with his head. "Have a seat, sir. FYI, you're being probed. If the boss likes what he sees, on your med scan and in your résumé, he'll let us know. And just between us? Unless you're using, hard-core, he's gonna wanna see you."

Of course, Shane knew that they were already scanning him— that they had been from the moment he stepped into the lobby. If the security head was at his desk, and not on a meal break, he'd already have had Shane's online résumé up and in front of him before Shane had given his name to the men at the desk.

And—jackpot—he'd barely even sat down before Goatee was calling him back.

"Right this way, sir," he said, leading Shane toward the elevators, where he pushed the up button.

This was almost too easy.

"You like working here?" Shane said. It was a question he would have asked, had he really been interviewing for a job.

"I like working," the man replied. "The pay's plenty good. And if you have a taste for . . . additional duties, you can earn a lot more in overtime."

"Oh, yeah?" Shane said, keeping his voice light as the elevator opened. "I was hoping that this facility had opportunities like that. Good to know."

The look that Goatee gave him was speculative, and it was so clear to Shane that the son of a bitch knew *exactly* what went down on the Brite Group's securely guarded floors. Which was where they were going. Goatee had to use a special key to unlock the buttons for the fortieth floor.

Shane jammed his hands into his pockets so as not to be tempted to wrap them around the man's throat as he asked, "What's the name of your boss? Who am I going to be talking to?"

"I'm not sure who's in the office right now," Goatee told him. "Whether it's Mr. Smith or Mr. Jones." At Shane's elevated eyebrows, he smiled tightly. "You learn, fast, not to ask questions with this gig. Just roll with it, and you'll go far."

"Mac."

God damn, but she had a headache. Mac opened her eyes, but the overhead lights were much too bright, so she closed them again.

"*Mac.*"

It was entirely possible that she was going to puke.

"You have to wake up."

Shit, that was Anna Taylor's voice, and in a flash Mac remembered. The gunship, the machine-gun fire, Shane—beautiful, honorable, heroic Shane—running full-bore up the hill as he shouted her name . . .

The little beige room where she and Anna had been strapped down, their clothing gone, wearing only flimsy hospital gowns . . .

Anna had warned her against using her power to break them free, and Mac had ignored her—until it was too late. Until drug-pumps in their arms had gone off.

But—good news!—whatever they'd been injected with hadn't killed them. They were both still alive.

In fact, Mac was feeling extremely alive. In addition to the headache from hell, she was strapped down to the bed again, and this time her restraints were so tight that whenever she moved, pain shot through her wrists and arms.

And that was really saying something, since one of her biggest talents was in suppressing the ability to feel said pain.

"Mac, *please* . . . What did they do to you?"

Mac forced her eyes opened and saw Anna strapped to the bed that they hadn't broken. Whoever had put them back onto the beds was gone—they were again alone in the room.

Anna was looking at her with something akin to horror in her eyes.

Mac looked down and . . . *"Fuck."* She was strapped down, and more. No wonder it hurt like shit every time she moved. Some-one had attached sharp metal hooks to the restraints, and they'd pierced the skin of Mac's wrists, the metal driven down through her flesh and then back out again, oozing blood.

It was pretty diabolically clever—if Mac tried again to pop the restraints, those attached hooks would tear her wrists wide open and cause massive hemorrhaging.

And although she had monster talent when it came to rapid healing, she didn't think that even *she* had the power to keep from bleeding out after an injury as catastrophic as that.

"The girl—she's back in my head," Anna told Mac. "She wants me to make sure you understand that we won't be given another chance. If you try anything else—anything at all—she says . . . They'll kill me."

Mac looked at Anna. "Tell her we want to see Nika. If she brings Nika in here, we'll do whatever she says."

"She wants you to lower your mental shields."

"Tell her I don't have mental shields," Mac said. "My telepathy is worth shit. If she wants to brain-talk with me, it's gotta be all her." She looked over at Anna. "And since when do *you* have telepathic powers? Even power-to-receive isn't something any old fraction can just do unless the sender's only a few feet away."

But Anna wasn't listening—she was clearly communing with the girl—a Greater-Than—who'd apparently chosen to be spokesperson for the Organization, God help them all.

So Mac took the opportunity to examine her restraints. No doubt about it, she'd need Bach-level telekinetic control to move her arms up as she gently unlatched the straps, and then carefully maneuvered those savage-looking hooks out of her flesh.

Yeah. So *that* wasn't going to happen.

It made her ill to look at the wounds, particularly since her skin was looking angry and raw around the metal—like it was the biggest piercing ever.

Years ago, Mac had tried getting herself pierced in a variety of places, to counter her lack of tattoos, but her body always read the metal as an unwanted invasion, and she developed an infection, no matter how hard she worked to keep it clean. And the moment she removed it—the earring or nipple ring—the hole instantly closed and healed.

But until then? It hurt like a bitch on wheels.

And no matter how she did it, removing these hooks was going to make her scream.

But *that* pain would be nothing compared to the anguish of having her heart ripped from her chest as she watched Shane Laughlin die.

Because he *would* come after her. Mac believed that with every fiber of her being—regardless of the fact that he'd damn well know that his doing so would mean almost certain death.

And the really stupid thing was that Mac knew Shane would have volunteered for this rescue mission even if she'd never used her voodoo on him.

He would have done it because it was the right thing to do, because he wanted to help, because he still believed in the power of goodness over evil, because he believed that America still had a chance to rise up from its current cesspool of greed and lack of compassion, to become, once again, a place where truth and justice and the common man mattered.

Mac had woken up this morning and had lain in bed for a while, just listening to Shane breathing, remembering his words from last night.

Can I tell you what it feels like from this end? Because, to me, it feels fucking real. It feels like . . . Connection, to the nth. It feels like joy, like truth. It feels like I belong somewhere again.

She knew exactly what he meant by that, because she felt the exact same thing.

Connection, to the nth. As if she finally belonged.

Almost as if it were real.

Mac had lain there thinking that maybe it would be enough—knowing that she made Shane happy, regardless of how it had started.

She had almost woken him up with a kiss—with a hell of a lot more than a kiss.

But she didn't trust herself around him.

When Shane was with her, she could imagine him talking her into doing it. Giving in. As it was, even while he was asleep, she was actually considering just going ahead and being selfish and making him her permanent boyfriend.

If they both lived at OI, he'd never tire of her. He'd never do what Tim did—because they'd never be apart for that long.

Mac wasn't a saint. She'd had that exact same type of relationship with Justin. What was the big, if she did the same with Shane?

People settled for less-than-perfect all the time, when it came to love.

Still, she hadn't awakened Shane with a good morning greeting of the orgasm variety.

She'd been too afraid.

Instead, she'd just slipped out of her apartment, not even leaving a note, knowing he would follow. Eventually.

But God, what she wouldn't give, now, to have that moment back so she could take a do-over . . .

"She's coming inside," Anna announced. "To talk to you. She says if you harm her—"

"She'll kill us, I get it," Mac said as the door opened, the many locks that sealed it clicking and popping.

"Not us," Anna corrected her. "Me. Apparently, they've discovered that I'm worthless to them."

Before Mac could question her and ask, *But I'm not?*, a young woman stepped into the room. She was heavily pregnant, and carrying quite a few extra pounds along with the baby that was growing in her uterus.

She was also carrying around a massive amount of hatred and fear. It was all Mac could do not to recoil. It was so strong, so dominant that Mac could read nothing more—no compassion, no love, no desire, no pride, no hope—not even any envy or jealousy. Just that relentless fear-driven hatred—almost as if this girl were little more than an animal who'd lived her entire life in a cage, in a really terrible zoo.

"Congratulations," Mac said, mostly to throw her off guard, because it was probably the last thing she'd expected Mac to say. Plus, she knew that reaching out to this girl-thing with true compassion and kindness would only incite her to bite. Figuratively. So she'd keep it shallow. For now.

The girl blinked.

"When's the baby due?" Mac asked.

The girl looked at the hooks in Mac's arms and laughed her disdain. "Like you give a shit."

"Looks like you're close," Mac said. "I've heard having a baby changes women radically. Prepare to be amazed."

"This is my third," the girl said, and the force of her hatred crackled around her. Just as absolutely, Mac knew that she was telling the truth. "I think you need an actual baby for that bullshit to happen. I'm just a breeder."

"Oh, my God," Anna whispered. "You poor thing."

The girl bristled. "I'm neither poor nor a thing."

"But you *are* on the wrong side of this fight, you know," Mac told the girl.

She just laughed. "I'm not the one with chunks of metal in my arms." She glanced over at Anna, and there was something in that look that made the hair stand up on the back of Mac's neck.

So she kept the conversational ball in her court. "Fair enough," Mac said. "So where's Nika? We'd like to see her, make sure that she's safe."

Again, the girl laughed her scorn. "What is it with you people? Do you really believe you have the power to make demands?"

This girl had no idea of the powers that Mac had, but Mac didn't say that aloud. It was better to let her—and whoever was scaring the crap out of her—think they'd bested Mac with their anti-telekinetic restraints. Of course, the fact that they may well *have* bested her with those painfully sharp hooks in her arms was entirely possible.

But it was a fact that Mac was unwilling to admit just yet. "Nika," she said again, pleasantly but firmly. "Now."

"She's not at this facility," the girl said, and yes, she was definitely lying. "But they are planning to move you to the same location. In China, I think—to avoid those annoying science nerds from Über-liar Institute." She looked at Anna. "Not you. Your journey ends here. Don't you just hate when they say that on *American Idol*?" she asked Mac. "After over forty seasons, you'd think they'd find something new to say. But Anna's really does end here. It's kind of ironic, since they went to all that trouble to acquire her." Back to Anna. "I don't really get how you could have a sister who's a fountain, and a friend who's a fountain, and yet be the furthest thing from one yourself. But—good news! You'll be leaving soon, just the way you wanted. Don't worry, it'll be quick. I've heard that bleeding out can actually feel quite pleasant. Compared to some ways of dying."

"Yeah, I don't think so," Mac said. "You don't get to control me—to order me to keep my powers in check—if you're going to kill Anna. She's your leverage. It just doesn't work that way."

"Of course it doesn't," the girl said. "And that's why you get to choose. Who's going to go with you to China, Michelle? Is it going to be Anna or Nika? Inquiring minds want to know."

TWENTY-SEVEN

What if he jokered?

That was among Elliot's biggest concerns, so he'd rigged a device that he strapped onto his chest that would automatically inject him with a fatal dose of a derivative of cyanide, should he experience the telltale symptoms. He set up the computer to administer a continuous jot scan, not just of himself, but of Stephen, too.

And then he sat on the edge of Stephen's bed—something he'd always admonished family members of patients for doing. *Pull up a chair, hold a hand, but don't crowd the patient,* he'd said.

If he survived this, he was never saying that to anyone again.

As he touched Stephen's arm, his shoulder, his chest, he could feel a slight buzzing, but nothing close to their usual connection.

Usual. Huh. Funny how he could spend a lifetime without something, and in the course of a few short days, it could suddenly become *usual.*

He leaned over and saw that Stephen's lips were dry, too dry, so Elliot rummaged in the drawer for the balm that he'd had Robert from Hospitality bring down from Stephen's apartment, figuring the Greater-Than would be most comfortable using his own products and wearing his own socks.

Even though he was unconscious and dying.

And okay, now Elliot was just stalling. Dry lips really wouldn't matter to Stephen if he were dead—which was what he was going to be, and soon, if Elliot didn't do something.

So he did something.

He took the syringe that he'd already prepared, and he tied the elastic tubing that he'd taken from the supply closet around his left bicep.

And he kissed Stephen, softly, sweetly, on the lips. "Love you always," he whispered.

And Elliot injected the oxyclepta di-estraphen directly into his own vein.

"Who's going to go with you to China, Michelle? Is it going to be Anna or Nika . . . ?"

"Nika," Anna said. "It's going to be Nika."

Mac looked over at her, her gaze hard, a nearly palpable warning. "Number two, it's not your choice," she told Anna almost sternly, then turned to the girl, Rayonna. Somehow Anna knew that the pregnant girl's name was Rayonna. "Number one, don't call me Michelle, little girl. You can address me as Dr. Mackenzie."

"The choice is yours," Rayonna said. "Dr. Mackenzie." Her tone was taunting, but Mac had scored a minor psychological victory of sorts.

"I choose them both," Mac said. "They *both* come with me."

"Anna's not worth the jet fuel," Rayonna said. "If you insist on both, then they'll both die."

"That's not going to happen," Mac said. "Nika's too valuable."

"She's powerful, which makes her dangerous," Rayonna said. "They're working, right now, on figuring out a way to put her into stasis—suspended animation. If she lives, they'll do the same for you, Dr. Mackenzie. So you see the need for leverage, as you call it, is only temporary. I'm afraid you won't get to see much of China, since you'll live out the remainder of your life in a stasis tank, fighting off drug-induced nightmares."

Dear God. "Kill her, Mac," Anna said fiercely. "Just kill this bitch now and try to save yourself!"

Something's happening.

Nika looked over at Joseph who was still sitting beside her in the shielded area he'd created in her mind. His head was tilted slightly, as if he were listening to something, hard. He stood up in one swift motion, letting loose a string of words Nika had never heard in that order before. And he didn't apologize afterward.

Instead, he turned to her. *They've activated your drug pump. They're trying to knock you out.*

She stood up, too. *Oh, my God—they did that before—it works so fast. You should go. Now! Before it—*

I'm keeping it from circulating into your bloodstream, Joseph told her. *But I can't do that for very long. Your body will absorb the drug in other ways. We've got about . . . three minutes, tops.*

Oh, God. Do they know? Nika asked him. *That we're planning to . . .* Escape. She still didn't want to think the word, in case they were somehow reading her thoughts.

Joseph didn't sugarcoat his answer. *They might.* He looked into the distance, and she'd learned that meant he was accessing information via his own physical body. *The illegal med scanners are still operational and the power grid's still up. That's not good.*

He turned back to her and gazed down into her eyes. *Nika, if I stay, this drug in your system will impact me. It shouldn't happen that way, I know, but it does.*

Then you should go, she told him, unable to keep her eyes from welling with tears. *You have to go!*

He didn't want to—she could see it on his face, in his eyes.

And God, what if, after he left, he was no longer able to get back to her? What if they moved her, somewhere far away, someplace where their connection couldn't activate?

What if he couldn't find her?

She didn't have to voice her thoughts, Joseph knew exactly what she was thinking, and he pulled her, hard, into his arms and hugged her tightly. *I will find you,* he told her. *Whatever happens, wherever they take you—believe this, Nika: I WILL FIND YOU.*

I do believe you. Nika wrapped her arms around him, hugging him back just as tightly. And she knew they weren't really hugging. Their physical selves were in two different places. But he felt solid and real as he rested his cheek against the top of her head.

And she wanted this moment—this somehow dangerously dizzying feeling of closeness and belonging and deeply abiding trust—never to end.

I'm so sorry, he said. *I promised I'd stay with you and . . . What the hell?*

Joseph pulled away from her, enough to look down at her with an expression of total surprise, his hands still on her shoulders. "What are you doing?" She saw and heard him so clearly, it was as if he'd spoken aloud.

"I'm not doing anything," she answered.

"Oh, no," he said. "Nika, you are. You have access to significantly more of your power right now. I can feel it. It's . . . unreal . . ."

"But it's good, right?" she asked him, gazing up at him.

Joseph smiled, and her heart leaped. "Sweetheart, it's fantastic. I don't know what you're doing, but . . . Keep doing it, for as long as you can."

Nika nodded as she looked up at him, but his smile faded as he swayed slightly.

"Neek," he started and she knew that, even though she didn't feel it yet, the drug was starting to affect him.

"Go," she told him, forcing herself not to cry. She lifted her chin. "I'll be okay."

Joseph touched her hair, her cheek, his fingers warm against her face. "I'll see you soon," he promised, and with a shimmer of light, he disappeared.

———

The pregnant girl just laughed at Anna's vehement request for Mac to wreak havoc, and Mac knew, without a doubt, that any attempt she made to appeal to the girl's humanity was going to fail.

And as the girl turned back to Mac and said again, "Anna or

Nika?" Adding, "And if you say *both* again, I'll open the door, and Cristopher will come in and kill this one right here and now." She smiled tightly. "Of course, if you say *Nika* he'll do the same. And if you say *Anna,* someone else will go into Nika's room and—"

Anna was ready to die. Mac could feel the intense emotion radiating off of her, along with waves of her love for her little sister.

Little sister . . .

"How about if I don't say *both,* but I also don't pick Anna *or* Nika?" Mac said. "How about, instead, I let you know a little something about my so-called worthless friend here? What if I told you that Nika's not Anna's sister." She paused for dramatic effect. "Nika is Anna's daughter."

Anna made a sound of surprise, but she was a smart young woman, and she understood why Mac should lie like that—that it would buy them at least nine months of time—because she added, "It's true. I was . . . raped when I was, um, *twelve* and my mother claimed Nika as her own."

Mac put it into plain English, in the event that the pregnant girl—ironically—couldn't put two and two together. "If Anna's had one child as special as Nika, it's likely that she'll have another, even though she herself is not a fountain." She tried not to choke on the word, it was so repugnant.

But the girl got it. The look on her face was one of pure horror and disgust. "You *want* to be a breeder? I'd rather be dead!"

She started toward Anna with such burning hatred in her eyes, that Anna said, "Mac?"

But the door opened, and a voice called out, sharply, "Rayonna!"

The girl stopped, but she stood there for a moment, just staring at Anna, her chest heaving with each ragged breath she took. And now the anguish that was pouring forth from her was so intense, Mac had to cling to the bed, for fear of pulling herself free and tearing the hooks from her wrists.

"Rayonna."

"You poor thing," she whispered to Anna, before she turned and hurried out of the room.

It was only then, as the man closed the door behind her, that Mac turned to look at him.

"You!" Anna breathed. She turned to Mac. "It's the man from Nika's dream!"

He was hideously scarred, but even worse, his emotional grid was similar to that of Devon Caine. With one exception. He knew *exactly* what it was that he did.

He was evil, incarnate, and he made Mac's skin crawl.

"So you wish to be one of our breeders?" he asked Anna in his oddly slurred speech. "We can certainly arrange that—consider it done."

And he took what looked like a hand control out of the pocket of his bloodstained lab coat and pressed a button.

"Whoa!" Anna said, as her hospital bed adjusted, releasing her legs from their restraints but then strapping her feet down into what looked like OB-GYN examination stirrups, as her knees were pushed up . . .

"Wait," Mac said. "You need to scan her. Find out when she's ovulating." She looked at Anna. She had been certain that the time that she'd bought them included a week—or more—of medical tests.

"That's not the way we do it here," the scar-faced man said with a grimace that was meant to be a smile.

———

Bach opened his eyes to find himself in the back of an OI van, parked just down the street from the Organization's Washington Street building.

For a moment, he was confused. He'd been having an impossibly vivid dream, in which beautiful Anna Taylor had been laughing and naked and pulling him down onto the bed in the room where he'd slept for most of his childhood. She'd kissed him and . . .

Ho-kay. *That* had been extremely realistic, but it was still just a dream, induced by the powerful drug that had been shot through Nika's system.

And it wasn't even *his* dream—it was a memory of the dream Anna had had—the one that he'd stood there watching, as if his feet had been glued to the floor.

Still he had to exhale hard as he sat up, which scared the hell out of Charlie, who'd been assigned to feed information to his seemingly unconscious form.

"Holy shit," Charlie said, quickly adding, "sir! Is everything all right?"

Bach had no idea how much time had passed, so he checked the clock on the computer screen. He hadn't been trapped in that dream for too long, thank God. "Nika's been drugged—I think they're planning on moving her. I had to get out—it was affecting me and . . . I need a current sit-rep," he ordered.

"The med scanners and power grid are both still operational," Charlie reported. "There's been no change."

"Any luck locating Mac and Anna?"

Charlie shook his head, no. "We only know they were brought to the Washington Street building—we tracked the helicopter to their roof port—it's still there."

"Tell Analysis to keep searching," Bach ordered. "Give me something good here, Charlie. Any word from Shane Laughlin?"

"None, sir," Charlie said. "But he *is* inside. Last report has him in the elevator, which is *very* good and—holy shit! Sir, apologies, you were looking a little green, so I just checked your jot scan? And you're integrating at eighty-one percent."

What?

Bach scrambled to look at the computer over Charlie's shoulder and *holy shit* was right. He'd spiked—and was continuing to hang there at that higher level.

"With all due respect, sir," Charlie said, "that's nine percent higher than your usual seventy-two. That's a *massive* increase. I don't think I've ever heard of anyone—*ever*—clocking in above seventy-eight." He turned and looked at Bach, his eyes wide. "What exactly did you do?"

"We'll worry about that later," Bach said, even though he suspected he knew. What he'd *done* was Anna Taylor—if only in his drug-induced dreams. Imagine that. Mac and Diaz were right about sex raising one's integration levels. "Right now, I'm going to see if I can use it—to make telepathic contact with either Anna or Mac." He had no idea if he was close enough to either of them, but he was going to try. "Do me a favor, Charlie, and put in a call to Elliot. I want him to know what's going on."

"I can't reach him, sir," Charlie said. "I've been trying for a while. I keep getting sent to his voice mail." He lowered his voice slightly as he turned to face Bach. "His message says that he's currently in with Stephen Diaz. I suspect, sir, that that's not good news."

———————

Stephen was on fire.

He'd been floating, drifting, farther and farther from anything solid or recognizable, but now the pain was back and he couldn't control it.

Still, it was better than the slow fade into nothing, than the waves of ennui and the ripples of oblivion that hadn't quite filled him because nothing could or would fill him anymore.

But now the pain could and did, and he didn't fight it, but he *did* fight. To stay. To be.

To live.

And when he opened his eyes, he saw flashes of lightning instead of gray. And with each beat of his beleaguered heart, he remembered all that he was and all he stood to lose.

And as Stephen fought harder and harder to stay, he realized that he was no longer alone. He turned and saw Elliot. And he knew—instantaneously—what Elliot had done.

And Stephen's grief and regret and burning sense of loss dwarfed the spears of pain that wracked him. But when Elliot reached out, his touch was powerful enough not just to soothe but also to heal.

Still, Stephen had to ask him, *Why?*

Elliot's smile was beautiful, his voice as gentle as a kiss. *You're needed.*

Stephen's heart broke. *And you're not?*

I'm still here, Elliot said, even though they both knew that what he'd done would surely kill him.

And Stephen realized that he hadn't changed the future after all. He'd merely delayed the inevitable.

———

The elevator opened with a *ding,* and Goatee took his key from the control panel, leading Shane onto the fortieth floor of the Organization's Washington Street building, where they believed that Nika, Anna, and Mac were all being held prisoner.

There was another security checkpoint right in the elevator lobby on that floor, manned, literally, by seven guards—all male, and all wearing the pseudo-cop blue uniform, all with weapons at their hips. As they wanded and then patted Shane down, he had quite a few opportunities to relieve several of them of their fire-arms, but he opted not to. He wanted to see just how much closer he could get to their security control room before he got this party started.

Goatee led him—conveniently—toward his target destination, through halls that were mostly empty. There were offices and what looked like lounges with their doors hanging open, and Shane spotted a man sitting behind a desk, on the phone, wearing the same lousy body armor that the corporate rulers had decided— over twenty years ago—was good enough for U.S. troops in com-bat zones.

There wasn't a Navy SEAL alive who hadn't opted to buy his own higher-quality gear—or who didn't know every chink in the common armor that was used worldwide. There was quite a long list of ways to kill a soldier wearing cheap protection—particularly if he or she felt invincible.

But right now, Goatee and Shane had reached a part of the hallway where most of the doors they passed were closed, and spaced farther apart. "Looks kind of like a hotel," he commented.

"It kind of is," Goatee helpfully told him. "The Brite Group is an international corporation—lotta visitors from overseas who need super-secure living quarters while they're in the U.S. We're also occasionally asked to take back-to-back shifts—when a shipment is being prepped. So we're sometimes housed here as well. It's pretty jam."

The hall they were in ended in a T—and Shane knew the control room was to the right. When Goatee started to lead him left, Shane stopped him.

"Before I go in to talk to Mr. Smith or Mr. Jones, I'd love to hit the nearest head." Which was also down to the right, according to the floor plans Shane had memorized.

But okay, that was confusion on Goatee's none-too-intelligent face—confusion and alarm—and Shane quickly translated his Navy-speak into plain English. "Bathroom," he said. "The head is a bathroom aboard a ship. I'd like to use the bathroom?"

Goatee laughed his relief. "Well, fuck it, brohms, glad you said so! I'm thinking *hit the nearest head*—which has gotta be mine, what what?" He laughed as he opened his jacket to completely reveal the weapon holstered beneath his left arm. It was strapped in with a single slender strip of Velcro. "I came *this close*"—he held up his right hand to measure out a half an inch between his thumb and forefinger—"to drawing on you."

The hall was empty, in all three directions, and Shane couldn't see any cameras—but there *had* to be cameras, unless there purposely *weren't* cameras for the sake of the anonymity of their overseas guests. He suspected that they were simply concealed.

Still, he'd lived long enough to recognize a truly beautiful gift when he was handed one.

So he reached out and helped himself to Goatee's SIG Sauer, and jammed the barrel into the space between the ill-fitting top and bottom of the guard's cheap body armor before his shit-eating grin had even faded from his pasty-ass face.

"Stay silent and do exactly what I say," Shane told the man, as he hustled him down the hallway that led to the right, "and I won't pull the trigger. You do know, don't you? That if I angle this right, the bullet'll get trapped by the body armor and bounce around— turn your pelvic area into total hamburger. It's something of a design defect."

Goatee squeaked his assent, and Shane moved their pace into triple time, even as, from down at the far end of the hallway, behind them, there came a shout, "Hey!" And then a classic, "Freeze, motherfucker!"

Shane didn't freeze. In fact, he booked it even faster.

———

Anna tried to tell herself that this wasn't about her. This had nothing to do with her—it was all about Mac and the way adrenaline would release more hormones into her blood, which the Organization would use to make Destiny.

It was about money, about greed, and yeah, okay, as the man with the scars opened his filthy lab coat and unfastened his pants, Anna knew that it was at least a *little* bit about her, because she could see from the glint in his eyes that he was going to enjoy hurting her.

"Don't do this," Mac was saying. "Don't you do this! Anna, shit, I am *so* sorry! Hey, you! Hey! *Hey!* Look at *me.*"

And it was beyond bizarre, because something happened. Something strange took place when the man *did* turn and look over at Mac. There was a shift in his body language. He stood a little taller, breathed a little differently, and seemed completely unable to look away.

Anna didn't know what Mac had done to him—but it was clear she'd done something.

"That's right," Mac said. "You don't want her. You don't need her. You only want me."

———

Shane almost made it to the control room. Almost.

And it was a damn good thing that he wasn't moving faster, because a security team of a half a dozen blue-uniformed men came pouring out of the very door he was heading for.

So instead he barreled his way into not the men's head, but the ladies', dragging Goatee with him and locking the door behind them—throwing both bolts.

It was a single-seater with a pristine sink and a toilet that no doubt got very little use. Not a lot of women working here—that was for sure.

Shane did a quick double-check of the map in his head as he gave Goatee a little stop-sniveling tap with the butt of the man's own handgun. He then dragged the unconscious guard by the feet to the opposite wall, because this one—to the immediate left of the toilet—was shared by the control room.

And when going in through the door was not a possibility— due to the fact that the team of guards were now banging on *this* door, demanding he come out with his hands up—that didn't mean the game was over. It just meant it was time to get creative.

Extra creative, since he had only twelve sticks of C4-flavored "gum" and two blasting caps.

There was a saying in the SEAL teams that Magic Kozinski had loved to recite in times of duress: *When a door shuts, a window opens. And if the window shuts, then it's time to blow a hole through the fucking wall.*

Shane rifled through Goatee's pockets, transferring several magazines of ammo into his own pants, and coming up with a dangerous little switchblade that the man had clearly been trying to work free during their race down the hall.

Wallet, ballpoint pen, pack of cigarettes, cell phone—Shane confiscated it all. He was traveling so light, it couldn't hurt. Plus, there was no telling what he'd need.

He got to work, slipping the detcord from his neck, using Goatee's knife to cut the little angel free, and sacrificing half of his explosives to create a Shane-sized hole, down close to the baseboard of the wall.

The fuse didn't have to be very long—there was nowhere to run for cover. But Shane did pull Goatee with his body armor in front of him as he lit the thing and hunkered down behind the toilet.

He checked the SIG Sauer, making sure that the magazine was full as he waited for the pop . . .

And waited, and waited . . .

It was taking too fucking long—impossibly long—but he was still careful as he peeked around the toilet . . .

To see . . .

The blasting cap was faulty. Had to be.

But if he used the second cap he'd brought for this, he'd have nothing to use to blow up the scanners and the power source.

So he cut another length of detcord and tried again with the same cap.

The third time was just an exercise in thoroughness—something useful for his hands to do as he thought about—really thought about—the potential ramifications of his Plan B.

Still, he didn't need to be a Greater-Than with powers to see through walls to know that the six guards in the hall outside the ladies' room had grown into a much larger number.

If he was going out through that door, he needed to be bullet-proof.

So when the blasting cap failed for the third time, Shane didn't hesitate.

He used the pen that he'd taken from Goatee, and he drew an arrow and wrote right on the wall that the bathroom shared with the security control room, *This way to the people you want to kill and the equipment you want to destroy.*

Just in case he jokered.

And then—with the exact same sense of purpose that he'd felt the first time he'd jumped out of a plane—Shane took one of the Epi Pens filled with Destiny from his pocket, opened the plastic, and drove it hard into his leg.

———

Nika felt Joseph reaching out to her, checking in, but she was still too woozy and he retreated immediately.

She heard some kind of alarm going off, and she wished that he'd stayed long enough for her to tell him about it, although, on second thought, it was possible she was imagining the sound. "Can anyone else hear that?" she asked the other girls, but the words came out all smooshed together and no one could understand her.

She didn't think they heard it, though, because no one was crying, and it didn't take much to set them off.

Except, then the door opened, and the crying started, but it wasn't the scar-faced man—instead it was the unhappy old woman. And she came directly over to Nika's bed, but then she stopped when she saw that Nika was looking back at her.

And she frowned and took out a fancy-looking cell phone. Whoever she called must've picked up right away, because she said, "And how am I supposed to get her ready to travel when the drug hasn't fully taken effect?"

Travel?

"And I'm telling you she's *not* fully unconscious—she's right here, blinking at me. For all I know, she's dangerous," the woman said. "Maybe she's built up a resistance. Just give her another squirt . . ."

No, *no*—if they gave her another dose of this sedative, it would be hours before Joseph could join her again. And she had to reach out to him now, to tell him they were getting her ready to *travel*.

So Nika closed her eyes and let her head loll back, even as she searched for him. *Joseph! They're going to move me!*

"Oh, wait, that's better now," the woman said. "Although why don't you give her another squirt anyway—just to be safe?"

As the man with the horrible scar began shuffling his way over to Mac, Anna closed her eyes, and with all of her might, she attempted the impossible. *Joe, please, if you're out there and you can hear me, please,* please *help us!*

For a moment, she thought she felt him, felt the familiar warmth, the slight bump and polite hesitation before he entered her mind. But then it was gone, and she was left only with the sense that he was too far away. Because she was only a fraction, he needed to be closer to establish that kind of intimate telepathic contact.

Across the room, Mac was saying, "That's right. Come on over here. Oh, yeah, right here . . ."

Somehow she was drawing the man toward her and away from Anna, and she couldn't let her do that. "Mac, don't. It's not going to change—"

"Anna, be *silent*." Mac smiled at the man. "I don't bite. Unless you want me to . . ."

———

"It's time to go into the building." Bach was done waiting.

His integration spike may have been an anomaly—but it wasn't truly a spike, either. Yes, he'd shot up, fast, and yes, his power was beginning to degrade, but that was happening slowly.

And while Bach would have liked to spend a day—or even just an hour—in the lab, testing his new limitations and abilities, it was go time.

Alarms were going off in the Washington Street building, yet the scanners and their source of power were still strong.

It seemed obvious that Shane Laughlin had tried—and failed.

Because the scanners were still running, the Organization would know—immediately—that the team from OI was coming in. So be it.

Jackie and her group of Thirties and Forties were ready but grim about the outcome as they headed toward the building. In a flash of inanity, as Bach walked with them, he wondered what they'd do if he suddenly sharply clapped his hands twice to get their attention, and then announced that they should pair up— quickly now—and find a nearby public restroom in which to engage in a little pre-battle coitus—in order to boost their integration levels.

How could he have been so wrong?

Of course, the answer came to him immediately. Because he'd wanted, desperately, to be wrong. Because, for decades now, he'd wanted no one but Annie. And since Annie was dead . . . *No one* had been his chosen companion.

But now, Anna—this woman who was so different in appearance from Annie, yet who shared a similar name and a beautifully similar spark of joy and hope and glorious *life*—had fallen into his world.

Bach's enhanced powers allowed him to feel her in that building, not as clearly as he felt her powerful little sister, but enough to allow him to find exactly where the Organization was holding her.

"Brian, Katie, Laurel, Frank, Rashid—your goal is to get into that security control room and take out those scanners," Jackie reminded her team. "Until that happens, each and every one of us is wearing a great big target on our backs. They'll know where we are, and where we're going."

As she continued, rattling off her team-members' names and missions—some were assigned to find Mac and Anna, some to try to locate Shane, with the majority seeking out Nika—Charlie, who was walking next to Bach, leaned close to say, "Sir, I think you should try, once more, before you go inside, to connect with Nika."

It was a smart idea. So Bach reached out and found . . .

A looming wall of darkness. A frightening swirl of nightmares and unconscious fears as Nika fought—as she continued to fight—to stay present.

But she was fading fast. Too fast. Plus, she was being moved. And Bach knew, with a certainty that made him feel as if he had some prescient powers that were awakening, that if they didn't move faster, the Organization was going to succeed in spiriting Nika away.

And he also knew he had to do it. He had to attempt to enter Nika's mind and fight beside her—and risk also being taken down by the sedatives she'd been given.

This meant he had to stay behind as he'd originally planned, which was a far harder thing to do than he'd anticipated.

"Go," he ordered Jackie. "Move! *Now!*"

And she led the team toward the building at a run.

"Charlie, get me back to the van," Bach commanded as he closed his eyes and plunged into Nika's nightmare.

Nika was lost.

She could hear Joseph calling her—or maybe that was just part of her bad dream. She could hear him, but she couldn't reach him—she'd never reach him again.

She could feel herself moving—she was being rolled down the hall, faster and faster, and she couldn't do anything to stop it.

Nikaaahhh . . . Joseph's voice was coming from farther away now. *Nikaaahhh . . .*

It was amazing.

The rush was incredible.

It roared through Shane's veins, spreading its power throughout his entire body, turning him into something . . . else. Something . . .

Greater-than.

He could feel the power tingling in his fingers and his toes, even in the tip of his dick, and he immediately recognized how dangerous this drug was—because he already wanted more. He didn't want this feeling—this power—ever to end.

He could feel his body using the drug to make him stronger, healthier—to erase any fatigue he was feeling and to heal the scrapes and bruises he'd gotten when Mac went all Rambo on the Organization's drug lab.

He had known there were no guarantees, when taking Destiny, as to what his skills and talents would be. But he was pretty sure one of his abilities involved both sex and Mac. Of course, maybe the drug heightened the effect her voodoo had on him—because he could sense her nearby.

Wherever she was being held, it wasn't far from this bathroom. He was pretty sure all he'd have to do was follow the tug in his groin and he'd find her.

Which was good to know.

Because his plan, post blowing the shit out of the scanners and the power supply, involved him freeing her and taking her home to make love to her for one last time before letting Elliot stop his heart.

But right now, Shane had to get into that control room. And the best way to do that was still to go through that wall. He focused on putting a hole into the damn thing.

And the toilet flushed.

Okay, great.

Apparently, one of his new talents was an ability to flush a toilet without touching the handle.

Way to go.

Shane concentrated again, closing his eyes and . . .

Whatever he'd done, Goatee started thrashing and moaning, which seemed kind of odd, until Shane picked up the handgun, intending to tap him on the head again.

But he dropped the damn thing, because it burned his hand. Jesus, it was *hot*.

And when he turned Goatee over, he saw that the man was wearing a gold necklace that had burned a chain-print pattern into his skin. It was red and raw and completely circled his scrawny pale neck.

But okay. That was good—that was *good*. Shane could work with this talent—the ability to heat metal. He just needed to learn how to focus.

He kept his eyes open this time, staring at the blasting cap he'd rigged against the wall, even as he worked to free Goatee from his jacket.

And he let it all heat.

Hotter. And hotter. And . . .

And his little bomb went off, not with a pop, but with a boom and a spray of plaster and chunks of concrete.

Shane used Goatee's jacket as a makeshift hot-mitt as he grabbed the SIG Sauer and dove for the hole in the wall.

TWENTY-EIGHT

Bach couldn't find Nika.

She'd been caught in the swirling chaos of nightmares and fear that was a side effect of the sedative she'd been given.

He could hear her—as if from a distance—calling to him. And it was breaking his heart that he couldn't reach her. But in truth, he was afraid of that total lack of control.

He was managing—somehow—to cling to the periphery of her mind, and thus escape most of the numbing and confusion-creating sensation. But of course he wouldn't find her there. He didn't stand a chance of finding her unless he let go.

Charlie—good man—had gotten him back to the van and was giving him regular reports both from Analysis and from the team that had entered the building.

"Power and scanners still aren't out," he told Bach in a loud clear voice. "Jackie reports they've made it past the guards in the lobby, but their elevators have been stopped, which they expected. The stairs are impenetrable, so they're continuing up to the forti-eth floor via the elevator shafts."

Using that route meant it would take them much too long to get there.

Bach knew that, any minute, Nika was going to be put on a private service elevator and taken down to the basement, where she'd be spirited out via tunnel.

So he took his fear and he swallowed it.

And he dove, headfirst into the maelstrom, calling Nika's name.

———

The man with the scar had forgotten completely about Anna, as Mac hit him again with a wave of her power.

As he shuffled closer and closer, she saw what she'd done to him, and she worked it, overtime, to hide her revulsion and her fear.

It couldn't just be sex that he wanted from her—it had to be more. It had to be powerful—it had to dominate everything he wanted and needed in his nasty little world. And he had to believe—completely—that whatever he was feeling, she was feeling it, too.

So Mac closed her eyes and thought of Shane—of the way her heart warmed when he smiled at her, at the comfort she felt with his arms around her, of the pleasure she got just from his presence in the room . . .

She loved him. God help her, she truly *loved* him. And she opened her eyes and made herself believe that this was Shane coming toward her, wearing some hideous Halloween mask.

And the man smiled back at her—at least she thought it was a smile.

If this didn't work? It was really going to suck.

———

Shane's aim had never been so true.

He'd always been good at clearing a room filled with bad guys. He had a solid sixth sense when it came to anticipating movement and eliminating the threat.

But today he hadn't wasted a single bullet as he rolled across the security control room and secured the door.

He'd taken the entire room in, in a single glance—the computers that ran the banks of scanners, the power source and backup generators, the rows of monitors showing not just video from the halls and public areas, but from the rooms where the prisoners were held, as well.

Which was why he didn't hesitate to drill each of the five men in that room with five perfect head shots. There was no question. They knew exactly what the Brite Group was, and what they did there.

So Shane ended them, without blinking.

He could see from the monitors that a small crowd had gathered outside of the ladies' room door—and from the looks of things, the big behemoth with the shaved head was in charge. The man looked formidable and may actually have had muscle beneath his layers of body fat. But like most rent-a-cops, he was all about the appearance and the swagger. He apparently hadn't done the math and put together the proximity of the bathroom to the security control room until he heard the telltale gunfire.

Now he'd stomped over and was glaring up into the camera that was positioned outside of the control room's locked door.

Shane scanned the other monitors, searching for Mac, Anna, and Nika, but there were too many rows of video screens, and the pictures flashed and changed constantly, dizzyingly.

So he focused on the scanners as he pulled the remaining C4 from his pocket—but then realized he didn't need it. With his new power to heat metal, he could simply fry the wires in all of the computer motherboards.

He let loose a blast and the astringent smell of melting electrical circuits quickly filled the air, even as he considered the best way to take out the power supply.

For that, he *did* use his remaining C4, strategically placed, although—damn—his second blasting cap had been blown to hell back in the bathroom. Still, with his ability to super-heat metal he could rig something makeshift, unless . . .

He took cover and focused and . . .

Nothing.

Although, one by one, the monitors were starting to flicker and go out, as their wiring overheated.

It was then, right before the picture vanished with a pop, that Shane saw her.

Mac. Strapped to a hospital bed and looking up at a misshapen man who approached her, his intention clear since he held himself in one hand, and a deadly looking blade in the other.

But the monitor went dark, even as Shane leapt toward the controls. "No! God damn it, *no*! *Mac!*"

But all of the computers were smoking now and the last of the monitors flickered and went out.

It was then that the C4 exploded, throwing Shane up and back. As the power went out and the electrical outlets in the room sparked and flared, he hit the wall with a crash.

———

The glint of the knife that the scar-faced man was holding in his right hand was Mac's first clue that this wasn't going down the way she'd hoped and planned.

Still, maybe it was a security thing for him, so she sent him another blast of love and sincerity.

"Baby, please," she said. "I know you're not supposed to, but I wish you'd free my hands, my arms, because I just want to hold you."

It was then that he laughed, and he stabbed the blade of his knife, hard, into the bed between her legs, so that it quivered there. "You think I don't know what you're doing?" he asked in that horribly odd voice. "You think I don't know that you're mind-controlling me?"

"But I'm not," she said, except her voice sounded breathless— and not in a *wow, I can't wait til you fuck me* way. "Baby, I'm not . . ."

"FYI," he said, as the lights around them flickered and then went out. "It doesn't work for me unless you scream." The emergency lights came on, casting the room in an even more artificial glow, and revealed the fact that the scar-faced man was smiling. It was awful. "Or bleed."

———

Shane was back on his feet immediately as the emergency lighting system clicked on, bathing the smoke-filled room in a dim bluish light.

He could hear the shouts of the Organization's security guards in the hallway, but fuck that. Mac was in peril, and he was going after her.

He used Goatee's jacket to shield his hands as he picked up the handgun, and he opened the door.

The behemoth was still standing right there, his surprise at seeing Shane written all over his ugly face. He raised his sidearm, and if he'd been any faster, Shane would have been dead. As it was, he just had time to send out a blast of heat, which made the man drop his weapon. In fact, most of them did, but a few got some shots off, even as Shane took out as many as he could before they ran away.

He felt the slap of a bullet graze his shoulder before he slammed the door shut again, and the thing was so fucking hot it practically cauterized the wound even as it made it.

Which, unfortunately, didn't mean it didn't bleed. It just didn't bleed as much.

So much for being bulletproof.

Still, he had to get to Mac. But how? Apparently his metal-heating talent didn't work outside of the room he was in—or all the guards would have already dropped their hardware before he'd hit the hallway.

Okay. Think. Or shit—experiment. What else could he do?

There was something called dematerialization, which would allow someone with that power to walk through walls. He could feel Mac—she wasn't that far away. Please, God, he just wanted to get to her, to help her. But again, he had to focus. And picture the floor plan in his mind. It would be a problem to walk through a wall and find himself in an elevator shaft.

He'd start out relatively easy and try to move back into the bathroom.

Shane took a deep breath and started to walk—and slammed, hard, face-first into the wall.

Son-of-a-bitch. Add dematerializing to the no-can-do list with bulletproof. And color him a moron for not checking first with, oh, say, his hand? But Jesus, he just wanted to get to Mac . . .

The smoke was getting thick, so Shane went back through the hole he'd made, into the bathroom where Goatee was still on the floor.

Maybe he could do that telepathic thing that Nika had done with Bach—leaping into his body and pushing his conscious mind aside. Possession, they'd called it.

Maybe he could possess Goatee, and walk himself out of here as a prisoner. Except, if he was going to possess someone else, why not go big?

Shane remembered the very brief audio report he'd accessed that detailed what Nika had said she'd done to leap into Dr. Bach's head. She'd used her anger to channel her power, and had focused on reaching out to Bach.

As far as recipes went, it was pretty vague. But if there was one thing Shane had plenty of right now—it was anger. So he closed his eyes and he pictured Mac.

And he pictured the man who'd been closing in on her with that knife.

———

"You really think I'd be stupid enough to take those hooks from your arms?" the scar-faced man asked Mac.

"Love is a funny thing," she said, then gave him a blast of her voodoo so extreme, it should have affected him in the same way that it had with Shane in the car, in the OI parking lot. It should have disarmed him, so to speak, but he just laughed.

Mac knew that as long as those restraints were on her arms, there was nothing she could do to stop him. Still, she couldn't quit. She couldn't stop trying, sending out wave after wave of her power.

Although, as he pulled his knife free from the bed and used it to cut her, just a thin line on the inside of her thigh, she wished for the first time in her life that she'd spent more time in training, in the telekinetics lab doing those freaking jigsaw puzzles. If she'd harnessed her telekinesis, if she'd learned to hone it and control it, then maybe she could have taken his knife from him and used it to slash his own throat. Maybe she could have picked him up and thrown him back against the wall with enough force to break his neck, without risking the wild randomness of her power accidentally yanking off those restraints and tearing open her wrists.

He dug deeper with his blade, and she made a sound of pain, despite her intention not to. She turned it into a curse. "Fuck you!"

"Mac!" Anna said, as across the room she started to cry.

"Look away, Anna," Mac told her as the monster used his remote control to adjust Mac's bed. "Turn your head. Don't watch this. And for God's sake, don't cry. He likes it when you cry. Think about Bach, okay? He's coming to get you—I know he is. He loves you—did you know that?"

"What?"

"Yeah, it kinda took him by surprise, too. He's pretty freaked. But he's the maestro—he's pretty smart. He'll figure it out."

"Do I bore you?" Scarface asked as her knees went up in the air, and her feet went back toward her butt.

Mac tried to keep her knees together—to no avail. So she looked at him as if she'd forgotten he was standing there. "Whoa, dude, yeah, I guess you kinda do."

She knew, in immediate hindsight, that that was too much, that she'd pushed him too far. Because he grabbed the knife and she knew that he was going to gut her with it. And she also knew she had to try to disarm him, which was going to kill her anyway because of those damn hooks, when suddenly he dropped the knife, and it clattered to the floor—and please, sweet Jesus, let him be having a massive stroke . . . Which he may well have been having, because he doubled over and then straightened and then doubled and doubled some more.

"Are *you* doing that?" Anna asked her.

Mac shook her head. "No."

"I am," Scarface said as he went back and forth a few more times. "I'm doing it. It's me, Mac. Shane." He coughed then, as if emptying his lungs of water or a great deal of smoke.

What? Mac was staring—she knew she was. But it couldn't be Shane. How could it possibly be . . . ?

"Don't play games," she all but spat at him. "Fuck you—*fuck you!*"

But the man took that remote out of the pocket of his lab coat and pushed the button that would bring her legs back down, even as he used his left hand to fumble himself back into his pants.

He turned and got a glimpse of Anna, and he quickly turned away. "Sorry, Anna," he said, coughing again, as he searched for the button that would put her legs back down, so that she, too, would no longer be lying there, flapping in the breeze, as if ready for a doctor's examination.

It was then he caught sight of Mac's arms. "Holy shit, what did they do to you?"

"Don't you touch me!" she warned him. This was *impossible.* Shane wasn't a Greater-Than. How could he have done this? It didn't make sense . . .

"I kind of have to," he told her, "if I'm going to get those hooks out. God *damn* them!" Again with the wracking cough.

Enough was enough. "Okay," Mac said, trying not to cry, certain she was calling this bastard's bluff. "Get the hooks out, asshole. *Do* it. Now."

"I get why you don't believe it's me," he said, matter-of-factly—and so like Shane that she almost broke down. "I admit I'm looking a little bit worse for wear, but . . . It *is* me, Michelle. I need to work fast, because Cristopher—did you know this asshole's name is Cristopher, without an H? He wants his wreck of a body back, pretty freaking badly, and I'm new at this so . . ." He carefully disconnected the hook that was in her left arm from the restraint that held her, and then sprang the restraint.

"Holy shit," she said. He was actually setting her free. "How . . . is this even possible?"

"Yeah, this is the part where you're going to be pissed at me," he said glancing up to look at her in a move that was totally Shane-like, except for the fact that he coughed again—and he was wearing Scarface's ugly-ass face. "After you went missing, I kind of volunteered for the rescue mission. But I didn't have an exit strategy, so I got some Destiny from Elliot, and I used it. To help, you know, save the world?"

"What?" Mac was barely aware of the fact that both of her arms were free from the bed—but still impaled by those awful hooks—as he added, "Smiley face emoticon?" and shot her a very strange version of that same toothy grin he'd given her that first night they'd met.

It was Shane—it was really Shane! She grabbed him by the front of Scarface's lab coat as he freed her legs. "What have you done? You could have jokered. My God, Shane, Destiny is horribly addictive!"

He nodded. "Yeah, well, I'm a former SEAL."

"What does *that* mean?"

"I don't know," he confessed, as he pulled away from her, to shuffle over toward Anna's bed, where he unfastened her restraints, too. He helped her down from the bed, then came back toward Mac. "I guess I thought it might sound more plausible and, I don't know, acceptable to you than the truth."

"Which is . . . ?"

"That I love you madly."

Oh, God! "But there's no cure! Death. Death's the cure." She was going to be sick.

"That depends on which addiction you're talking about," he told her, stifling another cough, as he examined the hooks that still pierced her arms. "The drug? Yeah, there's a cure. Elliot found one. Well, it's more like *maybe* a cure, but I'm optimistic. As for you? I'm pretty sure it's going to be death that ends *that* addiction." He looked into her eyes. "Hold on to me tight, honey, because this is going to fucking hurt."

———

Anna knew that Shane was right. It had to have hurt like hell.

But as she hovered nearby, hoping he wouldn't actually need

her help, he removed the hooks from Mac's arms. And then he covered the wounds with his hands until her bleeding slowed.

His breathing was sounding more and more labored, and his coughing was worsening, and when Mac could finally again speak, she looked up at him and asked, "Where are you?"

Shane had to know that she meant where was his physical form, while he was here in possession of this man named Cristopher.

But he just shook Cristopher's head as he handed Mac the man's huge knife, handle first, as his coughing continued to wrack him. "He's going to be back soon. I'm losing control. You've got to kill me."

Mac nodded, but Anna could see that she didn't want to do it—drive a knife into the body of her lover? Even if it wasn't actually her lover's body, it was still Shane who was in there. "You've got to get out of him, first."

"I will," he said, between his coughs. "But not until after you do it. I'm not going to let him have control until I know he's dying."

"But you don't know how it works," she shot back hotly. "What if once he starts to die, you *can't* get out?"

He touched her face so gently with one of those big misshapen hands. "Please, Mac. There's always a *what if*. What if I leave and he kills you both? You said it yourself. There's a chance that I'm already dead."

"But *you* said you're optimistic!"

"I am," he said, struggling to breathe. "Always."

"What if you stay in Cristopher's body," Anna suggested, "and take us to where they're holding Nika? Do you have access to his thoughts—can we find her that way?"

"I don't," Shane admitted. "At least not when he isn't trying to wrestle me to the ground to take his body back. I think you can understand why I'm not interested in inviting him to do that." He coughed again. "It's a great idea though—my taking you out of here, but I really am on the verge of losing control."

"You're losing control because you're choking," Mac told him fiercely. "There's a fire—it's nearby—I can smell the smoke. Don't make me have to search for you!"

Shane shook his head. "Please don't. There are too many guards, and you aren't completely bulletproof—not the way you need to be. You need to kill me—now, Michelle—and take Anna and get the hell out. I'll worry about me."

Mac shook her head. "No. You tell me, I'll kill Cristopher, Anna and I will come get you, and *then* we'll get the hell out. Together."

Anna nodded, even as Shane shook his head again.

"You're in the security control room, aren't you?" Mac asked him. When he didn't agree, she looked at Anna. "That's where we'll search first. Of course, if he's not really there . . ."

"Fuck. I'm in the ladies' room next door," he capitulated, but then admitted, "But I don't know how to get there from here."

"I do," Mac said. "I'll be able to find you. I'll follow your emotional grid."

"Oh, God," he said, coughing hard. But then his face and his eyes changed—just for a moment—as Cristopher struggled to break free.

Anna took a step back as Mac refreshed her grip on the handle of that knife.

Then Shane was back—but for how long? "Mac," he said. "Please. I'd do it myself, but I *really* don't want that knife in these hands."

Mac nodded as she gazed up at him, as tears filled her eyes. "I'm coming to get you," she promised.

"Please don't," he whispered.

"I have to," she told him. "I love you."

Shane smiled, and somehow he managed to make Cristopher look beautiful. "My day just got really good. I'm going to work extra hard to live. Please do the same."

"I will." Mac laughed, even as her tears escaped down her cheeks. "I'm so screwed, aren't I?" she said, and drove the knife, hard, into his heart.

———

Calm blue ocean. Calm blue ocean.

Nika knew that she'd never find Joseph if she didn't come out of this panic, so she breathed the way he taught her. Deep inhale, hold . . . Exhale completely.

Nice and slowly. Ten counts in, ten counts out. Over and over and over.

Nightmares still swirled around her—that same stupid dream with the ancient animatronic dolls from the Small World exhibit at Disney. She'd been having *that* dream since she was four—the way their heads tilted from side to side as their mouths moved, out of sync with the song.

David, coming by the apartment when Anna wasn't home, chasing her up the stairs as he called her those awful names . . .

Her mother, dead, lying in that coffin.

Calm blue ocean. Calm blue ocean . . .

———

When Mac opened the door, the hallway outside the room was dimly lit and filled with smoke.

She moved out into it, keeping a firm grip on Anna's hand, pulling the other woman along with her. She knew where to go. She could feel—Shane was close.

There was a lot of activity in the corridors—guards with guns who seemed to be leaderless.

At first Mac had considered the white hospital gowns they were wearing to be detrimental, but now she realized they worked to their advantage.

All they had to do was cower, and the guards would leave them alone—they had bigger fish to fry.

There was a crowd of guards outside of the control room—which was close to the entrance of the ladies' room where Shane was holed up. Instead of fleeing the smoke, they'd outfitted themselves with what looked like firefighter's masks, which was too bad. Mac had been hoping that the area would be clear.

But the entrance to the men's was around the corner, so she pulled Anna through the door.

Some clown was actually in there, taking a leak.

"Hey!" he said as he saw them, and Mac used her imprecise telekinesis to toss him against the wall, hard enough to knock him out.

Or kill him. She didn't particularly care which.

"Grab his weapon," she ordered Anna, who staunchly did just that. She even took off his air mask and went through his pockets, looking for more ammunition.

"Heads up," Mac warned as she grabbed hold of one of the urinals—there were three along the wall—and pulled, attempting to use her hands to guide her telekinetic power.

She ended up nearly crushing her foot and had to dance some-what wildly to avoid the pipes and pieces of wall that came with it, but her effort created a hole—one through which noxious smoke came pouring out.

She started to squeeze her way in, but bumped into Shane, whose eyes were watering, even with a piece of cloth tied up and over his face. And she ended up pulling him back with her into the men's room, instead. Pulling him back, and clinging to him tightly, gratefully—he was still alive!

He held on to her for a moment, too, but then pushed her away in order to pull off his makeshift mask—and vomit in the nearest intact urinal, even as he coughed and wheezed and hacked. And apologized.

Mac just held on to him as he finally cleared his lungs and took several deep gulping breaths—although this air was getting fouled pretty quickly, too.

"So much for the big, romantic, *hallelujah, we're still both alive* kiss," he said, glancing up at her with that expression that was pure Shane Laughlin. "But here's something almost as good. Check this out." He flushed the urinal without touching the handle.

Mac laughed despite herself. "That's some talent," she said. "What else can you do?"

"I'm still figuring it out," he told her as he pulled away to rinse his mouth in the sink, and to cough again. "I'm not bulletproof, and I can't walk through walls. My biggest guess so far is that I'm really, *really* great in bed."

She laughed again. "I was thinking more in terms of potentially life-saving talents?"

"I can heat metal and start fires," he told her. "Blow shit up without explosives."

"Telepathy?" she asked.

"I did what I did with Cristopher," he pointed out. "I haven't exactly had access to other minds to read until now, and I kind of always know what you're thinking anyway." He reached for her, pulling her close. "One step at a time," he told her quietly.

Mac nodded—because she *had* been thinking that even though they were both currently still alive, that status could change, fast. And even if they could go directly from here to walking into OI, the fact that Shane was now a Destiny addict filled her with fear and dread.

But he was right. There was no point worrying about that right now. They were facing so many obstacles between here and OI— any one of which could kill them.

Shane let go of her to cough again, turning to spit into the sink.

And Anna was there, holding out the mask. "Maybe this'll help."

Shane shook his head as he wiped his mouth with his hand. "You should put it on. But I'll definitely take *that*." He reached for the weapon she was cradling, as he turned back to look at Mac. "So what's our plan?"

"Get the hell out of here," she said. "Go find Nika and bring her home."

Shane nodded. "Works for me. Door or wall?"

"Ceiling," she told him, and blasted a hole right above the row of toilets, so they could use the stalls to climb up.

He smiled happily at her. "I love the way you think."

———

Nightmarish images continued to swirl around Nika.

Anna, crying in the bathroom, when she thought Nika was asleep and couldn't hear her.

Devon Caine, chasing Nika down the sidewalk as she heard her own labored breathing loudly in her ears, as she desperately tried to get away.

Her mother's face, hours before she died. She was so small and so still and . . .

"Anna?"

Nika turned, and oh, thank God. It was Joseph. She'd found him. Or maybe he'd found her.

"No," she said. "It's just me." Just like the last time they'd met inside of her mind, their words were both so clear, it was as if they were standing on the street and having a conversation.

He was looking at her so strangely, and he shook his head. "Yeah. Sorry," he said. "It's crazy—there are times when you look so much like your sister . . ." He laughed. "Of course, right now, I'm un-fucking-believably high, so my boot looks kind of like Anna to me. Still, as nice as it would be to linger here and listen to a little Pink Floyd, we really do have to hurry."

"Who's Pink Floyd?" Nika asked. And why did he think his *boot* looked like her sister . . . ?

Joseph laughed. "Some day I'll play you *Dark Side of the Moon*," he told her, "and tell you all about my cannabis phase, aka the wasted years. You can learn from my mistakes. Or not. Some mistakes we just have to make for ourselves, don't we?" He laughed and held out his hand to her. "Come on, Mini-Anna. We have to get out of here. Frankly, I have no idea how, but let's start by making sure we don't lose each other."

He wiggled his fingers at her, and Nika laughed even as she wondered at the fact that, had anyone else called her *Mini-Anna*, she would've gotten all up in their face for it. She reached for him and clasped his hand. . . .

And her world exploded.

———

Shane linked his fingers together and held his hands out so he could give Mac a boost up to the hole she'd blasted in the bathroom ceiling. But before she did more than turn toward him, it happened.

Some kind of massive explosion went down. It rattled the entire building, the entire street, possibly the entire city. Mac could hear glass shattering, and she was glad they weren't near any windows.

Pipes burst and water sprayed, and she lunged for Anna even as Shane did, too, and they all held on to each other as the floor shook.

The door popped open and Shane moved in front of both of them, clearly expecting an attack, but no one was there. He pushed himself forward, leaning against it, but it still remained unlatched, as if it had come unaligned.

When the blast finally stopped, the sprinkler system was going off, and Shane looked up at the water gushing down on them, like rain. "You have no idea how freaking hard I tried to get that thing to go on before," he said, but Anna interrupted him.

"Oh, my God. Your gun!"

Mac and Shane both looked down where she was pointing and . . .

The barrel of the weapon he was holding had been bent, as if heated in some unnaturally hot fire and twisted, up and around.

Shane looked at Mac. "I hope whoever she is who did this, she's on our side."

The water falling from the ceiling was, almost ironically but not unexpectedly, making the smoke from the control room that much worse.

Shane moved from his lean against the door, opening it quickly and peeking out before shutting it again.

He did the same move again. And one final time, before shooting Mac a *wait here with Anna* glance, then opening the door far enough to slip outside.

He was back almost instantly, pulling them out into the hall with him, where the air was slightly less smoky.

"Whoever did this," he said again, taking the clip out of the mangled weapon, and holding it instead as a club, "did the same to all the firearms in this area."

And sure enough, many of the guards who'd been out in the hall had tried to fire their weapons—and had them explode in their faces. Others of the uniformed men were unbloodied, but were still, somehow, dead.

The emergency lights were flickering across the wreckage, creating an even more hellish effect.

Theirs wasn't the only locked door that had been opened—all of the doors on the entire floor were ajar, and girls clad in hospital gowns like the ones Anna and Mac were wearing began to emerge. Slowly at first, and then faster, they poured into the hallways.

"Slow down," an odd-sounding voice commanded from the smoke at the end of the hall. "No need to panic. No need to run. You're safe now."

"Who is that?" Shane asked.

Anna answered. "Bach," she said, wonder in her voice. "It's Joseph Bach."

And yes, there Bach was—partly obscured by the smoke at the end of the hall. He was lit, but not by one of the emergency lights. Instead, the glow seemed to come *from* him, from within him. And from within Nika, who was standing beside him, holding tightly to his hand.

"Help is coming," Bach told the little girls, and Mac realized why he sounded so strange. Nika was speaking in exact unison with him—as if their voices were one and the same. "You don't have to be afraid anymore."

"Neek!" Anna called as she realized her sister was with Bach, as she ran toward them.

Nika looked up at Bach, as if asking permission to release his hand. He smiled down at her and nodded. "We're safe now," he said again.

And sure enough, the team of Thirties and Forties came pounding down the hall to surround them, ready to assist.

And it was the weirdest thing, but as Nika let go of Bach, to throw herself forward into her sister's arms, he vanished. He just disappeared—as if he hadn't really been there at all.

"*That* was weird," Shane said.

And Mac turned to look at him.

Shane smiled. "Yeah, right?" he said as he put his arm around her and pulled her close. "Like all the rest of this shit is normal."

Mac held him just as tightly. "Get used to it."

He laughed, and even though Mac wasn't telepathic, she knew what he was thinking. Nika, Anna, and Mac were all safe—along with hundreds of little girls. But the life-threatening part of Shane's day was far from over.

"Let's get you back to OI," Mac told him.

He didn't argue. He just nodded.

And together, they headed for the stairs.

TWENTY-NINE

Bach regained full consciousness in the back of the OI van, where Charlie was at the computer, monitoring the situation on the ground and gathering information from Analysis.

Jackie and her team of Thirties and Forties were working at top speed to clear the Brite Group's floors of all children and raw product.

Because Child Services had been privatized, and there was no way to be certain that the Organization didn't have connections that would allow them to kidnap the girls all over again, the children were being sent to the Obermeyer Institute, where they'd be cared for until their parents could be found. And for those girls with no parents, it was going to be their new home. A new beginning, surrounded by people who would nurture and respect them.

The dead guards and staff were of a lower priority than the kids and the drugs—but if there was time, they'd be photographed and fingerprinted so that Analysis could ID them at a later date.

But there wasn't a lot of time.

Dr. Obermeyer herself had put in a call to the Boston Police Chief, requesting he keep all personnel away from the scene for another few hours. In return, Bach and his OI team would continue to remain on call to the city force, well into the future, to take care of any dangerously jokering addicts who threatened the civilian population.

The Police Chief wasn't happy—he was, no doubt, getting calls from corporate "constituents" with ties to the Organization. But his dwindling troops couldn't handle the drug problem without OI's help, so he'd negotiated Dr. O down to thirty minutes.

And the clock was ticking.

"He's finally awake, ma'am," Bach heard Charlie say into his headset. "Hang on, I'll check." He turned to Bach and asked, first, "Sir, can I get you anything?"

Bach shook his head, even though he wanted desperately to reassure himself that both Anna and Nika were safe. But he knew they were. Even while he was not fully conscious, he'd heard Charlie report that they were being taken, under heavy guard, back to OI.

"No, I'm fine," he said. "I'm . . . What's my integration level?" It had dropped, considerably. He could feel the abrupt loss of power.

Charlie leaned over to check the other computer, and confirmed it. "You're down to around seventy-three, sir. You know, you actually hit eighty-five for a while there."

"I did?" That didn't make sense. Bach's legs were feeling sturdy enough to stand, so he came over and checked the computer himself. And yes. He'd spiked a second time—all the way to eighty-five.

He checked the other information on the computer, and—funny—that second, even bigger spike happened at exactly the same time that all of the windows had been blown out of the Brite Group's floors.

He vaguely remembered working with Nika to disable all firearms in the entire building, and to deliver a giant smack-down to any of the guards on the premises. He remembered being able to identify all of the men who were employed as the Organization's guards by their mental footprints—something he'd never been able to do before. And he'd made the choice, and it hadn't been a hard one, to act as both judge and executioner to all who knew and understood exactly what their duties there had entailed.

"Was anyone injured on the street below the building?" Bach asked Charlie now. "From the window glass?"

"No, sir. We don't know where that glass went, but it didn't hit the street or the sidewalk." Charlie cleared his throat. "Sir, if you wouldn't mind, Jackie Schultz has a question that's . . . well, it's a little odd, sir. She's found a room, on the security floor, that appears to be some kind of lounge, with a service elevator that goes directly to the basement." He paused. "Sir, the room contains three dead men—two guards and a man in a lab coat—who were killed considerably differently from the others."

"How differently?" Bach asked.

"Jackie's wearing a camera," Charlie told him, "so you can see, but I have to warn you, sir, the pictures are pretty graphic. All three of the men were beheaded."

And indeed they were. "Thank you, I've seen enough," Bach said, and the picture on the screen switched to that of Jackie, looking grim and pale.

"Sir, we've got a psych specialist—Dr. Rita Labrenze—in the car with Nika and her sister—they're nearly back at OI, so they have been talking for a while. I've requested that Dr. Labrenze ask Nika specifically about this room—without going into too many details—and she honestly has no memory of this particular event. I'm wondering if you—"

"No," Bach interrupted. "This is not something we did."

"With all due respect, sir," Jackie said, "Dr. Labrenze believes it's possible that neither Nika *nor* you would know if Nika had lashed out, unconsciously, perhaps—"

"I was deep inside Nika's mind at all times, Ms. Schultz," Bach said. "I appreciate your concern, but she didn't do this."

"My concern," Jackie said, "is based in part on the fact that you were battling the effects of a powerful sedative, while dealing with a huge increase in your personal integration. With all due respect, sir," she said again, "it's just something to keep an eye on."

"I will," Bach said. "And as long as I've got you—have you encountered any girls—prisoners—who are pregnant?"

"No, sir," Jackie said, then exhaled hard. "Oh, Jesus, Dr. Bach, *really?*"

"I'm afraid so. Nika encountered at least one. We're estimating her age to be about seventeen. I'm also virtually certain she's an untrained Greater-Than."

"I'll check again," Jackie said, "but . . . A Greater-Than being used in genetic experiments? And I know I'm making an assumption here, but . . . Chances are, sir, that she was spirited away at the first sign of trouble."

Or she'd ripped the heads off of her guards and doctor, and made her escape.

"If she *is* still there," Bach warned, "she could be very dangerous. She was working with the Organization, possibly under duress—but we don't know that for sure."

"Understood," Jackie said.

"It sounds like you've got the situation under control," Bach said. "If that's correct, I'll head out to OI."

"Absolutely. I'll see you back there, sir," Jackie said, and Charlie cut the connection.

Bach sighed and glanced at Charlie, who was watching him expectantly. And a little warily.

"I'm guessing," Bach said, "that you'd prefer to drive."

———

Mac insisted on going, first thing, to talk to Elliot.

Shane had a shower on his to-do list, along with a nice meal, a glass of beer, and about four hours in bed with his woman, definitely not sleeping.

Then, and only then, would he be even remotely ready to hit the hospital for his impending heart failure.

But Mac needed facts. And she had a boatload of questions, most of which, Shane was willing to bet big money, weren't going to be answered. Like, how long would it be before Shane went into withdrawal and needed more Destiny. Okay, that one Elliot probably knew. But Mac also wanted to know if it would be more or less difficult to subject Shane to the procedure that would stop his heart if he were simultaneously jonesing for more of the drug? And, wasn't it possible—if the procedure *wasn't* doable due to Shane's experiencing withdrawal symptoms—that injecting him with an additional dose of Destiny would increase his risk of joker-ing?

Which was when Mac shared some information that Shane wasn't previously aware of. While most addicts tended to joker upon injection of the drug, in rare circumstances, some addicts had been known to joker spontaneously.

Of course, that was an eye-opener for Shane—spontaneous jokering? And although it was clearly rare, it would undeniably suck if it happened to him and he killed Mac instead of made love to her.

So he followed Mac into the hospital and down to the room where Elliot was no doubt still sitting at Stephen Diaz's bedside.

Except when they got there?

It was Diaz who was sitting beside *Elliot's* bed.

"What happened?" Mac asked. She was stunned.

Shane was, too. Until he did the math. "Elliot took a hit of Destiny, too." Holy shit.

Diaz nodded grimly, opening his robe to show the nearly com-pletely healed scars on his chest. "With a higher integration level himself, he was able to boost my healing powers," he told them. He looked at Shane. "Apparently, he got the idea from you. As soon as I was healthy enough, he had me stop his heart and . . ." He looked down at Elliot, who was lying motionless in the hospi-tal bed. "It all worked, exactly as he thought. The relatively mild damage done to his heart was repaired as his system detoxed and burned off all traces of oxyclepta di-estraphen."

"But that's great," Mac said. "If it actually works—"

"To a point," Diaz said. "Because here he is, in a coma. Just like Edward O'Keefe." He dropped a bomb. "Who died two hours ago."

"Oh, shit." Mac grabbed for Shane's hand, and he took it.

"Yeah." Diaz nodded grimly.

"O'Keefe was in his eighties," Shane pointed out.

"Not when he died," Diaz said. "Elliot told me he had the health of a fifty-year-old."

"Has anyone run an autopsy?" Mac asked.

"No, not yet."

"Let's do that," Mac said.

"Does it really matter?" Diaz asked. "We won't have the results back before we need to stop Shane's heart." He looked at Shane again. "Elliot's going to die, and you are, too."

Mac grabbed Shane with one hand and the Greater-Than with the other, and pulled them outside of the room, slamming the door behind her. "You don't fucking tell a man in a coma that he's going to fucking die!"

"But he is," Diaz said just as hotly. "I tried to change the future, but I failed." He started to cry. "I would have died for him. Why didn't he let me?"

"Because maybe he believes that you both can live," she said, hugging him tightly. "*That's* the future he's trying for."

Diaz couldn't speak.

"Did you actually see him die?" Mac asked. "In your vision?"

He shook his head, no. "But I saw him dying."

"Well, dying people can be saved," Mac told her friend. "You also saw Anna carrying me away, but you didn't see the part where we both came back. Right?"

Diaz nodded.

"So come on, asshole," Mac said. "Let's go back in there and make sure Elliot knows that he's going to survive this. And then let's prep a room . . ." Her voice shook and she had to start again as she looked over at Shane and met his eyes. "Let's prep a room for Shane."

Bach didn't wait for the elevator. He took the stairs up to the Medical Center, where Nika was being checked by the doctors, where Anna was being given a medical scan, too.

She was already done and wearing an OI jumpsuit, just sitting out in the hall outside of Nika's room. She saw Bach immediately as he turned the corner, and she got to her feet and . . .

He was grinning like an idiot as he moved even faster, and now she was running toward him, too, and he held out his arms and she all but flew into them.

And they were both laughing, only Anna was crying, too, as she said, "Thank you, thank you, thank you for bringing Nika back to me," as she threw her arms around his neck, as he actually picked her up and swung her around, as he told her, "She's amazing, she's really incredible—and you are, too. We couldn't have done any of it without you—without your help."

Anna laughed at that. "Yeah, I was *some* help, huh? You've been so patient and kind and . . ." She smiled happily up at him. ". . . amazing. You're amazing, Joe. All of you are. But especially . . . you."

Bach knew that he should kiss her. He wanted to kiss her, and he knew she wanted it, too. But decades of *not* kissing the pretty girl made him feel awkward, and the moment was gone.

But that was okay, because she and Nika were going to live here now, and there'd be plenty of moments in their future.

"She's been asking about you," Anna told him as she pulled out of his embrace and took his hand to gently tug him toward the examination room. She peeked in the door, adding, "Good, she's dressed." She pushed the door open and pulled him inside, saying, "Look who's come to see you, Neek."

"Joseph!" Nika broke into a huge smile as she jumped down from the exam table and threw herself at him.

Bach had to let go of Anna's hand to catch her. She was almost as tall as Anna, but she hugged him around the waist as he hugged her back, smiling at her older sister over the top of her head.

"Subject's integration level has just spiked!" the doctor, a woman named Elizabeth Munroe exclaimed. "Excuse me, Dr. Bach." She pulled Nika away from him. "Nika, dear, I need you back on the table, sitting very still."

"What's going on?" Anna asked, her smile fading, as Nika did just that.

"I . . . don't know." Bach moved closer to the computer where he saw that—good God—Nika's integration level had jumped to nearly forty-five.

"Just like that," Dr. Munroe murmured to Bach, "she went from thirty to forty-five and . . . Dr. Bach, you're being jot scanned, too. You've had quite a significant increase as well. You're up to . . ." She turned and looked at him, her eyes wide. "Seventy-eight?"

"I'm pretty sure I spiked before I came into the room," Bach said. With his integration levels in flux, he'd ordered the computer to perform a continuous jot scan on him as soon as he entered the building. He backed up his record and . . .

Dr. Munroe looked over his shoulder, tapping one short but neatly trimmed fingernail against the computer screen. "No, sir, you're wrong. Here's where you spiked, and it's exactly when *Nika* spiked."

How could that be . . . ?

Bach looked up to find Anna watching him, and the expression on her face was . . .

"Computer," he said. "Access JB-one. Voice response on. What's my current integration level?"

"Seventy-seven, and falling," the computer replied.

"Please note any increase," Bach ordered, and reached for Anna, pulling her almost roughly back into his arms. She embraced him back, but it was decidedly halfhearted and more of a self-defense move—to keep her face from being crushed against his chest.

"Still dropping," Dr. Munroe said.

He released Anna and went to the table. "Neek," he said. "Another hug?"

She was far more enthusiastic as she hugged him again. "What's going on?" she asked, and the computer spoke over her.

"Seventy-eight-point-four-three-three."

Anna grabbed Bach by his arm, pulling him away from her sister. "I think we need to talk. Outside. In the hall. Now."

"Did I do something wrong?" Nika asked them both.

"No," Bach told her.

"Absolutely not," Anna said. "Just . . . I'll be right back."

———

Bach was silent as Anna closed the door tightly behind her. She just stood there, feeling sick, waiting for him to look at her, and he finally did.

"You know what I'm going to ask you, right?" she said.

"I do," he said quietly. "And the answer is *no.*"

She nodded. "So . . . Mac hooks up with Shane and her integration level goes through the roof. Stephen Diaz proposes marriage to Elliot—and I'm sorry, but I've got to believe that *that* occasion wasn't consummated with a cup of tea—and *his* integration level skyrockets . . . Am I really supposed to believe that you just *want* to have sex with my thirteen-year-old sister? That you didn't *actually,* or maybe *virtually,* while you were in her head—"

"You know me better than that," Bach told her, his voice rough. "Anna, my God, I honestly thought it was *you.* I thought my integration level went up because of your dream. Because of . . . What I wanted from *you.*"

"Apparently not," she said.

"I like Nika, yes," Bach said. "But in no way do I want to . . ." He shook his head. "That's crazy. I don't understand."

"What's not to understand?" Anna asked. "You touch her, and you spike. She touches you and she spikes."

"She's thirteen," Bach said.

"No shit," Anna said, her heart breaking for too many reasons to count. "You spent a lot of time with her. Deep inside of her mind. She's special—you said so yourself."

"I agree," Bach said. "But . . ." He shook his head again. "She's *thirteen.*"

"Then why did you spike?" Anna asked.

But he just kept shaking his head. "It's true," he said, "that I have a connection with her, but—"

"I don't make you spike," Anna pointed out.

"You should," he said.

"But I don't. Nika does." She took a deep breath. "We can't stay here," she realized.

"Oh, God," Bach said. "Anna, *no.*"

"How can we stay? Except there's no way we can leave," she said, thinking aloud. "Nika will be grabbed immediately and . . ." This time the Organization would kill Anna. "We're stuck here, aren't we? We have to stay." She took a deep breath, exhaling it forcefully. "Here's what we're going to do. Under no circumstances will any 'testing' be done between you and my sister, unless I'm also in the room. In fact, under no circumstances will you *ever* be alone in a room with my sister."

"Anna, come on, you know me better than—"

"Are we in agreement?" she said, trying not to cry as she watched him.

The muscle jumped in Bach's jaw as he clenched his teeth. "It's standard procedure here at OI—what you requested. Female students are not . . . It's standard."

"I'm glad to hear that."

"It kills me," he whispered, "that you honestly think I would . . ." He shook his head.

"I think," she said carefully, trying to keep her voice from shaking, "that my sister has the ability to make you a *super* superman. I think that's probably worth a lot to you—in fact, I know it is."

Now Bach, too, had tears in his eyes. But he didn't deny it.

"I think that I don't really know you all that well," Anna continued, "and that . . . I have to protect my sister."

"I understand." He nodded again, then added, "Anna, I'm so sorry."

And the stupid thing was that she believed him.

"Just leave us both alone for a while, okay?" she said. "I'm going to need a little time to . . . I'm going to need some time."

Bach nodded again.

And Anna knew that this was it. His chance to pull her into his arms and say, *The hell with spiking integration levels and the unbelievable powers that they bring. I want you. . . .*

But he didn't do it.

Instead he turned and walked away.

———————

Shane had vetoed his own plan to take a few hours and have the equivalent of a last meal, a last drink, and a last chance to make love to Mac.

The idea that he could joker—just suddenly, randomly—scared the shit out of him. But as Diaz and Kyle and the rest of the medical team prepared to stop and then restart Shane's heart, he did ask for a moment to talk, privately, with Mac.

Kyle showed them into the hospital room where Shane would recover. If he was going to recover, that is, instead of die.

As the nurse shut the door behind them, Shane looked at Mac. She was as tightly wound as he'd ever seen her—and he'd seen her pretty tight.

She couldn't sit still and she bounced from the bed to the chair to the other chair to the cabinet to the window, as Shane took off his boots and sat up on the bed, stretching out his legs.

"Whatever happens," he told her quietly. "It was worth it."

Mac turned from the window to face him. "How can you say that?" she asked.

"Because it's true." He shrugged. "This way? I don't know, maybe it's a good thing. We don't have to crash and burn."

Mac shook her head as she came back toward the bed. "That's really stupid. *Good news, I'm going to die so we won't have to have a bad breakup?* That's moronic. And I know you're not a moron."

"Not that I'd ever willingly leave you," Shane said.

"Then don't," Mac said fiercely. "Let's just take our chances with the drug. We'll have the doctors monitor your dosage—"

Shane was shocked. "Are you serious?"

"Yes," she said. "No. I don't know. God *damn* it! God, you *suck*!"

"You don't want me to leave you," he said, because he needed to be sure he'd heard her right.

She didn't answer. She didn't say yes, but she didn't say no, either. And she finally sat down on the edge of the bed. Close enough for him to take her hand. Close enough to intertwine their fingers.

Shane took that as an affirmative and smiled. "Well, all right," he said, but then asked, "Do you believe that I love you?"

Mac didn't answer him right away. "I believe that I love you," she finally admitted. "And if you're convinced that's enough—"

"I trust you," he interrupted her. "If you say you love me, I trust that you're telling me the truth. I mean, because there's really no way for me to know. Neither of us is telepathic, at least not the way we'd need to be to verify such a thing. So in the same way that you have to trust that my love for you is real, I have to trust you. It's a two-way street, Michelle."

She briefly closed her eyes. "Don't call me that," she whispered.

"It's a beautiful name," Shane said, "Michelle." And when he tugged her closer and kissed her, she kissed him back, sweetly at first, and then deeper, hotter, hungrier.

As always, he could sense her fear, and he pulled back to look into her beautiful eyes.

"I knew this guy from my SEAL team," Shane told her. "Scotty Linden. He saw this woman at a bar, and it was love at first sight. But she left before he could talk to her. We spent a full week scouring every resort on St. Thomas, looking for her. And all the time we were looking, Scotty created this . . . this *fiction* about her. Who she was, where she'd grown up, why she was perfect for him.

"Last day of leave, he finds her and . . . He's a good-looking guy, very charming, and he sweeps her off her feet. But then it's the morning after, and they finally start to talk, and he finds out she's *nothing* like he'd imagined. She's not shy or sweet. In fact, she's very opinionated and assertive, and he's scared shitless, because he's already asked her to marry him, and she said yes.

"So he kisses her good-bye, and he conveniently goes overseas. He's gone for months, only she e-mails him the entire time. And he e-mails her back, because even though he knows he's going to break it off, he's not a total asshole.

"So months pass, and he's still writing to her, and he finally goes home and . . . They've been married now for five years. He loves her, heart and soul, but it started out a total sham. But he never would've met her, let alone gotten to know her, if she hadn't caught his eye that night in that bar." He kissed her, and she didn't resist him, but he knew despite the pretty story, she was afraid.

"This is going to work," he told her quietly. "This procedure. And after it works, we're going to give this thing—you and me—a go. Okay?"

Mac closed her eyes. And said, "When you're with me, I have faith that this is going to be enough." Her voice broke. "But when you're not here . . ."

Shane kissed her again. "Then I'll just never leave you," he promised, his own voice rough, because they both knew damn well that he might be on the verge of leaving her forever.

She kissed him back, so fiercely. And then, because she couldn't do it with her mind, she slid down off the bed and crossed over to the door, and she locked it. As she came back, she unfastened her pants, and kicked off her boots. "I really don't think you're going to joker in the next thirty seconds," she told him.

"Thirty seconds," Shane said, laughing, despite the tears in his eyes. "I mean, I can do quick, and I'm always up for creative, but *that* would be a new record for me."

"Not quite," she reminded him, as she hit him with a wave of . . .

Hoh-ly shit . . . She'd done this to him before.

And he was no fool. He opened his pants and yanked them down his thighs as she threw one leg across him and straddled him and . . .

He came close to the very instant he was inside of her, and he knew she was coming, too. It was everything she'd made him feel back in the car and then some, because she was moving on top of him, laughing down at him through her own tears, *loving* him so absolutely. And Shane caught her mouth with his and kissed her as he just kept coming and coming and coming.

And he knew he had it right—that whatever happened?

It had been worth every minute.

Bach was on hand for the procedure.

It was over relatively quickly, with no complications—which was a plus.

Both Elliot and Shane were in good health to start with, compared to Edward O'Keefe.

Still, the old man's death was troubling.

Bach tried not to carry any negative energy with him as he went to see Mac as she sat vigil at Shane's bedside, as he stopped in to see Diaz and looked down at Elliot's too-still form.

But there was nothing he could do—no way he could help them.

So he left. He stopped in, too, to the observation room overlooking laboratory one, where Nika was beginning to explore her power, under the tutelage of Charlie and Ahlam.

Anna was in the room with her, reading a book. But she looked up at the mirrored glass as if she knew—somehow—that Bach was there, watching.

It was funny, the way life worked out—or didn't work out, as the case might be.

Bach went back to his office and shut the door.

It took one week, four days, seven hours, and sixteen minutes.

After the first few days, the doctors who came in—Munroe and Cleary and Masaku—started making noise about the sinking probability of a coma patient's recovery.

Mac had kicked their asses out of the room.

She played music she hadn't listened to in years, and she danced. She read aloud from books she thought Shane might like—classics by authors like Robert Parker and Lee Child—interjecting her own comments and color. She'd brought in her laptop and played movies, giving Shane a blow-by-blow of the action on the screen.

She exercised his body, gave him massages and acupuncture treatments, rubdowns of all kinds.

She slept beside him at night—curled up with her arms around him.

And she talked to him. And talked. More than she'd ever talked in her life.

And after one week, four days, seven hours, and sixteen minutes, she apparently said something that Shane felt the need to respond to, because he woke up.

It was a little crazy, because after one week, four days, seven hours, and sixteen minutes of telling him about the patheticness of her life even before her mom had died, it took her talking about something absolutely mundane—that she was thinking about painting her bedroom walls blue. She'd told him that she was just thinking about it, and she'd probably take another dozen years of living here at OI to actually get around to doing it, when Shane opened his mouth and volunteered to help.

"You sure about that?" Mac said, her heart in her throat, as she reached for the buzzer that would call the nurse. "Because you've been kind of busy lately."

It was then that he opened his eyes and he looked at her and smiled. "Am I alive or is this heaven?"

"You're alive," she managed, as tears filled her eyes.

Shane reached for her hand, tugging her closer. "God, that must've sucked."

Mac nodded.

"But I'm still here," he said.

"Yeah," Mac told him. "I am, too."

"I see that you are," he said, and then he kissed her.

And Mac knew that she was in trouble, because now the *really* hard part of letting herself love this man had begun.

———

Stephen knew from the shouting and noises of celebration coming from down the hall, that Shane had come out of his coma.

Yet Elliot remained unreachable, even after Stephen told him the good news.

Mac came by in the afternoon when Shane was napping, and

she made up excuses. Shane was a little bit younger than Elliot. He was in better physical shape. His Navy SEAL training had prepared him for this type of trauma.

There were a lot of reasons why it made sense for Shane to have woken up first.

And Stephen didn't believe any of them. "Maybe he still thinks I'm angry at him," he said as he held Elliot's hand. "I was so angry, Michelle."

It had been—potentially—the last time he was going to see Elliot alive. His last chance to say something meaningful, to tell him how he felt. Instead, he'd merely asked Elliot if he was ready before he'd hit him with enough energy to stop his heart.

I love you, Elliot had told him.

Right. Are you ready?

"I just want him back," Stephen said now.

"Give him time," Mac said. "He's going to be okay. Did you tell him about Shane?"

Stephen nodded. "Of course."

"That'll help," she said. "His knowing that it works. His theory, his procedure. That'll definitely help." She nudged Elliot's bed with her leg. "Hey, asshole slacker, get out of bed!"

Stephen laughed for the first time in nearly two weeks. "Is that how you woke up Shane?"

"Nah," she said. "I was talking about painting my bedroom. Crazy, huh? He wanted to help." She nudged Elliot's bed again. "Hey, Zerkowski, I bet if you wake up, the hottest guy at OI'll rock your world." She looked at Stephen and smiled. "How's that for a little incentive? Although—correction, you're the second hottest guy here, now."

"You're going to let Shane stay?"

She nodded, trying to play it nonchalant.

"You know, you're allowed to be happy," he told her.

"You are, too," she shot back. She kissed him on the top of the head as she headed for the door. "Because Elliot's gonna wake up, and then you're going to get married, and annoy the shit out of everyone because you're so fucking perfect together."

"I hope so," Stephen said.

"Count on it," Mac told him, closing the door behind her.

———

It took one week, six days, one hour, and four minutes before Elliot finally woke up, too.

Shane was up and dressed and taking his first authorized walk around Obermeyer Institute when it happened. He and Mac had just stopped by Bach's office when the word came down—that Elliot was finally back.

They both took a moment to compose themselves after hearing the good news—and Mac knew that Shane felt responsible for Elliot having taken his idea to shoot up, and run with it. It was a miracle that they'd both come out of it alive—and everyone at OI knew it.

This was not something they would try doing again.

"Do you mind if we, um . . ." Shane pointed to Bach's closed door, and she shrugged, so he knocked.

It took a few seconds, but Bach finally answered, and he shook Shane's hand. "Good to see you up and about."

"Mind if we come in?" Shane asked. "I know you're busy, but I had this idea and, um . . ."

Bach opened his door wider, letting them in, giving Mac a quizzical look that she responded to with a smile. She'd thought they were just out for a walk. But if Shane really wanted to do this now . . . ? She would stand by him.

Or sit by him.

As she sat next to Shane on the sofa, she asked Bach, "Are you okay?"

He was looking even more tired than usual as he took a seat in his favorite chair. "Rough couple of weeks," he said, forcing a smile as he turned to Shane. "What's up?"

"I'd like to work for you," Shane said, just point-blank, in true Shane fashion. "I've had a few conversations with the team down in Security, and I know there's a place for me there, if I want it— I appreciate your recommendation, but . . ." He looked from Mac to Bach. "I'd really like to be part of *your* team, sir. I know I'm not a Greater-Than, and I'll never be one, but I do bring my own set of skills to the table. I really think your entire crew could use some weapons training—not necessarily to use firearms, but to know what to do when they come up against them. Which is going to happen, because you know the Organization isn't just going to leave Boston. They're going to regroup and they'll be back in even larger numbers. And you better believe that from now on, anyone from OI is going to be wearing a target on his or her back. If I were you, I'd grow both your team *and* OI's general security. And I can help you do that. Plus, I think we've learned that it's always good to have a fraction on the team for unorthodox scenarios."

"Non-Greater-Than," both Mac and Bach corrected him, but then Bach looked at Mac. "You're okay with this?"

"Very much," she said. "I mean, I told him he could stay and be my boy toy, but he seems to want to be useful." She glanced at Shane and smiled. "*More* useful."

"What happens if you break up?" Bach asked, looking to Shane for the answer.

"I leave," Shane said promptly, adding, "In the extremely unlikely event that that happens."

"Or we learn to coexist," Mac chimed in. "You get to decide if we're pulling it off."

"In the aforementioned extremely unlikely event that a breakup happens," Shane said again.

Bach nodded. "I won't have drama on my team. And for the record? I intend to inform Drs. Diaz and Zerkowski of this as well."

"No drama," Shane agreed. "Message received and understood."

Bach stood up. "I'll have a contract drawn up. I assume you'll want to live on campus?"

Shane looked at Mac and smiled his happiness, as they both stood, too. "Yes, sir."

Bach held out his hand. "Welcome to the team."

The two men shook. "Thank you, sir," Shane said. "You won't regret this."

"Thank you, sir," Mac echoed, shaking Bach's hand, too.

They went out the door, closing it behind them, heading down the hall toward the lounge before either of them dared to speak.

Mac broke the silence. "You didn't even ask the rate of pay," she commented.

"Because I don't give a shit," Shane told her. "I got room, I got board, I got you—on top of that, everything else is gravy."

"This gig probably doesn't pay as much as cage fighting," she told him.

Shane laughed as he looked at her. "You are never going to let me forget that," he said. "Are you?"

She smiled into his eyes. "Damn straight."

"Seriously, Mac," he said, stopping her with a hand on her arm. "You have no idea how good it feels to be welcomed here this way. To have a place where I fit in, where I belong. I didn't think I'd ever have that again."

Mac just smiled at him.

And Shane smiled back at her, and the love in his eyes was beautiful—regardless of how it had started. At least she kept telling herself that . . .

"Do you think when Bach said *no drama*, he meant that I should avoid kissing the hell out of you in the middle of Old Main?" he asked.

"I think PDAs probably qualify," she said. "Especially when I start screaming *Take me to heaven, Shane Laughlin! Take me Navy-SEAL-style, like there's no tomorrow!*"

Shane laughed. And he took her hand, and they booked it, double time, back to the privacy of his rooms, where he kissed her, and—absolutely—took her to heaven.

Even though they both knew that tomorrow was coming, whether they wanted it to or not.

Since her explosion onto the publishing scene more than ten years ago, SUZANNE BROCK-MANN has written fifty books, and is now widely recognized as one of the leading voices in romantic suspense. Her work has earned her repeated appearances on the *USA Today* and *New York Times* bestseller lists, as well as numerous awards, including Romance Writers of America's #1 Favorite Book of the Year (three years running), two RITA Awards, and many *Romantic Times* Reviewer's Choice Awards. Suzanne Brockmann lives in Sarasota, Florida, with her husband, author Ed Gaffney. Find Suz on Facebook at Suz Brockmann's Troubleshooters World, and visit her website at www.suzannebrockmann.com.

ABOUT THE TYPE

This book was set in Sabon, a typeface designed by the well-known German typographer Jan Tschichold (1902–74). Sabon's design is based on the original letterforms of Claude Garamond and was created specifically to be used for three sources: foundry type for hand composition, Linotype, and Monotype. Tschichold named his typeface for the famous Frankfurt typefounder Jacques Sabon, who died in 1580.